JENNIFER CRYER

BREATHING ON GLASS

Little, Brown

LITTLE, BROWN

First published in Great Britain in 2012 by Little, Brown

Copyright © Jennifer Cryer 2012

The moral right of the author has been asserted.

A CIP catalogue record for this book
is available from the British Library.

ISBN 978-1-4087-0357-1

Typeset in Caslon by M Rules
Printed and bound in Great Britain by
Clays Ltd, St Ives plc

Papers used by Little, Brown are from well-managed forests
and other responsible sources.

MIX
Paper from
responsible sources
FSC® C104740

Little, Brown
An imprint of
Little, Brown Book Group
100 Victoria Embankment
London EC4Y 0DY

An Hachette UK Company
www.hachette.co.uk

www.littlebrown.co.uk

BREATHING ON GLASS

CHAPTER 1

Rhea began to keep a photographic record of the minuscule daily changes.

'Some day these will be the most famous cells in the world,' Lewis said.

'Celebrity culture,' someone called, from across the lab, and a gust of warm laughter took the edge off the air-con. Peering down a photo-microscope didn't have quite the paparazzi glitz the team longed for, but that evening the atmosphere puckered with the expectation that they would soon have a stem-cell line made from adult tissue. If they did, Lewis's words would come true. All around her Rhea heard the tense intake of breath as the research team geared up for the final push.

The students and post-docs around her were exuberant, animated with intellectual curiosity and idealism, but it had already been a long day and Lewis's eyes were losing their unfettered confidence. His shirt, which had been smooth and ironed that morning, was creased and showing its age. Crumpled linen, however expensive, and crumpled skin didn't make for a good look, but Rhea let it pass. His clothes were Amber's territory and she wasn't going to blunder into her sister's space. His research team, on the other hand, were definitely her business.

'I'll stay and finish the cell prep myself,' she offered. 'You lot get off to the pub and enjoy yourselves.'

When they left her alone with Lewis, they took their undeniable optimism away with them. 'They get their hopes up so easily,' she said, as she watched the retreating backs. 'I don't suppose today's results will be any better.' Lewis looked away quickly, but not before she had seen the flicker of resentment in him. However hard he tried, he could never hide his pique at the very things he relied on her for – her common sense, her caution. All those things that kept his research group firmly on track, he minded. They stood in silence as the youthful buzz dwindled to a few over-excited shrieks, and then, after the banging of the outer door, to nothing. Lewis looked at the culture flask as though he could charm a stem cell into reproducing perfectly, so that every daughter cell was an exact copy of its single parent. 'We can do it, Rhea.'

Recklessness and prudence swung disconcertingly between them. The wider the oscillations, the more dangerous they felt. At this stage in their work there could be no middle course. Success and failure were evenly matched enemies, but both threatening. To escape them, Rhea turned and went into the tissue-culture suite.

Tireless fans forced air into a cataract: an invisible wall that separated Rhea from the sample, half a gram of human tissue sucked from the thigh of a young researcher who was having a cartilage repair. The flow resisted her as she pushed her hands inside the tissue-culture hood but she pressed forward and breached it, her skin covered with latex gloves and the cuffs of her laboratory coat tight around her wrists.

Inside the hood, she touched the adipose tissue with her scalpel. Gently, gently, she stroked it. She knew better than to risk pressing down. Any pressure and the scalpel would give way; not the steel – that was strong – but the plastic handle would snap and the thin blade fly off, lacerating whatever it touched. As she transferred the dissected tissue into the bottle, a drop fell from the lump of fat onto the stainless-steel tray of the isolation cabinet. She wiped it away instantly before it had time to spread any infection, but even in those seconds, there was a smell of grease through the air curtain, soon obliterated by the disorienting edge of the alcohol she used for cleaning. She couldn't help breathing it in and felt its contribution to the air of unreality. The enclosed space created an illusion of the culture hood as a toy theatre with its brightly lit stage and its safety curtain. Cellular dramas, miniatures of survival, were played out there as she worked.

The half-gram of fat was invaluable to Rhea. With a visionary's clarity, she saw through it to the assortment of cells caught inside: the bountiful-bellied mature adipose cells with their loading of energy-rich fat, the tough, scrawny fibroblasts that made the connective tissue and, most desirable and least distinguished of all, the uncommitted stem cells. They were the important ones, still capable of developing into blood cells, or bones, whatever was needed. Grow your own spare parts? Surgeons everywhere held their breath, waiting for the science to do for the worn-out body what nature did for every new baby. Sensitive to being vilified for the use of embryonic tissue, medicine longed for technology to redeem it: to find the adult cells that could develop into any part of the body. And there wasn't a single researcher who didn't want to be acclaimed as the blameless saviour of human health. Every one of Rhea's colleagues was engaged in a frantic contest for that Holy Grail. Her friends might spend the evening in the pub, but in the morning they'd be in the lab early, vying to outstrip the competition.

All over the cell walls were surface markers, small molecular clusters that distinguished them from the other cells, moved information in and out of them. Identify those markers and you would have a means of separating out the stem cells, even the few that would be left in adult tissue. Rhea had developed a method of preparation that used minimal concentrations of the enzymes that broke down connective tissue and released the cells – the cell surface markers suffered little damage from the process. Filtering them through the net-curtain fabric she'd bought in a department-store sale, she separated them, at blood temperature to keep them alive. When most workers couldn't force their will on their cultures, Rhea could persuade hers. They flourished under her care: complete genetic blueprints of the donor in every flask.

She worked steadily, quietly, cut off in the ever-decreasing series of containment rooms that were like nested boxes, giving all her attention to what she was doing. Rhea didn't hear or see anything: the fans were noisy; the brightest light came from the lamps in the hood; no sound or shadow alerted her. But an over-whelming sense of presence made her look up towards the observation window in the door. Lewis was pressed up against the glass, his forehead flattened. Even he wouldn't come in and risk contaminating her work. His mouth made a *moue*. Through the wire-laced glass, it looked like a kiss, but Rhea knew it wasn't.

'Amber,' he was mouthing. Rhea smiled briefly and com-plicitly, with a flush of pleasure. They understood one another, she and Lewis, because they were the same: uncomplicated, with none of the unsettling attraction of opposites that existed between him and Amber. Or her and Dave: purposeful, impa-tient Dave. At least he understood about work. Lewis wasn't so lucky: his wife wouldn't be kept waiting for anything. He had married Amber within a year of meeting her and ever since then the irresistible allure of her sister and the interminable demands of his work had held him in joint thrall. Rhea had booked a slot for a previous set of radioactive samples to be analysed in the isotope suite that evening. The results could be crucial, but if Amber wanted him at home, he had to leave. The stress of not knowing the outcome would keep him on edge all evening.

'I'll phone.' The smallest nod was enough to create total

understanding between them. It was easy enough to keep up the constant exchange of research results: they were never further apart than a call or a text.

By the time she had finished the cell preparation she was tired. Her friends were in the glitter and camaraderie of the pub, but up here there was only her. She couldn't leave until she had set up her overnight counting. She felt stranded. But she wasn't far from home. The barest glance from the window showed the bar where she usually met her friends, and beyond it her flat, in darkness because Dave was away. She had only to touch the phone to feel close to him. The long sine waves of the communications industry looped between them. After his talk, he would be eating dinner now in a bar like the one she was looking at, a guest at another university. She didn't call him. He could enjoy this small professional freedom without her interrupting.

Rhea had developed a strain of bacteria that produced an antibody to the stem-cell surface marker. There was an elegance in the idea that nature could make its own reagents that gratified her, but she wasn't above manipulating chemical elements. She had labelled the antibody with radioactivity; months of work were crushed into a few microlitres. She would find out now if her antibody had found its target stem cells in her cultures. Let them have reproduced true. Let them be pure stem cells, she thought, as she loaded the samples into their racks.

The isotope suite was right at the top of the building, up a windowless set of stairs. Out were the pastel, colour-coded tiles of the lower floors, with their busy, noisy corridors, and in were austere concrete treads for the registered user. In all that emptiness, the only thing that Rhea could hear was the echo of her own footsteps; she might be the only person left in the building. She'd have liked Lewis to be there if the results were good: someone who'd be pleased for her. It was one thing to enjoy the isolation in the tissue-culture suite, with a dozen friends on the other side of the door; it was quite another to spend your evenings some-where that was constructed like a solitary-confinement facility.

The door to the isotope suite was painted a heavy-duty blue that jarred ambitiously with the waspish yellow and black of the *Danger Radioactive* warning symbol. The click of the lock release as she swiped her key card wasn't enough to open a heavy, lead-lined door like this; Rhea knew just how to lean her shoulder against it so that she could sidle in through the space that her weight opened up. As soon as she was inside, the door swung shut. Its dull thud was the last sound that could be heard from the stairwell. From the inside of that door everything – radio-activity, waste, the air you breathed, probably even the noise you made – was whisked away and cleansed before it could impinge on the uncontaminated world outside.

The scintillation counters were all busily moving sample vials in and out of their chambers. At each ejection they whispered intimately into their computer links, delivering numbers to data files and persuading Rhea that someone else must be in the room. It's the ghost in the machine, she joked, whenever the feeling threatened to overwhelm her. The incessant activity of the equipment used up the hemmed-in air and made it hot. It rolled down her throat heavily, inducing distaste, like nausea: the nausea of being tired and invigorated at the same time. But the feeling wasn't all unpleasant. It reminded her of something else dislocating: the end of a party, when the effects of the drink were beginning to wear off but you weren't finished with having a good time.

Yawning, she checked the racks queued up on the conveyor-belt. Her own vials were at the end of a long line already set up for overnight processing so there was no chance that she would have her results before morning. The samples at the front of the queue belonged to Stephen Glatton. He'll be at home, labouring over his Sudoku by now, she thought, marking the numbers in soft pencil so that he can rub out the mistakes. That way, when it's finished, it'll look perfect. By the time he brings it into work tomorrow, he'll have convinced himself that he solved it without any of the usual wrong turnings and dead ends. She lifted his samples off and substituted her own. A few keystrokes changed the machine settings from his to hers. By the morning I'll have my counts and I'll have put his samples back. He'll never know.

The first of her samples nudged its way forward and dropped into the counting chamber. Usually, she would have gone back to the lab now, left the machinery to go about its business, but she was nervous with anticipation. The orderly progression of her racks along the conveyor-belt would be reduced to a string of numbers that revealed success or failure. Her eyes snatched the first result from the screen and tried to read something into it, just to get an inkling of what the rest would be like. But it was impossible: the single number meant nothing in itself. She knew that she had to wait for the full set. Only then would she see them as a whole and feel the pull of the trend, like an undertow beneath the surface of the sea; the dangerous one you feel near to an estuary, where the competing forces of ocean and river have to come to an accommodation.

Let them all be stem cells, she wished again, but the words disappeared blankly into the space between the reinforced walls. She closed her eyes and let the rhythmic flurry of the machinery anchor her.

When the results eventually appeared they weren't at all the ones she had hoped for. She took the read-out downstairs and sat at her desk, easing through the figures as though her stare could massage them into something more compliant. The hint she had dropped to Lewis, that there might be something to tell him, twanged back at her, short of its mark. None of her samples was wholly stem cells. Every one of her vials showed promise, enrichment, but there weren't any pure preparations.

A cataclysmic failure might have been easier to face. You could always make a drama out of a disaster but all she could see here were tedious months of repeating the same process, a dreary edging nearer to the goal.

Never as good as she hoped, yet never as bad as she feared, her figures stayed solidly insufficient, refusing to budge over 55 per cent; 45 per cent of her cells had lost their unique stem-cell markers and become ordinary and useless to her. A pointless irritation at their stubbornness pricked at her. She wouldn't sleep tonight. It was dark outside, but only with the provisional, city sort of dark that never really thickens into blackness. At least there was something consoling in that: the way that urban energy never surrendered to nature, something that told you not to give up. If she phoned Lewis at home now he was going to be disappointed and he would have to hide it. He'd pass her over to Amber. She wasn't up for a sisterly chat with an Amber cosy by the fire in her new house in the country, the darkness so black around her that her lighted windows could be seen for miles around. Bad news and texts made a good enough match.

The adrenalin of exhaustion was making a racket in Rhea's head, drowning her stoicism. She decided to change into her trainers and jog home, a half-lit mile along the canal, and let the running sweat it all out of her. Running always unleashed her: even thinking about the steady rhythm of her legs, the glint of the recycled glass, like sparks under her feet, along the towpath was exhilarating. It made her feel elated and powerful; in fact, the hours she spent running were the only ones when Rhea felt she unconditionally inhabited her own body.

There it was, seeping through the crack in the doorway, the laboratory stench, the constant perfusion of chemicals. It sank into everyone who worked there, marking them out. Lewis had come home to her last night full of the lab, waiting for Rhea to phone with some results, smelling just like that. She filled the house with her own defences – perfumed oils lay in wait for him – but still the smell crept in, thwarting her self-possession. She made him shower and change his clothes, but it leached out of his skin in bed and hung about, lying between them. Sometimes Amber thought that was why she couldn't get pregnant; the stench got in the way somehow.

They couldn't smell it themselves but it bound scientists together, like the business of being attracted to someone whose immune system smelt the same as your own. Or was it the opposite? Amber couldn't remember offhand. She leant her face closer to the window panel in the door, careful not to touch it in case the smell attached itself to her. There was no sign of her sister. No doubt Rhea would know the answer, just like that. She would know exactly what could exert that unconscious draw on you: the comfort of the familiar or the fascination of the unknown.

Lewis's team scarcely glanced up from what they were doing: moving quickly from one workstation to another; slotting things in; pressing buttons. Sometimes she saw them joking and fooling about while they worked. Their energy flashed like intersecting laser beams. But that was when Lewis was there; he was the force they lined up around. It was the focus of his attention that held them so close, heads together, their eyes trapped by whatever he was looking at. Usually when she called in at the lab they were excited, engaged with one another. Today they were all self-engrossed and sober. No one was going to notice her and let her in. She checked around for Rhea again. Still no sign. And she hadn't phoned last night, only dropped a cursory text to Lewis. Her bench was empty, her pipettes lined up anonymously along the shelves; Rhea's space was defined by her absence.

If I've got to hang about, I could at least do with some coffee, Amber thought, but there was a notice on the door: 'No Eating, No Drinking'. No entry either, by the look of it. She gave the

9

door a belligerent shove, but it didn't move; she hadn't even rattled the electronic entry system. The steel fingerplate threw a reflection back at her: her own hand, pushing her away. She was definitely locked out. No one looked; she had no idea how she would get in. But she wasn't putting up with the indignity of having to stand and knock outside her own husband's laboratory door.

Alone in the dirty-water smell of the corridor, Amber knew impotence. Everything made her feel like an outsider. Soft footfalls made her turn anxiously, not wanting to be seen at a disadvantage. Katherine, one of Lewis's post-docs, smiled her shy, thin smile. Her skin was patchy with dehydration. She was carrying a large bottle of something dark and dangerous-looking, heavy too, yet it leant securely against her skinny little hip as she swiped her key card. Instantly the door opened and Amber was able to slipstream through behind her.

Once inside, Amber was met by puzzled looks, as though the researchers didn't recognise her. But they should all know her. For a tiny moment she feared her body had dissolved in the acrid air. She brought her hand downwards, certain that it would pass straight through her lost thigh but there was still flesh, warm and soft and solid to her touch. The glass doors in the cupboards shone red where they caught the colour of her clothes.

Of course, the researchers had been holed up in the laboratory day and night for months, and now that autumn was setting in, they wouldn't see much sun until next year. They were pupa-pale from the long hot summer's incarceration. Hungry holes of eyes took her in. She stared back. Lewis's team wore trainers, jeans and T-shirts and, thrown over them, the anonymous white lab coats that drained the life from their faces. She looked down at her own body, her dress: the red fabric shifted and curled with the movement of her breath as though it had a life of its own. She knew what they were staring at. Next to them, she probably seemed to be on fire.

'I'll wait for Lewis in here, if that's all right. No point sitting out there on my own.' There was a shuffle of half-movement, a turning aside and then a swivelling back again of bodies, half drawn, half confused, by the unspoken invitation to keep her company. But Amber understood instantly. 'Don't let me stop you if you're busy. I'll just wait here and watch.'

The lads retrenched to the safety of their benches but their attention kept detaching itself and wandering back to her. Amber took care to smile at each in turn, as though he was the only person in the room.

They were too scared to exist; that was their problem. Stem cells, they were always saying, as though the entire universe had been constructed around their great enterprise and they were intimidated by its importance. Amber had seen a stem cell; Rhea had given up her seat to let her peer down a microscope to look at a black scribble, like a diagram in a textbook. 'We won't actually know if it's a stem cell until we've got a whole lot more,' she'd said, while she flexed her shoulders and stretched out her arms to show the immense difficulties of everything they did. 'You can't tell by looking. We'll need to grow enough of them to check out every single detail about them.' The complications of stem-cell identification rose up legion in Amber's awareness. Her husband and sister could hide behind them for ever, and there was nothing she could do about it. They'd never had to face the real world, forced to adopt the sort of front that would keep paying clients trooping through the door of a public-relations company. She could do that. She could haul tired businesses out of the doldrums, make their shabby images shiny again, but it wasn't easy. Scientists had no idea what it took to be a flattering mirror for clients to admire themselves in. She gave such a lot of herself away, in exchange for her PR-industry salary.

Katherine coaxed an oblong plastic plate into the auto-analyser and tapped in her code. The ominous equipment responded willingly to her fingers; how confident this self-effacing girl was of commanding the ghastly thing. She sat next to it comfortably while her samples slid forward and the machine dispensed slugs of chemicals into each one. Amber perched on a stool as if she was in a cocktail bar while she studied the greedy sipping of the probes, the disdainful spit of their contents into the tubes.

'I wouldn't dare touch something like that,' she said. 'What does it do?'

Katherine did exactly as Amber expected: acted like a younger version of Rhea.

'It's amazing,' she said. 'You needn't be scared of it at all.' She patted the machine affectionately, as though it were a friend, saying, 'You check everything we do, don't you?' She turned back to Amber. 'It knows if you've made a mistake and tells you.'

Looked at from the inside like this, the laboratory didn't seem quite so threatening, not with the competent enthusiasm of Katherine beside her. All over the lab, people were cosying up to equipment that did just what they wanted. The deserted row of Rhea's pipettes, colour-coded for size, hung in front of Amber. It seemed only fair to them all that she should try one. 'Just with water,' Katherine encouraged her. 'Nothing to be frightened of there.

'First, you have to fit the tip to the shank, without touching it,' she said and Amber soon had everyone laughing at her incompetent antics as she struggled to manage the disposable tips. She was standing, the pipette poised in front of her, ready for another stab when the door opened. The man who had come in – he must have had a key card – didn't seem welcome. She felt the entire group stiffen as they saw him.

12

'Who's that?' she whispered to Katherine.

'You don't want to know.'

Everyone gathered together around the autoanalyser and there were a few moments of silence as the intruder stormed down the lab towards them, a few moments when Amber saw Katherine, Fazil, Andrew and Joe all glance towards Lewis's empty office and then Rhea's abandoned desk, looking for protection. The old feeling of being an incompetent in their world came powering back. She'd probably got them into some kind of trouble, fooling around like that. The interloper had tufty, scrappy hair, pale, insignificant eyelashes, and even before he spoke, his mouth began to dip like that of a man who had stood on his dignity once too often. But he belonged: everyone there knew him. Lewis's team closed together. Amber was sure this was some old battle, fought over and over again.

'What's his name, Katherine?'

'Stephen Glatton.'

Stephen Glatton was seriously pissed off; he was shouting the odds all down the lab.

'Totally unacceptable,' he ended.

Before that he'd said other things: *interference with order of counting, changed entries in the booking file*, complaints that Amber didn't understand, but *totally unacceptable* was part of the everyday ructions of a PR company. Amber was safely on home ground. Once he had said that, Stephen Glatton had changed himself from a threat into an opportunity. He was shouting at Lewis's research group, but she didn't suppose he would be quite so happy to take on the boss. He threw a booking list onto Rhea's empty desk. His face was mottled with frustration; the blotches gave him a skittish nervousness, as though he was handling some inherently unstable compound.

Skulking behind the benches, the researchers separated into two cohorts. The old hands pretended to search through their bottles and settled in to enjoy the confrontation; the inexperienced new kids shifted uneasily, embarrassed, but they couldn't pretend not to look. All of them held their breath. In the silence that stretched through the laboratory, a magnetic stirrer bar slipped out of control and clattered against the side of a beaker as though caught in the tautness of the air. Katherine, Andrew and Joe leapt to turn it off and the frantic whirl of activity provided cover for Glatton to dump a rack of vials on Rhea's bench.

'These samples have been left blocking up the counter all bloody night. I've had to take the whole lot off myself.'

His angry voice reverberated from the bare surfaces of the laboratory, hunting down the incompetent and the careless. It looked as if Rhea was in the frame. Not one of the students spoke a word. The equipment chuntered on, oblivious to the change in atmosphere. But Amber had tackled the pipetting and she wasn't having Rhea attacked: not here, not in her husband's lab, where she had just burnt off the persistent gloom of scientific angst.

She stood forward to defend everyone against the threat of its return; she reckoned she was safe behind the cling of her dress, her lippy, the intriguing smear of dark vulnerability that she smudged under her eyes every morning. And Glatton knew it too: she sensed wariness in his recoil from her. Now he wasn't on his own ground: she had him bang in the middle of hers. She stepped towards him again, threatening his position.

'This is a white-coat area for all users,' he said, eyeing the notice-board, siphoning off whatever doubtful authority he could from the safety instructions.

'I don't need one, not for my job.' Amber smoothed the red of her dress, ran her hands down her thighs.

'Really? I'd be interested to know what it is you do around here that doesn't require protective clothing.'

Worse than his words was the flit of victory that rushed across his face: the undisguised congratulation of his own hegemony.

Amber gave him her most innocent and disarming smile as she thought, Thank you, God, you have delivered the bastard into my hands. Then she shook him off with the most inconsequential shrug of her shoulders.

'Actually,' she answered, 'I sleep with the boss. How were you planning to improve your career prospects?'

They were still lauding her performance when Lewis and Rhea showed up. And the most amazing thing had been Glatton's reply. He hadn't taken offence. 'I'm probably going to be very nice to you', he had said, then flushed and half grinned so she'd been taken aback and let him off the hook. It was as though Glatton had a reversible personality and she had found the trick of turning him inside out. Astonishment and laughter rippled around her.

'But will he be very nice to the rest of us?' Rhea wondered.

'Only if she's here to frighten him,' Katherine answered, and Amber swirled with yet more pleasure because the attention was so very reassuring.

She glanced back at the Biological Sciences Building as she wandered out with Rhea and Lewis into the low evening sun. Seething Stephen was up there somewhere, watching them leave. From the look of him, she didn't think he had many friends. He'd watch the way they walked together, protected by family ties, and envy them. But that might mean he'd expect to join them and she didn't want him elbowing his way into their gang. The windows were in shadow; blank, they gave no clue. He'd been made to recognise the value of what she could do, Amber was sure of that – him and all the research team.

'He uses viruses,' Lewis was telling her. 'That's how he gets his adult stems to stay that way.' She let him drone on about work because it was Friday, drinks night, and his arch-rival had been defeated.

15

'Viruses? That doesn't sound good.'

'Well, it's not, is it? He puts extra genes into his cells with a viral vector. But when you put the cells into a patient, to repair their liver or their Alzheimer's disease or something, what's going to happen to the virus?' He answered himself: 'Who knows?' Lewis grabbed at Rhea's arm. 'But Rhea keeps her cells pluripotent just by giving them the right combination of hormones in their growth medium. No problem there. Our cells will be perfectly safe.'

No eating, no smoking, no drinking, no admittance. The safety of everything that Lewis and Rhea did was not immediately apparent to Amber. But the medical benefits, that was something else. If these stem cells could really repair broken bodies, what a difference that would make. And where would Stephen Glatton be when her PR had turned Lewis and Rhea into the aristocrats of medical research?

She shrugged at them, letting them know what she had already done for them; she had more than enough go in her for all of them.

'It's the red dress.' She explained it away as though it was nothing to her. 'Hot colours are full of energy.'

But Lewis had to have the last word. 'Strictly speaking,' he said, 'that's not true. It's the cold-looking blue light that has the most energy.'

Even on Friday night Lewis couldn't stop lecturing.

'Get over yourself,' she told him. She pulled an exasperated face at Rhea but in return got only a half-shrug of sympathy behind the scientific orthodoxy of Lewis's back.

Outside the bar, Rhea watched Amber sit down in the sun face-on, angle her legs so they could benefit from the full glare, then close her eyes as though the whole business of colour and light might be too much to bear. Rhea had the horizontal evening rays on one side of her face so she shifted her chair and straightened her white legs next to her sister's brown ones. Amber had this womanly maturity. Her body curved. Somehow it was never ashamed of its surfeit. The look-at-me clothes, hair that was curled and bleached. Amber made freckles sexy. Even the gap between her front teeth – Amber was scared of dentists, *injections*, she shuddered, so she had had no orthodontic work done – was no imperfection but made her more of what she was. Rhea felt her pale skinniness, her dark hair and oval face eclipsed by her sister's brilliance. So close together, subtle understatement couldn't compete with sheer exuberance.

She watched Lewis negotiate the paving dividing the bar from the canal side with three drinks balanced in his hands. They said you loved someone who resembled your family and Amber loved Lewis. He was moving carefully because every few steps he had to flick his head to shift the lank black hair out of his eyes. The awkward movement made the drinks spill and splash his trousers, which stuck to his thin legs. He didn't seem to notice the wet cotton as he angled his face away from the glare. His white skin burnt in minutes.

'You girls bask in the sun,' he said, 'and I'll just sit here and bask in the reflected glory.'

'Strictly speaking, you'll probably find it too hot.' Amber hadn't forgiven Lewis yet for correcting her about the blue light and he had to act chastened and take her hand, wrapping her fingers around the red of her cranberry juice, smoothing them into place until she relented and grasped the glass for herself.

While they made their peace, Rhea checked her phone. There were no messages yet so she laid it down, open and ready. The wooden bar tables had an antiquated, academic patina that reminded her of libraries. They were supposed to have been worn by the elbows of dispossessed Nonconformists back in the seventeenth century. Whole families had set off from this place for the New World. By the end of the twentieth century the city fathers had been seduced away from their Puritanism by the rewards of the post-industrial economy; they'd cheerfully sanctioned the regeneration of the whole historic canalside into a glorious playtime venue. The same post-industrial fervour had infected the university where Lewis and Rhea worked, and the knowledge economy had become the new religion, a fast track to grace. Americans, prominent scientists, were discouraged by the US legal system from pursuing embryonic stem cell research and now they were coming back across the Atlantic, looking up contacts like her and Lewis.

'Late morning in California,' said Rhea, checking her watch. 'The surf'll be up.'

They stared at her phone, willing it to ring. When an accidental bump from a passer-by made it tremble, it seemed as though it was working itself up to take the momentous call. Rhea trembled with it. She was the only one of them who had been to the States. She could think her way back across the Atlantic and right on to the West Coast where she had spent two exhilarating years working in the medical biotech industry. She closed her eyes and escaped the weak British sun. You couldn't hide from the sun in California. It flooded in everywhere, right through your skin, and sank into the very marrow of your bones.

The tremble was now for the memory of that excitement. There had been such jubilation about everything they did: work, morning runs along the beach, work, surfing, more work, dinner in oceanside restaurants, late-night work; she'd never been tired then. Money and energy had known no limits in the Californian sunshine. Even limits knew no limits; she'd had a lab of her own. Not like in Britain, where she'd done her PhD in the rain and on a tiny research grant, even though Lewis had done his best for her, ring-fencing his money and his time to give her what he could. She let the sun back in, squinting to look at him.

He smiled and raised his eyebrows. Now, the question was, what could she do for Lewis? Showing through the fine translucence of his skin was a brackish smear of worry. His salary was safe, but money for the other staff and recurrent expenses, equipment, chemicals had to be found outside the department.

Other groups were pushing ahead, maybe passing them by. She'd heard an item on the news: a clinic in Eastern Europe was offering stem-cell treatment to patients with all sorts of neurological conditions. *All sorts of conditions* was a give-away; even stem cells weren't a cure-all miracle. But there was always the nag of doubt. Could some other team have done it? It was so easy to find yourself left out in the cold. The possibility of losing now made a long ominous shiver run through her and she had to persuade herself that the warmth on her legs was Californian heat to chase it away. Only then could she feel her team's ascendancy. The backing that a successful biotech company could provide was colossal. The great banks of gene analysers, the wall-to-wall synthesizers, the computers that designed and then produced drugs targeted at any receptor you wanted: they were bulwarks against doubt. Only creativity was required of the human employees: creativity and anything that fostered it.

'Grunge alert,' hissed Amber, and Rhea opened her eyes. Stephen Glatton was pretending to wander along the towpath, his solitary evening clotting around him. Rhea shuddered. At the freshers' party last week, Glatton had put his arm around her waist – not openly and high up across her shoulders, as Lewis often did. He had snaked his hand downwards, hidden from the others. The movement had felt obscene; she had seen Dave's face in the mirror behind the bar, oblivious to the stealthy invasion, and had moved quickly to join him. Her job was a permanent university-funded post, but if Lewis lost his edge she would be transferred to another, more promising, team. Probably Stephen Glatton's.

Lewis might have had the same thought. He said to Amber, panicked, 'Don't let him join us. What if Vic calls when he's here?' and she ran her hand down his arm until it found his fingers and grasped them. It was closer than a kiss, more private, an intimate gesture of promise and protection. So powerful that even Glatton must have sensed its exclusion: he waved and sauntered on. Lewis and Amber stayed close, Rhea waiting behind them, until he was safely out of sight.

Rhea sat apart and kept her hopes to herself in case they came to nothing, but a feeling stayed with her, a narrow chance that Vic might consider their cells for medical trials. The fundamental change that patient involvement could offer them would fast-track their ambitions beyond anything they could imagine.

Lewis had been electrified when she had first come back from the US, bringing her industrial savvy with her. And now her old boss had been in touch. Big, slow-talking, fast-thinking Vic, all his years of commercial success comfortably shoring him up, wanting to talk to her about a link-up. The quivering of the phone, the way it surged up in anticipation of the US connection, made her heart bump against her ribs. The techniques she'd learnt in the States tingled at her fingertips. With Vic's money she could apply them to Lewis's work. This could be an important career move for her, bringing home this contact.

From his place in the shade, Lewis was watching her. She might be his second-in-command but she had outstripped him. If she could fix the money, there would be no stopping the two of them. He knew it too. He pulled her phone towards himself, into the pool of shadow made by the umbrella. When it finally rang he looked at her, calculating and warning.

There were things that Rhea wasn't allowed to say.

Technicalities mostly: the details of how her work was done – her methods of preparation; the formulation of the chemicals she had discovered to support stem-cell growth; the antibodies that identified cell-surface markers. Desperate secrets, all of them.

But Vic was after every last morsel of information. At the other end of the phone the beguiling transatlantic tones poured on, swathing her in blandishments. The satin sheen of the flattery didn't fool her but, still, it had its effect. There was seduction in the praise that she hadn't had enough of. It loosened her joints, the small muscles around her lips, but not her tongue. Her experiments were almost beyond doubt, but that wasn't the same as irrefutable. Rhea was too wary to give anything away; she had long lost the knack of idle abandon. The full-stop click of her closing mobile brought Lewis's eyes back to her. He had been monitoring every word she uttered.

'Vic,' she said. 'He wants to come over to the conference a few days early to have a word.'

Lewis pulled a face, not quite cool enough to hide his delight. 'He knows we're on to something, then.'

'He wants in.'

'Because we're only working with adult tissue?'

Rhea nodded, and leant towards Amber to disturb a spiderling from her sister's arm. She felt the warmth of living skin; everything about Amber was so near to the surface. 'You're going to come into money, Amber.' The spider spun its long escape route over the edge of the table, launching off into the unknown.

'Don't tell him anything else,' said Lewis. 'Better if you don't talk to him at all. Next time get him to contact me.'

Rhea gave him a sharp look. 'I can handle him.'

But Lewis stood his ground. 'He knows you so he thinks he can manipulate you.'

21

Rhea raised her eyebrows pointedly at her sister. 'Your husband thinks I can be manipulated,' she said, but Lewis was adamant, stiff with anxiety.

'I can't afford any mistakes. You used to work for him. He'll think you owe him.'

Owe him what, Lewis? I work for you. Am I supposed to owe you something? she thought, but she only smiled at Amber and shrugged. Lewis risked the sun and put an arm around each of them, drawing them in.

It was a warm evening, the last weekend before the beginning of term, and the great chestnut trees that led along the canal from the campus all the way to the quayside still held onto their leaves. The light was just beginning to fail. Returning students renewed their links, walking along the paved towpath touching with languorous contentment. A solemn pair of lovers in matched jeans and leather jackets leant over the industrial railings of the footbridge, reunited in their reflections, dropping votive pennies into the limpid water to disrupt the images and watching them re-form. As it grew too dark to see, they wandered on, towards the lights of the city, or home, to quiet and each other.

Rhea couldn't guess which. She was relieved that her ideas had worked out, too relieved to bother arguing with Lewis. Dave was coming home tonight after his couple of days in Nottingham. She wanted these soft edges, this feeling of being in between, the melting of day into night, because she could feel the start of something momentous.

CHAPTER 2

The story of her face-off with gamma-rated Glatton resounded through the department, waking up the listless moments between experiments. Because everyone was talking about alpha-Amber, an idea ruffled in her mind: that there was a place for her in the lab set-up, something she could do for Lewis and Rhea that they couldn't do for themselves. She rehearsed the scene conscientiously, lining up the details to their best advantage so that Lewis and Rhea couldn't avoid seeing that she was indispensable to them.

'Why did you want to be a scientist?' she asked Lewis. A throb of tension pulsed in his temples, turning the faint blue veins livid. 'It's not an exam,' she said. 'I just wondered.'

He shrugged as though it didn't matter. 'I suppose I wanted to discover things.'

'But what about you? Do you want everyone to know who you are? Do you want to be important? Lewis, do you want to make money out your work? Because if you don't, believe me, someone else will.'

He couldn't admit easily to personal designs in any of this. The moral safety of a medical mission excused him from any responsibility to himself. Or her. All of Lewis's past, all the exams he had studied for, all the grant applications he had written, especially the ones that had been turned down, all the late-night and weekend experiments when she'd been left alone clouded his features before he answered: 'Yes.'

She had finally coaxed the true scale of Lewis's ambition out into the open, mewling and naked. Amber could feel the future taking shape around her; she could soothe and clothe it into something decent and glowing. 'A stem cell.' She blew softly on his hair. 'The tiny thing that is the start of everything.'

Already she could imagine the way she would present it: a single cell held in the cup of a human hand. Whose hand? Lewis's? Rhea's? Her own? No nail varnish. The hand that held the future of medicine would be unadorned, competent, clean. Would it be a female hand? She paused. No. The female hands would hold the patients that were going to be saved by Lewis's research. His hand, then? But there was a better idea. A child's hand. A baby grows from a stem cell. That one cell divides and produces all the other cells of the body, heart, liver, eyes, skin, hand. She took Lewis's hand between hers. His fingers were thin and long, but his knuckles protruded, unexpectedly large, almost swollen.

'Do you think you're getting arthritis?'

'No.' Lewis flexed his joints experimentally. 'But if I do, I'll take some stem cells from my cartilage and grow myself some new knuckles.'

It seemed to Amber that she could almost see the few remaining stems that were scattered throughout Lewis's body, in his skin, his heart, inside his bones and teeth; he was so transparent to her.

'Could you really?' she asked, and let him tell her that he couldn't, not yet, but that he almost could.

'It's just that if you take adult stem cells from, say, the bones, you can't turn them into just anything, as you could with embryonic stem cells. They've already moved some of the way towards being determined.' Lewis grimaced at the idea that the cells he prepared weren't totally flexible.

'They don't do it to get at you, Lewis,' she pointed out.

'But we have to find a way to grow them so they can turn into anything. Don't you see? We could cure almost anything if we could do that. Grow people new nerves for Parkinson's disease, new brains for Alzheimer's patients, new hearts, everything. All from your own body.'

'Better than someone else's.' Amber felt a vague distaste at the idea of a new heart from someone else, never mind a brain.

'What if you had some brain cells from Glatton?' she mused. 'Do you think I would still love you?'

'Christ, Amber. Don't even joke about it.'

They were sitting in Lewis's study at home. Far away in the kitchen the oven timer began to shrill and Amber rose. She knew that her sister had arrived back from the States with this adult-stem-cell idea buzzing around her head. Now Lewis was laying claim to it. She folded the two thoughts tightly together and tucked them away where they couldn't contradict one another. Lewis and Rhea, constantly needing to be reconciled. But she knew how to present their discoveries. If they could do it, she could make sure everyone knew about it. And she needed a decent new initiative to present to her boss because some of her work projects weren't going well. She hated the fusty hand-shakes and bored businessmen. She loved what Lewis and Rhea were doing. Tailor-made spare parts for the sick from their own bodies. It was an operation to be proud of. Even Warren, her boss, would be awestruck when he understood its impact on medical science. He'd be desperate for their portfolio.

By the time Friday had come around again, she realised that the evening, heading for home, was when she was happiest. Birds, flocking to roost, formed black nets to gather up stragglers; commuters used the journey to create a clear space between them and their jobs. Amber glanced in the rear-view mirror, back towards the city. She thought of the crush in Oswald Street, the gathering of footloose friends, crowded into bars, the pushed bodies and pretended intimacies. The cringe-making competition for the most triumphant day. Then later, when you'd left and the drinks flushed the others from their hidey-holes, the tawdry speculations about your private life would come spinning out, like sugar, brittle and sticky, lingering to be used against you some other day. Embarrassment at the shallowness of it all grasped her. She sloughed it off and turned onto the slip road. Grow Your Own. Spare-part Surgery. She hadn't hit on the phrase that would describe the scale and beauty of Lewis and Rhea's achievements, but there was time. And a weekend always seemed an eternity on Friday night.

The motorway receded. In front of her, dotted across the countryside, welcoming lamps were switched on in windows. This is my world now, she thought. I belong here and it can be whatever I make of it.

An elderly cyclist was riding one of those workaday bikes that old men rode slowly, pedalling their way to and from home. So much more dignified than the pumping Lycra-clad buttocks you struggled to avoid in town. He was cresting a small hill, perhaps a hundred yards away. The road was empty so Amber tweaked the accelerator. The car gathered speed, the move through the automatic gears as smooth as precision engineering could make it. A slight turn on the wheel and it swung out obediently, just the right amount to avoid any oncoming traffic. She overtook the old man and moved back into place. It was getting cold. She stretched for the climate-control button. Everything behind in order, a quick check, a glance in the mirror. Oh, God, she couldn't see the cyclist. She stopped the car.

Failing light. Vague, gloomy shapes. A spasm that closed her throat and clumsy, shaking legs as she ran back along the road. The bike was stretched out on the verge, its front lamp shining up into the sky. The old man: nowhere.

An ambulance would come screaming; it would take a long time out here. Then it would speed away to the hospital or – would there be no hurry? – to the morgue. *Oh, God, I was really careful*, she'd say to the policeman. *I was watching him*. And his face would take on the disengaged, accusatory expression that he used whenever he had to deal with protesting suspects, as contemptuous prosecuting counsels rose to their cold-eyed work behind him.

'Christ, where are you?' she croaked. Across the hedge, staring at her in his own paroxysm of alarm, was the old man, one hand clutching at the trailing greenery.

'You all right, pet?' he asked warily.

Amber's knees buckled haphazardly, with no particular connection to her legs. 'I thought you were hurt,' she said.

The old man grinned, the last of the light catching his long teeth. 'It's very kind of you to be concerned,' he said, 'but I just stopped to pick some blackberries for my missus. She likes them, see, and there won't be many more now.'

He might have heard the shudder of relief that rattled her bones. Grateful for the falling dark, Amber hoped he hadn't noticed anything strange. The car door was standing wide open into the narrow road; she hurried back and slid inside, closing it before anyone could come along and tear it off.

Grandad's death had given her the money to move out here and concentrate on getting pregnant. She dreaded the thought that she had constructed a terrible bargain: a life in exchange for a death. Fate would want paying for something like that. She felt the hard pinch of anxiety that always came with getting what you wanted.

*

The best part of twenty miles inland from the city, two from the nearest village and protected by a circle of hills, Snitter Heugh was everything she wanted. Early on Saturday morning, it was hardly light and Amber was outside, enthralled by it all. Her house had been given its name, the Old English for Snowy Ridge, some time in the far distant past but she hadn't lived there through a winter yet; it had been hers only through a busy summer. Lewis had been at work all the time and the garden had been neglected. After Mr Darell had moved away, no one had thought to cut back the spring bulbs or the perennial borders or prune any of the hedges that broke the winter wind, so they had all grown unchecked. Such benign neglect, coming after years of careful cultivation, meant the autumn garden was in full fruit: the spiked holly that kept out the next-door cattle was splattered expectantly with red berries, arching their way towards Christmas; bulging seed cases yellowed, prescient of coming summers. Amber picked one and rubbed it between her fingers. It split open and scattered its seeds into the waiting earth.

Lewis and Rhea were working – playing – she thought, day and night to get ready for their conference and the American, the money man. Amber knew something about money. It made the world go round, however Lewis and Rhea tried to deny it. In the end, she would have to help them with Vic, but today she could lean against the brown stone wall and feel the heat it was absorbing from the sun. The stones were square cut, large for house walls. Everyone knew that they'd come from the Roman villa a couple of fields away. She could see the stunted remains, worn low by centuries of attrition; the sense of history intrigued her. She couldn't stop imagining the men who had cut those stones, building something that had lasted nearly a thousand years. They must have walked on the very paths she used now, swearing and sweating.

'Sweating?' Rhea had said, slapping her down. 'You haven't

been up here in the winter yet. They were probably freezing most of the time.' She had reluctantly conceded the swearing. 'Yes, you'll have got that bit right.' Amber moved her shoulders against the roughness of the stones, trying to rub some of their strength into herself: persuading Lewis and Rhea to do the smart thing at the conference wasn't going to be straightforward.

Up here, morning came fully formed. Once the sun had tipped the hills there was nothing to hold it back. It flowed across the wide valley bottom unimpeded and filled every hollow and cranny; in the city, gloom could linger most of the day in closed rooms and back alleys. The light was gaining strength, promising a fine, bright day, far too good to waste. I'll ask Rhea and Dave over, she decided. Once the house was full it would attract luck, more life. For now, it was too big a space to fill by themselves, by herself, really, because Lewis was still in bed, sleeping off the corrosive effects of too many hours in the lab.

She waited until nine o'clock to call; Rhea and Dave would be up, but not busy yet. They'd be at the table in Rhea's flat, weekend breakfast crumbling around them, both too distracted to talk. Talking would come later, when they had forgotten about the week's worries, or at least managed to clear them to one side. Sitting quietly on her kitchen step, holding her breath, Amber could hear the rasping of cows' tongues as they tore grass on the other side of the hedge. It didn't matter if you were too tired to talk as long as you had that to listen to. They could sit out before lunch and relax. Rhea would appreciate the break.

Dave answered the phone.

'Good morning,' she said. 'I'm calling to let you know that you have been selected to receive a day out in the country. Lunch will be provided by the famous kitchens at Snitter Heugh and served *al fresco* by . . . me.' There was no sound from the other end of the phone. 'It's a lovely day up here, Dave. You and Rhea can have a total chill-out. I've already done the cooking.' Amber paused,

29

leaving space for an appreciative riposte, something funny and clever that would get the day off to the right start, but nothing came back. She gave the phone an irritated little shake. 'Dave, are you still there?' she said, into the void of the dead line.

She had to call Rhea's mobile to get an answer.

'What's the matter with your phone?' she asked. Rhea's voice was blurry; she sounded half awake when she said nothing, as far as she knew, and Amber realised she was still in bed. 'Why aren't you up, Rhe?'

'I'm having a lie-in, that's all.'

Amber knew that Rhea wasn't having a lie-in. Lewis might like to stay in bed but not Rhea: she got out of bed as soon as her eyes opened and made herself something to eat. Rhea was always too hungry to stay asleep.

'Why? Are you ill? I wanted you to come over for the day. It's such nice weather, we shouldn't waste it.'

Rhea sighed and said, 'I'm all right but I don't think we can make it, Amber.' Her voice was untypically sour.

'It'll do you good.'

But Rhea wasn't having any. 'I'm all right,' she protested. 'I went back to work after you left last night. It was really late so I slept in the spare room. I haven't woken up yet. Don't worry about it.'

Chinese lanterns caught the morning sun with a throb of orange. Amber couldn't let go of the idea of Rhea and Dave made happy in her home: a luminous vision that they just weren't signing up to.

'I wanted to talk to you about the conference.'

'We can't come over, Amber, but I'm fine. You come down here, if you like. We'll have coffee in town. Come on the train. Lewis can drop you at the halt and we can meet at the station coffee shop.'

Rhea's voice had turned steely with resolve; Amber accepted

that there wasn't going to be a celebratory day at Snitter Heugh:
that a glorious something was already over and done with. She
appealed to Lewis. 'What do you think is wrong with her?'

Lewis shrugged, car keys ready, jangling at the ends of his
fingertips. 'No idea. Girl stuff, I expect. Probably wants you to
go on the train so you can have a boozy lunch together.'

Apart from that, Lewis was puzzled, at a loss. Or more likely,
she thought, not bothered. She could already read, in the dart of
his eyes towards the study, his eagerness for the hours he would
have to himself. He was more at home with research than with
people. But she wanted company. The sisters had always been
close; with their mother, they had formed a tight little knot
against the world after Dad had died and it had never unravelled.

She already had an inkling of why Rhea wouldn't come to
Snitter Heugh. The scenario spread itself out to her. There was
only one picture that all the pieces fitted. Rhea was sick in the
morning; Dave was worried to death. Her sister was pregnant.
On top of that, Rhea still had to protect her. She didn't want her
to drive. Rhea was afraid of the impact the unwelcome pregnancy would have on her infertile sister. The hurt deep inside
Amber drew further back and hid itself, unable to acknowledge
such a debt.

She was overcome by the effort that this was going to cost
her, to be pleased for Rhea, who wouldn't be pleased for herself,
and at the same time to hide her own grief. Her body felt outside her control; it wouldn't co-operate. Rhea had been right
about the train: she wasn't fit to drive.

Years of suppressing anguish rolled out before Amber. She saw
herself suffocating in the background of Rhea's motherhood. At
christenings and birthday parties, during holidays and school
concerts, she would always be a ghost at the family banquet.
She was doomed to frighten people by trying to join the feast.
She put on her jacket, as though she had never done it before.

Fingers, elbows, shoulders, joint by joint she worked herself into the sleeves. She paired the buttons charily with their holes. This was how it would be from now on.

Sitting on an empty train, Amber watched the countryside disappear and change into suburban houses. Weekend families were at home, pottering in the garden, cutting lawns and cleaning cars, because this was an ordinary Saturday for them. If those people were to go out, their houses would wait patiently for them: plates would stay put in the kitchen cupboards, clothes in the wardrobes or airing on the radiators, even the food in supermarket storage jars would remain the same, just as it had been left. But while she was away from it, her own home, the focus of her hopes – she couldn't not know that now – was going to change irrevocably. All the things she'd optimistically assembled would transform themselves into jeering changelings. By the time she got home, her sister would have told her and everything would be different.

As soon as she saw Rhea, she knew she was right. The awful green jacket that had fitted loosely was strained across the last button. The pale face, the tired eyes, her dark hair hanging limp and despondent, all helped to drive the truth home. It was like being in school again with some new teacher standing you up in front of the whole class and asking if you were going to be as clever as your sister. Amber had understood then that her best chance had lain in being a good girl; she understood now that she was going to need everything she could muster even to be able to put on the pretence of being good.

She rehearsed her public-relations face, empathetic, understanding, in a distant, professional sense, as she crossed the station forecourt, but Rhea turned, the coffee machine spitting steam and fury behind her, and waved so wanly, but with such a brave effort, that Amber's resolve fled. A harassed barista saw the change and looked back uncomfortably to his fuming machine.

The first of all the embarrassing and humiliating incidents in store for Amber had already happened; she cringed in shame.

'Whatever's the matter?'

'Nothing. What's the matter with you?'

Rhea and Amber swapped concerned looks to and fro across the tiny table, a silent, sisterly auction for jurisdiction. It was Amber, as usual, who gave in and spoke first. 'Why couldn't you come to Snitter Heugh? It's a lovely day.' She looked up at the station roof where dirty windows leaked a sullen light into the concourse. 'It would do you good to get some fresh air. You're so pale you must be . . .' but she couldn't say the rest. She stopped and waited, braced herself for the news.

'Dave. I didn't want to come with him.'

So that was it. Dave didn't want the baby.

The coffee shop was small but it wasn't friendly. Too many strangers had tramped through it and gone away without leaving anything of themselves behind. It had been the same when they were little and Dad was always ill. Nurses and neighbours had replaced their mother. It was an article of faith with Rhea that a baby needed parents to love it. She said she had been Amber's mother, in fact. Shining through Amber's mind came the glorious idea that she could repay her sister, take on the baby. The thought of nursing the lonely little one glittered urgently, only to fade, the presence of Rhea prohibiting it. Amber tried to replace it with an image of herself smiling at Rhea's news, happy for her, but it wouldn't take shape. Her lips felt stiff and intractable, hardly able to let her articulate what had to be said.

'You know,' she forced out, as she reached across the table, 'you can tell me, Rhea. I won't mind.'

'You'll find out soon enough, anyway.'

There were some things you couldn't hide. Amber's gaze strayed to the strained button. It was open now. Rhea's hand hung loosely across her abdomen. Amber was able to manage a consoling smile for a sister. But her heart was fluttering. She couldn't look at Rhea's face. She looked away for a moment so that she would only have to hear the news. Rhea was talking to her.

She was saying, '*Dave and I are splitting up.*'

The rest of the concourse was silent. The clamour of arrival and departure stopped. Amber had to blink to make sure it was still there and then, miraculously, it went on its way again.

'Why?'

It was an accusation. Amber flung it out into the void where it reverberated and came back at her. Rhea was silent, gathering the thin packets of sugar into a pattern, alternating white and brown in radiating spokes, with a hole at the centre.

It couldn't be endured, her sister's aversion to facing the truth. Amber brought the whole calamity down on herself. 'Just because you're pregnant?'

Rhea's face registered alarm, fear and incredulity in turn. 'Amber,' she laughed, 'why would I be pregnant? You've got babies on the brain.' She piled the sugars back into the dish and rubbed her hands emphatically.

Amber was weak with the ineffable relief of a sacrifice reprieved. It meant that she was equal to whatever else was needed of her. She moved her chair, put a protecting arm around Rhea's shoulders and felt her stiffen at the close contact. Usually she hated it when Rhea brushed her off. This time she tried not to mind.

'Come on, what happened? You were fine last week. It can't be that bad.' Rhea pulled against her, impatient, discomfited, but Amber kept her arm firmly in place. 'You've had a row,' she said. 'It happens. It's nothing. You'll get over it.' She shrugged her shoulders to prove how unimportant this would turn out to be, and Rhea escaped her arm.

When Amber discovered that Rhea was throwing Dave out because he had found himself another job, in Nottingham of all places, she couldn't stop herself laughing.

'Oh, Rhea.' Tears hung behind her eyes; she smiled widely, just to make sure there could be no mistake as to the reason for them. 'What's wrong with that? His contract's nearly up. Aren't you glad he's got a permanent job?' When Rhea took too long to answer, stirring her coffee, as though it was to blame, Amber's good nature filled in the silence for her. 'You can commute at weekends. Then, when you've finished this project, you could look for something nearer to him.' The ominous cessation of the coffee stirring cautioned her. 'If you wanted to, that is.'

Limply, and too late, she sat quiet.

Rhea was already gathering her things and making to leave. 'He didn't even bother to tell me,' she said. 'The first I knew about it was last night, when it was all sorted. Everyone in the university must have known except me. I feel such a fool. Who was it sat plotting with him and promised not to tell me? I'd like to know that.'

'I had no idea, Rhea, and neither did Lewis, or he would have told me.'

Amber pulled her sister back into the uncomfortable plastic seat. The barista looked across in consternation, fearful that he was going to have an incident on his shift. Amber gave him a conciliatory smile, like the smile she usually gave Dave when Rhea and Lewis were too full of themselves to notice, and the lad turned back to the bottled-up fury of the espresso machine. *Oh, can't you see, Rhea? Dave needs a life too. He only wanted his turn.* The words formed themselves on Amber's lips, bubbling up to be said, but Rhea was piling cups and clearing away the debris, her eyes darkening and threatening.

'Rhea, you can't trash your whole relationship over a job interview.'

Finally Rhea sagged. Her face collapsed into deep, hurt lines. 'It's not the bloody job interview. It's that he didn't even tell me. It's as though none of it was anything to do with me.'

'There must be an explanation. Why don't you have a proper talk, just the two of you?'

Rhea shook her head. 'I don't want to talk about it.'

Amber wondered privately if Rhea had wanted her to come down to talk to Dave, to help patch things up. 'Why did you want me to come on the train?'

'Because you would have parked your car at the flat and I've told him he may as well go right now. I didn't want you to run into him packing.'

'Come on, Rhea, you haven't thrown him out already? You can't just let that be it, after all this time.'

'That's what he said,' snapped Rhea. 'He said we could work something out. But, believe me, after what he's done I can end it just like that. I don't need him, you know.'

That implacable tone. Amber knew it all right. It had cut her down all her life. When Rhea made up her mind she stuck to it, whatever it cost. No going back with her, no second chance to make amends. There was a long quiet spell. Finally Amber reached across the table and put her hand on her sister's arm, but it was as if Rhea was encased in transparent body armour, visible but untouchable. Who else would rather be alone than risk not being loved?

'He does love you, you know.'

Rhea raised her eyebrows. There might have been the splintery glint of hurt but Amber knew that the subject of Dave was closed between them.

She used the best china that evening, and a tablecloth covered with butterflies and flowers tied with fancy ribbon bows that had come to light during the move. Whenever their mother had not wanted to talk, she'd embroidered things: butterflies, crinoline ladies. Easter flower extravaganzas had provided a bulwark against the constant attentions of their grandparents. After Dad's death, Mum had disappeared into needlework, to avoid giving offence. As time went on her bunker had developed into a haven and she'd become involved with Guilds. The old-fashioned linens had turned into great mystically patterned hangings, exhibited in galleries and stately homes. The paternal grandparents had thoroughly approved of this turn of events, involving, as it did, no new husband to usurp their son's place. They'd continued to pay his share of the firm's profits to dear Stella. 'Unstinting', their mother had been heard to say, in a confidential undertone to her friends. Amber wondered if she had minded the pressure to preserve her widowhood, that born-again virginity, and, the grandparents had subtly implied, her income, or had she truly found pleasure in the colour and texture of this absorbingly female art?

Amber had never sewn, hated it. At school she'd been forced to produce a row of rosebuds to decorate an unwanted bookmark. They'd felt like barbed wire to her as she stretched them out across the schoolroom canvas. She blenched now, shamefaced about her hysteria with Rhea. She set the table with determined pulses of kindness: Lewis's knife – he liked the slim modernist cutlery; the electric salt grinder, a present from work colleagues; two glasses bought with Granny on a trip to Bath. She left the places for Rhea and Dave empty, waiting, promising herself she would fill them soon.

Rhea reached back to remember, back past Dave, back past her work with Lewis, further back than her life in the US, to when she was a student. Amber was still at home with Mum so she was by herself and thought only her own thoughts. Foetuses swayed in her memory. Preserved, and grey from the formalin, they watched from their glass jars. She caught at the image and tried to hold it still in her mind. They were displayed in a glass case outside the anatomy lecture theatre. It was old and unsteady and the jostling crowd of students often knocked into it. Then the small bodies would revolve slowly, drawing her attention. It seemed indecent to stare back at them. But now a wall of photographs had replaced the display case: snapshots of babies born in the fertility unit. She stood transfixed.

'Lovely sight, aren't they?' A nurse looked at her, kindly but concerned. Rhea smiled briefly and moved on, trapped in the woman's thoughtful gaze. The memory of those foetuses weakened her, took her back to being a student without the right to an opinion. Now she would have made a fuss, had them removed, but there wasn't any need. Their images had been replaced by new babies, made possible by science.

'I've an appointment with Eleanor Bonworth,' she explained, and the nurse nodded, misunderstanding her confusion, and followed her into the clinic.

Eleanor Bonworth brought the cord blood herself. It was still warm and full of stem cells. And it was with this gift of blood that Rhea had been able to make the antibody that identified stem cells. Without that, she would have had no means of knowing which of her cells were the valuable ones. Full of life herself, Eleanor handed it over and leant comfortably against the reception desk. The worried nurse found some urgent task behind another door and Rhea felt whole again.

'I was looking at the pictures of your babies,' she said.

'Not mine, Rhea,' Eleanor corrected her, with her disarming smile. 'They belong to their parents. I only do the techie bits.' The fertility consultant was as far from Rhea's image of techie as anyone could be. Plump, middle-aged and dressed in garish colours, she was everyone's idea of a career mother. Perhaps that was why she was so successful. Rhea stowed the big vial of cord blood in her vacuum flask. 'I could send you the results,' she offered.

Eleanor beamed. 'I thought you'd never offer,' she said. 'I was beginning to think they weren't any good.'

'They're getting better all the time. The cord blood has been crucial. You can't imagine how important it's been.'

'Oh, my mothers are pleased to let you have it. They say it's a thank-you for their babies.' Eleanor looked towards the ward. 'Why don't you bring your results up to show me? We can have lunch.' A web of understanding spun between them. An uncontestable link between research and patient. 'Soon,' Rhea said, 'we'll be able to store cord cells from all babies and use them to treat them for the rest of their lives.' Perhaps by the time Amber had her baby.

On the way back to the lab Rhea kept thinking of her sister. She knew that Amber was being typically thoughtful. She phoned every day and never mentioned Dave; she was being supremely tactful because she would be dying to get the full, unabridged story. But she kept out of it. She chatted about work, Rhea's flat, Stephen Glatton, her home improvements, but every one of these 'safe' topics transformed itself into a funny story with a sad hollow at its centre. Insufficient yields, empty spaces, that awful man, not enough money: all of them led to awkward silences that Amber blew away with jokes. It was touching to be so considerately managed, but it was irritating too.

Rhea's mind had never been so badly behaved. If she wasn't careful, she found herself going over and over it again and again: the way that Dave had got himself another job without telling her. There must be some people who'd known: his referees for a start. She stared uncontrollably at the Business School, wondering if they'd been sworn not to tell her, or if Dave had just trusted to luck that she wouldn't find out. Might he actually have moved away without telling her? It seemed so.

The routine of the laboratory kept her going. But away from the bench she was at a loss, so she stayed at work where the aircon lulled the room into cool and Rhea into calm. The idea of two outputs from one system pleased her and she worked constantly, letting the circuitry take the strain. Forgetting herself and slowly improving her cell yields at the same time: how could that not be right? Fortunately the cord blood wouldn't wait. She gave it all her attention, switching on the centrifuge and leaning into the concealing hum of the accelerating rotor. Leaving work as late as she could, Rhea ran home in the evening and counted every pace: the unbroken rhythm and steady accumulation of the numbers permeating her.

Afterwards she duveted down, warm in the bed that she and Dave used to share, but still it took such an effort to sleep, such a long leap across humiliation and anger, that she abandoned the effort, leaving the blinds open to watch the sky. The days were cooler and more bearable now, but it seemed the earth, fully charged by the preceding summer, had to rid itself of all the surplus heat. The nights were suffocating and she always felt queasy. If she did manage to dip into sleep, it brought no relief. She would wake up shortly afterwards, alarmed by the noisy grinding of her teeth. Her jaw ached, and when the clocks went back in October, and her colleagues enjoyed an extra hour of sleep, Rhea endured it.

It might be tiredness that was making her feel cold all the time.

'Rubbish,' Amber said. 'It *is* cold. Look at the weather. I need double-glazing.' Even while she watched the kitchen blinds move in the draught from Snitter Heugh's original-feature sash windows Rhea deciphered the message as *I need a baby*. Home refurbishment as displacement activity was easy to understand. Rhea thought she herself had learnt all there was to know about displacement activity in the last few weeks of trying not to think about being miserable: in fact, betrayal boredom was setting in. She climbed onto a chair and tightened the cord on the blinds to stop them flapping. Amber looked a little disconcerted at the makeshift solution. 'You can always borrow a cardigan, Rhea. Any one you like.'

In Amber's bedroom – it was Lewis's too of course, but he wasn't allowed quite the same ownership rights – there was a gloomy clothes press, bought at an auction. It could never have been made to hold a wardrobe like Amber's; the blues and the greens and the deep, startling pinks shimmered agonisingly inside it, where there should have been greys and browns and sombre, regal purples. Rhea grabbed a pashmina, turquoise and peach like tropical coral, and dislodged something under it. A lemony flutter to the floor: a soft threaded ribbon that she knew, puzzlingly, had to be from a baby jacket. For a sudden moment Rhea thought, She's pregnant. A whole world of Amber fulfilled was hidden in a clothes press and she, Amber's sister, had been deliberately excluded from it: a re-run of the Dave scenario.

Bitterness engulfed her, but even alone, she slapped the glaze of indifference over her face. Before she had got it securely in place, she knew that it couldn't be true. Amber wasn't pregnant. She had said so, and she would never lie about a thing like that. She must have bought the jacket as a talisman, imagining that baby arms would come along to fill those little sleeves.

Rhea could remember Amber as a girl, casting the I Ching for a fascinated crowd of school friends, getting them to throw pennies in the air, then writing down her mysterious runes with them hanging on her every word. She said the future was already out there and all you had to do was to reach forward and touch it. Her fingers – she was into Goth at the time and they were tipped with great blobs of black varnish – were perfect for the job. Lewis, the house in the country, the baby clothes: they were all part of the same process. Rhea pushed the lemony froth back, piling the pashmina on top – she buried it as deeply as she could, so that Amber wouldn't be upset – and then she took a cardigan from another shelf.

The sisters slouched down together on the sofa. Rhea hated wearing someone else's clothes, especially Amber's. She hadn't put her arms into the cardigan sleeves so it slipped from her shoulders and crumpled onto Amber, where it belonged.

'That cardigan looks better on you than on me. I may as well give it to you.' Neither of them moved.

At the edge of Rhea's vision was Amber's wanting face. Rhea knew what she would be thinking, but couldn't mention. 'Why don't you do something about it?' she asked.

Amber's face sprang into life. 'I am doing something,' she said. 'I'm always doing something about it. Poor Lewis is worn out.' They both dissolved into laughter: the first laugh untinged by compassion that they had shared for weeks.

'But he wants a baby, too. He'll be there for you both.'

As Amber subsided into a comfortable humour, Rhea pressed her. 'The tests won't hurt, you know, and they might uncover something really simple. You ought to find out.' She was unable to disguise her belief in the value of a methodical, scientific approach.

Amber was still reluctant. 'But what if they say no? There's no hope then, is there?'

False hope: it was a situation that Rhea never wanted to be in again. 'At least you'll know the worst. What's to lose?' Amber didn't answer. 'I had to face up to knowing . . . about Dave. It was the not knowing that was worst.'

'I'm not sure, Rhea. You're better at knowing than I am. Knowing is what you're really good at, actually.' Amber's voice faltered with the certainty of unfulfilled need.

Rhea couldn't forget the hidden baby jacket and all it

represented. As in running, there were muscles you didn't know you had until they started hurting. It was the same with your feelings. Being left out, the last to know, went a long way beyond hurt pride; it burrowed down to something so far beneath, so well hidden, that you didn't know it was there until it moved and left you suspended alone over a precipice. Dave had undercut all the certainties in her life.

'I'd give you a baby, if I could,' Rhea answered. 'Anyway, I bet medical science could. At least think about it, Amber.' She kept her face calm because Amber's eyes were searching it, trying to find an answer.

'Do you really think it would work?'

'Why shouldn't it?' said Rhea. 'I'll talk to Eleanor Bonworth for you. She's lovely. You won't find anyone better.'

The knot between them tightened.

CHAPTER 3

If I don't laugh, I'll probably cry. Normally when Lewis read he drained the life out of the book. Not this time. *Investigations into Infertility: Part I: Male* had got the better of him. Its detailed descriptions of the infinitesimal malfunctions that compromise masculine fecundity had left him feeling perfectly limp. The authorities had installed CCTV cameras to deter student mis-behaviour in the library so he'd squeezed himself into a secluded corner of the stacks where there could be no extant record of his reading. Now he felt as though he were loitering in a doorway, wearing a dirty raincoat, and it didn't coincide with his preferred image: bright young academic, pushing for a chair and flaunting the sexiest wife in the university. In fact, it made him look like a no-mark wannabe.

This was something that happened to other people: the sort of people who didn't put the effort in. He'd always worked hard and he couldn't understand how he'd come to this.

'Norham!' his mates would shout, breath clouding in the freezing air of the school playing field, as they kicked the ball, expecting him to pick it up. Lewis had always thought there was a bit of class to his name. It was a place, like Warwick or Leicester, and dukes were once addressed by their place name when the king called them to his side.

Now some monstrous nurse would shout, 'Norham!' expecting

him to stand up in front of a waiting room full of people and go to submit his reproductive tract to intimate investigation. He squirmed, and the book fell to the floor. As he groped about under his seat, the thought struck him, with the unwarranted weight of a foul blow, that when his tests were run, all the lab rats would know who he was.

'Norham,' they would say, sleaze lifting their voices. 'He works over the road in stem cells, doesn't he?'

Their grubby hands would pluck at the cover of his report form and work their way through the results. Sperm count. At the thought, he let out a groan. 'The bastards!' And then he had to look up nervously, sure he had been overheard. Obviously he couldn't use his own name. He needed an alter ego: the bloke they knew at lab booze-ups couldn't be identified as the patient whose sperm they were peering at.

Long-haul Lewis, working all hours. Innocent enough words but they had sharp elbows. When he had first been allocated an office, the only available space was a corner of the lab. The university maintenance men had erected a couple of partitions – plywood and glass – but no one had thought to order any blinds, so every passing student could look over and watch Lewis at his desk. Grateful for any space of his own, he hadn't made a fuss. Instead, he'd stuck posters over the lower part of the windows and ducked behind them. Even so, unpredictable transmissions penetrated his flimsy screen, clearer on some days than others. Sometimes, by chance, he would get a helping of some student smartness that had never been meant for his ears. Sometimes he was intended to hear the whinges, the deviously voiced complaints of his research team. He tried to take notice because he hadn't forgotten his own years as a post-doc, but it was impossible to know what to do for them. They were never satisfied. If he'd had more funding, more prestige . . . If only everything wasn't always just another few steps into the future. Lewis heard more grumbling than he liked through the lash-up of a partition.

Now, in the library with the incriminating volume balanced between the table and his knees, it was the unheard that was occupying him: Amber and Rhea, forever plotting together, shifting apart whenever he approached. He suspected that they had planned the infertility investigations together, then laid a trail of goodies in his path so that he had gobbled his way into these straits without a thought.

He'd come across Amber clearing out the bathroom cabinet, her bottles of flowery remedies piled into the bin. 'Rhea says alternative medicines don't work.'

He'd walked straight into that trap. 'She's right. Homeopathy is rubbish, but if it helps you to believe in it . . .' He had kissed her and acknowledged the familiar, seductive power of her perfume, but she had pulled away, businesslike. An efficient expression had held him at bay.

'I think you're right, Lewis. We should do everything properly, scientifically. I think we should have infertility investigations.'

At first Lewis agreed wholeheartedly. 'What a woman,' he'd said. 'Sex and science.' Only later had he realised it meant him too. And, later still, that Rhea had had something to do with it.

He'd been sitting outside the operating theatres one evening, waiting for some tissue. He'd been working late, because of the offer of a biopsy sample, some bone cells from a hip replacement. The patient was a surgeon himself, getting on; it seemed that the older you were, the more convinced you became of the importance of bio-donations. This character actually rang the lab, looking for a chance of immortality, and offered them a bit of himself. He said he was having some cartilage for his own research and, while they were sawing his bones up, he didn't mind parting with a bit of his marrow. It wasn't so often that

46

they got the offer of something like that, just the stuff of stem cells, although the younger the donor, the better they liked it. This particular surgeon reckoned he had been rejuvenated by an affair with a research assistant – probably giving him the bone marrow of an embryo. Rhea had grimaced and said she'd look for the evidence in the cell cultures, not the bedroom. The guy had offered half a kilo of fat from his beer gut too, but that had to be declined. Rhea had said she just couldn't face it. On the way up to theatre to collect the sample, Lewis had pictured him, with his hammock of belly, in the blue patient's nightshirt, asleep on his stainless-steel bed, and he knew why Rhea had been so reluctant.

The list was running late. It was half-term: a thirteen-year-old had been messing about on the railway line and not got out of the way quickly enough when the London train had come through. One of the theatres, and several of the most experienced surgeons, had been taken by the emergency so Lewis was left waiting in the corridor, wondering who the youngster might be, remembering his own foolhardy youth. He'd had a few narrow escapes himself, times when he'd acted long before he'd thought things through. It was only afterwards that you understood how small a gap there was between getting away with it and a catastrophe. His parents had always known it, and had warned him time and time again about the railway line, but this lad would have slithered down the embankment without the slightest fear of what came next. The first thing would have been a remote shudder of the rails, something that had nothing to do with him, and then the devastating noise exploding out of nowhere, wrapping itself around him and tossing him away. He probably wouldn't remember anything after that, and now the anaesthetic would lie on him, thick as a blanket, keeping him away from himself. Lewis could smell the soporific of medication in the air. Only the night-lights were on: they lit the linoleum flooring, making it gleam with a homely cleanliness. In the dimmed light, the warm, balmy air and the sense of exclusion and postponement, he had begun to drift towards sleep.

The double doors had banged apart and one of the trainees came stumbling out of theatre. He sat, his hands hanging between his knees, his head down.

'Tired?' Lewis had asked him.

'Wiped out. We're losing the kid, and it's manic in there.' As he moved to sit up straighter, his operating-theatre clogs squeaked against the floor, a note of distress and alarm. 'I felt faint. Nothing to eat all day.'

After Rhea had processed the sample, Lewis had seen the young medic again, downstairs in Reception, searching through his pockets for change for the tea machine. Still haggard, he greeted them with a thin, discouraged smile that told them he had just seen his first death. He needed sustenance, rest, consolation.

'I've got a cereal bar,' Lewis offered, holding it out. The lad had reached to take it just as Lewis moved towards him. They had collided, and fumbled together, then laughed as they tried again to pass the bar between them.

Just then the parents of the boy who had died came out of the chapel with the priest. Lewis didn't think they'd seen anything – they were deep in the rawness of their loss; their heads were bowed and the priest was talking quietly into their ears, soothing the cacophony of despair that must have been ringing in their minds – but a burst of mortification stopped Lewis laughing and shuffling around.

The grieving couple had stood close together. In a slow, sad wash of understanding Lewis recalled that those two people, between them, still contained every one of their dead boy's genes. He had been the child of their bodies and he would never really be gone from this world until the two people who still held the root of his life were dead too. For now, the most important thing for them might be to stay close, to stay alive, so that something of their son would too. They would never stop being his parents.

The cereal bar was handed over, and he had separated from the medic, both of them too embarrassed to exchange more than a cursory goodbye. It was in the car park, into the tumble of his shame, that Rhea had said, 'I've had a word with Eleanor Bonworth, Lewis. She'll be glad to see you and Amber. She says you're nowhere near to giving up hope.' For the first time, Lewis recognised the unsoundable depths of Amber's longing for a child to love.

Still, he hadn't appreciated all the indignities that the tests involved. He put *Infertility Investigations* back on the stack and slunk into the lab. With his manhood at stake, Lewis had to know for himself. He had to conduct a private sperm count in his own laboratory. Luckily, the students were somewhere else and he was able to put one of the counting chambers into his pocket without having to explain to anyone why he wanted it. It was heavy enough to weight his trousers unevenly and kept bumping on his leg. His hand clutched downwards in anxiety, expecting it to break, but when he got back to his own office he didn't dare take it out and slip it into a drawer: Rhea, Katherine and Fazil were working just beyond the glass partition and ready to notice every move he made. He wandered into the tissue-culture suite, but Andrew was bolting together the media sterilising equipment. He wrenched at the spanner so that it slipped from the nut and clanged against the supporting rods on its way to the floor.

'Shit.' Andrew had become belligerent lately and attacked the framework as if it were an enemy. Bending forward, he turned and noticed Lewis. There was an unspoken challenge in the hunch of his shoulders and the turn of his attention back to the loose joint. Fazil came in to see what the fuss was about, picked up the spanner and eased the nut into place. 'Treat it kindly,' he said, just as Glatton turned up.

Lewis leant on the bench and heard the clunk of the counting chamber striking wood. All the heads turned to him; this close, even the contents of your trouser pockets weren't private. He hated sharing the space, especially with Stephen Glatton. The man was smirking into his incubator, saying, 'Looks like things are going well here,' and Lewis took it as a comment on his team-management skills. He made a clumsy attempt to reassert himself.

'You'd better redo that joint,' he told Andrew, nodding towards the ragged tape.

But Glatton must have seen Andrew's balled fists and glare of resentment. 'As long as the thread hasn't stripped.' He sniggered at the trouble he'd been able to cause.

'It would have been stripped if it had been one of your lot.' Lewis sneered. 'You're never around to supervise them.'

'The thread's fine,' Fazil pointed out. He began to undo the nut, picking away at the torn sealing tape.

Glatton's lips pursed a little as if he were going to speak. Go on, spit it out, Lewis thought. Tell me how we'd be stronger if we joined forces and faced the competition out there shoulder to shoulder. But Glatton must have thought better of it; he took advantage of the confusion to carry his precious cells into his isolation hood, where he couldn't be followed. Lewis felt brainless. The extractor fans whined, as though they were struggling to keep up with the tension in the atmosphere; Andrew glowered at everyone; the incriminating counting chamber hung ready to judge Lewis.

'He doesn't trust his group to be able do their own isolation work,' Lewis offered, to Andrew and Fazil, hoping to raise some team camaraderie, but they both pretended to be occupied and refused him the support he thought he was owed. This was everything that Glatton had wanted.

Lewis was an only child. His research team was the nearest he'd got to the comforting ruck of being part of something bigger than himself. The playground tribes, with their big brothers and multitudinous cousins, had intimidated him and left him isolated. He felt it now, all fury on top and underneath an empty space that he might collapse into, with Glatton giving him a shove, Fazil and Andrew standing around the edge, looking down.

Back in the lab he complained to Rhea and Katherine, 'All these communal facilities are putting our cultures at risk. I hope Glatton's keeping that virus of his isolated.' The girls glanced up, blankly.

'Have you seen this?' Katherine and Joe crowded close to Patrick, one of Stephen Glatton's post-docs, who gurned triumphantly and pulled up his sleeve to reveal a newly healed tattoo. The DNA helix on his forearm twisted as he flexed his muscles. It loosened and tightened in a sickening parody of its biological function. Joe and Katherine put out their hands to touch his arm. Only Rhea stood apart.

Lewis fled to his office. He felt diminished. His team was struggling to maintain any sort of standards in this place. They weren't going to create pure stem-cell lines without decent facilities, the right sort of colleagues around them. If he angled his head so that he couldn't see the tissue-culture suite, everything in his line of sight belonged to him. His workspace, his people. They were quietly busy now, pushing forward the frontiers of knowledge. Behind the tissue-culture-suite door Stephen Glatton was waggling his tubes of virus around, claiming success and encouraging Andrew's disaffection.

Dragging in Lewis's pocket, the counting chamber unbalanced his equilibrium. Utopian and impossible, the vision rose before him of his own laboratory, privacy for his team, the chance to pursue his work without constant interference.

He spent the afternoon alone in his office. Then he had to pretend to go home, and skulk back, late enough for the lab to be empty. Even so, he had his excuse ready: a forgotten paper he needed, slipped between his filing cabinet and desk, where he usually kept his briefcase.

Lewis wished he could tell Amber. Whatever the embarrassment, he knew now that fertility testing was something he couldn't deny her. If things went against them, if one of them was unlucky and some accident of biology made a genetic child of their own unlikely, the Amber he loved would find another way to love one. He envied her the way she robbed Fate of its power by circumventing its decrees, while he was compelled to break himself against them. There was always a long pull, and it was a steady, slow pull towards her. Sometimes he welcomed it, but sometimes he had to resist, because if he let it have its way, he might disappear into Amber. The space he left, the place in the outside world that should have been his, would be filled by someone like Stephen Glatton, taking over his people and jeering at his loss of himself, even while they envied all that Amber brought him.

It needed only a drop from the tadpole jar of his semen on the slide. He bent his head to the eyepiece. It was Rhea's microscope, adjusted to suit her eyesight, and Lewis could only just make out something buffeted by Brownian motion, the random thrash of molecular energy.

He changed the focus to accommodate his own vision and something more purposeful came into view.

Another subtle adjustment to the resolution, the difference between yes and no, and there they were, everywhere. Sperm were beating a path across his view: determined, fierce and gloriously unrestrained Lewis-spermatozoa.

If there'd been the least possibility of celebrating a sperm-fest, Lewis would have seized it. He'd have cracked open champagne and invited friends – strangers in the street would have had glasses pressed into their hands – but, actually, as he thought it through, there wasn't much chance of a party. He couldn't leave the results on Rhea's desk for her to find in the morning. He could hardly rush home and tell his wife what he'd done: the furtive, messy business of procuring the sample at work, then checking it yourself could seem just a bit sordid, after the event. He would have to keep it to himself. The sperm thrashed on while the snaky tail of the lie he was going to tell Amber coiled around him. Some day soon, he would have to pretend to be concerned about his part in the investigations. He quailed, but then he remembered that this was what Fate had decreed. And it wouldn't be fair to let her know that he had checked himself.

Yes, he was exonerated. And he had a result. He decided he ought to allow himself a drink on the way home, congratulate himself privately and get over it before he saw Amber. That way she would never know. His resolve stiffened all round; he would take *Infertility Investigations: Part II* out of the library and make himself fully conversant with the procedures, *Female*, so that he could prepare Amber and, at the same time, make sure he couldn't be patronised by Rhea's friend, the fertility consultant.

When he reached the canal-side bar, music was blaring from the doorway to attract the serious drinkers: students and the trainee lawyers from the nearby legal quarter who had a lot to forget before they were ready for bed. Lewis wanted to remember. He wanted to fix this feeling of affirmation and preserve it for the rest of his life. He felt that a man so unconditionally in charge of his own destiny couldn't reward himself with a drink in a student bar. An aura of entitlement persuaded him that something more sophisticated would also have a fitting sense of restraint. He drove on to the Ashfield.

In the space between the two bars, a mile of modern high-rise development and safely out of sight of the university buildings, Lewis enjoyed his rolling swell of elation. He loosened his grip on the wheel and let his jaw unclamp. There was a surge of lust and he toyed with the idea of going straight home – the provoking allure of Amber's body was never going to shimmer with its tinge of anxiety again – but as he came close to the Ashfield, a dark hot hatch, blue merging into night, hurtled from the exit across his path. He had to brake sharply as it cornered wide, and at the last moment, he swung off the road and into the car park.

The bar at the Ashfield always had a muted look; the air was opaque with restraint, the furnishings subtle. Low candles glowed discreetly on the tables. Lewis asked for whisky, then held the glass to a candle, watching the light reflect through the crystal and the liquid. It made an amber pool, shadowing across his hands. She would be waiting; she knew how to get everywhere, right under his skin, always just drawing back the right amount to make him move forward. He dared not disappoint her; he ducked his head and stared into the fire because her boss, Warren, was leaning on the bar. She had eyes everywhere. If Warren recognised him, she would hear about his private treat and he began to formulate his excuse.

A tight group of men emerged from the dining room, circling the fireplace, then heading for the comfortable seats by the window. 'He's up for a knighthood,' Lewis heard someone say and his interest was spurred. There was something lupine about the type: they all swerved together, as if someone had given a secret signal. Lewis was lost in the wonder of serendipity as he recognised the university's senior managers.

His head of department's eyes registered Lewis and slid away, back to his intimates. Twitching, those eyes flitted back, sheep-ish now with the acknowledgement of their elitist exclusion.

'Lewis.' Featley left the group. His face had been scoured by too close a shave. His grey hair and steely gaze made him look metallic and indestructible. Featley had a reputation for ruth-lessness. Nothing got in the way of the head of Medical Science's imperceptible progress towards greatness. His lips split apart. 'What brings you here, if you don't mind my asking?' He turned his head, monitoring the reactions of his deserted colleagues, and Lewis realised, with a child-like relish, that his boss thought someone else had invited him.

'Drink?' Lewis asked, waving his glass resolutely towards the bar.

Featley vacillated, his head still swivelling in uncertainty. 'Oh, I, er, think someone might be getting me one.'

Lewis could see post-prandial drinks shuttling across the bar, settling into welcoming hand-clasps, sealing a fine agreement of expansive geniality. 'Well, I will,' he said, with decision, and got to his feet, leaving his boss to follow behind.

With four courses and coffee tucked away, the senior man-agers were stolidly enjoying the Ashfield's range of single malts. Dinnerless and jubilant, Lewis joined them just as the director of finance was singing his soft Irish lament of poverty.

'A genetics institute? You'll be needing to find someone with a bit of clout to put up the funding. My coffers are bare.' The circle of raised eyebrows brought the formula of a self-deprecatory smile to his lips. 'Bare-ish, anyway,' he amended, aligning himself back into the communal perception. 'Have you approached the Regional Development Board?'

'We never have any luck there.' Featley's stubborn lips pursed. 'We're too speculative for them. They want quick returns. In and out, that's their motto.' He breathed out a long, heartfelt sigh. 'A genetics institute takes years to turn a profit.'

'Maria had to rush off,' someone offered, into the silence that followed, and there was a thoughtful raising of glasses, a confirmatory sipping of drinks.

'Had to get back for the kids. She can't join in, really, can she?'

Maria was the sole woman on the senior management team, famous for her dark blue sporty car. 'She's against the whole idea of a genetics institute,' Eriksson moaned.

Lewis scarcely heard them. He could see the blood corpuscles milling behind his eyes; he could remember the hectic motion on the microscope slide. He could feel his time coming. 'A money man, a Californian, is coming over from the States. He's interested in setting up a stem-cell trial with me.'

The fast arrest of their lazy gazes when he mentioned US biotech support for his project, the stilling of the wolf pack, alert to the possibility of prey, was compensation enough for Featley's rebuff.

Featley looked put out. 'Of course, we had been thinking of Stephen Glatton,' he demurred. 'A solid record, good contacts with the Japanese. He's a very safe pair of hands.' He tailed off without any noticeable support from the others.

'Is yours the same project that Glatton's been pushing?' the director of finance wanted to know.

'Certainly not,' Lewis answered. 'Much safer, already much nearer to the patient. I've had my people working on this for almost ten years, now. That's how long it's taken to get anywhere near to commercialisation, but I always knew it would. The rewards are unimaginable.'

'We'll talk about this tomorrow. Perhaps you could get something together, Featley?' the dean suggested, as his imagination stalled. He gave a nod in Lewis's direction. 'He's one of yours, I expect.' They all drifted away to taxis, to home, bed and their dreams of ermine.

Left alone, Lewis celebrated with another drink, and then another. Each glass made it seem more possible that he could attain the impossible, an independent laboratory where his group could flourish untrammelled. What couldn't they achieve with the seclusion and security that US largesse could buy them? All he had to do was to come up with a coherent pitch. Warren's presence seemed suddenly intentional. Who better to come up with the apposite phrase, just the angle to lure the attention of the unbeliever? You wouldn't have guessed it, looking at Warren slouched against the bar, restlessly rotating the beer in his glass. He had thick, very curly hair, caught in a ponytail; it gave him a dreamy, romantic look. When they had first met, Lewis had been tempted to warn him that it was dangerous to wear your hair long and tied up, that it made it easy for someone to grab you in a fight, but he soon saw that there was a toughness, almost criminal, about Warren that meant people would keep their distance. And he had seen why Amber was so valuable to him: her easy manners smoothed his rough edges and mollified the clients he alarmed.

As Lewis made his way across the bar the carpet felt thick, an impediment, like walking on a beach. The memory of the fight with Glatton dogged his footsteps. Warren could be a daunting adversity if he chose. But thick carpets were the reward for overcoming that sort of hesitation, surely. He walked carefully, telling himself it was air he felt under his feet, not sand.

Amber's husband wasn't a welcome addition to her boss's evening. As Lewis approached, Warren crouched back into himself, ready to pounce. But there were highlights of bright colour on his cheekbones, as if he, too, had been caught out in the wrong place, and Lewis nodded towards the swinging doors. 'Evening meeting,' he said. 'Got to do it.'

Warren, standing alone at the bar, with no colleagues in sight, nodded assent. 'All right if you haven't kids.'

Lewis winced, unsure what Warren might know about *the investigations*. His appearance, which said he might swing a punch as easily as sketch out a poem, might open the way to any confidences from Amber, but Warren looked at him with undisguised frankness, as though there were something he might let Lewis know about himself. 'I've got one, of course, our Polly.' Lewis remembered Amber telling him how she had seen Polly once on the street, walking home from school by herself. While the other children jostled in groups, she dragged her leg, awkward and alone. The same school uniform, the same lessons and the same journey home, but a difference that Polly lived with every minute of her day. A traffic accident had severed nerves that hadn't regrown. A feeling of prerogative rose in Lewis at this fluent docking of their separate privations. He smiled, and the multitudinous swarming tide of his semen sample was still carrying him along when he said to Warren, 'I can help her.'

Warren looked away. He erected automatic barriers of distrust and silence, and Lewis felt proud. The stupid, piddling thing with Glatton was child's play; this was business between men. With another whisky legitimised into his hand he explained to Warren that his stem cells could colonise Polly's withered neural pathways and make them whole.

'It's a lot to take in,' Warren said.

The bar was quiet now. Rooms like that were never meant to be empty. They were meant to be so full that everything was kept, packed tight, in its place. In the vacuum that had been left behind when the customers went home, Lewis sensed his feelings expand to fill the incongruous space. He opened his mouth to tell Warren about his sperm test, then didn't, because Warren said he didn't want Polly to be experimented on. The barman was watching them, waiting for them to leave, and he was listening too.

'It wouldn't be like that,' Lewis said, and the barman went back to wiping his glass.

Warren patted Lewis on the arm, taking charge of him. 'We'll talk about it,' he said, 'when we've had time to think.'

Out in the car park Lewis fumbled for his keys. Uncoordinated fingers dug around the lining of his pockets, groping for the fob. Christ, he thought, I'm drunk. I can't drive home. He stood in the slash of light from the kitchen door. Grey-faced workers were filling the bins with the day's waste and Lewis felt nauseous. It was too far for Amber to come and pick him up; he didn't know what to do. But there was Rhea, not a mile away and plenty of taxis around; she wouldn't be in bed yet. The phone had hardly started to ring when she answered, and Lewis knew she would rescue him, that she would be able to comprehend his need over the airwaves.

The taxi driver took an amused interest in Lewis's plight when he dropped Rhea off. His eyes lit with professional envy as Lewis pointed out his car.

'I'll leave you to it then,' he said grudgingly. 'I can't see my missus being so obliging.'

In the car he felt too large for his own body. Sitting in the passenger seat where the belt was adjusted for Amber meant that he had to breathe hard against the constriction.

'God, Lewis, you stink of whisky.'

He exhaled again, noisily and deliberately. 'You might get drunk on my breath.'

'Let's hope I've got more sense. One of us has to be sober enough to get you home.'

Lewis luxuriated. How he loved being driven in his own car by Rhea. The over-close embrace of the seatbelt, the way he was unexpectedly gathered up and pressed back into the seat whenever she accelerated, made him feel swaddled. 'Sorry,' he said.

Rhea obligingly put her foot down. 'I've phoned Amber. You're staying with me tonight.'

Lewis gave the belt a little tug to relieve a sudden pressure on his chest. 'Why?' he asked cautiously. He set himself to reviewing his options. He might be in the doghouse at home. He tried to remember if it was a baby-trying night, but the detail of the schedule had slipped somewhere out of his reach. There was another bewildering thought. But then, even drunk and hungry, he couldn't seriously imagine that Rhea was making him an offer.

'Because I'm not driving all the way up to yours. You're lucky I came out at all. How come you got this wasted anyhow?'

Lewis was prepared to acknowledge his misdemeanour: transgression seemed like triumph tonight. 'Drinking.'

It seemed a perfectly sufficient answer to him but Rhea shot him a dirty look.

'It's just that I thought there would be a dinner at the meeting, and there wasn't. I haven't had anything to eat.'

'Well, I'm not cooking at this time of night. You'll have to get a takeaway.'

Lewis couldn't keep the smile off his face. Its stupidity filled the car, annoying Rhea.

'It's supposed to be a punishment, Lew. You deserve to sleep in the car park.'

'Oh, it's a good punishment, Rhea. Honest.' His luck was getting too good to be true. He probed for the flaw. 'Am I in trouble? What did Amber say?'

'No, she was OK. She just said she couldn't remember you telling her about a meeting tonight.'

He nodded ponderously. 'Last-minute thing.'

Rhea curved the car around a sharp corner, so that Lewis rocked gently to and fro. He wanted the journey to be never-ending. He wanted to go on, forever feeling the unfurling of possibilities that had been tight inside him, while Rhea drove him, smoothing the way forward.

There was still a kebab shop on Waterloo Road, although it must have been five or six years since Lewis had been there: certainly not since he had been married and subject to the health police. A group of students was gathered in a semi-circle outside the shop, posing and posting photos of themselves. Lewis moved through them and into the shop, feeling like a successful man looking back on his impecunious youth.

He ate his doner kebab in Rhea's kitchen while she made tea.

'The deans wanted to see me about some idea they've got,' he said, 'for making money out of biotech.'

'They haven't a clue,' Rhea answered. 'The Americans are years ahead. Wait until you meet Vic.'

'I was wondering about him. We're going to lose Andrew if I don't find some more money to pay him. He could help us there.'

Rhea looked at him in disbelief. 'Oh, there's more to it than that, Lewis. I've been on the phone to Vic again.'

An oversized bite of minced lamb might save him: he wouldn't be able to answer until he had chewed, swallowed, rearranged his mouth and hidden his dismay that there was something Rhea hadn't told him. But there was a deep pool of unknowing between them about Rhea's time in the US, when she had been widening her world view and he had been at home with Amber. Without Rhea, Amber had centred herself on him, and for a while that was good, until she began to be just as busy as he was, and making money. With Rhea back, there was a reinvention of their lives, and the exciting thing about her was all the stuff she didn't tell you.

'If we can get the stem cells pure enough, he's prepared to handle the clinical trials.' She held out her hands, palms upwards, a gesture of offering, but drunkenness was spinning Lewis down. What was she giving him? Alms, arms? Words staggered in his mind. Palms, that was it. But a picture was emerging. Rhea's stem cells ready for use in patients?

'I'm going to persuade him, Lewis, if it's the last thing I do. The deans would never take on that sort of responsibility. We don't owe that lot anything.' She gave a quiet snort, to herself, really, as if she thought he was some sort of apologist, and didn't bother to look at him. He had to reach over the table and touch her hand to make her pay attention.

'I'm getting sick of making the effort all the time, and not knowing if it'll ever come to anything,' she said straight into his face. 'That lot have never been any help to us.'

'You know what deans are like. They're all delayed gratification.' Lewis could feel his speech slurring in his mouth. For a moment, he tasted the sour flavour of being old. 'You wouldn't think they could afford to wait for anything at their age, would you?'

'At their age, waiting is probably all they can do,' Rhea said, and took her hand back. She stirred the tea and pushed it across to him.

A sweet smell rose from the cup: camomile, honey and vanilla, Amber's bedtime drink. The ghost of her filled the space between them. In a drunken daze he watched the steam rising, confused by the juxtaposition of Rhea and Amber. Lewis's body always held a physical memory of Amber. Under the swell of her breasts you could see her ribs. The four fingers of his hand fitted into the spaces between them so that he could feel her bones. Amber, masked by her image, her makeup and her clothes armour against everyone else, was so open to him. The knowledge that he was allowed to touch the skeleton that held her together made him quail. But inside Amber there was something else, something so brilliant that it was like glacial ice, harder and more refractive than any other sort. And that was the thing that mesmerised him, reflecting light onto anything that came near. He shuddered with lust.

'Does she make you drink herbal tea at night?' asked Rhea.

'No, nothing . . . Whisky,' he tendered, halfway between a statement and an enquiry, not certain himself which he had meant. It seemed such a liberty, so late at night. But the ghostly tea was poured down the sink, and as the smoke and peat smell of the whisky replaced the cloying vanilla, Rhea became herself again, smart and clever, pale-skinned and dark-haired: Modigliani-faced Rhea. Everyone said that it should be Lewis and Rhea who were the siblings: they looked so alike.

'I won't tell Amber,' she said, as she passed the glass. 'I'll take your secret to the grave with me.' She raised her eyebrows. Lewis wondered if it had been like this for Rhea and Dave. She had tea; he had whisky. And in the kitchen at night, they avoided talking about something. Amber was always asking him if he had phoned Dave or heard from him, but he had never really thought about it until now, when he was watching Rhea, by herself, pushing the glass casually across the table as though it was something she always did.

CHAPTER 4

Someone was rapping on the other side of the door. However hard she grasped at the handle and pulled, Rhea couldn't open it and the tapping went on. Sharp, insistent taps that faded as she struggled to listen, until they transformed into pats, soft, tentative pats, as though hands were searching for an entrance: a hollow sound instead of the solid drub. The stroke of sleep mixed with the thump of reality.

'Rhea, it's late. Are you awake?'

'I am now.'

Rhea had to lean back on her pillows to take it in. Last night she'd slept without stirring: the first time since Dave had left. Perhaps it was just the security of having someone else in the flat. Ensconced in the spare room, Lewis had displaced the emptiness. He deserved to have woken up with a hangover, exacerbated by a stomach recoiling from the toxic takeaway, but she could hear him bouncing about in the shower. You couldn't hear much through the rooms of the flat – it was in a purpose-built block with concrete walls – but the water pipes seemed to connect everything. Showering was an unexpected exposure. She could tell that he'd switched to power mode, the spray thickening to a drumming as loud as the rapping in her dream.

She closed her eyes against the furore, trying not to listen herself out of the calm she felt, lying still while someone else was busy. Lewis had brought tea, saying, 'You're a star, Rhea. I was never as glad to see anyone as I was to see you last night.' Still lying with her head against the pillows, still drugged by sleep, she was unwilling to make any effort to drag herself clear and interrupt the seductive drift from reality.

Amber had been three, left behind when Rhea was taken to the hospital to see Dad. 'Too small,' Mum had said, 'she won't understand,' and the neighbours had jumped in to take care of her. The seaside, that was the thing. They would take Amber to the seaside. But Rhea was torn between the honour of going by herself with Mum and a trip to the beach. She clung to her bucket and spade, reluctant to surrender them. Next-door crouched down to level things out, and promised her, 'When you come back, you can come with us while your mum has a rest. Ice cream. A paddle. It will take her mind off things,' they'd said, standing up again and talking over her head.

Now Rhea couldn't even remember the visit to the hospital but she hadn't forgotten the walk across the flat, grassy park towards the beach and the long distance from which she saw Amber. Her sister was digging furiously, with desperate concentration; wet sand flew into the sky from her spade. Amber looked up and saw Rhea coming and desolation broke into boundless relief. She opened her arms, as wide as they could stretch, and she ran and ran over the scrubby turf towards her sister, as though her entire world had been set to rights. Rhea thought of it now: she had been tall enough and strong enough to pick Amber up and swing her round so that the beach and the sea and the sky – the entire universe – had revolved around the two of them.

She knew that no one would ever be so pleased to see her again. Not Dave, that was for sure, and she knew that this had always been missing: nothing had been able to match that feeling of being utterly necessary. She couldn't recall the rest of that day, just the sense of dread, and standing between that abyss and her little sister. She opened her eyes when the noise of the water stopped and was replaced by Lewis's voice. That Amber's husband had said the very thing – *I was never as glad to see anyone* – it had been like another setting to rights.

'I'm all done. It's your turn.' He hesitated outside her door. 'I'll get out of your way, Rhea. I'll wait for you in the café by the bridge.'

He was gone, and Rhea got up in the awareness of absence: the sudden, unexpected absence of Lewis and the gradually accepted absence of Dave.

Amber might have called to check up on him. Rhea scanned her phone for messages. Nothing. She flicked to her contacts list. First – of all her friends, relatives and colleagues – was Amber, right up at the top. A sense of augury gripped tight, squeezing her chest, alarming her all over again with its warning. It's not an omen, she told herself. *A* is the first letter in the alphabet, that's all.

The fridge door shut with a low hiss, like a sigh of relief or resignation. Whichever. Relief and resignation had become so intertwined in Rhea that she couldn't distinguish them. Last night she'd run along the canal bank to get away from herself. The water had been fretting out an oily mist. By morning the fog would have gone but Rhea had known she had a night to withstand first. She'd stamped her soles hard on the pavement, as though she could dent the surface, but her trainers were too compressible and she couldn't hurt herself like that. She'd run the tension out of herself: it had oozed out in her sweat and she had showered it off.

Eventually she'd decided not to try to sleep. She defied it, and that, with Lewis's drinking, had done the trick. Sleep had crept up behind her and pulled her down so completely that when Lewis had woken her in the morning she had thought it was still night.

They walked to work together, along the towpath. The summer had been kind so the leaves on the trees were full of sugars. When they had changed colour they hadn't sunk into dingy brown: they were flaming with red and glowing with the deepest yellow. The colours above her were so vibrant that she didn't notice the brown mulch of fallen leaves underfoot. Rhea wandered beneath the trees and was surprised to see them at all; all summer she'd been too distracted to notice them, but they had gone on just the same, doing their own work. Now the season was almost over, they'd changed in a final exultant flaunting of all they had been. Even Lewis was in no hurry to get to the lab: he was delaying their arrival, pointing out to her the tubes in the grass from which the crane flies – spreadeagled everywhere – had emerged. She couldn't see the camouflaged escape tunnels at first but he lent her his sunglasses and they leapt into view.

Rain clouds were hovering in the west and a light wind was blowing, but on the towpath it was sheltered and sunny. Two young men in fluorescent jackets stopped cutting the grass and examined the ground to see what Lewis had been pointing out. Catching Rhea's eye, they smiled at her, the sort of uncomplicated, early-morning smiles that passers-by often gave, and that she had forgotten about.

'It's a lovely day,' she said to Lewis, and meant it.

He was unshaven, his shirt was crumpled and, without his sunglasses, his eyes were crinkled, as though the shabby ripeness of autumn had got into him too. A different, dishevelled Lewis looked back at her. Dissolute and happy, he said, 'It gets better and better.'

Rhea craved the laboratory. Ever since Dave had left, when she wasn't at work, she had felt an enveloping homesickness for the certainties it engendered: once she was there, uncertainty would evaporate in the fervour of activity. Usually she arrived first into the cool and quiet of loneliness and switched things on until the room was alive with the companionable hum of the water baths and the centrifuges. But this morning she walked into the lively pulse of work that was already under way. Warm, curious glances greeted her; they sparkled off and paused on Lewis, but it was to her that they returned, Rhea, who was so much more likely to come up with an explanation as to why she and Lewis had turned up together. Nothing escaped friends who were together twelve hours a day; there was no hiding place. They knew more about your life than you did yourself.

The hair falling down Rhea's back was still damp and it caught and tangled as she ran her hands down it, pushing it out of the way, longer, finer and straighter than Amber's. She liked her own hair better. What it lacked of Amber's magnificence, it made up for with its muted sheen. She let it trickle through her fingers and thought, It won't do them any harm not to know something.

She opened her lab book: another dozen cultures ready to harvest and check. If she didn't start straight away, it wouldn't be finished before lunchtime when she needed to set up the preparations for tomorrow, then help Katherine with the gel apparatus. Every day was tight, all the actions packed in together, like stones in a wall. Move one and the whole edifice would collapse.

A shift might happen at any moment, she knew that. Researchers were temporary loyalists. As long as you paid them they were committed to your side but their fidelity was stretched once unemployment loomed. They had all watched in disbelief as someone indispensable was replaced by a cheaper model. The speed with which the new person became part of the team only made it worse, when they thought about it.

Stephen Glatton beat her into the culture suite. The windows in the doors were there for safety reasons, so that you didn't go barging in on someone holding a big bottle of sulphuric acid. But they made everything visible. Rhea hadn't planned to spy, but all the same she left her fingers slack on the handle and her eyes roaming the view inside. Glatton was getting ready to run the autoclave, with his tattooed post-doc in attendance. He switched on the water supply while Patrick set the temperature and pressure dials, the two of them standing close to reach the controls. Now he was opening the cupboards, lifting out the clean glassware, loosening the screw tops. Patrick took them from him, fitting on the foil covers and applying autoclave tape. The calm routine of their co-operation could only be the result of familiarity. They were comfortable, easy together. Long, winding ropes of communal effort joined even the Glatton team.

Fazil came out of a cubicle with a tray of cell cultures that he had been washing; he left them on top of the incubator and disappeared back behind the partition. Patrick shifted and edged around the bench to look at the bottles. His curly hair fell down his face, hiding his expression from Rhea, but Glatton smirked across to him and shook his head.

'Leave it.'

Glatton looked up and saw her watching. He seemed shocked, not as though he had been caught out but as though his privacy had been violated, and Rhea dropped her eyes. Outside, the indigenous seagulls patrolled their territories, oblivious to the internecine disputes indoors.

'I need to wash my cells, but I'll wait until you're done,' she said.

She brought out yesterday's samples from the cold room: two hundred tubes in each rack, each waiting for a hundred-microlitre squirt of the next reagent. It was difficult to do the same thing to four hundred tubes without missing one, but Rhea didn't need to think about it. A short circuit between her eyes and her hands had developed over years of practice. It didn't involve her brain, and she passed the time by keeping an eye on the others.

Fazil had finished and was putting his dirty glassware into the dishwasher. Katherine and Joe were scanning yesterday's gel runs, but Andrew had abandoned his on the bench. One of the gel tanks was fizzling out of action with an electrical fault. Andrew brandished a beaker full of thin tubes, already tagged up for loading and deteriorating with every second of the delay. He glowered. He squatted down, rummaging through the cupboard for a spare set of leads, but he had no luck so he glared upwards, red-faced for lack of an answer.

Only Rhea had a personal set of equipment. That was the difference between staff and the temporary employees, who could be disposed of as soon as the grant money ran out. Of all the post-docs, Andrew was most at risk: thirty-four, getting too expensive to be attractive to another research team and with only a few more months left on his project grant. At odd moments, Rhea caught the others watching him with neurotic fascination, gauging their chances of sharing his fate. If they didn't get more money Andrew was going to be just another post-doc with his brilliant future behind him. He was in constant turmoil; worry was turning him bolshie, not tank leads. At this rate, they'd be glad to see the back of him.

Before she could offer him her equipment, Andrew was in the office, standing at the desk and leaning forward over Lewis, jerking his head in staccato bursts. Lewis's hands went up in a conciliatory gesture. He had an alarmed smile on his face. He rose and sent a silent appeal across the room towards her. *Come and save me again.* Everything normal, the ordinary ups and down of laboratory life; the tumultuous churn of the academic assembly line. She raised her eyebrows and then her pipette at him. *You say you're the boss, you'll have to manage. I'm busy.*

Joe wore boots fastened with dozens of buckles right up to his calves. They were far too heavy for the laboratory but, along with his new nose-ring and his Mohican haircut, they were

70

integral to his image. The boots always squeaked on the composite flooring: she knew it was him before she raised her head.

'Come and look for me, Rhea. What do you think?'

She went with him into a culture suite that looked as though it had been turned over. Flasks of cells had been taken out of the incubators and left lying about the open benches. All Joe's bottles of medium were opened and upended, pouring their contents away with a warm, yeasty smell. Rhea turned the taps full on to wash it away. Joe saw her shocked grimace.

'It's all right,' he reassured her, when it so obviously wasn't. 'No,' he went on, 'all my cells are dead. Every last one.'

Rhea had to refocus the microscope to suit her eyesight. She thought it might be a bit high because the orange light of the phase contrast was blurred and she couldn't find the bottom of the plate to bring the shiny, black-edged cells into focus. Moving the eyepiece didn't help much: all she could see was the medium, and floating about in it, swirling away whenever she shifted position, the curled-up remains of a dead culture.

'It has to be an infection.'

She couldn't see any yeast cells, swollen with their budding and dividing, or any swarms of bacteria scurrying around, clustering and sticking fast to the debris. But she couldn't think of any other explanation and she helped Joe dump his cultures in the biohazard waste.

Once that had been dealt with, Rhea checked all the other plates. Only Joe's were affected, but she took samples from them all as a precaution. She had a miserable apprehension that something unwelcome had penetrated their sterile firewall. It whirled around her like the intruding smell of a stranger in the familiar space of their laboratory.

She saw Joe's eyes darken with embarrassment.

'We'll have to tell the others.'

This could have happened to anyone, but it had picked Joe.

Dirty technique? Plain bad luck? There had been mutterings from Katherine about the bacterial risks from nose piercing. But, most probably, poor Joe hadn't done anything to deserve it. That wouldn't make a public confession any easier.

'We can't risk it spreading, Joe. They'll need to take extra precautions.' He nodded his unnecessary consent.

The quickest way was to take the samples up to the hospital for testing. Rhea knew the diagnostics technicians well – she'd often advised them on any advances in cell culture that might read over to their own work – and they might process her samples quickly as a favour. Twelve thirty. If she could get up there before they started to sterilise their equipment, they might even put the tests up today. She hurried out through the lab. Katherine and Andrew were moving their glassware, quarantining it behind autoclave tape. Joe had already gained outcast status; he was loading his into the washer for an extra hot cycle. Fazil helped him as if he had a special duty of care to the youngest team member. He was already a father, a photograph of two little girls stuck to the cupboards above his bench. Rhea tried to smile at him, to catch his eye, but he bent determinedly, as though sheer force of will could wash trouble from the reagent bottles and save Joe. Rhea dreamt of disposable plastic ware, but it cost such a lot that Lewis had bought a scientific dishwasher. And they could put glassware through the autoclave. There was nothing that a good sterilising wouldn't sort out, Rhea told herself. At a high enough temperature and pressure, everything succumbed, eventually.

'Everything' seemed to include Lewis. By the time she got back from the hospital, it was raining and he had got wet coming from some meeting or other. He succumbed to maudlin sentimentality. Last night's whisky was leaking out of his liver, finally having its way with him. 'Rhea . . . ?'

72

An unasked question dissolved in the air between them. She waited, enjoying the struggle Lewis had to reveal himself. The two of them had always lightened their long hours by the competition to be top dog; for months on end that was all the fun they had at work. This sudden intimacy had the odd flavour of too sugary a coating on a bitter pill.

'What?' She waited.

Lewis put aside some papers that were on his desk, playing for time. Or maybe he was putting aside that whining tone because when he spoke his words were serious. 'I've had Andrew in here.'

Rhea's mind flew back to the scene she had watched that morning: Andrew hanging over Lewis hadn't been the routine fracas of laboratory life, then. 'You know there are only a few months to run on his grant? He wants a definite commitment that I can still pay him next year. Otherwise he's after another job.' Lewis's face was gloomy. 'We can't afford to have him take his eye off the ball now. Not with the dates coming up.' There was a calendar on the wall with the dates marked in black. Next to it hung a project plan, with the work schedule of each member of the team. They had used the colours of the rainbow for themselves: red, orange, yellow, green, blue. Without Andrew's yellow they wouldn't hit the target in time.

'As long as he's here, he should be pulling his weight,' Rhea said, but the weight of ambiguity slowed her words. A glance out of the office showed Andrew preparing a fresh batch of culture medium for the whole group. Commitment was a two-way process and Andrew needed his own chances too. She offered her best shot straight away, 'The clinical trials that Vic mentioned . . .' before caution kicked in and reminded her that he hadn't actually promised anything.

'I knew you'd say that.' Lewis squeezed her arm. 'What would we do without you?'

It seemed safe enough to believe that it would be fine, standing in the office. But beyond the door hordes of people were scrabbling after every advantage. 'We can't promise him anything, Lewis. It's not in the bag yet.'

But Lewis was full of confidence again, reassuring her. 'We've got stuff on our side: things to offer. The university's building a genetics institute. We can get a slice of that.'

Vic. A genetics institute. Finally. Rhea felt lucky. 'I'm going for my run,' she said. 'Want to come?'

'I'll race you,' said Lewis, stretching his arms. He might act a bit nerdy sometimes, but Rhea suddenly saw that her brother-in-law could be opened out into a series of extravagant, fantastical shapes when he wasn't absorbed in work. She'd been running regularly for the last few weeks and she knew that Lewis hadn't. Between that and the delayed hangover, she guessed she could beat him. She saw herself running first, out front, leaving him struggling behind. It felt like a great end to the day.

'I'll beat you,' she said, pushing him back into his chair.

Rhea was changed first. Waiting for Lewis by the cinder track, facing into the wind, enjoying its strength, she thought it a good sign. She'd been brought up on windswept beaches; she was relying on the weather hindering Lewis more than it would her. He came out flexing his hamstrings, loosening his extensors, but Rhea had already done that, and she knelt down to tighten her trainers and check her ankle supports.

They exchanged complicit grins; Lewis probably thought he could win too and they were both enjoying the attention from the laboratory windows. She felt the skittish flash of excitement that shot between them: their old competitiveness. They were both on their mettle. They counted in unison. One, two, and off after three. Rhea felt her legs spring forward as though they were leaving the rest of her behind. Crunch, crunch, crunch. They pounded the familiar track. All the times she had pounded it on her own seemed to have left some energy in it that bounced back into her feet now.

The comfortable, familiar rhythm set in. Twenty-two, twenty-three, she counted to keep herself steady. After fifty she lifted her head and looked to the left. Lewis was just behind her, breathing down her neck, but that was right where she wanted him, pushing her, keeping her pace up. Rhea planned to keep him there until the halfway mark, to let him think he was making ground. Then she would tire him with a slow pull away, and humiliate him with a final burst when he had nothing left to give.

When she made the first turn, the wind and wet slapped her hard in the face. It had started to rain heavily so that she couldn't see the roofs of the warehouses that were supposed to become the Genetics Institute, but she knew where they were. She wondered if Lewis was as sure of winning as she was. She could hear his breath rasping, so she knew that he was close behind and getting tired. Ready for the pull forward, Rhea pressed her head down. She put her shoulders into her chest, her chest into her hips and her hips into her legs, and found the force to pound 10 per cent faster. Even in the wet and the gloom she sensed Lewis at her left shoulder, so she pushed harder. Her heart was beginning to thud so she concentrated her mind on talking it down with counting, fifty-six, fifty-seven, but the faster she ran, the faster she had to count and the faster her heart boomed through her ribs.

When she could see the Medical School, she could still hear him next to her. He had kept pace with her all this way and she began to think he must have been training secretly, and playing with her. The smell of Lewis's sweat was easily distinguishable, but by then she couldn't tell his breathing from her own. Her breath grated, his breath grated, his foot punched, her foot punched. She grabbed at a moment and turned to see where he was, and he was staring right back into her face. His eyes locked straight into hers. Her heart thumped, or was it his? She couldn't tell. She couldn't even count separately from him. Everything about them pounded together up that track: leg, foot, leg, foot. Neither could break free of the bond.

When they reached the end of the course, Rhea wrenched herself away from him and leant against the railings, putting her head back so the rain could wash down her. She tasted salt and she had no idea which of them had won.

'It's your own fault,' Amber said. 'You've both got exactly what you deserve.'

Rhea saw the expanded Lewis had been tucked back into his box. Flexing his calf, he winced and looked to Amber with the 'sympathy-darling' expression he affected whenever she was there. Not that it did him any good.

'You're like a pair of kids,' Amber complained. 'Neither of you can admit defeat.'

Lewis and Rhea didn't admit defeat with folded arms and hangdog laughs; they exchanged clenched-fist salutes, then collapsed onto the sofa and the sanctuary of the weekend supplements.

Rhea only pretended to read. Property development and a spat between a pair of celebrity economic analysts about the reliability of their sources couldn't hold her attention. It was only Amber who needed to see the bigger picture. Rhea and Lewis had to obliterate it. Everything, absolutely everything, that didn't advance their work had to become irrelevant to them if they were going to triumph. Once the cultures were pure the clinical trials would vindicate them. The cultures not reproducing pure, she had her own ideas there. A clean slice of effort would cut through all the residual mess. If she submerged herself sufficiently, she might emerge bearing something precious.

She wanted this so much that it felt like a purification rite, something she would come out of reborn.

'What are you thinking about?'

Grandiose ideas took a swift, cloddish plunge into reality and Rhea admitted to nothing. But Amber couldn't bear silence: she had to have someone to talk to, so that she could feel she still existed. She only felt alive when she could feel concern or sympathy for someone else. Lewis knew it too. He reached across and laid his hand on her arm, so there was a palpable link between them.

'I'm thinking about how lovely you both are,' he told her.

'You must be after something,' Amber said, 'and you're going to get it.'

The overstretched muscles in Rhea's calves twinged as though they had been reminded of some further effort they didn't want to make.

Lewis loved them. While Amber held up board after board, titled Spring Conference 2004, set with pictures of cells in all their stages of differentiation, then photos of old people, smiling happily and gliding around at tea dances, he leant back on the sofa, entranced.

'I'm sure Warren will step up. He'd love to see the company in something like this,' Amber said.

There wasn't going to be any limit to Amber's promotion of their opportunities, but Lewis wanted her with them. He made an indulgent gesture. 'We can do something for his daughter. Between us, we can do it. We've got everything we need.'

He looked at Rhea too, and she knew he was thinking about her bringing Vic into line.

While he smiled in self-congratulation, Amber shifted uneasily, fraying at her edges. She would be thinking about her baby, the one thing she wanted for herself. They went back a long way, Lewis and Rhea, longer than Lewis and Amber. But nothing like as long as Rhea and Amber. Her sister deserved to be part of it.

'I'll do my best.'

'I'll certainly do mine,' said Amber.

'And me,' from Lewis.

And it seemed a pact had been forged.

As Lewis walked through Reception, Professor Featley stood at the head of the stairs that led to the upper echelons, beckoning urgently into the lower reaches. His stage whisper carried further than most of his official pronouncements.

'I need a favour, Lewis. The vice chancellor's having one of his receptions but I can't make it. Would you mind giving up your Friday evening?' Lewis was spirited up to the second floor where the suite of professorial offices was situated, next to the scruffy, peaceful library. Sofa scientists, those professors, closeted in serenity. How he had always longed to join them, as far away from the hassle of the laboratory as possible.

The night of the reception was the first time that Lewis had been to the dining room in the Vice Chancellor's Court. The VC was standing by the door, shaking hands, so perfectly positioned between the oak panelling and the halogen light focused on a predecessor's portrait that the blandishing wood and the clear beam combined to give his bald head an ethereal glow, almost a halo. But the painted image of the old man, retired for twenty-five years, possibly dead by now, still exuded belligerent power. It glared down from the wall and diminished the current VC, for all his genetics institute.

Lewis shuffled Amber into the forming tailback. The deans of the Medical and Dental Schools and some female *apparatchik* from Neurobiology, whom he had noticed with a sweaty smear of schoolboys trailing after her on open day, were ahead of them.

Lewis trained his eyes on the little tableau in front of him and strained forward. The deans disbursed effusive congratulations: such ungenuine delight in each other's successes. They were all enhanced by the reflected glory.

Then the real business began. Brief words were exchanged, just below the threshold of his hearing. A harpist was twanging away in the background, obscuring the conversation with her wretched overtones. Lewis edged nearer. *Restructure*, he heard, or was it someone's botched operation, *re-suture*?

He couldn't be sure, but he thought he could feel consensus filling the air. Cosy agreement bloomed out from the close circle of inclined heads and they parted. The VC was businesslike, patting arms proprietorially. Some deal was done, but Lewis couldn't tell what. Bland, unfocused glances came his way. He took them in, turned them into a comfort, a sure acknowledgement of his claim to be taken into consideration soon.

The young neurobiologist was dispensed with efficiently; the VC was smiling, his eyes gliding from Lewis and greeting Amber with a practised familiarity.

'Glad you could both make it.'

The wood panelling and the spotlight were casting their favour on Amber now. She glowed under the attention; even the dour old portrait seemed to soften, watching her, and Lewis felt the possibility of preferment as he mounted the last few steps. He put his own professional smile in place, holding out his hand. 'Thank you, Vice Chancellor. We wouldn't have missed this for anything.'

The VC didn't keep them long. A crowd of professors was turning raucous at the buffet and Lewis didn't feel like pushing his way through the calculated laughter. He'd expected a warm beckoning from the deans, a discreet invitation to meet them, next week, perhaps, but none had been forthcoming. He might have been invisible.

Lewis remembered, when he noticed Amber bending attentively to listen to the neurobiologist, that her name was Helen Something-or-other. She had presented a paper at a departmental seminar on the development of neurons. Won some award for it, Young Scientist of the Year maybe. He went to join them. But Amber wasn't fascinated by the details of nervous-system organisation. Helen, it turned out, had been near enough to hear what the deans had said to the vice chancellor. They had been talking about their plans for a new genetics institute. The VC had been all in favour, apparently, had said that the university could only benefit from co-operation with industry. Outside agencies would be approached for their support, but he had insisted, specifically, that it would be only at chief executive level. Amber was astonished. She pressed Helen: 'Is it sorted, then?' she asked. It seemed there had been mention of papers being prepared, ready to be discussed at administrative planning meetings already ensconced in directorial diaries.

Lewis's diary was on his desk in his office, virginally empty of administrative planning meetings. His lips pressed themselves together in case his thoughts had ideas of escaping through them. He felt as though he was laid open on a dais at the centre of the room. Everything was receding from him, the chattering and scraping of forks and clinking of glasses disappearing into the distance. The harpist was playing still, and lisping the dirge of a deserted girl. The plaintive notes were the only clear sound left in the room.

'I'd heard some talk,' he got out, turning aside from Amber's dumbfounded look. 'It's all a bit theoretical yet.'

A silence came among them. Helen didn't volunteer any more information, Lewis didn't ask, and Amber proffered a bowl of peanuts, picked over and half empty.

CHAPTER 5

There were rowan trees at Snitter Heugh. The soil was barely a few inches deep over the rock base but the rowan had evolved for thin conditions, so the trees survived. The summer was usually short: often there was only a sparse ration of sun but every year the berries burnt red. Amber loved watching them darken and swell at the edge of the roadside but the birds didn't: even now, with winter approaching, they avoided rowan berries and left them so that they shrivelled on the tree.

Families had to be nurtured on whatever there was. She tried, but Lewis and Rhea were often unavailable to have happiness foisted on them, she thought wryly. They were too busy to realise they weren't happy, and so many things were intruding and getting in the way of Amber's plans. She was coping with the new house alone. Fat flies appeared in the kitchen; she heaved out the vacuum cleaner and began poking the nozzle around the windows where the damned things were buzzing.

Lewis didn't see the point. 'Don't bother. You're fighting a losing battle,' he told her, as though she didn't know it.

A pathetic bleating was coming from her phone, which wanted to be charged. 'Just leave it, Amber. It's not as though there's any decent coverage out here anyway.' But she couldn't ignore the desperation of the plea, so she stirred and went to plug it in. It might have been a frown that passed across his face, the threat of some encroaching worry. Lewis, always distracted or busy; Lewis, still not included in meetings about the Genetics Institute. When she'd left the sofa, he had too. Without turning, she knew that he was by the sideboard, pouring himself another whisky. When she went back to him she would be able to smell it, the smoky breath that reminded her of garden fires, heat mottling your shins and face, the cold wind whisking it away behind your back.

'It's for my nerves.' He laughed, excusing himself. He held out his fingers, feigning trembling as evidence of his need for medication. The unmentioned appointment at the fertility clinic next week unsettled the atmosphere.

'Are you scared?' she asked.

'What's to worry about?' answered Lewis, lowering himself carefully onto the sofa, holding the glass aloft, deliberately steady now. 'Twenty-three per cent of all couples have fertility investigations.'

'What's to worry about, Lewis, is what they're going to say to us. We might find out we'll never . . .' Her voice weakened.

'Let's face it, we won't find out anything yet. It'll only be a chat. It'll be ages before they do anything.'

She could sense his detachment, the sanguine reliance on 'ages', a time that might never arrive. Lewis's eyes strayed to the television remote control, and Amber's baby began to recede into the distance, shunned by its father's dismissal. She would have to call them back, closer to her. Amber curled around Lewis, feeling for the fit of their shapes, the appeasing match as he shifted to accommodate her. Her shoes were on the floor, and as she lifted her feet onto the sofa to escape the nip of the draught, Lewis's hands drew forward to meet them.

'You're cold,' he said, chafing her ankles. 'Perhaps you're right, and we should think about double-glazing.'

Amber had poured all the money she had inherited from her grandfather into buying Snitter Heugh, and then her salary. Even so, the mortgage was stretching things. There was always something seriously expensive needed to bring the old place up to scratch and Lewis had never been paid anything like what he was worth. The weather had exposed the house's deficiencies. Sash windows strained against their cords; draughts scurried around the kitchen, biting at ankles. The entire place juddered with foreboding: double-glazing would solve most of its woes.

'So, suddenly we don't have to worry about money?'

Lewis was right back with her now, the baby waiting in the wings for her to summon it. She sat upright and held his face between her hands: fair, fine skin, but dark, rasping stubble that roughened whatever it touched and reminded you of something enduring and abrasive. Something that felt thrillingly male. 'You've got something nice to tell me, haven't you?'

She breathed the Lewis smell in. It was hardly ever a chemical stench now he didn't work at the bench; he was usually in his office, making arrangements about his research direction. There might have been the smell of money, or aftershave. They were often mixed in the business of PR. 'Is this credit-card action? Or have you got promotion?'

'No – and no.'

Same old caution. Her feelings were always laid out, a hand of cards on a table, while Lewis's were close to his chest. The wariness that weighed down Lewis's voice began to drag on hers. 'No movement on the Genetics Institute yet?' Lewis shrugged noncommittally and Amber had to push and probe his studied nonchalance. 'There is, isn't there?'

Lewis didn't admit to anything but he let her feet go and dug about in his pocket. 'I thought you'd be stressed about the clinic appointment so I got you a surprise. Close your eyes.' In the dark, Amber took the present that came still full of the heat of his body. She cupped it in her hand. It fitted easily, with its supple, flimsy wrapping and its hard, silky inside.

'I chose it especially for you. It had your name on it.'

The best surprise was that Lewis had given it to her. For a day or, at any rate, an hour he had stopped thinking of work. He had imagined what it was like to be her and brought her a present. A seamless band wrapped them together, close enough to hold a baby until it took root and grew. When Lewis was asleep he thrashed and tossed about the bed as though he was in it alone. Amber clung to the edge, lying still because he didn't even know she was there. She had him to herself now, even if it was only for a short time. Opening the present, looking and admiring, wasn't important, because it didn't matter what it was. But she opened her eyes.

'If we have any luck at the clinic, I'll always think of this when I see our baby.'

She didn't take her eyes from Lewis, watching the glow of him having accomplished something so perfect.

'We could try tonight, just by ourselves,' he suggested, and she pulled him to her. 'But look at your present first.' He was loose with anticipation so that his fingers slipped as he disturbed the soft wrapping. 'It's as amazing as you are. It's a necklace of amber.' The paper fell back and the amber glowed, sensuous, as if it were lit by its own inner light.

'It's lovely. I'll always wear it. It's like an amulet.' Now Amber's fingers touched the paper, folding it back to let the tawny light smoulder on its whiteness. 'Look at it glow,' she said, but Lewis was pulling the paper apart and showing her.

'Look, you haven't seen everything yet,' he said, exposing the bare jewel.

A hideous insect leapt forward and stared Amber straight in the face. She pulled away and the whole thing fell to the floor.

'Oh, no!' she cried.

'Don't worry.' Lewis retrieved it. 'It's been like that for a hundred million years. It won't have broken now.'

He cradled the omen with care. 'I knew you'd love it. Your mother chose the right name for you. You keep things safe.' He pulled her hand and the necklace towards himself and kissed them both. 'Think how long ago this insect was alive, but the amber has preserved it. If we got it out, I might be able to sequence the genes: that's the genotype. And we can see what it looks like: the phenotype, how the environment has manipulated the expression of the genes. I could know everything about this little fellow.' His eyes were bright with satisfaction. Lewis was lost to her again, engrossed in his own vision of science, another hopeless attempt to drag her into his world. He might know all about genotype and phenotype but he understood nothing about reality. She'd moved into his world, taking on his PR, but he had no idea how much she wanted him to come into hers, rooted in the excitement of a man and a woman really and truly making life.

Lewis held the necklace up and the insect glared at her with its ancient eyes, beads full of agonised pleading for release. He would hang it around her throat. Amber reverberated with the chiming fear of something trapped fast inside her: genotype, phenotype, whatever, dead for longer than anyone could remember. Just as it had with her baby, the softness in her had hardened around it, trapped it inside her, and Lewis had no clue as to how that felt. He was touching her breast now, communicating feelings of his own, his fingers swollen and clumsy, but they might have been touching someone else for all she could sense them.

All night the insect nourished itself on the heat from her body, its slippery surface wet with her and Lewis's sweat.

The next morning Amber hoped she hadn't got pregnant under its influence. The feeling grew in her that the baby wouldn't have been hers in some way. But in her hand the amber glowed red; the most expensive sort of amber there was. Lewis had given it to her as a promise. *When we are rich and famous*, he always joked. This gift had added, *when you are pregnant*. She was too frightened to keep it on and too frightened to leave it off. To please Lewis, she told herself, she wore the necklace under her top at work. All day long it hung, heavy and satiated, between her skin and her clothes, and it made everything go wrong.

A day like this needs a decent burial, she decided. She couldn't just walk away and leave it there waiting for her tomorrow. Amber looked at her face in the mirror. It wasn't something she wanted to see – a face that looked as though it should never have come into the office today. But she couldn't take her face off. Restoring her makeup helped. A tinge of defiance fleshed out the blusher. Since when had anyone in PR faced up to the bare truth? She pushed the necklace further down out of sight.

Before she went home, she called at Rhea's flat.

'I'm hacked off,' she informed her disconsolately, and threw her coat onto the sofa, where it landed, draped over the sag that still marked Dave's place. 'You would think that, after all I've done for that company, Warren would let me use their printers for an hour or two.' She plunged down into the single armchair that co-operatively took up her shape while Rhea avoided her eyes.

'So the boards are off,' Rhea said, and her shrill note of triumph caught in the large vase on the table and made it ring.

'No way,' Amber said. 'I'd never let you down. We're running behind on the Howie contract so I said I'd stay late again tomorrow to catch up. I'll run the boards off at the same time. He can't exactly complain, can he?' After I've explained things to him properly, she thought. There were graphs and reprints and computer printouts on Rhea's table, all explaining stem-cell research, but not to her or Warren. The way to approach it was

86

through people; its impact on someone like Polly. If it was left to Lewis and Rhea, their efforts would never get out of the lab. Amber felt brave: a body that was going to be laid bare by infertility testing and maybe given a child by it was a strong one. That insect around her neck couldn't bring her down.

'Do you want some tea?' Rhea asked, making off to the kitchen. 'Oh, look, I'm out of your camomile stuff. Will you have something else?' she called, increasing the gloomy disquiet she'd left in the living room. Amber followed her into the kitchen to find her sister gazing at the empty packet. 'I gave the last of it to Lewis the other night when he stayed.'

'You wouldn't get Lewis to drink camomile tea.'

'He poured it away.'

The kettle boiled and switched itself off.

'Anything will do,' Amber said. 'I'm not fussy.'

'Ordinary tea for both of us, then.' The note of triumph returned to Rhea's voice, as though she had got her way again, cutting the ground from under them as though ordinary was the most they should hope for.

Amber wasn't going to let that happen. 'Did you know that Lewis had got me a present?' She could feel a quaking in her stomach as she said it, as if the words had unsettled a dependable symmetry. She could see Rhea watching her, working out the answer she thought would suit her best. Her sister had a face like a map, if you knew how to read it. Rhea would be thinking as she spoke, trying to have the same thoughts as her sister so that she could make her a present of whatever she wanted to hear. Amber felt weary. The burden of gratitude for all these gifts was wearing her out.

'We could have a drink,' Rhea said, the bottle of wine already in her hands.

'No, thanks,' said Amber. 'I'm driving.'

'Right.' There might have been uncertainty, a premonition of

87

pain in Rhea's voice, as though she was the one who expected trouble now.

'It was a scientific specimen.'

Rhea sighed and didn't answer so Amber crossed the kitchen impatiently. She looked outside at the night. 'The present that Lewis gave me, it's a scientific specimen, like a blueprint of the universe,' she said, 'phenotype and genotype both at once.'

That gave Rhea something to think about. 'Who told you all that?' she snapped.

'Since when did I need somebody to tell me everything? I worked it out for myself.'

Amber shifted uncomfortably at the untruth, at the glare in Rhea's eyes that warned her to keep her distance from the private territory of work. For a moment Amber had a glimpse of that world: a picture of Rhea at work with Lewis, the pair of them wallowing in their abstract teasing out of the mechanics of life, the reduction of biology to a series of intimately controlled laboratory experiments. Rhea would have encouraged Lewis to buy the necklace for her, to keep her happy in her own little world. They would have been speaking for a while, thinking of her, then dismissing her as they turned back, vindicated, to their elevated calling.

'Actually, I've read a couple of Lewis's textbooks to help me with the boards. I'm not stupid, you know.'

The words had come out harder than Amber had intended, untempered by her superhuman effort to be reasonable. She wondered if Rhea had noticed. She had: her face was buckling. Her feelings were pulling it around because she couldn't keep that world all to herself.

The wretched specimen thing was caught: Amber was trying to drag it over her head, but it wasn't going to come off easily. It tangled in her hair and caught there, clinging while she struggled to get rid of it. 'Just look at it. Look.'

'Wait.' Rhea took the thing in her hand, the necklace. 'Wait.'

Amber had to stand there, and keep still, until her hair was untangled and the necklace slid smoothly into Rhea's fingers. With it gone, she retreated to the living-room sofa and watched from a safe distance. Rhea was staring the creature out, awed. 'Amber, it's fabulous.'

Tears magnified the perplexity in her sister's eyes. Amber knew then that Rhea hadn't chosen the present: she'd never seen it before this moment when it had ambushed something in her. She was surely thinking of Dave, of the dent in the sofa where he should have been sitting. Now the necklace truly seemed a cruel, taunting thing dangling from her fingers: a nemesis for them both.

Amber tried to save them from its grim hold. 'Lovely? A dead thing staring at you like that?'

'It's made of amber. It's got everything about you in it. I never thought Lewis would be romantic.'

The insect watched them from its cell, stupefied by Rhea's hypothesis.

'Well, it's precious because it's ancient, isn't it?' Rhea went on, holding out the necklace, with its amber and its insect stuck with each other for all time. Amber tried to smile to show she understood how Rhea felt, but only a baleful stare came back at her, barring her from any contradictory opinion. The wrap of her sister's fingers around the necklace looked like a dangerous trap, baited with false promise.

'That's just the sort of thing Lewis says.' Amber pushed her face close to Rhea's. 'Well, I don't like it and I'm going to tell him.' The disapproval she registered in Rhea's silence drove her on. 'The thing is, Rhea, Lewis likes being frightened of me. You didn't know that, did you? It's the only way he knows he's alive.'

It seemed so true once she had said it, that Lewis liked being frightened of her, even though she had said it only to defy Rhea.

Rhea, with her studied cool, knew how to get to you. This will hurt, but it's for your own good. There would be a sweet and a sticking plaster with a smiley face on it, and you would find yourself bewildered, trying to believe her.

When Amber had gone Rhea took refuge in surfing the net. Even there, shame fingered her, making her shield her face.

I don't think I'll ever be able to have a baby. I've just had my first round of progesterone and have been diagnosed with ovarian hyperstimulation syndrome. Could anyone tell me what this means?

Flashing on the screen, in moments, came the answers.

It happened to me too, but now I have a six-month old little girl. Good luck.

It happened to me too. I still haven't conceived but I haven't given up hope. Good luck.

There was a Freudian slip in the third response, a lapse into baby talk that Rhea found agonising.

Goo Luck.

She put her hands over her eyes and pressed but the words were still there, burnt on her retina: after-images of despair.

Eleanor had pushed the web address on her, saying that the emotional dimension of infertility was under-considered in her experience; how often it proved to be a significant barrier to conception. Patients needed emotional support. Too much knowledge could be a burden, she had supposed, but not for a scientist like Rhea.

Rhea couldn't bear to know so much about other people's sadness. She closed the website down before any other desperate woman could expose herself. She hadn't meant to infiltrate their generosity and spy on the women's tenuous hopes, yet their disembodied hurt had sidled too close, latching on to someone who had no right to it. Pulling it closer and pushing it away felt equally shameful. Dazed by the choice, Rhea clicked on her stats programme and watched the numbers scurry around the screen, then resolve themselves systematically into manageable columns. An answer was cross-hatched into those figures somewhere, if only she could find it.

She checked her email: some of it from friends and colleagues; lots of it from opportunistic spammers with the know-how to breach her computer's firewall, but nothing from Vic. There was something menacing about his silence; you hated it but you didn't want it to end. An absent Vic might mean he was off being wooed by some other group but a present Vic would certainly mean admitting that Joe's, and now Fazil's, cell cultures were dead. She'd already begun the delicate and distasteful business of examining minutely every single procedure that Joe and Fazil used but she was no nearer to understanding the cause, operating in an atmosphere of disfavour only because of her constant intrusions.

The bottle opener that was like a friend, laughing and spreading its arms in welcome: every time Rhea saw it, she was swept back to the memory of her little Amber running towards her in delight and found that she was carried away on a tide of love. Adult Amber, with her new wardrobe of thwarted emotions, was something else. Her body had a mind of its own and her feelings didn't belong to her any more. They belonged to the pivotal urge that had taken her over. Rhea tested her own abdomen and felt its flat integrity with a vague emptiness. She and Lewis would have to take up the slack until Amber got what she wanted or found a way to live without it, at the same time as sorting out the lab problems.

'It's good news. There's nothing in your cultures, Rhea, not a single thing.' Microbiology was the only department that cheered negative results. Rhea wasn't so sure. Some bug that a decent dose of penicillin or streptomycin would cure was the best news she could hope for – because the contagion was spreading. Katherine and Andrew's cells had given up the ghost too, with the same mysterious symptom: no sign of infection. Only yesterday they had hurried her into a corner and confessed, secretly, with Stephen Glatton looking over, wondering what was going on.

It was hard enough keeping any sort of problem quiet in the department, but now the honeypot smell of money rolled around the corridors, along with the rumours that Lewis was expecting some, attracting a constant procession of visitors to the laboratory. There was Glatton, for a start: he'd taken to hanging about at all hours under the pretext that some collaborative project could be fixed up. His cultures were thriving. Glatton watched and pretended not to, while the trouble with their cells festered like a dirty sore and she tried to hide it. Glatton was practically a fixture around the place now. Him, and the tinnitus of anxiety.

The humid carbon-dioxide breath of the incubators mixed with the brothy smell of medium as she opened the incubator door. The stainless-steel shelves, wiped with bactericide until they gleamed, gave no clue as to the cause of the trouble, and the medium covering her cells in their transparent flasks was no longer red but a clear and used-up yellow: a reliable sign of growth.

'How do you do it?' Lewis wondered, slipping in beside her.

Even while he was asking her, she knew she couldn't tell

him. There was no way she could explain how she did her culturing. The words you would have to use didn't work in the laboratory: when Rhea checked her cells, she just thought about how they were doing from their own perspective. If Fazil or Andrew or Joe or even Katherine saw their cells were struggling they would immediately subject them to extra washing, extra feeding, an increased vigour in their regime. But Rhea thought it would hold them back, all that punishment. If her cells seemed sparse and fragile, she trusted them with a little peace until they seemed to feel better: not the sort of care you could talk about.

'Treat 'em mean and keep 'em keen.' She covered her embarrassment with a joke but Lewis couldn't see the funny side of the failure of his hopes.

Usually Lewis didn't admit to worries, and never showed uncertainty, but he couldn't hide it now. There were a couple of flasks of her cells on the bench. He lifted his hand towards them but hesitated and drew it back as if he were afraid to pick them up, as if his touch might be the contaminating one. She was the only person who could grow cells now, but as long as Vic was incommunicado, Rhea didn't have to admit it. And she didn't want to confess because no one was going to invest in a research group with a jinx like this hanging over it.

'You're what's standing between us and disaster, Rhea. I couldn't manage without you.'

Lewis's voice was scarcely more than a whisper; it disappeared into the past as though it was afraid to remain, the way things were now. They stood together in silence, in a space that was addled by their desolate empathy. Anxious chatter spiked in the lab, reminding them to be concerned for the others. Rhea spoke quickly and softly, as if that could protect them from having to know. 'Don't worry them about it. You and I, Lewis, we'll keep on until it's sorted.'

Lewis was hugging a large sheaf of paper to his chest. He clutched it even closer as Stephen Glatton passed between them on his way to admire his cultures.

'What are they?' she asked, nodding towards the bundle.

'Handouts.' He grinned heroically. 'I've just got them off the photocopier. There's nothing like a warm lecture.'

The way Lewis put on a brave face made Rhea feel better too. She poked her finger at the paper. Yes, it was still warm. She glanced at the clock: ten to twelve.

'You've left it a bit late, haven't you?'

The space outside the lecture theatre would be filling up, dozens and dozens of students all waiting for clever, sexy Dr Norham to deliver his warm lecture. She could see that he knew it, and was going to take consolation from his hour of hero-worship. She had to keep worrying about the cells for both of them.

With Lewis out of the way for an hour Stephen Glatton slid out of his isolation suite carrying a thick, colourful promotional brochure. Under the guise of departmental unity it didn't take him long to lay it on the bench where she could see the banner announcement of a Mark II version of the latest array technology. *Fastest Throughput* it promised. *Keep ahead of the competition.* Glatton was prepared to admit to her, *in private*, as you might say, that it was expensive. So stunningly expensive that he would rather it was bought as a general departmental initiative, although he was prepared to contribute some of his own grant money. He'd explain all this to the deans at his meeting about the Genetics Institute but he wanted to get things off to a proper start.

'Do you think you would have any use for it?' he asked. 'Do you need to know which genes your cells are expressing?'

It gave her another sleepless night. She had seen the quiver of excitement in Glatton's entire being. Even he didn't get that size of frisson from taunting someone else. He was on the verge of a serious breakthrough. If he needed array technology he was investigating the mechanisms his cell used to change. He must be absolutely confident he had stem cells, while hers had never reproduced truly, and no one else in the lab had any. In this business there were no consolation prizes. All the sacrifices were for nothing if you weren't first. Their only hope lay in Vic. When he came over for the conference he had to be so impressed that he poured resource into them, so fast that Glatton was left behind.

Wretchedness made her brittle with determination. Washing glassware was soothing. The water poured with a constant drum into the stainless-steel sink, splashing the surround as she rinsed and tipped, tipped and rinsed. Her hands were numb from the cold. She fumbled with a bottle and it slipped to the floor. Rhea sighed.

There must have been something heart-rending about that sigh, because Katherine abandoned her DNA extraction. 'I'll do that for you. It's only fair.'

Fair? It seemed such an unexpected concept in the rough-and-tumble of research, but Katherine hadn't lost sight of it. She took the bucket, too full of soaking glassware, water slopping onto the floor, and carried it to her own bench. The feeling must have been infectious; things like that could take hold and spread throughout the group. Everyone wanted to help Rhea, now that Katherine had pointed out how much she was doing for them. But that was the home team. They would be kind, but peer review would be merciless: the smallest crack would be probed until it opened into a chasm. If Stephen Glatton found that their cells were dying he would want them banned from the joint facility to protect his own work, and if he was really doing as well as he claimed, he would get his way. She could sense the fracturing of the ground under her feet even while she was standing at her sink. Rhea touched her fingers to the bench. Wet, slimy. She was too busy to clean up behind herself.

There has to be a rational answer: It's not the evil eye.

In some part of her mind an idea was forming. It felt like the slow roll of a wave along a flat beach, working towards her. But as it came near, it would let go of its tight curl and splash away, its potential dissipated and lost. She felt the beginning of the swell now. *I couldn't manage without you*, Lewis had said, so quietly that the words soaked through her. She stood still, so that not the slightest movement would ripple out to disturb the wave's delicate equilibrium, but the usual thing happened. The drops of water sparkled apart and she was left to finish clearing up.

They were claiming their boasting rights: that was all. Natural and necessary. Figures were being bandied around, gross exaggerations, surely. Lewis could hear them inflating at every telling, and at the same time, the morale of the romancers rising to ever greater heights. The same was true of the rivalry between them: the grosser the achievement, the more exaggerated the performance of those telltale gestures. Gimlet glances and squaring-up postures ballooned as the glasses emptied. Lewis restricted himself to a single drink; Amber would tolerate no repetition of last time's drunken episode, but he had treated himself to the Ashfield on the way home with a mounting sense of desperation. He hoped to meet, by miraculous coincidence, the senior management team, to gain confidence and succour from their interest, but the crowd in the bar were sales reps, sparring after a taxing month: not so very different from the senior-management team, actually, but of little use to him.

Those sales targets would be raised next month, and they would have to be met somehow. He watched the drinkers winding themselves up, accuracy and probity disenfranchised to the greater good. Ever-increasing expectations hounded Lewis and, so near to losing his whole career, even one drink might induce a haze of compelling recklessness. But he was going to find a way through this disaster. Whatever it takes, he promised himself, whatever it takes.

When Rhea had arranged for the fertility consultant to give a talk about fertilisation and cellular development as part of the department's seminar programme, Lewis had taken it as sorted that he would host the speaker. It was a perk. The department would pay for a decent meal, and it usually fell to the most senior researcher in the speaker's field to entertain the guest, but Featley had made a great show of asking Stephen Glatton to look after Eleanor Bonworth. The relish with which Glatton brightened up and offered a party, at his own house no less, was gruesome. His pale lips turned down in distant contemplation of his triumphant evening. 'Food,' he muttered, and Lewis imagined the curled sandwiches and doughnuts that Glatton normally ate for lunch transferred to a grubby sideboard in a back room. He wasn't even going to drink at this party. He would have stayed away, if he had dared, but who knew what might be fixed up behind his back? Whatever it takes, he reminded himself.

Amber was cautiously thrilled. 'On the one hand, it might be the perfect way to meet Dr Bonworth. On the other, it might be better not to mention about us having treatment.'

'Don't mention it,' Lewis warned. 'She won't want to talk shop.'

The caterers had delivered salmon roulade.

'I know you don't eat meat,' Glatton fawned over Amber, 'and there's no gelatine in the desserts.' Amber left her close admiration of the exquisite dainties as though the taste of them was already in her mouth.

The sight of his wife unfolding with gratitude for this thoughtfulness reignited Lewis's own resolve. But whatever-it-takes didn't include Amber. Stephen Glatton embraced his victory with undisguised glee: his trouncing eyes slid everywhere, from the waxed floors to the shuttered windows and polished mirrors of his glass and wood home. There was a faint Scandinavian chill about it that drew people closer. The guests clustered in groups and cast admiring glances at the bespoke bookcases and the paintings on the walls. The large room was under-furnished, as a man's house was bound to be: no Amber to dot the shelves with pretty dishes, only a few strong, dark lines of sculpture.

Eleanor Bonworth and Featley had been seated by the fire. In the pool of warm light their faces were softened and their heads moved together in a delicate balance. Featley looked every inch the academic with his cautious posture of rationality, ready to take issue at the drop of an opinion, but Eleanor leant back comfortably in her chair, her skirt pulled tight across her knees, making a wide, inviting lap. You might tell anything to someone like her; probably that was what happened in the clinic. People told her things they certainly wouldn't tell their mothers. How else could she make their dreams come true? He caught the rhythm of her and Featley's conversation – polite, collegiate, the sort of talk that made actually saying anything impossible – with a sense of disappointment. He'd be glad to see Featley enticed from his professional reserve.

Joe and Andrew stood alone, holding empty glasses. Their faces flushed with apprehensive bonhomie as Patrick approached with a full bottle and the offer of integration into the conclave of senior post-docs. The lads might admit to anything here, just to feel included among the rising stars. Their lips opened soundlessly as they dealt with their over-filled wine glasses, but it wouldn't take much for them to be spilling out the truth about the dead cells. The despondent could gabble like stand-up comedians, if only someone were kind to them. He probably ought to join them to make sure no one was.

But Rhea guided him across the room. 'My sister's husband.' She introduced him to the group at the fire. The fertility consultant's face remained impassive; she gave him the same impartial smile she had been giving Featley and an amused nod of recognition to Amber. At least her large, calm body didn't shift with curiosity about his sperm count.

'Lewis,' she said, and held out her hand.

The use of his first name surprised and pleased him. In the clinic she'd called him Mr Norham, but only indirectly when she'd asked the nurse to show him where to leave his sample. Should he transcend the professional boundaries or respect them?

'Eleanor, I did enjoy your talk,' he said, concentrating on the work-related spirit of the occasion.

'I wish I had heard it.' Amber hadn't been at the seminar but suddenly she was the most interested person in the room. Her voice ached with longing, open and on the surface.

With a gesture of kindly intimacy Eleanor patted her arm. 'It was just about conception. That's all I ever seem to talk about, one way or another.' There wasn't any way out. Lewis was going to have to stand and listen while Amber quizzed Eleanor about the pertinence of their sex life.

'But what did you tell them about conception?'

Eleanor laughed. 'Nothing they didn't know, probably. It's difficult to pitch things right for a professional audience, like your husband and sister.'

Lewis felt the connection he longed for, the equal recognition of experienced colleagues. The indignity of the fertility tests might have faded completely if it hadn't been for the dead cells and the feeling that he might not warrant recognition much longer. He tried to see what Featley was thinking but Amber leant forward, blocking his view. 'So, what did you tell them about conception?' Amber repeated.

Eleanor paused as she searched for words. 'There is one thing that often surprises my audience. Most people believe that the mother's egg has only one set of chromosomes. They imagine that it needs another set from the father to make it whole. But that's not true: it has two sets. The egg has a redundant set, eased aside in a polar body.'

Could Amber follow this? Lewis looked to see and she was spellbound. There was none of the patronising boredom she showed when he talked about his work.

'Do you mean there's no need for men, then? We can have babies by ourselves?'

He pitched in to play his part. 'No chance. The sperm cell might have only half as many chromosomes, but it's the one that has to do the work. All that swimming uses up the energy in its tail, so when it touches the egg, the tail drops off, and the mitochondrial DNA – that's the sort that you always inherit from your mother, Amber – falls away with it. The egg doesn't divide by itself. It's the all-male bit of the sperm that penetrates and activates it.'

His voice was too loud. The room was quieter now. People looked their way, bemused and straining to hear the end of the story. Stephen Glatton came over to find out what the excitement was about, and Lewis couldn't stop now. 'It's only then that the two sets of DNA in the egg discover their fate,' he went on. 'One set has its own nuclear envelope, it gets to stay, but the other is pushed to the outer edge. No one knows why one set gets chosen and the other is banished to the perimeter,' his hands indicated the two competing factions, 'but the unlucky one never gets to join with the male. It just wastes away.'

Amber's eyes were wide. 'You mean that happens to everyone? That there's this ghost inside you?'

Eleanor raised her eyebrows. 'I wouldn't put it quite like that.'

But Amber would. She gaped at Rhea for her opinion and Rhea wouldn't be outdone.

'You have to wonder how it is for that spare set of maternal DNA,' she mused, 'falling apart in the zona pellucida. It's the other one of you, a person who might have lived your life quite differently.'

There was an excited, triumphant conclusion to Amber's understanding. 'Perhaps she's still there inside you, wanting her way instead of yours.'

It was worrying and yet, Lewis thought, the science was right. It was all in the interpretation. Talking about processes as though they were people and knew what they were doing had a dangerous edge. He touched Amber, made of those very processes, to caution her, and she glanced at him. She knew what she was doing. Amber always had this effect on people. Even Featley indulged her shamelessly. Right there in front of Lewis and Stephen Glatton, he picked up the drama of her conceit and let his scientific objectivity go: 'The one that stays, you know, it doesn't bind to the male straight away. Like Eleanor said, the mother's and the father's DNA sit tight in their own nuclear envelopes, weighing each other up. Then the cell begins to split. There are going to be two cells so they have to get on with it, commit themselves to a common purpose and share themselves out.'

There was an eddy of confusion and Lewis felt nervous. 'We're teasing you a bit,' he said. 'It's not quite like that. It just depends how you say it.'

Featley understood Lewis's warning. He was suddenly shamefaced.

'Lewis has been instructing me,' Amber told him, business-like now. 'I'm doing the PR for the spring conference, about the

101

stem cells. It would be good if you would look over it too, to give just this sort of human angle. And I'd like to able to include something about the Genetics Institute business. The department always needs good press.'

Rhea smiled apologetically at Eleanor, and Lewis remembered that they were friends already; the cord blood that passed between them had given them every reason to meet.

'Eleanor and I have been talking about the idea of setting up a cord-blood bank,' she explained, drawing her sister in. 'We could store stem cells from every baby born in the hospital, and by the time they're grown-up and need them, I'll have worked out how to use them. We'd be the first hospital in the country to do it.'

'Hold it. You hadn't said anything about that.' Lewis was alarmed, but Amber was all for it. Just the sort of thing people wanted to know, she assured them.

Featley was impressed. 'Umm. We'll have to see what we can do.'

Away from the warmth of the fire, the chasm between the brilliance of Amber's vision of the future and Lewis's research team's desperate reality seemed wider than ever. Andrew and Joe were huddled over their drinks with Patrick. Lewis's only consolation was watching Glatton look glumly at the post-docs laying waste to his buffet.

'If you would have a word with him.'

But he didn't want to talk to Warren about the way his stem-cell research might help Polly because he couldn't guarantee that it would, now the cells were dying, and he didn't want the narrowing of Warren's weasel eyes at his loss of face. Lewis could still remember how it had felt when Amber's expectations had had the power to lift him out of himself, right above the sludge of actuality that had clung to his feet whenever he tried to move. If he closed his eyes he could remember it easily: the opening of doors into places he had never imagined. How the fantasy worlds in which she was completely at home became the arresting, then ordinary landscape of his life. The eclipsing of Rhea by her sister had been sudden and complete. So much so that he had hardly noticed when she'd gone to the States. He'd been glad there was nothing to pull him back down to the dullness of habit. He longed to feel the surge of exhilaration that had made him powerful and unbeatable, but when he opened his eyes again, there was Patrick, juggling with the centrifuge tubes. The red caps flashed for a while but the light plastic was uncontrollable, and however much the tattoo on his arm writhed and twisted, he couldn't keep the tubes in the air. He soon dropped one and then the rest followed it to the floor. If Patrick imagined that circus skills would earn him a living, he must be deluded.

From their slumped postures he guessed his team had a collective hangover. They thought Glatton's party could count as a success because no one had liked him for the extravagance of his buffet or the restrained elegance of his home.

Joe's socialist principles meant that he felt particularly bad about having taken advantage of so much bourgeois excess. 'He can't have earned the money to pay for it. He's not old enough.'

'You mean he's not good enough,' chipped in Andrew.

'Actually,' offered Katherine, 'he's older than you suppose.'

At first Lewis thought she was talking about him. He and Glatton had been appointed on the same day to form the nucleus of the department's stem-cell initiative. He'd always thought of himself as the senior partner, just topping Glatton in age and experience. Within a few years the assumption had settled into an incontrovertible fact. He was still getting over it when Katherine went on, 'It's not his house, actually. It's his parents'. They're abroad.'

So Stevie'd had a party while his mum and dad were away. Lewis shrugged as if he had known all along. The realisation that Glatton wasn't wealthy and richly endowed with good taste didn't quite make up for the fact that his cells flourished regardless. The array technology that he had on appro was being set up in the clean lab. Access was to be on a need-to-use basis, a notice on the door informed the curious, *Applications to Dr Glatton*, although Lewis knew that the department would pay only a quarter of the cost and Glatton would need to hustle for the rest.

'I'm sure he's at the bottom of it, somehow.'

'Do you think Glatton even knows about our cells?' Joe asked.

'Did anyone mention it?'

Thankfully, shaken heads all round, except for Joe's. His bristly plume was still, his eyes dark and full of resentment. If eating and drinking had made Joe a class traitor, Stephen Glatton was going to get the blame for it.

'He seems to know an awful lot about everything. I wouldn't be surprised if he was interfering with our stuff.'

Lewis had already given a good deal of his thinking time to wondering if there was something sinister about his group's problem. He'd tried the idea out on Rhea, choosing a time when she was frowning over her methods book, turning the pages and comparing them to Joe's and Katherine's, then Andrew's and Fazil's, wondering all the time what she was doing differently. 'Nothing?' he suggested. 'It might be something else altogether.'

She looked around, her face lightened with expectation. Briefly, they were joined by the need for him to be right.

'What if Glatton's infected our cells with that bloody virus he and Patrick tote about the culture suite?' he said.

She swept it away, telling him in her grown-up voice that it was more likely to be the chaos than the conspiracy theory, leaving him feeling childish and over-reactive. He tried to defend himself: it might have been an accidental infection; no one had mentioned deliberate sabotage, but some damage had been done. She couldn't look at him. Rhea turned pages stubbornly, determined to find an answer in the methodology. Lewis was glad to have an ally now, but he wished it hadn't been young Joe.

Rhea was still all misgivings. 'You can't go accusing someone,' she insisted. 'We haven't any evidence.' There was a straightforward way of solving that problem. Lewis would demand a sample of Glatton's virus and run the gels to check whether he could find viral DNA in their cultures.

Joe went with him to confront Glatton. Lewis was grateful for the back-up but he would rather it had been Rhea. Her presence might have taken the sting out of the accusation; she would have known how to put it so that it wasn't an accusation, only an innocent idea that had drifted by. Joe's hair and Patrick's tattoos were probably the most innocent things in the laboratory, but it wasn't going to seem like that when they went head-to-head about whose fault this was.

He scraped together his evidence in the knowledge that it was negative. That there wasn't any other explanation was his main line of attack. The intrigue of the situation, the possibility of its resolution by sudden and bold means, gathered itself in his mind so that by the time he spotted Glatton and Patrick, leaning on their incubator, their white coats hanging loose across the door seal as they shifted their arms and made themselves comfortable in his team's space, he was certain of his own position. He went straight to the point.

'You'll have heard that we've had some culture trouble.'

Of course they'd heard. Sparks of having heard flitted through their eyes, ready to ignite. Lewis huffed and blurted out his predicament, running all the arguments together, not allowing any of them their proper chance for impact. 'There's no other explanation,' he insisted at last, conscious of the weakening of his own polemic. 'No bacteria, no fungus. The cells must have been compromised by a virus. You're the only group using one. It has to be yours.'

Glatton allowed the point with a shrug, but then he grimaced and twisted his pale lips in his reluctance to take things further.

Lewis was uncertain of what this meant. Had Glatton conceded or – and this hit disastrously at Lewis's determination – hadn't he a clue about what the problem was? Glatton turned to Patrick and asked him to get some of the viral DNA. Patrick flexed the muscles of his torso, and the gangster-movie dimension of the scene dawned on Lewis. Even so, the tide of ridiculousness didn't sweep him away. It urged him on. He was acutely conscious of his own sidekick, Joe, poised and expectant at his side. All the boyhood fights he had imagined but never consummated welled up inside him.

Patrick came back with the minuscule tube, no more than a needle, its ampoule-like nature as potent as – well – genetic material. Lewis found the grace to laugh at himself. He tittered nervously as Glatton passed it to him, saying, 'It's an artificial construct. We buy it ready prepared so we've never had any live virus to infect anything.' He nodded fondly at the tube. 'A bit of a gene made in a synthesiser from a few chemicals. Patrick will give you the firm's address. If you want any more you can buy it yourself.'

Lewis's embarrassment intensified in the heat of the anger that this brought on. Where did Glatton get the sort of money to pay for ready-prepped materials? Machines like coffee-makers made artificial genes if you could afford them, and saved you all the trouble of handling viruses. Joe's emo-mask remained impassive but he had to be resenting the months he spent preparing the sort of stuff that Patrick got with an email. A groan escaped him as he thought of Andrew hearing about this. It might have been a cough.

'Pop it in the fridge,' he told Joe. 'I'll just check Rhea's cells. They're all we've got.' It was a final effort to hang onto his dignity, played out in front of Glatton and Patrick so that they would understand the scale of his predicament. They all stood around as he extracted the cultures from the incubator and focused the microscope.

'At least . . .' The words collapsed in his mouth.

Every one of Rhea's cultures was dead.

Disbelief settled like a sedative. It threw back the small quanta of light and saved Lewis having to see. It stilled the incessant oscillation of sound waves so that he didn't have to hear. Best of all, it infiltrated his skin and then his blood–brain barrier and pacified his worst torturer, his own thinking. He sat suspended in the soft, muting throes of incredulity until long after the others had gone home. He still breathed and if he put his hand to his chest he knew his heart was beating, although it felt slow and uninterested. He sat very still, trying not to disturb the merciful oblivion that had enveloped him.

It was the only way he knew to exist. If he moved, the mist would swirl and disappear, and the world would crash through with all its pain and humiliation. Better the opaque white of nothing than the clarity of reality. Years of work were strung out behind him, and in front of him there was nothing. A great blank spread across his thinking. He couldn't find a rational explanation: it was as though a plague had descended to punish him.

Stephen Glatton's incubator stood proud and jeering in front of him, defying him to touch it and feel its immovable strength. He opened the door carefully and breached its innards. He took one of the flasks from the middle shelf and slipped it under the microscope just as he would have done with his own cultures. There was nothing at all to distinguish these cells from his own, except that Glatton's were burgeoning. They had the same dark membranes, the same protrusions anchoring them to the plate, the same rounding up ready to divide. And all alive.

On the way out he passed the lavatories and, on an impulse, he went inside and stood in the cubicle where he'd wanked out his semen sample. It hardly seemed possible that his life had been crammed with promise so recently. It couldn't all have disappeared into Glatton's clutches. He kicked the door savagely and it sprang back at him because it hadn't been locked anyway.

CHAPTER 6

The whole of Lewis's group gathered together for the final ritual of disposal, gazing at one another in an elaborate tangling of innocence and guilt. It felt like retribution, undeserved, and for a crime that had been so subtle and inconsequential that they didn't know they had committed it. Team solidarity was never as solid as when someone else joined the accused. Joe's pariah status had been revoked. Once Katherine's and Andrew's and then Fazil's cultures had died, he had been absolved of exclusive identification with blame. The price of Rhea's inclusion had been the loss of her cells too.

No trace of her cultures was to be left in the laboratory. They were to be annihilated, with whatever had killed them. Disposal was an upsetting business: piling all the cells, and everything that had been in contact with them, into the biohazard waste. Their entire collection of non-disposable glassware had to be sterilised. Rhea led the whole group, all of them carrying the sealed bags down to the industrial-scale facility, set in concrete in the basement. The autoclave produced reactions of awe in the youngest members of the team. They turned to Rhea with bewildered expressions – Surely you don't expect us to run this, the aggrieved set of their mouths was saying – and she realised that it was probably older than most of them. But the grotesque old thing still had its insurance certificate and she had operated it constantly until they had been able to afford the tiny, user-friendly units that lived upstairs in the lab.

It took two hands to lower the autoclave lid. Rhea did it herself while the others stood watching: watching the tightening of the massive bolts and the checking of the ungainly safety valve. And watching her too. There was a querulousness about them as they distanced themselves from such a brutish task. Their speechless sideways glances betrayed their discomfort with someone who was so plainly at ease with the monster. Their gracelessness – it wasn't her fault that she had needed to learn all this before technology had become so sophisticated – made her graceless. She fumbled with the valves and stabbed at the isolation switch on the wall. There was something profoundly depressing about being the only person who knew how to manage this infernal anachronism. She put on a face that she knew wouldn't fool them.

'A clean start,' she said. 'I'll unfreeze some of the back-up supplies, but not until we've decontaminated everything again.'

The aftershocks of the catastrophe were rumbling around the lab. Andrew deserted, scuttled off to the library. Fazil was swabbing the benches. They couldn't possibly need any more cleaning but it gave him something to do. Katherine was loading the dishwasher again. The celebrity status of being the only one to have any success fell clear away from Rhea, but at least it didn't seem to matter to Katherine. She came trooping down the lab to collect Rhea's washing-up, as usual.

'Thanks.' It seemed little enough to say to the only person in the lab who could still raise a smile, and Rhea didn't want to burden her with the job of going back down two flights of stairs to switch off the autoclave, so she went herself.

The basement was littered with junked equipment. Old centrifuges, missing some vital component, and the spectro-photometers that were used for measuring colour reactions, out-of-date and no longer useful, were piled around the walls. Rhea could remember using some of the specs when she had been a student, but already they looked as though they had lain undisturbed for a hundred years. Once something was out of commission, it disintegrated faster than you would believe. She opened the covers to look for the prisms that directed the light beams in them. Highly refractive glass could split daylight, and perhaps even the fluorescent torrent in the over-lit basement, into perfect rainbows. She had taken one from a pensioned-off machine like these when she was a post-grad, but it had got lost in the move to the States. The feeling came to her that if she could replace it, she would go back to being the sort of person who had made those rainbows, and everything else would go back to normal. How could it not, with the laboratory full of coloured light? While the autoclave cooled, she searched each of the discarded specs, but every one of the prisms had been taken already. Some other student was having their daylight split into arcs that bounced vividly around bare laboratory walls.

'Rhea?' A call for her came faltering around the basement, made hesitant by the accumulated rubbish of the recent past. She pushed the spectrophotometer lids shut, secretly, holding them carefully at the last minute as they slotted into place so that they wouldn't make a noise, as if she was doing something wrong. More pointless guilt for another uncommitted crime, and it was only Lewis looking for her. The same free-floating anxiety that she was feeling must have brought him down to help her.

She opened the safety vent and let the last of the pressure into the air. In the hiss and spurt of the old autoclave, Lewis's voice lost itself in the noise of the escaping steam. Rhea shook her head and shrugged her shoulders. He was gazing expectantly in her direction but she had no idea what he had said.

111

'I was looking for a prism in the old spectrophotometers,' she shouted, and Lewis raised his hand to show that he had understood. He took it as an instruction and began to check the specs, methodically opening them in turn. The commotion of the steam was everywhere. Rather than shout across the room again, Rhea crossed to him and said into his ear, 'I've already done it.' Lewis started in surprise and scanned the basement uncomfortably, as though he was afraid someone might have heard her. 'I've already checked the specs,' she said, as the steam finally died away. Her voice had sounded loud and vexed in the sudden quiet. Lewis bent further over the metal casing, delving deeper into the innards of the machine so that she couldn't see his face.

'There's bound to be one somewhere.'

Rhea pulled him up, saying, 'It doesn't matter, Lew,' and dusted off his lab coat.

She realised it must have been a while since he had worn it because it was tight across the chest. He was burrowing into the equipment again, still hoping to find a prism, and the coat seams were strained across his back, as though it belonged to someone else. Perhaps he had put on weight, she thought. She couldn't actually remember when she had last seen Lewis work in the lab. He kept his back resolutely turned, but muttered into the mechanics and electronics. 'We might have to think about Plan B,' he said.

When she pointed out that it really didn't matter because she could always buy herself a prism from the New Age shop he stood up and said it did matter, with such a serious expression that Rhea was disconcerted.

'I've thought of a way out. You can't tell one cell line from another, not by just looking at them. No one would ever know if we bought in some new lines and labelled them up as though they were the stem cells, just while Vic's here.'

Rhea started to laugh, as though it was a joke between them, but she knew already that it wasn't and the *faux*-giggle sounded like a snigger. Lewis turned away, unable to look her in the eye, and while he wasn't watching, she rearranged her face into an unconcerned smile and led the way back upstairs, pretending she hadn't heard.

Side by side, Lewis and Rhea watched Katherine and Joe unloading the dishwasher.

'They rely on us. We can't let them down.'

Rhea looked at Lewis and knew he wasn't talking about the prism. 'Oh, Lew,' she said, 'We can't do anything like that.'

All the commotion of the cleaning had calmed Rhea; it was as though her brain had been scoured of the debris cluttering it. The glassware that Katherine was stacking out of the washer was sparkling clean. It reflected a sharp, clear light, glinting in the racks, almost as bright as a prism. Scalding water vapour from the machine was clouding the glass partition, individual droplets coalescing into running streams. The wave that rolled towards Rhea gathered itself and didn't break.

'That's it,' she said. 'Katherine's started putting my washing-up in the machine. That's why my cells have died.'

How could it have been so easy? Only Rhea didn't bother with the new dishwasher. She quite liked standing at the tap, cleaning her own glassware; that was her thinking time. They had used the wrong detergent; something hadn't rinsed away and had poisoned their cells.

Excitement prickled all over her skin. It was like a plasma ball, the sort she had played with as a child. Wherever you touched it, that was where the energy rushed. It was this taut-ness that held her, bound her life, made her quicken.

At the end of the day Lewis visited the culture suite, hooking out one of the high laboratory stools to keep her company while she gave a final check to the fresh cultures. They didn't mention Plan B again. It seemed like the product of a fading nightmare: a time apart that had no hold on them now. It was only a few months until the conference but, by working non-stop, they could do it. They fell into easy step as they walked along the corridor together, the automatic lights flickering on seconds too late so that their shadows kept leaping in front of them in a disordered relay race for the exit.

Lewis's mouth tightened.

'Amber?' Rhea anticipated his thoughts before he spoke. 'Don't worry. I'll give her the injection tonight.'

So late in the year sunset came early. In the half-light shadows hazed before them. When Dave had gone, Rhea had run to the laboratory for cover. She left it now with Lewis, the knowledge of her dishwasher discovery tucked tight under her coat. It was simpler than love, more certain anyway, and she didn't need anyone to share this. That knowledge warmed her from the inside out, so that in spite of the frost it felt like the sudden leap of the sun towards summer.

Stephen Glatton was crossing the quadrangle; she and Lewis turned instinctively in on themselves to avoid him and stepped sharply into a narrow service road that ran to the back of the building. At the same time a delivery truck turned the corner: a truck with dual headlights, bright to her dark-adapted eyes, so she couldn't see the driver behind them. He hit the horn; they'd slipped off into the dark and been caught in this fractious light. She crushed up to Lewis in a doorway as the lorry slowed and carped into low gear, its long overhang passing inches from their faces and blocking out the view. When it had gone, they waited in the untroubled space it had left behind. Things were glitteringly clear, the way they were only in the bareness of winter. Rhea could still hear the rapping of Glatton's leather soles on the frozen paths, but the noise was retreating. He couldn't have seen them.

'I can't stand that creep. You don't like him, do you, Rhea?' Lewis asked. The thickness of the re-established dark insulated them from public scrutiny. The truth was less of a hassle here than in the busy lab. Glatton was certainly a rival, but was he really a creep? Rhea knew that Lewis would be wondering where Glatton had been. A meeting about the Genetics Institute?

'Remember the way he rolled over for Amber?' In the dark she could feel Lewis bridle. 'It might come to him or us,' he said. 'Best keep it simple.'

Satisfaction at solving the tissue-culture problem melded with gratitude at being associated with Lewis, always that bit ahead of the curve, rather than tag-along Glatton. Wherever Glatton went he left something stressful behind him – something you couldn't see or hear, but you could feel it. Your nerves knew it was there, shadowing you.

Rhea tousled Lewis's hair, somewhere between a dissolving sadness and an emerging happiness.

He laid his arm across her shoulders. 'Stick with me, baby.' He was looking back, making sure that Glatton had gone. 'And don't let that nerd collar our post-docs while I'm away.'

She laughed. She rattled her filing-cabinet keys in her pocket and they separated as they wandered back into the empty twilight of the quadrangle. Glatton's footsteps had dwindled to nothing, and as they parted, Lewis and Rhea exchanged a look of mutual commendation.

The garage provided paper towels to wipe your hands but the dispenser was empty. Rhea forgot that she wasn't wearing her lab coat and rubbed the grime down the back of her jeans. It didn't matter; she could take them off as soon as she got to Amber's and have a shower. With the cell-culture problem solved, the broken concrete forecourt felt like solid ground beneath her feet, and if the cold crept upward through the thin soles of her indoor shoes, that was something else Amber's house would dispel. At Snitter Heugh there would be food and clean sheets, because Amber knew how to spoil you as no one else could. Here she was, looking forward to a night's retreat with her sister. But even while she was looking forward to it, Rhea looked back towards the city. Over the hills, edging the horizon, a thin line of reflected light glowed red up into the clouds. Amber had pointed it out first. 'See that, Rhea? It makes the whole city-thing look like the entrance to Hell.' Amber would never stay over in Rhea's flat, as though she felt it wasn't a proper place for someone who wanted a child. Rhea felt the nervousness that Amber's spoiling brought on.

Already tendrils of Amber were spreading themselves into the countryside: new life, new friends. Then, if the infertility treatment did any good, there would be a baby to occupy her. Rhea felt the pivot of Amber's affection waver dangerously between suffocation and abandonment. She was reassuring herself: filling up the car for her eventual escape home.

Darkness hid the state of the house and made it seem elegantly romantic until the security lights blazed on. Then you could see how run-down it was. Rhea wondered how long the rural adventure would keep her sister happy. Even for Amber, labours of love had their bounds, and she'd get no help from Lewis. At the same time she felt spasms of affection for them both. And the steady beat of optimism for her own future.

Amber had put some sort of aromatic essence in the guest room to create an uplifting ambience. While Rhea changed she padded around, folding clothes, stacking them on the bed.

'I've put your jeans in the washing-machine for you, babes. They'll be ready by tomorrow.'

Amber, who couldn't leave you alone. You only had to drop your guard long enough to shower and she had rearranged your laundry, then your life behind your back. Nothing to worry about, Rhea reminded herself. For the next few hours, she could just give in. The smell of Amber's essential oils drifted around with her, enveloping her in their enervating taint of abdication.

Amber sat on the edge of the bed, indulging her liking for physical closeness. Lewis had gone to Manchester, but she would have come wandering in even if he'd been there. She hated being alone, even for a short time, and without him, she would be roaming the house looking for someone or something else to be connected to. Amber didn't speak, just watched, her eyes roving over Rhea's face. She couldn't pass a mirror without looking for herself in it, checking she was there. If the mirror was someone's eyes, so much the better.

This was the first time they'd felt able to chat together since Rhea's split with Dave, but there was silence. They both waited.

Amber stood up again and began putting Rhea's clothes into the drawer. 'Are you all right now, Rhea, about Dave? Do you miss him? Or –' she closed the drawer and Rhea's clothes disappeared '– are you ready for the next instalment?'

'Give me a break, Amber. I've been really busy all day and I've only just got here.'

But Amber wasn't put off so easily. She stood closer, so that Rhea could feel her warmth and hear her raspy breathing, the sound of her childhood. 'I was talking to Mum. We both thought it would be best if you could meet someone at work. You'd be as bad as each other.'

The dragnet of scrutiny closed around Rhea.

'It wouldn't be much fun for me, though,' Amber went on. 'You and him and Lewis. I liked Dave.' She ignored Rhea's grimace; she brightened. 'At least Lew could report back to me.'

'You'd better let Mum know that you've both got it wrong. And, personally, I can't see Lewis spying for the pair of you.'

Which of them knew Lewis best? They watched one another, each occupied by the same thought. They sighed and looked away. Lewis and their mother. They could share that problem.

'He's wary of her,' Rhea said at last. 'The mother-in-law.'

Amber looked shamed. 'I don't know why.' She excused her husband and mother in the same breath. 'I've always thought . . .'

'I know,' said Rhea, and took her hand. 'He only wants to impress her.' They both paused at the immensity of the task Lewis faced: living up to the memory of their father and his bequest, the income from the factory, even after his death.

A day dangled in their memories: the two of them with Mum, Lewis off parking the car.

'You'd be pregnant in no time if you weren't working so hard,' their mother had said. 'Just don't tell Grandpa. Don't let him know Lewis doesn't make enough to keep you. He won't like it, you know.' And there had been Lewis's tense, hurt face, hanging behind her shoulder, realising that she didn't think he was good enough. If he hadn't minded until then, he always had afterwards.

'Why don't we do it now?' Rhea asked. 'Get it over with before supper.' Amber was unwilling. Rhea pushed: 'Go on down and fetch it while I get dressed.'

Amber wanted her injection but she didn't. She stood up too slowly and her fingers steepled as though she was praying for deliverance. She radiated confusion, so that Rhea's skin crawled with it too. 'Go on,' Rhea urged. 'I'll be down in a minute.'

'Will we do it downstairs?' Amber asked. All at once it was *we*. They were in this together. When Lewis had been there, it had been *us* and *you, Rhea*.

'Yes. Whatever. We can have something to eat afterwards.'

When Rhea got into the kitchen Amber had set the table, the

two places opposite one another with a covered dish of pasta between them. She poured a glass of wine and offered it to Rhea.

'I'll have one later. You have it now,' Rhea said but Amber shook her head.

'I won't have any, just in case it makes a difference. I don't want there to be anything to regret afterwards. If it doesn't work, you know.' She put down the wine and nodded towards the fridge and the IVF injections, eager, but reluctant too.

The enormous brushed-steel American fridge was out of place in the shabby kitchen. It took up the whole of one wall. Rhea guessed it was for all the local, pesticide-free produce Amber was making a religion of these days. Now it held the cocktail of chemicals that would force her to super-ovulate so that her baby could be made in the hospital laboratory. In Rhea's mind, there was a clear, strong image of cells flourishing under her own care, the unexpected mixture of high and low tech that had saved the research project. The memory of the wave that had carried the solution to her filled out until the kitchen disappeared and she could see and hear the water, tumbling as though it was laughing. And the real, liberated laughing of her friends. Lewis had gone to Manchester happy.

'This is so going to work,' she said, hearing the force of confidence in her voice. 'Between us we can do it, you know.' For once she let herself be swept up in the enormity of it. The great metal door swung open under her hands and light splashed into the warm fug of the kitchen.

She got the cardboard box out quietly and started to prepare the injection, knowing that Amber's ambivalent eyes watched her while she worked.

'Baby ingredients,' she said, as she held up the syringe. Amber didn't flinch. Rhea brought the needle point to her sister's leg. Amber's skin was going to be a used sort of skin

119

soon. It was starting to be creased and fragile and it was going to wear out until all those soft-scented creams couldn't hide the damage. But not yet. Rhea brought the needle nearer. 'Don't look,' she said, but Amber twisted her head to see and her body shrank. A muscle in her thigh, the quadriceps, went into spasm, pushing the needle and Rhea's hand away.

Rhea held the leg tighter. It was firmer and stronger than it looked – everything about Amber was – but held tightly like that, her sister relaxed and the muscle softened, accepting the intrusion. A lot of people gave themselves their injections but Amber was reluctant to do so. She would trust someone else when she wouldn't trust herself. Rhea closed her thoughts down, in case her sister could hear them, but it was already too late.

'Do you think you could push a needle into your own leg?'

'Yes,' Rhea said, but her answer had a sad, disappointed sound. She felt surprised, and displeased with herself, as though there was a fault line of truth in the *yes*, something she hadn't quite grasped. She couldn't imagine her own body softening the way Amber's could; she felt it would harden, then shatter suddenly. Fragments of her would embed themselves everywhere.

'Do you suppose it will do any good?' Amber asked, in a casual, incurious voice, trying to hide the depth of her need for reassurance.

'Why shouldn't it?' Rhea answered.

They were sisters, after all. They ritually exchanged guarantees that everything would be fine, aware that they didn't know whether it would or not, both casting spells for the future.

Amber stood over the pasta, spoon poised, ready to cut into it. 'I want a baby so much that I'm frightened of myself.' There was a pause while she grimaced. 'And I hate my job.'

'But you're really, really good at it,' Rhea told her. 'One touch from you and somebody's whole image is transformed.'

'That's all PR comes down to, transforming the grubby into the pristine.'

At Amber's ambiguous tone a thin veil of sadness settled over Rhea. Always an undercurrent of blight that she couldn't quite dismiss. 'You always know how to put things, how to get people on your side.'

'What you're saying is, I've made a career out of being a manipulative bitch.' She took a long drink out of Rhea's wine glass. 'It doesn't count if I have yours, does it, Rhea?' She rubbed away the ring that the wet glass had left on the table. 'I love this table,' she said. 'It's not just a table, it's generations of living.' Her fingers probed the grain.

'I don't think so,' Rhea told her. 'Blokes in warehouses make them look old like that. They whack them with chains.'

'Chains?'

'It's only a table. I don't suppose it felt a thing,' Rhea said. 'More chic than shock.'

Amber shifted uneasily, but her fabricated grin turned into a real smile. 'Only a pretend, then?' she said.

Rhea wasn't sure whether Amber had been talking about the table or herself. The absolute understanding that had always been at the core of their evenings alone, even after Amber's marriage, hadn't come back. Sadly, Rhea traced its loss to Dave's presence. He'd managed to create more distance between Amber and her than Lewis ever had.

The hormone injections were making Amber unpredictable; she was so very easily bruised.

Rhea gave up trying to make sense of it and didn't attempt to talk. Amber could speak at any time. She was talking now, in her quiet, tender voice that pretended to tell you everything. She talked about babies, and how much they mattered, how nothing was as important as a new life. 'Who do you think the baby will look like?'

'Lewis.' Amber was sure. 'His dark hair will blot out my carrot tops, won't it?' As Rhea was like Lewis – dark, yet pale – the baby might look like her if it was a girl. How Amber would mind!

'We'll have to clone you, and then there'll be another Amber.' But there wouldn't be another Amber, would there? Because there was no Amber without a Rhea, and, a rueful recognition this, no Rhea either, without a corresponding Amber. Ravelled together, they shared a past.

At the idea of cloning, Amber shuddered with the mixture of pleasure and disgust she specialised in.

With the culture dilemma resolved, Lewis was fully prepared to have a chat with Warren – it was a taste of what his life might become – but not in the lab. His workspace had a private dimension, nothing to do with Warren. It wasn't as though he liked the man. Lewis had always thought of him as the pushy type whose main strength was his tenacious grip on everything that went on in his company, but at any mention of Polly, Warren's fingers plucked helplessly at his earlobe.

'Isn't there anything the medics can do?' he asked, expecting to hear about an operation that might make a difference, best done in a year or two when she'd grown a bit, but Warren shook his head.

'She should never have been like that.' Warren hit the table with his fist. He had a closed-down expression, not daring to see the alternative life that might have been Polly's, but Lewis saw a patch of tissue, aching to be regrown. He looked around the staff club, full of postgraduates enjoying themselves, but who knew what lay behind that easy humour, waiting for a quiet and lonely moment to make its presence felt? The tables were plastic so the lifting and lowering of glasses made a constant noise, like people talking a long way off; the quiet moment didn't come for most. Warren didn't have that luxury.

'The technology isn't ready yet, not for patients. But we're well on with the research.'

But that wasn't much good to Warren. Polly was growing up; she'd want to go to gigs and out clubbing, and Warren, God help him, wanted to say no for the same reasons as every other dad.

'As soon as we can arrange clinical trials, she'll be the first. I can promise you that.'

A mutual sense of impotence drew them close.

'There have to be steps,' Lewis warned him. 'You could trawl the net and find some clinic that'll take your money and any risk you want with your daughter.'

'Polly.' Warren insisted on her name, insisted on the warmth of her, her voluble silences and the drag of her leg. 'If I don't look out for her, who will?'

Warren had agreed that Amber could do the publicity for the conference and Rhea felt the extra responsibility.

When they couldn't get the cells to grow, she'd tried all sorts of different media formulations, thinking that was the problem. With Polly in mind, she didn't care how much work it would be. 'I think I'll give them another go,' she said to Lewis. 'The cells are growing so well now, I'm thinking I might be able to culture a single cell. If it's a stem cell, the strain from it might be a hundred per cent pure.'

'We've never been able to grow a single cell before, not without helper cells.'

'That's what I think is different now. All that trouble might have been worth it.'

It wasn't a good idea to get over-enthusiastic. It could easily all come to nothing. But Rhea couldn't hold back a grin. 'I think it'll work. Really, I do, Lew.'

They were both on their feet.

'Polly.'

123

'We'll get it done for her in no time. I'll help you.'

As good as his word, Lewis stayed on to help with the cloning. He had been out of the routine lab for months now. Suddenly he was in it all evening and critically out of practice. There was a period of dislocation: his former expertise and precise technique hadn't exactly disappeared but had retreated perceptibly. He hovered behind Rhea in baffled silence as she worked. She adjusted her expectations. 'You could do the washing-up,' she suggested, as she prepared another plate, and he agreed readily. To get it done, Lewis was prepared to do the most menial tasks there were, but with the conference so close, there was never going to be time to make a significant difference. If she was going to get this up and running, she would need some help and she wasn't ready yet to share her ideas with Katherine, who was far too friendly with Stephen Glatton, whatever the truth about the dead cultures. Katherine's bright, evasive eyes were too eager to please. The sight of them raised the spectre of Dave and his final, guilty cajoling, but Rhea hadn't time to dwell on it. There was too much to do and the tube of living cells was smooth in her hand, at the same temperature as her blood so that she could barely feel it. She tilted it to mix them evenly. Lewis came to help her plate up the cells but he hadn't put in the practice that she had; a drop almost fell from the pipette, and then it didn't. There was a tremor and it finally let go. Lewis looked disturbed. His fingers pulsed on the pipette dropping the cells too quickly. There'd be a dead patch on that plate in the morning.

'The trick is to squeeze very gently,' she told him, 'hard enough to push the cells out, but soft enough not to cause damage.'

There wasn't enough room for two people in the cubicle and they were too close together. Cells liked company: they released chemical messengers to contact one another and that increased

124

their survival rate. Rhea had grown heart cells when she was a student. She'd start with a spare covering of them on the bottom of her plate and when they had grown dense enough to touch one another, a spark of recognition would pass through them and they would begin to beat in unison, in her tissue-culture flask. As she peered down the microscope, Rhea had always thought they were happy then, giving her a Mexican wave. Lewis and she were sharing the same air. There was a film of sweat on his face and Rhea knew how dangerously close they were.

She took the pipette from his hand and, slowly, just touched the tip to the bottom of the plate to make the cell's passage easy. Invisible, protected by their wall of forced air, she could imagine them already putting down feelers, anchoring themselves while she and Lewis struggled to stay afloat.

These cells were eating money: the cocktail of factors she had devised to thwart nature had cost the rest of their grant income. It had to work. Five hundred and seventy-six cultures, each with a chance of being pure. She and Lewis sat close and bent together to check every one.

It was almost a party. A celebration anyway, according to Eleanor. The embryologist had hair cropped so close that you could see the plates of his skull. He set himself up in the corner of the room, a fitting symbol of the latest in reproductive technology: more like a replicant than a midwife.

'At least he looks intelligent,' Amber murmured. She was already sleepy from the pre-med and the owner of the shorn head spoke slowly and clearly to her.

'I'll be checking your eggs to see how many of them are viable. If you phone in the morning, I'll be able to tell you.'

Lewis was in the corner, supervising the assistant, making sure that she was labelling the Petri dishes properly, alarmed about all the things that could go wrong. 'You'll be certain to fertilise them with the right . . .' There was a pause while he groped for the phrase but the embryologist had heard it all before.

'Sperm,' he called across the room. 'Don't worry you're the only couple in today.'

Everyone focused on the labelling, making sure that the right samples would be brought together. Lewis said he would supervise. It was impossible to think that he wouldn't be there when his own children were conceived, and Eleanor looked over, surprised. Perhaps she hadn't dealt with a father who wasn't awed by her expertise before. She picked up Amber's wrist, peering hard at her name band. Only Rhea was watching her sister, noticing the relaxing of her body away from the eggs inside her as if she was wanting to let them go. Amber was floppy now.

The anaesthetist knew Lewis. 'Don't worry, we've not got it wrong yet,' she said to him. Feeling among friends, she didn't bother to hide her needle so at the last moment Amber panicked and held tight to Rhea.

Rhea stayed and watched Lewis, checking and rechecking the labelling. He would be more sure than many men that his children were his own. Until DNA testing most could never be certain who had fathered their wives' babies. Had they loved them any less?

It was all on television. Eleanor watched the screen and manipulated her pipette through the tubes and canals of Amber's anatomy. Her ovaries had fifteen or sixteen eggs all ripe and ready for harvesting. 'It's a healthy crop,' Eleanor said. 'We're going ahead.'

Lewis looked on, concerned, as the embryologist plopped them from the pipette. He placed a restraining hand on the technical arm. 'The trick is to squeeze just hard enough to get them out and gently enough not to damage them,' he said.

Rhea heard him take her words and make them his own. Lewis was afraid of giving up control of his babies to the expert. Already they were precious to him.

The embryologist nodded slowly. 'I've looked after thousands of babies, you know. Not many men can say that, can they?'

The air thickened with calm and concentration. Lewis pored over the Petri dishes, his focus so intense that the pool of liquid with its invisible egg became clear and bright to Rhea too. She wanted to show it to Amber, but she was only half conscious and the anaesthetist was bent over her, talking her back into the room. Eleanor put away the equipment. It was all done.

Lewis was confusing the trainee embryologist. With a pang, Rhea saw her look at him with a mixture of attraction and nervousness. The eggs in those dishes would be his children; she could see how thoroughly Lewis had taken charge of them. Even separated from Amber they could never belong to another man. After the penetration of his gaze, they already had Lewis in them. Rhea knew that Eleanor would ask in vain for spare eggs to be donated to a needful, infertile couple. Lewis wouldn't be able to let any part of her sister go.

CHAPTER 7

Lewis was trying to forget how much hung on Vic's presence, but every now and then his smile slipped and anxiety kept his shoulder joints up to his ears. Vic's shoulders, naturally, flopped easily around the microscope. His hair was grey, the same colour as most of the equipment, as though they had grown alike over the years. Only his hands looked out of place. The delicate controls elided into fragility next to their bulk, but Lewis saw how they loved his confident touch: the microscope responded with a subtle precision.

'Yes!' Vic's voice boomed into the corners of the lab, rattling the glassware. 'There they are. Looking good, Lewis, looking good.' The cells did look good.

Now that all the washing-up was being done by hand they grew constantly; it was difficult to keep up with them and Rhea was struggling to keep the separate strains under control. Her records lay at Vic's right hand, all the details accurately noted in a systematic folder. She pointed to an entry. 'You can see,' she explained. 'I only seeded these yesterday and they're overcrowded already.' Vic could see. It was perfect, except that they weren't all stem cells: every day a few slipped out of control and lost the ability to develop into absolutely anything; they committed themselves to becoming fibroblasts or fat cells.

Lewis waited for the inevitable question, smiling for all he was worth.

Rhea answered it without the slightest hesitation. She looked Vic straight in the eye – he was sitting at the microscope and she was standing next to him – and told him 50 per cent, more or less, as though that was the most amazing thing in the world. Vic lumbered to his feet and put a heavy, mindful arm across her shoulders. 'Not bad,' he said, 'but it'll soon be higher, if I know you. You'll develop a pure culture.'

'I've got a few ideas to be going on with,' Rhea said to Vic, measuring her words carefully. 'Come and meet the others.'

They ambled off towards the writing desks together, carrying Lewis's future with them. He had to hurry – the fire door swung idly against him, holding him back. When he caught up, Andrew and Joe were half standing, trapped between their desks and chairs. He'd never noticed before how narrow the space between the desks was. Vic's frame wouldn't squeeze through that passageway. Lewis just knew it would never even try to go there: it would wait until you came to it. Vic looked relaxed and patient but he must have been wondering how they could produce the sort of results he expected, working in such cramped conditions, while Joe and Andrew tussled with the furniture and scraped their way out of the warren.

'Seventy-five per cent,' he told Rhea. 'If you can make that, it's worth us starting to run the pre-trial checks.'

In a thrilling instant Lewis experienced the shift that success could bring about: the attention of medical staff concerned for their untreatable cases, the astonished relief of patients and the profound gratitude of desperate parents; the adulation of other scientists. Envy would be part of this and he welcomed the idea of their resentful admiration.

Vic was even more encouraging. 'The other twenty-five per

cent might not be a total bust. We can run some array-technology checks to see if they're still expressing the right genes. My lot have had some promising results with that.'

'Array technology? The department has already got the kit on appro, and we've got a quarter of the money to buy a set-up ourselves, but we still need to find the rest.'

Only feet away Glatton's post-doc, Patrick, was butting in with the expression of the seriously overlooked. The scrape of his chair shocked them out of their complacency. But Patrick wasn't Glatton, not yet anyway. He couldn't directly contradict Lewis in front of the American. 'I think you'll find it's ours,' he said, leaving room for doubt.

Vic's big eyebrows rose and hovered around his hairline while he thought, and then he bent towards Rhea. 'It would take some of the pressure off my people if you could do the experiments over here.'

In an impenetrable circle, money, space and success bought each other. 'How am I going to do it?' Lewis fretted, and paced around the office, stirring up more agitation with every turn. Rhea sat at his desk, flipping over the pages of the calendar.

'Me, I suppose,' she said. His eyes fixed on her, full of the sort of wishes you don't believe will ever come true. 'I wasn't making it up when I told Vic I had a few ideas.' The ideas that raised purity from 50 to 75 per cent never came to fruition in a couple of weeks; she had to take that into account. 'He's giving us some space. He won't press for a few weeks after the conference.' Lewis's eyes flickered briefly, but long enough for Rhea to understand that other things lurked in them. If Vic gave them the money for an array set-up, it would be a joint venture with Glatton. He'd been quick to follow up Patrick's preliminaries with a full presentation of his own, explaining he needed to check that the virus wasn't being expressed in his cells.

'My talk has got to blow his out of the water,' Lewis said.

If the funding was to come to them, he would have to expose Glatton for the fool he was; his wheedling his way into Vic's attention shouldn't have been tolerated. But what could you do? Like a viral genome, he managed to insinuate himself everywhere.

The mission of the spring conference was to be inspirational. It was meant to send the participants back to their laboratories primed with enthusiasm and confidence, resolved to do even better. It had achieved all that for Rhea and Lewis long before it started. Amber had hardly seen either of them for weeks. Hints of the work they would present had finally got Lewis involved in the Genetics Institute negotiations and he couldn't leave Rhea to cover all the lab work so he had been even later than usual, every night.

At the conference Amber showed the research to Warren. He might have been putting a businesslike front on things but his eyes narrowed as they searched the displays, trying to spot the one that held out hope for Polly.

'If they can do anything for her . . .' His voice was flat with discouragement. The graphs and tables of figures and black-and-white photos of endless bands claiming to be genes were too far away from his girl. Science was trapped in those two-dimensional grids. But Amber had set it free. At the entrance to Reception, the two banners she had designed hung on each side of the door. They towered above her like a triumphal arch, proclaiming the benefits of stem-cell research. Every single delegate had to pass between them and every single delegate's attention was caught. People paused to admire them and a queue built up.

'Once again,' Warren said, as he left, 'you've stopped the traffic.'

The draught from the doors opening and closing made the banners waver and Amber felt dizzy. They were huge; she went upstairs and leant on the balcony railing to admire them. The enormodrome of a hall was filling up. Everywhere groups of people were milling around, exchanging greetings. Clusters formed spasmodically around the exhibits, broke up and re-formed elsewhere. She scanned the crowd for Rhea or Lewis but they had disappeared, leaving the young scientists to look after their stand unchaperoned. There was a constant shifting. Aspirations, apprehensions, allegiances were in flux under her gaze.

A formal posse of elder scientists moved together, inspecting the posters systematically, but the young people were volatile. They flitted around, attracted to this group, then that, taking up and abandoning positions as they searched out the place where they would fit. How could you not feel sorry for them, jostling in that arena? Their temporary contracts would be up all too soon; they had to scrimmage for new jobs. Disgust swept over Amber as she realised she was watching people flexing their credentials, having their brains felt up: a buyer's market, with the post-docs up for auction.

Katherine was there, gesticulating towards her poster, explaining it, pointing out the photographs, then offering a handout to some old guy in jeans. He glanced at it dismissively, put it down and slouched off without bothering to speak. Katherine looked crestfallen and Amber set off for the exhibition floor to console her. The rebuff of Katherine's efforts stuck in her throat; she felt sick with empathy; shades of loyalty darkened Amber's vision. As she struck out for the stairway, though, the steps seemed to move too, away from her. The eddying bodies below rose up and fell back. She struggled against the downward pull, but by the time she reached the hall her eyes felt like lead; keeping them open became a colossal, unsustainable effort.

Faintness dissolved Amber's strength. By the entrance there was a row of chairs. She sank into one, but from her half-closed eyes she saw someone coming towards her, a grey pin-stripe suit, a raincoat over his arm, alarm in his face. These seats must be for important guests; she shouldn't be sitting there, but the more she tried to get up the further she sank down. She was on the floor then, still sinking. She didn't want to be engulfed. She was fighting against it, but it was too heavy. The weight took her down and she slipped to somewhere underneath.

It was even darker. The darkness sucked her into itself, but she could hear the delegates; she knew they were still there, somewhere above her. With a last effort she kicked and surfaced. Her head was out, but her eyes wouldn't open yet. Her body stumbled up, by itself.

She was blind. She made for the door and her eyes opened, a slit, but she was feeling her way rather than seeing it. Still, there was an impression of bright light outside, spiking the air. She pushed her way towards it, but long before she got there, a determined quiet came and drew her aside.

Oh, what is it now, Amber? Rhea thought. Can't she just text? Colleagues were trying to speak to her; visitors were crowding around, trying to attract her attention. *Where is the lecture? Who is on first? Where am I supposed to be?* The extra demand – the conference telephone – grated on her nerves. She gave it a fractious scowl.

'What does she want?' Caroline, the receptionist, followed her stare.

'She's not on the phone. She collapsed. We couldn't bring her round. She's been taken to hospital and we couldn't find Lewis or you.' Caroline was looking around as though she expected Lewis to appear now. 'I thought you must be together somewhere. I told them I'd find you.'

Amber would have fainted. It wouldn't be the first time she'd gone in for some stupid diet. Rhea determinedly moderated her feelings, but Glatton was clipping across the floor, Lewis scurrying to keep up behind him.

'He was in the café,' Glatton informed Caroline. 'I've fastened the doors open and I've got a university van waiting.' A path had been cleared. For them? Rhea moved automatically along it.

'Will you tell everyone, Rhea? Explain what's happened?' Lewis was holding her back. 'Look after the others at their poster session.'

'Lewis, I'm coming to the hospital with you.' Lewis seemed surprised, as though this was the last thing he was expecting, but Glatton was ushering them along. 'She'll want to see the two of you. You need everybody you can get at a time like this.'

'Yes. Oh, yes, both of us.' Relief softened Lewis's face.

They followed Glatton, who broke into a trot, and Lewis was straight after him, stumbling at every step. Glatton paused to let him catch up, then walked alongside, shepherding him past the desk, keeping Lewis on the path to the door. When did he get so thoughtful? Rhea thought. Usually he was an officious pain.

Lewis was on his mobile to the hospital as they hurried out through the gaping doorway. Now Rhea was carried along in the current of panic – this wasn't just another faint. 'Ovarian hyperstimulation syndrome?' Lewis was saying. The worst suspicion invaded Rhea's mind. She could see that syringe. She had given Amber her injection the night before, while Lewis was downstairs with the conference guests. The sudden flush: she had dismissed it as Amber's eczema or a touch of her asthma, familiar enough to be insignificant. It might have been the first hint of this. If only she had taken more notice. The excitement of seeing old friends who didn't know what they were going to hear tomorrow had distracted her so that everything else had seemed trivial and the moment had passed, barely noticed, certainly unmentioned.

Glatton was fierce with responsibility. He thrust the van out into the traffic and got a blast of horn. 'Don't take any notice,' he said. 'I'll get you there. Obs and Gynae?' He quizzed himself, running through his personal sat-nav, the sort of thing he prided himself on having at his fingertips. Then it all clicked into position. 'I'll take you through the delivery entrance.'

He switched on the hazard lights and swung right. The traffic was snarled up. The school run was in full swing and the road was choked with four-by-fours ferrying kids towards the private schools that clustered around the teaching hospital and the university. Every child sulking out of the window, every mother bright with exhaustion, the whole city seemed to be dumped in front of them, especially to block their way.

Rhea rubbed Lewis's arm, but she didn't dare to look at him. The flush of last night's injection haunted her, so she focused on the scene outside: engines idling, kids stoking themselves up with over-indulgence. She stared outwards until the van jolted forwards.

Glatton had found his gap. 'Conference to ward in twenty minutes.' He was monitoring his own performance, dropping them off at the works entrance.

Rhea led the way through the maze of underground corridors, a common short-cut for staff: ducking under the heating pipes avoided the crush in Outpatients. There were rumours that colonies of Pharaoh ants lived down there, coddled in the dark and the warmth. Rhea had always scoffed at the idea, but suddenly it seemed possible that the shadows might incubate unknown horrors.

When they reached the crowded hospital, it seemed comfortingly unambiguous and honest. Except for the chaos in A&E. Electronic monitors did their best at reassurance. *Your waiting time will be approximately forty minutes* scrolled endlessly above their heads, and they broke into a jog through the long, anonymous corridors of Cardiology. They should have been familiar, those corridors, she had passed through them countless times, but they were unrecognisable now. The doors, propped open or closed against them, had a quality of belonging somewhere else. Instead of being welcoming and familiar, all of it seemed strange.

They got to the ward as Amber was being wheeled out of Examination. At the sight of her prone on the steel trolley, Lewis moaned and Amber turned her head, her eyes wandering around the ceiling. While Rhea stood aside, he went to her. Dr Bonworth came out of her office, wiping glove powder off her hands with a towel. Seeing Lewis bending over his wife, she joined Rhea.

She was slipping from his grasp. Lewis's hands were chilly and damp when he touched Amber. He spoke her name and a small contraction of her pupils convinced him that she had heard him.

He stared into her eyes but he couldn't stop the lids closing. She kept drifting away, breaking the link between them.

He clung to her hand.

The porter pushed the trolley and Lewis jerked sideways down the long ward, clutching her, bending over her and staring, until they reached an empty bed. The covers were turned back in a neat triangle and he realised it was waiting for Amber.

The finality of it hit home: Amber was to be kept here, separate from him, cared for by experts. He released the grip of his gaze and she smiled weakly.

'We'll just get her settled in.' The hospital process was unfolding; he felt conscious of having nothing to contribute. Dr Bonworth manoeuvred him back up the ward towards Rhea, who waited, leaning against the door. Their eyes met, briefly, then Rhea glanced towards Dr Bonworth's office so he knew where he was supposed to go.

The insouciant calm of a medic closing her door on the ward was the most disturbing thing Lewis could remember, so devastating that he was paralysed by fear.

'Lewis.'

His body bridled at the sound of its own name, and the thought of Amber left in that bed. Why weren't they doing something? 'What's going on? Where are her notes?'

Amber's file was lying on the table, open. Dr Bonworth closed it and made a decisive little show of laying it in a drawer and slipping the drawer shut. Instead of speaking, she turned towards the viewing window and watched her beds, scanned them with an unhurried efficiency that matched the purposeful hum of the hospital routine. She kept her back to him, checking on Amber being settled into the ward, with an air of contemplation. 'We aren't quite sure yet,' she said, without turning. 'It might be completely unrelated to her treatment.'

Lewis's lunge forward took him by surprise; he only just stopped himself grabbing Dr Bonworth and shaking the truth out of her. Experience must have alerted her: she turned to face him, holding his eyes with her professional distance. But Lewis was having none of it. He wanted action; he wanted answers. He trawled desperately through his mind, searching for a clue. Eleanor Bonworth demurred, her impassive face giving nothing away.

'We have to bear in mind some sort of adverse drug reaction. We're already doing everything we can,' she said, her well-trained neutrality keeping him away from his wife. She must have practised that skill over the years to protect herself from the knowledgeable husband. And what a skill it was. An atavistic fear of her black art consumed Lewis. She might have been a witch doctor filled with supernatural licence.

But she consulted her medical grounding and recited a litany of tests that were being carried out on Amber. The half-understood plainsong did its work. Lewis felt endlessly grateful that there was an established protocol for this sort of thing. Eleanor Bonworth's vocation was life; he swallowed the idea that dying might be in her trade too. The procedures in Medical Biochemistry meant that emergency requests were pushed to the front of the queue. Already the sample vials would be moving steadily forward on the hospital's analyser; already machines were busy, picking up samples of Amber's serum. Her name would flash on the monitor and her results would race into the printer. The technicians wouldn't glance twice at it because they had everything under control. Eleanor Bonworth would assess the numbers and make her move on the steady ground of science.

'What do you think?' he asked her.

'We can't be certain yet. It looks as if there might be some abnormal immune response. I'll know more this afternoon. It might be ovarian hyperstimulation syndrome, Lewis.' She softened. 'It might just be dehydration. She says it was very hot in the conference hall. We're rehydrating her. All her vital signs are stable now. Let us do our job.'

Lewis's hands flew up in surrender. Professionals, firm and absolving, they were what Amber needed. There was no room for panic and overreaction. 'All right. But be straight with me. You must have something to go on.'

There was a pause as she measured him with her eyes. Then she shifted him aside and got the notes out of the drawer. Lewis understood that there was no way she needed to remind herself of what was in them. He had the impression of being handled tactfully and kindly, but then again, he feared she was playing for time, delaying the moment when she would tell him the truth. He was so strung up that if she waited long enough almost anything she said would feel like relief.

'Eleanor?'

'I'm worried. This shouldn't have happened but we've got most things steady. I've got to warn you, Lewis, I can't promise we'll be able to rely on her ovaries after this.'

Too many words for Lewis to make much sense of them. His attention span had dropped to moments. But he thought of the fertilised eggs, safe in their frozen chrysalises. Fifteen babies were more than enough for anyone. Through the window he could see Amber, floating troubled under the influence of her illness. Rhea bent over, drawing back the long hair falling across her face and saying something to her that made her smile, faintly and distantly, from beyond the drugs.

'Do you think I'm bothered about her ovaries? I don't care. It doesn't matter, Eleanor. Just make sure she's all right.'

Eleanor Bonworth and Lewis joined Rhea at the bedside. They sat around Amber, her fan swathing each of them in turn in humid air. Eleanor tried to talk to Amber. She asked her, quietly but very deliberately, if she had felt ill the day before. Amber couldn't answer. Her lips quivered but her eyes closed again before she could say anything.

'Did she complain after her last injection?' Eleanor asked Lewis. He tried to remember, he tried manfully, but last night had disappeared from his memory, eclipsed by the last hour.

'You didn't give her the injection last night,' he heard Rhea say, and as he turned to look at her, he saw Eleanor's face stiffen with annoyance.

'Perhaps you haven't been able to keep up to the schedule. She's meant to have one every night.'

Rhea faced into the draught of tepid air; it swept the hair back from her face so that her skin stood out, strained and dark-shadowed under the eyes. 'Lewis was downstairs last night with some conference delegates. I gave it to her.'

He'd been too busy schmoozing Vic to see to Amber: he remembered now. Rhea must have sorted her out.

Eleanor made a brief note. 'And how was she, Rhea? Any flushing, visual disturbances, blank patches?'

He stroked Amber's arm. It was roughened; eczema was swelling under her skin and the stroking disturbed a smell, the dainty scent of the soya oil that Amber used in her bath. She had soaked in it that morning when neither of them had had any idea of what was going to happen. He had taken her towel and held it away from her to keep her like that, warm and fragrant, the triumphant day still to unfold in front of them. She'd slipped through his fingers then, just as she had now. 'There are more pressing things to do, Lewis, if we want Vic on board. You have to prioritise.' For a moment he hadn't thought so, but Amber had pushed him out of the door. 'If this doesn't come off, Lewis, you'll regret it for the rest of your life.'

'Her eczema was flaring up,' Rhea volunteered. 'It would have been bothering her.'

Eleanor Bonworth nodded encouragingly. 'We'll keep an eye on it.'

Amber was sleeping then, lulled by the seep of the drip into her arm. Let her rest, that was the best thing. 'She'll sleep now, but of course you can stay if you want to.' Eleanor left them to themselves. Before they went home, the lab techs would ring the test results through. Then everything would be clearer.

As soon as she was out of the way, Lewis jumped up and seized Amber's chart. Pulse: high. BP: lower. Respiratory rate: almost normal now. Temperature: still raised. He checked the dosage information on the drip. 'I hope they didn't make any mistakes labelling those vials,' he said to Rhea. She took his arm and sat him on a chair by the bed.

Amber looked peaceful now. The sides of the bed had been raised to form a sort of cot to stop her falling out but it cut her off from him, put her away. He sat watching for what seemed a long time.

Rhea began collecting her things, her bag, and the brush she'd been using on Amber's hair.

'Are we going?' Lewis was surprised, but relieved that she thought it was time for them to leave. She would know the right thing to do; he appreciated that he was hopelessly out of his depth. He had stood in the way while Eleanor had organised Amber's treatment and Rhea had soothed him into accepting it. His only contribution had been to ruffle everyone's feathers and take their attention away from their patient. He felt awkward under their gaze. The ward was oppressive with female concern. Before she left, even formidable Eleanor Bonworth had dropped her guard, when she embraced Rhea, promising every care. Other women, the patients, scattered support through the curtains as they made their slow trips from bed to day room. Nurses peered over in sympathy, saw Lewis and mentally airbrushed him from the scene. It was almost as though the sisterhood wanted Amber to be ill so that they could nurse her back to health.

'They'll take care of her,' he reassured himself, while Rhea grasped his arm and guided him out through the door, along the corridor and down the staircase.

'We're only going down to the canteen for a few minutes, Lewis. Didn't you see that the nurse was coming to do her obs?' She gave him a brief hug, pulling him together as though it was only to be expected that he wasn't in charge of himself.

The hospital concourse was crowded with visitors and patients in their nightclothes. Their faces had the blankness of people with endless time to fill. Lewis glanced guiltily at his watch. Too late for his talk. He should have started by now. The best help he could give was to secure their prospects, his and Amber's too. She couldn't come home from the hospital with their entire future in jeopardy. The responsibilities of fatherhood had begun their lonely and tortuous journey into his life. He would have to bear them alone.

'Perhaps I should go back, if you can stay here,' Lewis said, as firmly as he could, but his voice had an overstretched sound, nervous and panicky.

'No, you shouldn't,' snapped Rhea, too fast for thought, but then she backed off, pillowed his landing with 'We should phone, let people know that Amber's all right.'

'Need to let Vic know,' Lewis agreed. 'And organise the group. I ought to see to them, Rhea. You know what they're like.'

At the thought of the bereft research team, struggling to hold the line against the competition without his leadership, Lewis was out of the door, joining a huddle of smokers and closet telephoners under the porch. But his calls were different. He didn't need to check what time dinner would be ready or whether he should bring a takeaway: he had serious business in hand; his whole future was at stake.

He stood alone in the middle of the hospital lawn with his back to the light, seeing his shadow elongate and blur in the low afternoon sun. It was solitary, extended out on the grass. He had only himself to rely on. He pulled himself upright before he opened his phone. He told himself he had a job to do. Amber depended on him, he assured himself, and then there was Rhea's job, his responsibilities to her. His mother-in-law's gibe intruded – but if everything went well enough Amber would be able to leave work. He could give her the chance to take care of herself properly. He felt sure of what he needed to do.

By the time the calls were made, it was four o'clock.

'I'll be back by seven,' he told Rhea, 'to see Eleanor. I'll let everyone know that Amber's in the best place.'

She lifted his hand and palmed something into it, something small and cold she had taken from her handbag. For a moment he thought of lipstick as she closed his fingers around it. 'It's the flash drive,' she said, 'the back-up copy of your talk. You might need it.'

She had given him permission. With her blessing, Lewis felt vindicated. He didn't mention his presentation, just nodded in appreciation, incredulous with relief at having been granted his release, but all the time, he wondered if he could cut the talk by 50 per cent. The people he really needed to hear it would still be around; they could spare half an hour. He fingered the flash drive in his pocket; its tiny competence encouraged him. He could produce it and just begin to talk, a small apology on his lips, a man under extreme pressure, coping. Alongside this confidence, magnanimity suffused him. He would pay public tribute to Rhea. She backed him up at home and at work.

He was conscious of the coming together of a melded whole. He and Rhea were standing close; he didn't have to move. He kissed her cheek, then her lips. The dry brush felt like a kiss to himself, a gift to seal a bargain that would save them all. They were so close in this that they were one person. Between them they could take care of everything.

'You'll stay with her until I get back, won't you? Look after her?' he said as he left.

When Rhea went back up to the ward Amber was half awake. 'Thank God you're here, Rhea. Lewis would only panic.' She gestured faintly around the room, at the sickly green walls and the iron bed rails. 'He wouldn't have a clue.' For the next few minutes she kept opening her eyes, fastening them on Rhea, then closing them again.

It left Rhea alone with her thoughts. She couldn't stop them zeroing in on Lewis and the conference. Amber seemed profoundly asleep now; Rhea could have left, dealt with the conference and been back before her sister knew it. But that was what bloody Lewis was doing. And Amber's eyes might open, checking that Rhea hadn't left her.

Thank God you're here, Rhea. The soft touch, the iron grip that Amber exerted.

Something was happening outside in the corridor – Rhea could hear it, but she couldn't see. A woman, gasping. At first Rhea thought she was having a baby: the panting she'd seen on television, the cries of pain and triumph. But Eleanor Bonworth's voice cut in: 'In here.' Authoritative and firm. 'You'll be fine, my dear. Perfectly normal.'

A trolley sped past. A woman in a blue silk robe, her head raised from the bed looking for Eleanor, who came promptly behind. They were gone in a moment. A door crashed as the trolley barged it out of the way, then thumped as it swung back. It was quiet again. The ill woman had disappeared, swallowed by the hospital labyrinth, as though nothing had happened. Rhea looked down at her sister, still there, but drained into anonymity by the white, hospital-issue gown. We should bring her some clothes, she thought. Why hadn't bloody Lewis gone home for Amber's things? She remembered the kisses he had given her: unmindful, unexpected. She bent forward to the sleeping princess and passed them on to her.

Amber turned in the bed and rubbed at the needle in her hand. As Rhea soothed her, she wondered if the saline in the drip would feel cold and alien in Amber's veins. No, of course not. It was perfectly constituted for comfort. Science had made it compatible with life. No need to speculate about what might happen to Amber. She was in the proper place; all the expertise counted for something. Rhea believed that.

So, instead she worried about the conference. It would be noisy: people talking, their tongues tapping like keyboards and words springing out. Words grouping in sentences, gathering into ideas. There would be a circle of excitement, the tapping getting faster, then slowing as each person reflected, dissecting out the ideas, discerning what they meant to them, what they could take away with them. All that going on without her.

Rhea was alone. Amber, deep in sleep now, was lost to her. Nurses tripped in and out, ring-fencing themselves with taut little smiles that said, *Don't talk to me, I'm very busy*, and at the far edge of her hearing she heard a telephone ring. She wondered if it was the results back from the lab. Amber didn't stir. Amber didn't hear it. Nothing tugged at her attention as she slept, and drifted through her dreams.

A mass of student bodies blocked the way, but Vic's unmistakable voice was pounding somewhere near by, providing a solid background to the over-excited chatter. The crowd surged towards the bar, shifted, so that the sound came closer and Lewis could make out the words.

'He's that kind of guy, some of his ideas could do with a retread.'

He was worn out by the gruelling day, knackered by the effort of simply holding everything together. It occurred to Lewis that they were talking about him. He let the crush of other people's bodies support him because he could scarcely hold himself up. It obliged. More and more people crowded into the space behind him. Music pumped from the loudspeakers. Lewis's anxiety ratcheted up in the noise and the press until he felt he couldn't bear it. He looked around himself, and felt disgust. What sort of man left the hospital where his wife might wake up and ask for him? He began the long struggle back towards the exit.

'Here, Lewis.'

Katherine had spotted him and his colleagues eddied closer. They exuded the nauseating intimacy of alcohol and attention-seeking. Lewis felt drenched in dismal sobriety. He half expected to repel them, but they were too well oiled to mind his misery. The racket around them was incessant.

'How's Amber?' Katherine asked. She stood too close and shouted into his ear. He closed his eyes against the assault. When he opened them, she had backed away, offended, and turned to Vic.

'Rhea phoned. I've passed on the news to everyone,' he explained, in his slow drawl, while the rest of the noise seemed to hang fire until he had spoken. Lewis's presence seemed surplus to requirements.

He pulled the memory stick from his pocket. 'My talk.' He smiled and shrugged, then everyone turned away from him, an incomprehensible presence that had no place among the rational and the committed. He couldn't recognise his own team. He had to look at this selection of strangers and wonder which of them would come to his side and which were up for a betrayal. Not one of them met his eyes.

'No problem,' said Vic. 'I've taken care of everything. Caroline's sorted you out with another time. Stephen came to the rescue and filled your slot.'

Glatton had been the keynote speaker? Lewis fumed. Vic had the knack of taking everything on to himself, as though his brawny frame was the only one with the strength to bear it. The arrogance that bolstered that confidence. The way it made Vic look in charge of him. There still hadn't been any real detail about what he had come over to organise, only hints that slithered away when you tried to pick them up and left you clutching air while he moved on to the next person, charming them into his magic circle, mesmerising them with his dangled promise of funding. Vic could stuff his funding. Or give it to Glatton.

Lewis realised he couldn't see Glatton or Patrick. It wasn't possible that they'd gone home to an early supper after a day like this. The most important delegates would be dining with the VC. Glatton and Patrick were sitting in his and Amber's seats. The outrage he felt was magnificent. It sprang up without hesitation and apprehended him. It blotted out his worry for Amber and the paltry tangle of plans he had for making good his absence. But when it died away, consumed by its own fierceness, he knew that his loss was incalculable.

Lewis was going to have to accept a graveyard slot during the final poster session. The international group gathered around Vic were full of sympathy: they wouldn't hear of his worrying himself. As long as his wife was well, that was what mattered. Plenty of time to catch up on the work later, they assured him, as they moved on seamlessly to urgent consultations about their own projects.

Excluded from the discussion of the talks he had missed, consigned to the marginal hinterlands of domestic troubles, Lewis peered around for a seat, a drink. Vic went to buy the young people beer; it was agreed that Lewis, in his state of family crisis, would have to make do with orange juice. The drift of his colleagues' attention was the price of his absence, but he was surprised by how quickly it was exacted. Conflicting loyalties were confusing them and they might spin off in any direction. He could see the excitement in their eyes, as if they revelled in the disturbance, and the fear of Amber's state came back to him. Nothing seemed controllable any more, not by him at any rate.

It overtook him like cloud rolling down a hillside. He wasn't supposed to be here. Amber was ill with an undiagnosed condition. Anything might happen to her. The calm on the ward was a pretence, designed to keep him subdued, and he'd fallen for it. Amber's asthma with its unexpected urgencies that she passed off too lightly had let him avoid the truth, just as he was being avoided now. He left without saying goodbye.

Back at the hospital, he tried to talk about it to Rhea, but she wouldn't listen. She didn't even seem pleased to see him. While he'd been away, Eleanor Bonworth had told her that Amber's tests had been satisfactory. Ditto her obs. Still, she was sleeping, Eleanor had observed. They would keep her for a couple of days. She wondered if they had got to the bottom of everything. When Rhea had explained this to Lewis, he turned back to the bed where Amber was watching them.

'Lewis,' she said in surprise. 'You're here.'

'I had to go back to the conference to get the car.'

'Am I going home, then?'

Rhea stood behind the bed, shaking her head at him.

'Not yet, darling. In a day or two. You gave us a fright, you know.'

'Oh.' Amber's head fell back. She was disappointed, but she patted the bed, wanting him to sit with her. 'The talk, Lewis. Did you sock it to them?'

'I cancelled it. I said I'd do it Wednesday night. If you're all right, that is.'

The variation on the truth came out smooth and blameless, but it was for the best. It wouldn't do to let Amber feel she had backed him into a corner.

'It wouldn't have mattered. Rhea was here with me, weren't you, Rhe?'

Amber drifted away again, left them watching each other over her bed.

'Is the talk on Wednesday, Lewis?'

'Yes, during the final poster session.'

Rhea looked at him with resignation. He shrugged it off but

she was persistent. 'Everyone will have skived off and gone home by then, won't they?'

Rhea kept doing the very thing he didn't want her to do. She picked away at his disappointment so it became more and more real. She kept talking trouble into existence.

'Probably,' said Lewis.

He was quiet as he gave her a lift to collect her car and pretended to concentrate on driving, although there was hardly any traffic.

'No one's said much about why it happened,' she told him.

'It's just one of those things,' was his answer. 'They did explain there was a risk.'

'They didn't say anything about the chances of her still having a baby, after this, I mean.'

'Baby?' He had all but forgotten about that now: he had far more important things than babies to worry about.

CHAPTER 8

Caller ID: Unknown. After the phone had blipped all evening with texts – *didn't want to bother you with a call but thinking of you both* – Lewis knew that something awful had happened. The hospital wanted him to come immediately. The roil of apprehension that would soon give way to fear edged closer.

He was still dressed and his car keys on the bedside table in Rhea's spare room, as if all this was already known and he had only to go through the preordained steps: slip out of the flat without waking Rhea, start the engine.

It was only when he got to the hospital that he felt his muscles quaking unpredictably, stopping him leaving the car. None of this is about me, he told himself. No more dramatics to draw attention away from Amber.

Eleanor was there so Lewis knew straight away how serious it was, even though she moved calmly and smiled at him when he went in. Someone was adjusting the oxygen flow to a mask that was strapped to Amber's face. A nurse pressed the tentacles of a monitor to Amber's chest, and as she pulled the sheet aside Lewis thought for an awful moment that his wife was impossibly pregnant. He turned to Eleanor, confused.

'Fluid in the abdomen, on the lungs.'

A technician came and took away four vials of Amber's blood. Another arrived with a covered trolley and couldn't get it into the cubicle. There was a crash of stainless steel and the thump of rubber wheels on the architrave around the door. The pneumatic hinges wheezed, and it was exactly the same sound as Amber's breath. Then the monitor noise started fluttering. The registrar rushed to Amber's side and bent over her head. Eleanor nodded to the others and took Lewis away.

Outside, she sat him down on the metal bench in the corridor. He could still hear hurried movements inside the treatment room, but no voices. Nothing that was being done there needed to be talked about. He imagined the meeting of eyes, the imperceptible shakes of the head that meant the difference between the sustaining of life and the inevitability of death.

'We need to drain the fluid, Lewis. The pressure on her lungs is unsupportable.'

He couldn't stop himself saying it: 'She'll be all right?' But there was no reassuring cuff to tell him to stop being such a silly boy. Why had he expected one?

Eleanor spread out her fingers as if she held something down. 'We'll do everything we can.'

Amber felt so close to him out here that he thought she must be dead already. It was only her body that those medics were probing and pumping and taking stuff out of. Her soul was out here in the corridor with him, holding him, waiting for it all to be over. They would be together then.

Eleanor came back, tired. The lines on her face deepened as she sat with him. 'I think the worst might be behind us. You could sit with her for a while, Lewis.'

Amber was still surrounded by equipment; he reached out to hold her hand. It was cold and waxy, as though she was dead. The technician came back to take another blood sample but couldn't get it out of her vein.

'It's always like this in the middle of the night,' he observed to the nurse, as he went off with scarcely enough to do his tests.

Talk to the unconscious, people said. They might be able to hear you. In front of the staff and all the people who probably knew him, Lewis whispered, 'Don't leave me here, Amber. I can't bear it.'

The phone was furious, so agitated that it shook in his hand. Nine voicemails, all from Rhea. He deleted them one by one. Once Amber had been stabilised, everything that had gone before was wiped out. It was all going to start anew now. Lewis could feel only humble and grateful.

'If you don't tell me where you are I'm going to kill you, Lewis. I'm going mad with worry. What the hell do you think you're doing?'

Even anger felt like love, which it was.

'I'm coming now, Rhea. To get you.'

They drove to Snitter Heugh together. Lewis didn't know whether it was a good idea or not. He harboured doubts about whether Amber would be allowed to abandon the hospital-issue gowns.

'She'll feel better in her own clothes,' Rhea told him. 'Mine won't fit her,' and then the journey took on the aspect of a pilgrimage, a contribution to Amber's recovery.

Lewis seemed surprised that his night in the hospital hadn't changed the entire world.

'Well, Rhea, it's still there,' Lewis said as she turned into the gate at Snitter Heugh.

'Waiting for you.'

'Waiting for Amber.'

He wanted to pack her things himself and left Rhea alone in the kitchen to listen to the bony rattling of the plastic covering the outhouse roof.

When they got back to the hospital Lewis had left Amber's

bag in the boot so Rhea sent him down for it. She went on climbing the stairs alone. She had an uncomfortable feeling about the hospital bag: that she should have packed Amber's things herself. She wished she'd protected her sister against the risk of Lewis finding the baby jacket hidden in the wardrobe. It wasn't something he could even begin to understand.

Ward eighteen seemed deserted when she reached it. There was no sign of Eleanor or any of the nurses; all the doors, to the tearoom, to Examination, to the offices that lined the corridor, were closed. No one was on duty at the nurses' station, so she began to look for Amber herself.

The first room she tried had only one occupant, the woman she had seen the previous night, in the blue silk robe. She was sitting in bed now, watching television, absorbed in the afternoon chat show, and didn't notice Rhea staring. In the next room there were four beds and four women. Three were sitting primly in their sheets, talking lightly while their fingers browsed segments of fruit held in paper napkins. They stopped talking and turned enquiringly towards Rhea. They must have expected a nurse, come to deliver medication or to take them off for some procedure, because Rhea felt she wasn't someone they wanted to disturb their picnic.

They glanced expectantly at the fourth bed, where a large elderly woman was lying, gazing blank-eyed at the ceiling. She turned her head and struggled into a sitting position. Rhea turned away, embarrassed at her intrusion, but the woman called after her, said her name: 'Rhea, don't go.'

The words stumbled through Rhea's mind, reawakening something once familiar but now dormant. When she turned back she saw Amber, an Amber who was forty years older. Her skin had a pharmaceutical drear: too many painkillers, too much pain? Her graceful limbs were swollen and heavy. Urbane, elegant Amber had to clamber about the bed to sit up. Her lips

153

fumbled for the phrase that would hold Rhea back. There was revulsion in Rhea, a pulling away from the blighted body. Fear invaded her, the sort of fear that comes from flesh too close to your own: you have to feel its mortality whether you want to or not. She looked down at herself, needing to see that her own body was still the same. She was unwilling even to approach the bed; her hands were afraid to touch this old, bloated sister.

The picnicking ladies abandoned their snacks to watch her. With food raised halfway to their mouths, they held their breath.

'Amber, lovely,' Rhea said, 'I couldn't find you.' There was a sigh of release as the watchers subsided back into their convalescence.

Her sister's face struggled to arrange itself into a smile of welcome. Helping her to sit, Rhea felt the slackness of Amber's joints, as though her arms and legs were coming loose from her body. The movement stirred the air around her and the familiar smell of soya oil rolled from the bed and surrounded Rhea to assure her that it was truly Amber inside the sheets.

Amber's hospital gown was twisting; it dragged her back down the bed. She tugged at it, uncomplainingly, but as soon as Lewis turned up she asked him if he had brought her things.

'We should have thought earlier,' Rhea apologised. 'Sorry, we've been all over the place.'

Amber insisted she had been fine. She hadn't cared what she wore yesterday, anyway. The drugs had left her voice lifeless, and although Rhea still had to look hard for her sister, without the dramatics that normally surrounded her, the same kind Amber was speaking: the Amber who smiled a grotesque smile and asked how the talk had gone before she said anything about herself.

'Don't you remember that I cancelled it?' said Lewis. 'If you're well enough to stay with Rhea, I'll give it tomorrow afternoon.'

'Oh, you go too, Rhea,' Amber said, in a dull, thick voice, as though the air was too heavy to breathe. 'I'm fine here. I know how long you've been working for it.'

A fresh blaze of liberation leapt in Lewis's eyes. He seemed young suddenly, all unfulfilled promise that could be brought to life by a single touch. Amber looked so ill and in need of love. Guilt-ridden, Rhea wanted to go with him.

'We'll keep an eye on her,' chirruped the other inmates. 'She'll be fine with us.'

Rhea helped Amber to change into her own pyjamas, a silvery grey that dulled her flushed complexion. The neutral colour soothed her swelling and gave some fluidity back to her body. By the next day Rhea felt that she and Lewis could leave the invalid and go back to the conference.

There was a steady exodus, not a flood, but a straggle of delegates making their way down the steps, toting overnight bags and, no doubt, various degrees of fulfilled ambitions. A couple of the British teams that Lewis wanted to talk to had been dispirited by the advantage that money and size had given the overseas competition. They had drunk too much at the conference dinner the night before and had decided on the spur of a muddled moment to get straight back into their laboratories. The conference centre had a well-thumbed look; the excitement had gone home with the big names. Lewis and Rhea exchanged grimaces of frustration before they made themselves go in.

His team was just mooching around. 'Don't worry,' he told them all. 'We've got the results. That's what counts in the end.' The bodies, the separate faces, merged together in a collective wish to believe him. They were concentrating on replacing the image of meteoric success with another, more measured, version. A sigh escaped them and they were smiling bravely.

Rhea stood close, as though the group's disappointments were her concern too. Lewis was conscious of how they always rallied to her call, how much he needed her on his side. If she left a desk after helping someone, an untroubled pair of eyes would follow her. His team murmured as it deflated around him, but it felt like assent.

Lewis delivered his talk to an almost deserted auditorium. His voice fell into a void: what had seemed slick and professional turned on itself and became stale and pedestrian. Without a virtuoso sounding board to absorb his ideas, they drained away between the empty seats, and when he reached for his conclusion, it just wasn't there.

There was a thump as Joe tried to turn on the house lights and hit the wrong switch. Caught in a spotlight, with the steeply raked seats rising around him, Lewis was dazzled and the very thing that should have happened seemed real. His shoulders could feel the claps of admiring hands, and the auditorium echoed with congratulations, repeated again and again. He felt it so strongly that visions of the future wrapped themselves around him; the room hung on his every word. Then Joe got the switch right and reality reasserted itself. Watching the delegates leave, he felt their lack of interest. That was the only difference between those two realities, he thought, the flick of a switch. Your results are the same. It just depends which switch gets flicked, or who is standing there when the light goes on.

The people who knew him stayed behind: Vic, his research team. Stephen Glatton was sweating triumph. It was so easy to lose your grip. You were away for a couple of days and a lifetime's work ran like sand through someone else's fingers.

Vic lumbered down the steps, slowly because of the weight on his knees. Moving downhill was difficult for a big man. Lewis wondered if he should go up to meet him but the look of concern and disappointment on Vic's features held him still. Nothing would persuade him to make the first move, because part of him wanted the fatherly sympathy that was being offered. Vic had seen him collapse. No amount of walking towards him would blank out that sight.

Glatton hadn't any scruples. His strawy thatch bobbed around Vic's chin as he bounced down the stairs, one step ahead. 'They've had a harrowing time. We need to look after Lewis and Rhea,' he muttered, but state-of-the-art acoustics made sure that everyone heard him.

Vic did his best to console him. As a sign of the confidence he had in Lewis, he offered him an immediate grant so that he could join with Glatton to buy the array technology. Rhea looked stunned, but she pinned a determined smile on her face. Glassy and false, it embraced Lewis and Vic but somehow excluded Glatton, who was sincerely obliged.

He phoned Amber standing under the conference-centre canopy because the rain was pouring down. Reception was poor under the metal roof; none of this had been in the plan.

'Never mind if half the seats were empty, as long as Vic was there. He's the only one who really matters,' she told him, the dubious connection making her words unreliable. Even in a hospital bed, Amber was gathering strength and making a come-back, as if she didn't know what she might have lost.

Lewis wasn't convinced. He drove himself back to the hospital and thought that everything seemed distant – the world carried on like a film, one that he wasn't in.

Sore eyes and low blood glucose were making him feel chaotic. Amber, on the other hand, lay peacefully, her body composed. Now that the bloating was receding, Eleanor had shown him the scan of her ovaries. Inside, where it mattered most, was still swollen. But the frozen eggs would wait. The timescales that protected their potency reached further than the effects of fertility drugs. Amber's body would recover. Rhea, when she arrived, thought so too. Perched on the hospital bed, she said that Amber might have red-haired children because her own hair had been that colour when she was a child.

'Grandfather used to call her Gingernut. He only did it to annoy Mother, really. She always said it was auburn, that her Celtic ancestry explained it.'

Lewis had been pretending to read while Amber slept until Rhea had arrived. He put aside his file, making way for her. 'But your hair isn't red.'

'I take after his side of the family.' Rhea laid claim to Amber's hand, lifting it from the counterpane. 'The sensible ones.'

'Her hair's fair now.' Lewis realised he had never looked closely before: he'd made do with more of a general impression. He did a swift, forensic sweep of Amber's head. 'It's right down to the roots,' he said triumphantly.

'That's only because she put so much effort into it. You've never even seen her real hair colour, Lewis. She started bleaching it long before she ever met you.'

Lewis knew he was being punished, that he should have woken Rhea when he had gone to the hospital alone. She had usurped his place now, next to Amber, and bent, speaking close into her sister's blank face.

'Do you remember, Amber, when Dad was ill and I looked after you?' Then she turned back to Lewis. 'There were all sorts of things I didn't know, and no one had time to see to them. I never knew when we needed to have our hair cut and it was always hanging over our eyes.' Rhea brushed her sister's hair aside. 'You do have red hair really, don't you, Amber?' Then she stared at Lewis, right through him, challenging him to argue. But he couldn't hold the look that violated his privacy and turned away so that she laughed, unvanquished, and put out her hand to touch his hair. Lewis used to have a whole lot of hair, cut into a flopping fringe. Amber had arranged for it to be restyled, ready for the conference: reduced to a buzz-cut. He often found himself running his hands nervously over his head, searching for his lost hair. He was still trying to get used to it. 'Like a mole,' Rhea said smoothing her palm over the crop. 'I thought it would be bristly. You never expect it to be so soft, do you?'

Exhausted and confused, Lewis leant towards her. But Rhea retreated and the moment passed. 'Go home,' she said. 'You're worn out. I'm having a drink with Vic. I'll see what more I can do.'

He let himself be tidied away, back to Snitter Heugh and an empty bed.

During the time that Amber had been in hospital the weather had turned. A vicious wind snatched wildly at the bushes and rammed torn-off leaves into the gullies and ditches, catching him unprepared. He was knocked off balance. As Lewis's car sped in through the gate the security light switched on and bounced off the paving. Looted leaves flew around, forced by the unpredictable gusting, as though everything was being swept away. It was difficult to step out of the car into this maelstrom. He scuttled for the shelter of the walls.

After the first glass of whisky, if he thought hard enough, Lewis could believe, briefly, that none of this had happened. He almost managed to convince himself that Amber was still at home with him and that he hadn't missed the key opportunity to give his talk. But the second burnt away the illusion, leaving him gaping at the truth: his chance had gone and he had blown any hope of rescuing it. Glatton would really have something to crow about with his post-docs now.

In an act of restitution, he set about torturing himself systematically. He imagined the reproaches of his research group, who had chosen to work with him because he was so good that he never took his eye off the ball. Until now.

Then resentment of Amber's obsession with pregnancy stirred, rumbling from some low place. He poured more whisky. It seared his throat and he took pleasure in it. Lewis had always dreamt of a girl like Amber, a woman who would keep him awake. Something about her now had made him afraid to go to sleep.

The morning dumped puddles of muddy light around the bedroom. Lewis hadn't drawn the curtains when he went to bed and there was no stopping the day trampling its way in. He turned his eyes from the whisky glass by the bed, remembering how the dregs of his fury had turned to fear. He pulled the duvet up closer. It still smelt of Amber, as though she might appear at any moment and slip in beside him, warm and fragrant from her bath.

Her hairs were still entwined with the embroidery on the pillow, blonde, honey and ash. Not hers at all, it seemed, but put there by her hairdresser.

Wrapping the strands around his knuckles, feeling their thin, tight pull, Lewis wondered if he could see any red in them, if Rhea was right. There wasn't a trace. He was glad that Amber had transformed herself into something for him. The woman-liness of the artifice gave it the sophistication that had civilised him during their marriage. The realisation that all this had been done for him, constantly and quietly, while he'd been distracted by work, gave him an unexpected, opulent impression of love. Last night's desolation faded.

The phone rang while he was in the shower, the one place in the house where he wouldn't hear it, so all he got was a message.

'Meet me at the hospital with Amber's clean night things, eleven o'clock. Put them in a decent bag. You need to see Vic. Eat some breakfast, Lewis.'

You need to see Vic. It was a start. Abandoned hope was resur-rected faster than Lewis could believe possible.

The precision of Rhea's directives cut a clear path through the fug. Eat some breakfast, she had instructed. Lewis was hungry, having missed dinner last night. He trawled through the refrigerator shelves: eggs, mushrooms. That was about it. Amber only did veggie food, but Lewis had been known to sneak a bacon and sausage sandwich from the Medical School refectory. The thought of the calorie hit from the forbidden fat, rich with the ancestral flavour of all the bacon and sausages that had ever been fried on the canteen hotplate, cheered him up and he put the healthy food back into the fridge. He ate a couple of muffins that he found in the pantry and forwarded Amber a psychic message about the benefits of blueberries.

Nightdresses. Easy. He opened the right drawer straight off. It was pretty empty because he'd already delivered most of Amber's stuff to the hospital and the nightdresses that were left were Amber's best ones. He lifted them carefully, trying to keep them folded as she had left them, but the silk slithered and fell from his hands in an untidy heap. He grasped them more firmly, and saw, at the bottom of the drawer, the necklace he had given his wife.

Wonder filled Lewis's soul. He could see Amber nestling his gift among her silk lingerie, hoping for something of him to seep into it. For a moment he stood still, stunned by the beauty of her reasoning. Ugly twinges of guilt about the way he'd thought of her last night prodded him into further action. Decent bag, Rhea had said. He found something suitable in Amber's wardrobe: a glossy carrier with ribbon handles that looked just right for best nightdresses. When he got to the refectory, the woman behind the counter noticed it and smiled at him as he picked up the bacon and sausage sandwich. Older women invariably had a soft spot for Lewis. He knew they thought him young and vulnerable; he'd enjoyed a good deal of surrogate mothering in his career. He looked down sheepishly at the carrier bag.

'Someone's lucky,' she said. His faith in himself began to return.

The refectory tea was scalding, and the polystyrene cup wasn't going to let it cool any time soon. A newspaper left on the next table caught his eye. He read the headline: 'Refugee Crisis in West Africa'. He reached over for it and when he turned back Glatton was taking a seat at his table.

'Another crisis,' Glatton said, nodding towards the paper. Then, 'How's Amber?'

'I'm just going up to see her now,' Lewis answered, 'with Rhea.' He smirked at Glatton's raised eyebrows, the gurn of envy.

'And Vic,' Glatton announced. 'I've just left them together in the foyer.' Lewis still couldn't drink the scalding tea, and if Vic and Rhea were already waiting for him, there was no time to eat the sandwich. He had to pick up the carrier bag and his briefcase and make an undignified exit.

Vic was standing by the stairs, creating an obstacle for the flow of bodies that passed around him. Even in the busy foyer he was surrounded by a perma-calm. Nothing seemed to touch his self-belief. Behind that big body and that self-possessed lack of tact, Rhea sheltered, part of it, her hand on the stair rail as though she owned it.

'Vic wanted to call on Amber,' she said, her voice streaked with warning. 'He knows how ill she's been. We've all been worried, haven't we, Vic?' She glanced upwards into Lewis's face, asking him to say yes. Vic was giving in, Lewis knew, but it was for Rhea. She was gathering them together, shepherding them up the stairs to the ward where Amber would complete the business. He realised what the warning was: he should keep quiet and leave this to them.

Vic didn't seem out of place in the women's ward. His frame spilt over the hospital chair but he balanced his forearms across his knees and made himself comfortable, working his mastery on Amber too. She sat up in the bed and began to talk of coming home. With Vic holding her hands, moving them up and down, weighing them against one another, she became all optimism.

'But you take care of yourself,' he cautioned. 'And you take care of this husband of yours. He's had a fright.' He folded her hands together and gave them back to her, as though they had reached a decision between them. 'I want you to think about something. Promise me you'll think about working for yourself.' His jowls swung as he turned his head in Lewis's direction. 'I've seen those banners she did. Everyone was talking about them. What's a girl like that doing wasting her time in someone else's business?'

A great bolus of fatalism settled itself in Lewis's stomach as he saw the ease with which Vic was able to dismiss Warren. Then he realised, to his own surprise, that he had no idea where Vic's fatherly advice had come from. Did Vic have a wife, a sister, a daughter? He must have had a mother. Vic had arrived from the States surrounded by his entourage of eager young assistants, unencumbered by any family responsibilities. The thought, the loosening of bonds, the freedom that it involved, startled and roused him. Like a stent slipped into an artery, the idea expanded, cleared the way, then let too much blood through so that it rushed to his head.

Lewis chauffeured a fragile Amber home through that steady state of wetness where drizzle hangs suspended in the air. But there had been a blizzard of emotional farewells to contend with. Women she would probably never see again had clung around her, cloying the air with their good wishes. All this time there'd been staccato bursts of gunfire from the television news, but they hadn't noticed. Women and children in Africa were running from huts into the sights of horsemen, who hitched rifles aloft with one hand while they hauled on reins with the other. Horses reared and turned as the scramble for cover dispersed the victims. Huts blazed. For the moment, the people seemed to have gained cover in the clumps of spindly trees. Lewis had stood captive to the horror, but all around him the women in the ward had gone on kissing air.

Lewis had turned to Amber, appalled, and she had gazed back at him before he had time to look away. The staunch line of his disapproval retreated immediately, but she had picked up her case and gone past him, twisting back into the ward for a last goodbye.

The car ran smoothly, responsive to the road. Amber's joints weren't going to feel the slightest jolt from the uneven surfaces of the long commute. That was what money does for you, smoothes the way, Lewis thought. Money earned by Amber's grandfather had once seemed his of right, something to prime the pump of his own success. The convertible it had bought felt like an extension of his body; the power of the three-litre engine funnelled through his fingertips and out on to the road. It took only a change of gear and a hint to the accelerator for him to be launched ahead of himself. Amber was oblivious. The baby train rattled on, regardless of his exhilaration.

Outside the drizzle was heavier. Greasy dirt smeared across the windscreen but the automatic wipers swept the glass clean. The car was powerful and heavy. Still, it glided on the slippery surface. The road spun away and the car straightened again as a touch on the steering pulled it back, in spite of the wet and the rural mud. Lewis stole a glance at Amber. She sat calm and unconcerned. Her hand crept forward and covered his knee while they faced outward, defying the road and the weather to outmanoeuvre them. The compliance of her fingers as he moved to brake reassured him. Amber wasn't frightened. Absorbed in her own world, she had handed herself over to him: she for the baby, he for his work. She pressed his knee as if she knew he had understood and they went on, together and separate.

When he opened the door and ushered Amber inside, a damp smell rolled towards him. Amber's hair was frizzy from the rain. When she went near to the fire it caught the light, which made it look red. Rhea's Amber, not his.

'Can you remember when you didn't live here?' he asked her.

'No,' she said. 'Can you?'

Lewis had to be busy. He filled the kettle. This house was Amber's. It didn't belong to him, even though his name was on the deeds, legally signed and sealed in the lawyer's voguish office in town. There'd been glass from ceiling to floor in that office, everything out in the open, but when he wandered too near to the window, the five-floor drop at his feet had made him giddy. And that was without thinking about the size of the mortgage or the cost of the renovations.

'I can't remember anything before I met you, not much anyway.' Amber was laughing in the low, winning way she often did. 'I love this house. It was all I could think about when I was in the hospital, coming back here, with you.'

Amber was tired after the journey. Her joints were still swollen, and when he touched her, Lewis could feel the inflammation. Things can seek out your weak spot. Eleanor had gazed at her patient's angry skin, her pulsing joints. Lewis helped her to a chair.

'I'm just glad we got you home at all. Eleanor said that this sort of thing can be worse when you're pregnant. It's lucky you're not,' he told Amber.

Once the words were out Lewis knew he had meant them. A baby was the last thing he wanted. As soon as he saw how true it was, he wished he hadn't said it. To make amends, he went over and touched Amber again, this time tentatively.

'Who are you calling lucky?' she said, in a way that made him

165

feel it was all his fault. 'Lewis, we've got to give this baby thing one really good chance. I'm thinking I should pack my job in so when I get the embryos back that's all we'll have to think about.'

'It doesn't matter to me whether there's a baby or not. I'll love you just the same.'

She didn't speak, and knowledge seeped into Lewis. He took it to mean that unless the IVF worked she wouldn't love him just the same. There was a silence while he convinced himself of it.

Emotion was faster than reason. The feeling of never being enough was always ready to claw its way upward. It sprang up so fast that Lewis took a step backwards, as if to escape it. 'There's just the two of us now,' he said. 'Aren't we happy?'

'Yes, we're happy,' answered Amber, wearily. 'You know what I mean.'

There was a moment when Lewis's feelings hung in the balance, but the exhaustion in Amber's voice swayed him. They were both disappointed. Amber wanted a future that he didn't really believe in: one in which the house was full of life and noise. A future he watched from a distance, too far away to be touched by it.

CHAPTER 9

Amber was putting away groceries with exaggerated care, the way you do when your mother's coming: tins strictly segregated at one side of the shelf, flour and sugar packed in plastic boxes to keep them safe from damp, or mice, or whatever it was that she thought might come creeping in to spoil them. She did it slowly because her joints hadn't quite recovered and sudden movements still jarred. Lewis sighed as he got up to help her. The house around him was scrupulously tidy: the sort of extreme domesticity that made him uncomfortable.

'Think of it like your lab,' Amber told him, as though it would make it better to have Stella invading his workspace too. 'Come on, Lewis, it's not as bad as all that. I'm going to enjoy being looked after by my mum. You're always busy.' Amber made a great pantomime of finishing the groceries herself.

Years later, he was still flinching at the remark that had implied he didn't earn enough for Amber to leave work. It wasn't as though anyone believed Stella's outlandish ideas about women working but some deep part of Lewis wanted his mother-in-law's respect. The muscles around his jaw clenched when she floated through the station barrier but it was his eyes Stella's sought before Amber's or Rhea's. She smiled at him before she looked at her daughters. Lewis took her suitcase, his free hand lifting automatically to her arm. He felt her delicacy, the bird-like thinness of her bones through her clothes. It was as though she carried a personal world of privilege with her. Entitlement was woven into the very threads of those garments.

Stella had never stooped to working. You could say that she had wafted through life, totally insulated. He was mortified and excited even to think it, but it was true. She kissed him with a practised lightness. 'I'll see to everything, Lewis,' she said, with precise elegance. 'That's what mothers do.'

He hurried to open the car door but she had done it; she fitted herself neatly into the seatbelt, composed, legal and ready to go. She must have seen the tight marks of alarm on his face and guessed what he was thinking. He ducked into the driving seat, hiding a smile tainted with embarrassment and gratitude.

He took them home along the coast road. The women sat together in the back, half talked, half listened to one another and Lewis focused on his driving. It was that time of the afternoon when the light was beginning to fade, but it wasn't dark: the worst time of all for accidents, but no one demanded his attention. He was able to watch the road disappear past him, shapes looming up, then left safely behind. Rhea was quiet. Amber and her mother were entertaining each other. In the mirror, he could see their heads close together. Under the watery light their hair was the same colour, the white mother and the bleached daughter.

'Oh, look at that!' Stella cried.

The dredgers on the estuary had been draped with coloured lights. In the evenings they looked more like Cleopatra's barge gliding to port than the dirty old workhorses they were in daytime. Darkness and a few fairy-lights were all it took to transform them.

'Why do they do it?' Lewis wondered, puzzled by the idea of climbing the high rigging for such an unnecessary task.

'Aren't they the signalling lights,' Amber said, 'so other ships can see them in the dark?'

'It's only to be expected.' That was his mother-in-law's explanation for anything that was unexpected, and difficult to fit into the ordinary pattern of things. She smiled contentedly and didn't seem to find anything incongruous in dressing up a dredger like a Christmas tree.

Lewis parked the car, and as they stood on the sand dunes to admire the view, he hung back so that they could have the best of it. There was always a wind from the sea and their words blew towards him. 'I'm so pleased Lewis brought us this way, darling. I wouldn't have missed it for anything,' Stella said. 'He's done the right thing, you know.'

Now that Amber had left work Stella was delighted with her son-in-law. Amber was delighted with her mother, immured in Snitter Heugh. Only Rhea seemed disgruntled and impossible to please.

'Stay with us, dear,' Stella said. 'I'm sure Lewis won't expect you to go to work while I'm here.'

Expectant glances came his way, all expecting different things. Lewis felt a profound surge of uncertainty, mixed with the strong, warm smell of cooking meat, so powerful he was transfixed. He looked blankly at them.

'It's nothing to do with Lewis, Mum. I've got my own job, you know.' Rhea wouldn't stay away from the lab, whatever he said. It was a relief that something didn't depend on him.

Stella opened the oven door to check on the joint. Men didn't like vegetarian, she had told Amber. No, not poultry, Lewis was entitled to something stronger. Venison was natural, Amber. Deer weren't badly treated. She had given her daughter a wry look. A man's life was made from darker meat, it said. So the close-grained haunch was served, with its provocative gravy, especially for him.

In bed that night, Amber laughed. 'It's me who's ill and she's got you spoilt rotten.'

'Look and learn,' he said, and she threatened to smother his complacent grin with her pillow. In the end he was almost, but not quite, sorry to see Stella leave.

It was a given now that everything Lewis did took precedence: his research was crucial for all of their plans. Amber went to the clinic alone. A new nurse was eyeing up the accumulating patients. Every now and then she would make a swift, predatory sally into the room and fish one out. The woman would disappear for a while, then return looking cleansed and brightened. When Amber had woken up in the hospital after being so ill, she'd felt light, as though she could defy gravity. In fact, she'd felt so insubstantial that she could have floated upwards and looked down on her own body. The idea of leaving herself behind had been a profound and liberating relief: not as if she had died, but as if, suddenly, it was the first time she had ever been truly alive. Was it possible that you could escape the incessant itch of your skin and the seething of your joints? Spared a womb, would you be spared, too, the interminable clamouring for a baby? For a time, ignoring her body had felt like an unlimited release. She ached for the peace of resignation. Hopelessness and quietude crept seductively close. Maybe those women the nurse had beckoned had been rescued from themselves.

Once she had got home the pain in her joints had subsided. First her shoulders, then her hips and knees. It was as though it had been gradually absorbed into the ground of Snitter Heugh. Only the arches of her feet hurt now. She knew the blessing of skies that stayed still, and ground that didn't spin away when you stood up too quickly. Often, though, her brain ached. In the cold, dark mornings she walked the two miles to the village. While Amber had rested, her mother had woven a long, wide scarf, hazy with the colours of the heather and the sky that had been cloaked by the wet weather; Amber wrapped it around herself and trod softly so as not to jar her fragile equilibrium.

Inside the post office there was coffee, served at tables that were still covered with last year's cloths patterned with spring flowers, and cakes with sell-by dates that stretched to next spring. The even-tempered voices of other women wove a steady, uncomplicated rhythm, drawing her back to the undemanding friendships of the hospital ward. Each day Amber bought coffee and sat down to rest before the walk home. The fug of warmth diffused the stabs of her joints to a more bearable discomfort while the caffeine eased her headache.

At first, the other women glanced her way, then continued their conversation. Soon enough, they smiled, and within a few days they were tentatively admiring her scarf, fingering the weave, acknowledging her mother's artistry. The subtle blend of colours transmuted into the minutiae of Amber's life. She found herself telling her new friends everything: her absolute need for motherhood, the recent move and her isolation, what with Lewis and Rhea so busy. They might have been bored and left her to her problems. They might have shunned the miserable incomer. But that wasn't in their natures: they repaid her with a matching warmth, folding her softly into a communal understanding.

'Don't give up hope,' they counselled, sure voices cancelling the cautious prognostications of the fertility experts. 'Mostly, you just need to give nature a bit of encouragement,' these women assured her. Their confidence in a happy ending was manna to Amber. Their merriment in the trials of delay lightened the bald truths of medical statistics. How old was she? Only thirty-two? Some of those women had given birth when they were well into their forties.

Their reassurance penetrated deep into Amber; their patience undid the tension of her sinews and allowed her to be tired. In the afternoons, she drifted in and out of sleep. Thoughts and dreams curled together in a daze of ease and paracetamol. She knew then that hope wouldn't die in her; it kept surfacing, sensing warmth and returning to life. Her arms, legs, lungs, womb: they added up to what she was. When she looked in the mirror, she saw a face, but it wasn't hers. It was the face she had before she made herself up in the morning: the face that only Lewis had seen.

She was back in the hospital now, but this was Outpatients: no ties could survive in the anonymous coming and going of strangers.

The nurse was still watching. Her face wasn't exactly pretty, her mouth was too uncompromisingly honest, but it was one of those arresting puzzles that you can't take your eyes off. She was right not to use makeup. You shouldn't hide a face like that: you had to let it stand up for itself. This woman waited in the clinic doorway, half in and half out, without making any effort to disguise her interest in Amber. It was uncomfortable to be studied so thoroughly, so Amber watched back. The nurse didn't look away.

'Mrs Norham, isn't it?' Her voice was husky. Like her face, it didn't ask for allowances to be made. You could buy into that brown, northern brogue, or you could walk away and leave it alone: she wasn't going to change it to suit your ears. She had a brave smile. It hinted of something unhappy in her background, the determination to be cheerful in the face of some unknown hurt. Intrigued, Amber followed her into a small consulting room.

'Dr Bonworth has asked me to have a few words with you before she sees you.'

A half-smile came to her paradox of a face: the satisfaction of being trusted by the consultant. Amber visualised the two of them together, studying her case. They must have been collaborating to do their best for her. Professionals like them could read between the lines of the notes. It took a long time to be that astute, but this woman wasn't young; not old either. Perhaps she had children herself. Or perhaps she knew what it was not to have them.

'I'm Rachel Fenbridgeter. I'm running a trial for a new infertility treatment.'

'Yes,' Amber said, 'I'll sign up for it.'

Consternation made the nurse's face reticent. A shuffle of the papers on her clipboard was meant to disguise her loss of direction. 'It's certainly encouraging to have such an expression of confidence, but you understand that this is just a preliminary discussion?' Amber nodded. She could go along with all the palaver of medical ethics if it got her a baby. The nurse was suitably mollified. 'We've all noticed your positive attitude to your treatments. Dr Bonworth will explain your test results to you. This new fertility regime is very gentle, but if she thinks there's any question of risk to your health, we won't go ahead.'

'But gentle,' Amber pleaded. 'It could be perfect for me.' Nurse Fenbridgeter still shook her head. She belonged in a world like Lewis and Rhea's: what counted were test results, measurable things. She couldn't contemplate the intangible, the PR spin that could put you on the right or wrong side of acceptable. She hadn't been outmanoeuvred by a professional before.

'There might be an allergic thing complicating matters,' Amber offered. 'We had moved house, you know. I've always been prone. You can't imagine the dust.'

How wrong Amber was. The nurse most certainly could. She

had only recently endured the most awful move herself. In fact, the only thing she couldn't imagine was how some people could leave their home in such a state. Amber smiled, the consolatory glow of recognition seeping into her face and finding its complement in Nurse Fenbridgeter's intriguing features. A shaft of sunlight cast the shadow of the window frame along the faded wood of the desk.

Sunday school. That glow. The shadows on the whitewashed wall had come from the taper Amber had guarded, very carefully, in the mottled brass holder that was given to each girl on her birthday. The smoke curled upwards towards the vaulted roof and the child's hand, steadied by the weight of responsibility, pressed the flame against the black wicks of the big altar candles, melting away yesterday's hardened wax until they spurted into today's life: eight of them, one for each of her eight years. She'd looked back to admire the path of light she had left behind her.

'That's your goodness,' her mother had told her, and Amber had felt herself a shining angel. I'll never be naughty again, she had secretly promised, clasping the taper in rapture. Virtue had beamed out from her.

'Of course, I've changed to a totally organic diet. And I do *t'ai chi* every night before I go to bed.'

The nurse shook her head in appreciation. 'If only all our patients were so responsible.' She looked as though she might be going to tell some lurid tales about the behaviour of other would-be mothers, but thought better of it. Even silent, her mouth wasn't quiet. It assured Amber, *I won't burden you with this*.

It was settled. Nurse Fenbridgeter would refer the application to Eleanor, with her recommendation.

Now, at the thought of the nurse's face, the quick suggestiveness of her voice, hope gained another foothold. *We've all noticed your positive attitude,* she had said. Light-headedness vouchsafed Amber a clarity that wouldn't let her give up. She could see sharply, as though everything had been washed, that Vic was right. She should work less. Better to shed the whole grimy business, quit putting a decent gloss on the unacceptable, but she had promised to do the publicity for Lewis and Rhea's work. Still, she would give herself a fresh start, a final, pure effort to give pregnancy a chance. Before she left, Rachel placed a light hand on her arm. 'It would be good if we could make some progress on your anaemia.'

Amber's new friends from the post-office café were all very willing to help on this one.

'You don't need to be a vegetarian to support animal welfare,' Esmé assured her. 'Look at our farm.' Amber stopped to catch her breath and, at the same time, to marvel at her new boots: thick-soled walking boots that had let her climb for two solid hours without chafing.

Esmé's Labradors panted around her feet, hankering to go on, but up there on the hillside, cold snatched the breath from your mouth and Amber needed her inhaler. The moorland sheep leant solidly into the wind that blew with unremitting ferocity. But stoical sheep had held their ground like that for centuries, outfacing the weather to tramp their narrow tracks between the patches of short, spare grass. Amber turned into the wind and pushed the hair out of her eyes.

As they climbed down to the valley, Esmé called the dogs close to her. 'These are new flocks. The old hefted sheep had to be killed in the foot-and-mouth outbreak. This lot don't know their way about yet. If they get scattered, they won't be able to find their way home.'

The incomer sheep picked their way across the springy grass. Scree spread down the slopes and made walking difficult.

Amber, Esmé and the two dogs had to climb upwards again to avoid it.

'Foot-and-mouth,' repeated Amber. 'Was it that bad?' For once Esmé was reluctant to talk.

'That was when these two got so fat.' She rubbed the backs of Dina and Dee-Dee, scratching through their coats so that her fingers disappeared into the furze of sandy hair. 'We hardly ever went out in case we spread it around. You just felt guilty all the time, but there was nothing you could do.' The dogs were rubbing against her legs now, comforting her. 'We had to go to the supermarket one day and on the way back, as we came across the bridge, they started killing the Flinbridge pigs. They were screaming so loud you couldn't get it out of your head.' She gazed into the valley as though the sound was still lurking in it, biding its time among the cotton grass and the tussocks of heather.

But anaemic Amber had to build herself up if she was going to become pregnant; she was determined to eat meat. She lifted a ham from the oven, vulgar and coarse with the huge knuckle bone protruding from its hood of fat. Its surface was covered with eruptions: tiny, vicious detonations all over it, where fat and water and heat had clashed head on. The smell rose stronger.

'You sit down.' Rhea watched her hesitate. 'I'll see to that.'

Fat glistened under the blade of the knife; the soft pink meat came into view. Then there was Rhea, unconcerned, unfazed Rhea, flipping it from knife to plate, passing it across, speaking as though pushing dead animals into your mouth was the most natural thing in the world.

'Quick. Straight down, and don't even think about it.'

But Amber recoiled from the tiny puddle of fat and the flopping flesh.

Rhea understood immediately how difficult fat was for her.

The fat was the worst part. If you'd been a vegetarian for ten years you couldn't eat it, even if you wanted to. The blubber was cut away and swept from the plate without a word. Amber raised the softly striated muscle to her lips. She touched it to her teeth, her tongue, and immediately she was invaded by that sweet saltiness; she ached to take it into her. The Flinbridge pigs screamed at her across the valley, betrayed. In a scald of panic she backed away.

'You don't have to if you don't want to.' Rhea's arm was round her shoulders, hiding the sight of the corruption. 'Veggies do have babies, you know.'

'Oh, Rhea, I do want to. I want to do everything possible. But I'm scared. I know it's the right thing to do but it's the wrong thing too.'

'You could just keep taking the iron tablets.'

There was a gurgling spurt of steam from the joint as though it had an opinion on that. The hot smell of salt and sugar blocked out the stench of the lab. The irresistible lure in the ham snared her; her body demanded she do it.

'No. I want to eat it.'

'Well, then.' Rhea teased the ham apart with her fingers and buttered two tiny squares of a loaf. Four minute, sacrificial shreds of meat were placed deep in the heart of the floury bread. 'Just one bite. That's quite enough to start with.'

Amber looked at the proffered morsel. It was tiny. How could it hurt anyone? Rhea's hand was still, steady. It reminded her of the way Rhea always sorted things out, as if she didn't think anything of it.

On the day that Amber had started school, the new infants had been led in single file through a long, dark corridor, then ejected from a door into the playground. She'd turned back to see the other children behind her popping out into the sunshine, one by one, like peas from a pod, each one alone. She'd thought she was going to cry, but then she'd seen Rhea leaning on the gate. She was talking to her friends and, without pausing, had held out her hand to her little sister. How good it had felt to be the only new starter with someone waiting for them.

It was such a tiny thing, a little bread, a little butter, an infinitesimal scrap of something else. Rhea made things easy for her. Amber kept her eyes on her sister and didn't look at the sandwich. Rhea looked back, smiling very lightly, not saying yes, not saying no. Her fingers made the decision for her. While she looked away, they picked up the food and put it into her mouth. A glorious burst of flavour, longing fulfilled, a deep relief stretching into her very bones.

The ham had a metallic taste, like mercury fillings. Rhea said that indicated the presence of some obscure trace element. She said it ought to be doing Amber good and that she could imagine the molecular complex wending its way around Amber's digestion, passing through the cell wall and embedding itself in an enzyme, the enzyme that was crucial to the initiation of a pregnancy. Once that switch was thrown, there would be a cascade of other switches, reaction after reaction: the tiny ball of cells taking shape. Amber closed her eyes, and when she opened them again, the kitchen felt tiny. She had ballooned, huge and powerful, to fill the space, as amoral as nature itself.

Rhea held the meat, examined it from every angle. Satisfied by her inspection, she began carving, handling the knife comfortably, stroking at the ham so that it separated and fell away at her touch. Amber felt her own body, solid and unyielding. She could scarcely believe that something as domestic as cooking was all it took to turn flesh and blood into food. Rhea spread the slices across the plate.

'Well done,' she said. 'Whatever it takes.'

Yes, thought Amber, I'm having a baby, whatever it takes.

Hunger grew in her; her own flesh demanded more. She measured herself against Rhea, never flinching, doing whatever it took. The meat was cooling. Rhea was ahead of her, already organising the next move.

'You could pack it up and freeze it. Just try a little bit whenever you feel like it.'

Amber stood in awe of Rhea's ability to reduce hot flesh to neutralised packages in cold storage.

The newly purchased array technology lived in Glatton's half of the lab. It gave him the opportunity to treat Rhea with elaborate courtesy when she went to look at it, showing her the shelf where the instructions were kept, offering her a personal photocopy to take away and generally making her feel as though she didn't own an equal share. He opened up to her, now they were on the same side, so to speak, and admitted, with a squalid imitation of modesty, that he suspected his cultures were pure stem cells. There was just a slight question of their degree of commitment.

'Once the arrays are up and running, we'll know if they're expressing the right gene profile.' Vic, it seemed, didn't mind if Glatton's cells weren't able to turn into absolutely anything. As long as they could repair destroyed nerve cells, they were good enough for him. Between that, and the totality of his condescension, Rhea thought Glatton's domain a perfect imitation of Hell.

The effort of research was disproportionate to the returns. Everyone was sick of it. The weather was dirty and the windows were crusted, blocking off the outside world. They had spent so long cloistered together that they had forgotten the outside world existed. Or if it did, it was a watered-down version of the life they lived together. So much so that a phone call felt like an intrusion.

The pulse of intimate conversation beat in their own lab, Lewis explaining that he wouldn't be home for dinner again. Lewis had an anxious cough. Exhaustion had meant he couldn't fight off the infection. He needed to see his doctor but he had been too busy. Antibiotics might clear it up, but then again, realistically, they might not. It was one of those things you couldn't shake off. Like a worry you couldn't get out of your head, it lurked and came back at you whenever you were tired. Lewis raised his hands in a show of resignation. Katherine and Joe exchanged knowing looks and turned away as Rhea tapped at her computer.

Hidden behind a password, she had a spreadsheet that predicted the financial cost of each percentage-point rise in the purity of their stem cells they would gain by plugging away as they were. It was far too much. The salary bill alone was astronomical. Fazil, Katherine, Andrew and Joe all came to work with a fat price tag attached to them, and spent their days drifting around their benches as though weighed down by the magnitude of the burden. Even the stirrers turned slow and desultory. Lewis made frantic efforts to cheer them along, nervy with indecision.

There was no choice about working so late. Once Amber's illness had interrupted their schedule, they had to make up the time. When the others had gone home in the evening, they sat together in his office, in the tiny realm created by the lightbox, like a miniature cinema. Rhea looked at negative photographs of gel run-outs, comparing them one with another until she could be certain where they differed and where they were exactly the same. No mother could have looked at her baby more carefully, at the tiniest details of its anatomy, the creases on its wrists or its flailing feet. As long as they sat still, they worked in a gloaming half-darkness, but as soon as either of them stirred, the movement-sensitive lights would bolt on and they would be shocked back into immobility, like a pair of convicts caught in a search beam.

There was scuttling in the corridor. The lab doors burst apart to let in Glatton. One by one the lights jerked on, tipped off by his approach. His cocky walk grated on Rhea's inflamed nerves. If Glatton had brokered some deal with Vic and Featley, that was exactly how he'd walk. He wouldn't come out and tell you: he'd let you find out by degrees. More fun that way. The signing-in list lay open in the porter's lodge every evening. She was going to check it as she left, to find out who else had worked late.

'I thought I might find you two here.'

Rhea closed the results file. 'Well, it's not exactly rocket science, is it, Stephen? This is where we work.'

He nodded grudgingly, as though he wasn't prepared to concede anything. He tried his luck with Lewis. 'I've been hard at it myself. I just wondered if Amber would let you out for a drink before you head home.' There was silence. Glatton broke it himself. 'Rhea?' he asked.

'Sorry, Stephen, we're absolutely slaved.' She stood up and piled file on file, certain now that he was only there to check the state of their involvement with Vic. 'Another time.' Glatton shrugged and turned his back. She had told him what he wanted to know.

In the uneasy quiet he left behind, the lamps flickered out again. Now there was only the gleam of the lightbox in the darkness. For a moment it seemed that the light was too light and the dark too dark. They didn't mingle anywhere. Gradually her eyes adjusted: shades of grey began to appear and centrifuges, fridges, freezers and incubators took their places around her. She laughed nervously. 'Does Amber still let you go for a drink, after last time?'

'Yes, but it's me, isn't it? I can't trust myself.'

The lab settled and sighed around them. Rhea sat next to him and played with the results sheet. 'It's just as well you've got us to keep you right, then.' She patted his arm, but kept it sisterly. In the half-light she could see his skin, so like hers. His right hand and her left, one each side of the printout. They might have been a single pair.

'Amber,' she said, 'is she all right?'

'Yes. No.' Lewis's voice faded with doubt. 'I mean, she's fine, but she's still a bit shaky. She takes all these long walks with her friends. She's going on about double-glazing. Honestly, we can't afford it, but she says she'll catch pneumonia from the draughts in that house.'

'It's her asthma. She's scared, Lewis. We've had some bad times with it. You've got no idea. Let her have her double-glazing. It'll keep her happy.'

Rhea was looking at the disappointing figures again.

'Are you going to show Vic the spreadsheet?'

'Only if he asks.'

'We won't say anything to him?'

'Not yet.' She sighed. 'Something will turn up.'

Amber kept peering out of the windows at the distant land-scape because the inside of Snitter Heugh brimmed with absence. It was empty without Lewis and Rhea but still it cost money. Even the bare trees and the grey skyline, often teasing her by appearing and disappearing through the mist, were better company than a pile of invoices. Unpaid bills had such a look of reproach; they were threatening to escape their intern-ment in the box file and spread themselves across the kitchen. She had five hundred pounds tucked into a drawer in the bed-room, in case she couldn't get to the bank. She brought the roll down to pay an instalment to the builders, fingering a sum of money that would have been trivial to her when she was earning regular bonuses at work. Her credit card wasn't acceptable: there was a reality about banknotes that suited the local economy, but she had expected the money to feel heavier than it did.

There couldn't be much work in the country – she'd had no trouble finding someone to install double-glazing, although she preferred to believe it was because the neighbours had taken to her. Belonging had become the leitmotif of her existence and paying up was a non-negotiable requirement in village life. Likewise, colossally expensive double-glazing. Mullioned windows didn't come cheap, but the local planning regulations were exceptionally strict on character preservation. She guessed it was a ploy to support the local economy.

'Luckily,' Sarah Pindon had told her, 'our Simon and Martin do all the big houses around here. But I'm sure they'll see to yours, if I ask them.'

Simon and Martin were fantastic company, always ready with an intriguing story, full of fun. Their good humour was enough to scare away draughts and anxieties, never mind their steady, committed approach to home renovations. Every problem had a solution as far as they were concerned; you just had to work out what it was and do it. They'd just finished their first coffee of the day when the scaffolders turned up. Amber opened the kitchen door to see how many more cups were needed but Simon was on the step, blocking her view.

'There you go.' Under the cover of his clipboard he thrust two empty mugs into her hands, keeping a watchful eye on the men unloading the lorry. 'We'll have our next cup after they've gone.' There was a definite hardening of his features as he peered at the scaffolders. They scowled back, angling their bundles of long grey poles to get a better look at Amber. Simon leant forward, putting himself in their line of sight. 'They come from Flinbridge way,' he told her. 'We hire their scaffolding, but we have as little to do with them as we can.' A satisfied grin invaded his face as Amber's smile fled.

'They've always been bandits over there. Rustle your cattle before they'd look at you.' He paused for dramatic effect. He had told this story before, Amber guessed. 'Time was,' he said, 'that lot came over the hills and burnt everything we had.' The bandit scaffolders looked willing enough to Amber. They were heaving poles and clamps from the lorry, a bit carelessly, she thought, dropping them, rather than lifting them down and laying them in order on the ground, the way Simon would have done. Still, that didn't make them arsonists. Martin popped up behind Simon, wanting his part in the story.

'They burnt the Abbey School down once,' he added gleefully, 'with all the kids locked in it.'

'You weren't there that day, then.' Amber laughed and Simon joined in.

'All a long time ago, nearly a thousand years, but we don't forget, do we? It pays to know who your friends are.'

So it was true. One day – was it sunny, Amber wondered, or rainy and dark? – men had come across the hilltops from Flinbridge and burnt down the school with all the children locked inside. She glanced towards the horizon. It was clear and bright; you'd see anything that moved. Had anyone been watching and thought nothing of their first glimpse of the marauders? They might have mistaken them for ordinary travellers, or the innocent shadows of passing clouds. The unexpected hardening of Simon's features at the sight of the Flinbridge scaffolders leapt up at her. Was that how the twelfth-century villagers had looked as they realised it was a raiding party? Martin and Simon had sold her a crucible they had reclaimed – liberated, Lewis sneered – from an old ironworks, knowing that she had been making paper at Snitter Heugh.

They had roots in this place, roots that stretched deeper than she could imagine.

'We'll have some more coffee when they're gone.' The cups clinked in her fingers. Simon and Martin stood between her and the strangers.

She folded the five hundred pounds. The notes were new, stiff, unused to being handled. It was difficult to stop them springing open the envelope. Amber had to press firmly to seal it. Simon didn't bother to count the cash when she passed it to him. He glanced downwards and she knew he had an instinctive sense of its value. She saw him peel off some notes and pass them across to the scaffolding men for a sweetener as they climbed up into the lorry and left.

No one had been able to protect the Abbey children. She thought of Polly: what might Lewis and Rhea be able to do to help her? The scaffolding shell clung flimsily to the stone walls of Snitter Heugh, the poles reedy and insubstantial. Simon and Martin whistled as they tore the wrappings from the new window frames and folded the waste into the back of the van. Amber needed to belong here. She would make the house into a fortress against the world.

CHAPTER 10

Rhea's car climbed out of the city, away from the coastal plain towards the hills. The difference in height had a significant effect on the seasons. In the city it was well into spring. Primroses flowered demurely in sheltered suburban gardens, but at Amber's the buds would still be tightly furled until the wind had fallen and the temperature had risen. The journey between the two worlds had an unearthly aspect, the reversal of time.

It drew Rhea backwards, to a need she thought she had left behind: other people. How much easier it was to stay at work in the lab. She would be safely ensconced there tomorrow. Already she was looking forward to warming up the vials, then sitting at the microscope, watching cells that had been frozen into suspended animation round themselves up. They would lose their jagged edges and smooth out before your eyes. Then they would settle down on their plastic plates and begin to divide. The next time you looked, where there had been four cells, there would be six, eight. Once you'd seen that happen, you could never forget just how powerful life was: how it could come back from a frozen nothing and flourish, if it wanted to. It had to want to: Rhea had always understood that. It was important to her, sitting at the microscope, to know that it wanted to.

When she arrived, the house had undergone a change, and not just the windows: the door was new, made from massive oak planks, riveted instead of nailed. The step was still the same, though, worn in the centre. Amber would have kept that step, low in the middle, so that a child could climb it. She hadn't given up casting charms at the future.

Amber's footsteps were careful as she came out to meet Rhea. Lewis followed her, a few feet behind her trailing skirt and scarf. She turned back to him and stood on her dress.

'Be careful,' Rhea warned, as Amber slipped and crashed against the edge of the door. She tottered, and Lewis jumped to help her.

Hard wood brushed tender skin. There was nothing at first, then a thin line of red welled from her lip. It was a light, shallow cut, but the blood flowed freely. Lewis took her to the kitchen, lowered her into a chair and turned to the sink. 'You're not quite back to yourself yet. Eleanor said to take things easy.'

At the mention of Eleanor, Amber put on her pouting, tearful smile. It had to be the baby thing. What else brought Amber to the brink of tears? Lewis kept leaning towards her, his wife, to listen more carefully, or leaning back, to look at her face. Rhea had never known him so absorbed in another person. This was the place in the world that he and Amber shared; a place that existed only for the two of them. It made her think of Dave, how he and she had turned away from each other and hidden themselves. There had been no welcome for a baby there.

'I've broken my tooth! Oh, no! Christ! Look, it's come right out.'

A piece of tooth lay in her hand. Lewis flushed suddenly, sweat on his face. He picked up the fragment and looked at it curiously.

'God only knows what it's going to cost,' Amber said.

Lewis shrugged. 'It doesn't matter,' he said, uncharacteristically. 'We can't do anything about that.' He placed the tooth in a plastic bag from the kitchen drawer, zipping it away. Why would you keep a broken tooth? Rhea hated to see him clinging to a bit of Amber; there were baby teeth at home, the baby shoes that their mother had clung to. It was ghoulish. 'Throw it out, Lewis,' she said. 'You can't glue it back on.'

Lewis was suddenly angry. 'I know what a crown is, Rhea.' He put the bag into his pocket.

'Lewis, phone the dentist. You'll come with me too, won't you, Rhea? Lewis hates anything like this.'

There was a photograph of their wedding on the wall. Amber and Lewis legally joined together. Lewis was looking straight at the lens, but Amber was turning towards Rhea, bestowing her bouquet. *You next*, she had said. What a commotion Bridezilla had made over that wedding. She'd had Rhea go over every detail with her for months. Bored or busy, Lewis was expert at keeping out of the way, and sometimes Rhea had wondered whose wedding it was: Amber and Lewis's or Amber and their mother's.

'It's because of the meat,' Amber was saying. 'It's my own fault. I shouldn't have started eating it.'

Lewis had his car keys ready, willing to play his part in the drama of his marriage.

'He'll see you in half an hour. I'll drop you both off, and call at the lab for you, Rhea. Check on the cells, then pick you both up again.'

'You should go with her, Lewis. I'll see to the cells.'

But Lewis was even more determined than Amber. His lab key card was already in his hand. Rhea remembered how he had shaken at the sight of Amber's split lip.

'It's all sorted, then. You can come with me.' Amber gave a watery smile. It was sorted, as far as she was concerned. *Oh, get off the stage, the pair of you*, Rhea thought, as she wrote off the rest of her day.

It was dark by the time Amber was safely home and Rhea was driving back to the city alone. Rain began to pit against the windscreen, bright little spots ringing with light. Lewis had checked the lab. The incubators were safe; the temperatures were all running at blood heat, the carbon-dioxide levels were just right, all the monitors were green, the alarm systems showing sleep mode. But Rhea knew Amber would be lying awake, goaded by her broken tooth and her empty womb.

Lewis felt the strain in his jacket seams, and as he collected the stuff for his meeting at City Hall, he hoped he was moving inexorably into a heavier-weight version of himself. He and Vic had been invited to a funding meeting about the Genetics Institute.

Traffic lights were squirting cars onto the ring road, but they jumped to red as Lewis passed them. Bright sun flounced in and out of the clouds, giving him a headache. He squeezed his eyes shut, and when he reopened them, some runner, too arrogant to break his rhythm, was grunting madly straight through the lights and careering into his path. Lewis jammed the brake pedal into the floor as hard as he could. The judder of the brakes was like a bad aeroplane landing, the rough and sudden thump on the tarmac – welcome in its awfulness because the alternative was so very much worse. The car stopped, the belt kept Lewis firm in his seat, and the would-be athlete was off, fingers in the air.

All the traffic stopped. The formidable engines grumbled discreetly. They weren't at their best, idling: they wanted to be off, over the speed limit. Their owners vacillated between two equal desires: to keep them under control and to let them have their heads. Lewis's heart fibrillated, partly in fright, partly in anger. The driver to the right hooted, then lowered the window and shouted, 'Up yours!' Accelerating too fast, Lewis's car leapt into the junction to a cacophony of horn blasts.

After the spiky disquiet of the streets, the smooth red walls of City Hall were soothing. The bricks shone red: engineering bricks, fired with the utmost care by Victorian artisans. The traffic still whined in its anxiety to move. Lewis stared at the solidity of the bricks and took comfort.

In the entrance hall, a uniformed messenger assumed responsibility for his progress, punching the entry code into a keypad, chatting to Lewis as he did it, his body turned towards his guest. Lewis could have seen what the code was; it wasn't a secret from someone like him. There was no need: he was to be guided through the opened door and accompanied all the way to the Council Chamber.

· The spotlights for the photo session were already switched on, giving the dais the feel of a stage. As he walked past them, Lewis couldn't help but enjoy the tug of celebrity. Spotlights at his right and left would merge into a single illuminated rostrum beneath his feet. The public seats, on the other hand, were consigned to dismal obscurity because the windows were covered with what looked like very old and dirty net curtains. But as a breeze came through the open casements they flapped heavily and fell straight back: those curtains were blast protection.

The vice chancellor repeated his usual platitudes, with just enough variation for the audience to be able to believe he knew who they were. This was the university showing itself off to the city, the obligatory period of ritual boasting when the VC enumerated his institution's achievements, counting out awards and honours from a checklist he carried within him. The embrace of his vision spread wide: the city had gained international recognition for economic regeneration projects that were paramount in countering the decline of its traditional industries. He spoke without pause over a hovering police helicopter, which must have been outside the range of his hearing but kept Lewis on edge with its irritating whine. At last, the chairman announced lunch.

There were eggs, constructed from sausagemeat and mock caviar. It was always like this – nothing was ever what it seemed outside the lab. Still, *faux*-authenticity was obviously good enough because the fanciful creations proved unexpectedly strengthening. Conversations sprang up everywhere, but Lewis didn't know anyone near to him. He searched around, embarrassed to be alone in the middle of the networking.

'Lewis?'

One of the university enterprise team was by his side. It appeared that City Hall had a problem on its hands. 'I said you'd have the answer.'

A circle of interested faces formed around Lewis. He looked back expectantly. Nothing happened. Everyone was waiting for him to take the lead.

'I'll do my best, but you'll have to tell me what the problem is first.'

There was a flurry of consensual jollity, as though it was thought politic to laugh at his jokes. One of the council delegates, a wiry man with an eager, thrusting manner, edged forward, taking it on himself to speak to Lewis.

'You may have read about it in the *Examiner*.' How confidential his manner seemed, for something that had appeared in the local rag. 'The dog that mauled a baby.'

'Yes.' Lewis had seen the article. His wife, Amber, he said, had been upset, then relieved to read that the child – a little boy? – had survived relatively unscathed.

At the mention of the words 'baby' and 'Amber', Vic's antennae must have picked up a signal: he joined the group. The spokesman opened out to his audience: 'We intend to prosecute the owner, but he's claiming that the dog isn't a pit bull, that

191

actually it's some Peruvian breed, renowned for its good nature.'
He turned back to Lewis. 'What we thought,' he went on, 'was
that we might be able to prove something with DNA, but we've
been wondering . . .' He paused, looking back at his colleagues
for support in the municipally unmapped regions of genetic
analysis. The question came out in a scamper: 'Dogs don't have
DNA, do they?'

The cheer and hoot from the crowd when Lewis told them
that dogs most certainly did have DNA turned heads all around
the room. Lewis was off, back to his folder, fetching out the
DNA profiles he had brought with him, just in case, showing
them how to find the differences. They clustered around him.
He couldn't resist the comprehensive levels of attention.
Gratified, he delivered his undergraduate master class in the
subtleties of genomic differentiation to an admiring audience.

Vic hovered in the background, an unspoken warning against
offering what you couldn't deliver.

'OK,' said Lewis. 'If I'm honest, there are no sure ways of
telling what breed a dog is by DNA analysis.'

'Thanks,' the council guys said, and Lewis offered to leave
them some handouts on the topic.

It didn't seem to matter that he hadn't helped them with
their problem. By the time they sat down to the negotiations
there was a general air of something having been sorted out. All
that was left was to fill in the detail.

When it came to the celebratory photograph, it was to appear
under the headline 'City to Boost Stem Cell Research'. There
was a division on party lines: council to the right, university to
the left. Lewis made a quiet joke of it, then he had to give up
his place in the front row to one of the lawyers, a girl, prettier
than him. He did it with grace and, in return for his chivalry, she
edged sideways and he slipped in next to her, which was a perfect position: she was tiny and made him seem tall.

He felt tall. She had to look upwards to thank him, and as he acknowledged her, his eyes slipped further down to the curve of her neckline. Smallish, rounded breasts: not like Amber, not like Rhea. For a moment, he feared he might touch her, but it passed, and he was left to move his eyes back to her mouth. Still, to be so challenged, and at the same time to feel so controlled, proved that he could accommodate excitement and calm.

He composed himself for the photograph, feeling prepared for whatever might come next. A warm thought nuzzled at the back of his mind – he could always look down again.

He did just that as the young man glanced up from his camera and said, 'Ready?'

The photograph didn't come out immediately. The police helicopter with its upstaging whirr had been tracking an armed gang who had robbed a jeweller's. When the raiders heard the clatter of the blades, they had taken a member of the public hostage. This routine bout of criminality pushed the story of the final steps towards agreement on the Genetics Institute right off the front page, and the complication that the hostage turned out to be diabetic and in need of insulin injections bounced it right out of the news altogether. In fact, the whole episode might well have been forgotten completely, but the university enterprise team told the journalist that a new pancreas could be grown from stem cells and managed to get the photograph reinstated on a moribund news day, a couple of weeks later.

The mornings were getting lighter, and as she ran along the towpath seagulls wheeled overhead. They came inland for the spring tides, away from the storms at sea, and fed on the exposed sandbanks. Under the stress of finding nest sites and breeding, they tormented one another with their anguished cries and reminded Rhea of her sister and brother-in-law. The

193

special-care baby unit seemed a haven of enlightenment. In the adult high-dependency unit it was fraught, but here everything was kept quiet because such new-formed ears were only used to sounds under water. The tiny limbs twitched as though they remembered swimming.

The parents were traumatised. They were very young. They hardly noticed Eleanor and Rhea come into the cubicle because all their attention was focused inside the incubator with their baby. Perhaps they too were only hearing distant, liquid sound that had little to do with them and seeing shapes and colour drift incomprehensibly in and out of their view. The baby had no coverings; there was a clip on its navel, to keep the inside in.

The grandparents were volubly distressed. The grandmother had her hand across her forehead. She looked at Eleanor and gestured towards the tubes and wires, the outlandish para-phernalia that trapped her at the edge of the room. 'I wish we could pick her up. I hate to see her attached to all of this.'

'Everything we can do, we will do,' Eleanor reassured her.

They were neat, clean people. There was a smell of shoe leather and new clothes in the confined space. The baby would have a nursery at home, new stuff from a department store. The wrapping would still be around it, keeping it pristine. On the top of the incubator there was a pink rabbit; they must have known that the baby was a girl. She imagined them plucking the toy from a basket, white with a broderie-anglaise frill, and bringing it here, just as they had been plucked from the round of family visits, night feeds and laundry that they expected, and been brought to this inexplicable pass.

The grandmother looked anxiously for another opinion because all her reference points were absent when she watched a baby whose cradle was an electronic safety net. The mother came and placed her hand on the transparent plastic lid, the

194

nearest she could be to her child. Had she held her, slippery and warm, for a moment as soon as she was born, then let her go?

There was a connective tissue of tubes, colour-coded, manufactured umbilical cords; drip bags, gently deflating, replaced breasts, leaving the mother sore and estranged, but sublimely protected. Rhea looked at the monitors. Breathing, heartbeat, acid base balance, glucose and calcium levels were being monitored and held steady. There wouldn't be any convulsions to cause brain damage. The medical impedimenta held the sick baby more safely than the mother, or the grandmother, ever could.

She shuddered – it was the feeling of someone walking on your grave – when she remembered her own childhood. Her mother's self-absorption had cut a swathe through her own self-belief. And always Amber to care for, a joy and a burden, but in the end it had strengthened her.

'If we could store cord-blood stem cells after every birth, it might make a difference to a child like this,' Eleanor said.

On the way back to the fertility unit they passed the store where the fertilised eggs were kept, and Rhea couldn't help feeling she was part of a marvellous synergistic enterprise; it added up to so much more than the sum of its parts. Those cells weren't a baby, but how many wombs were waiting for a chance to make them into one? The phrase *each child a wanted child* nestled in her mind. All her years of science ended, eventually, in this compassionate engineering. She thought, It's a form of love.

When she got back to the university there was a camera crew at the gates. A television series about a diplomat's family was often filmed there; the grandiose gates stood in for a foreign embassy, only to be entered under the strictest security. A limousine swept past her. Actors in evening dress waited in the main entrance to greet the arrivals, giving it an elegance she never saw when it was occupied with staff intent on their illicit cigarettes under the canopy.

The steps up to the department were crowded with what looked like students demonstrating. At first Rhea thought they were part of the filming but there were no barriers and she began to climb through the avenue of placards. The demonstrators began to shout, but not at her. Rather, they shouted for the sake of it, and they were too close for her to hear what they bellowed from the bottom of their lungs. A placard was thrust forcefully in her way and she caught the words EMBRYO and SHAME, in yellow paint. She glimpsed Lewis at the window, waving her on. She stumbled and the concrete swooped up towards her.

At the last moment she was saved. Two separate pairs of hands held and righted her. Two faces, belonging to middle-aged women, different from the young people all around them, were close to her and looked at her, puzzled and sad. Lewis yanked the door open and pulled her inside. The women let her go but their eyes followed her. The walls of the reception area were glass and there were no blinds. The university prided itself on academic levels of transparency. The public had always been welcome to gaze at what their money was spent on. The security man turned the door key and the protesters turned to one another.

The foyer was full of people. Andrew, Featley and the dean pushed her to a chair and Lewis gave her a mug of coffee with sugar in it.

'For shock,' he said. He looked appalled. In his hand was a folded newspaper; he held it out, showing the headline: 'University in Embryo Research Breakthrough'. 'They're demonstrating against us,' he said. 'They think we're killing babies.'

The article claimed that Lewis and team had made stem cells

that could cure diabetes and explained, for the benefit of any readers without a background in advanced cell biology, that stem cells were the building blocks of the human body. Indeed, they trumpeted, we all came from stem cells in our mothers' wombs. All the activists in the readership had gathered at the university to protest at the destruction of embryos.

Amber had come in to advise on any PR issues. In fact, so many people milled about that Rhea had difficulty keeping track of them. They gave an impression of energy and importance. After all the dreary, lonely work of the last years it seemed that the world was finally taking notice of what they were doing; it was just a pity it was about blame. She didn't believe that a few cells were the same as a baby, not like the living ones she had seen. Amber, on the other hand, was in uncertain sympathy. She hovered between the dilemma of wanting to do good and not wanting to do harm. She still wasn't pregnant. The increasing depth of her disappointment gave her a shrivelled look. She had been to the edge and peered into some abyss that others couldn't imagine. With that knowledge came a particular moral status.

'I think they might have a point,' she pronounced.

Stephen Glatton listened, still fascinated by the way Amber had turned him inside out with her 'sleep-with-the-boss' insouciance. In a sort of reverse *Schadenfreude*, he was determined to take their misfortunes and make them his own. His cells, he claimed, expressed genes *like* an embryo. Could this be interpreted as questionable?

'Interpreted as what?' Lewis couldn't stand his pernickety sense of importance. 'If he's worried about the protest, why doesn't he get out there and take the flak like the rest of us?'

Glatton preferred to examine his conscience endlessly with Katherine. Even Amber was dismissive of his scruples. 'Did you get your cells from an embryo, Stephen?'

197

He looked at her with doubt, probably one of the most complex emotions he had ever experienced. 'No.'

'Then you needn't concern yourself.'

Glatton was bashing on with the array technology; it might be that his cells were ready first, their gene expression showing no trace of viral contamination, and Vic would take them for the pre-trial checks.

Amber took Rhea aside. 'Lewis might lose everything.'

Joe and Patrick spent the morning with their bicycle-lock chains hanging ready over their chairs – in case anyone broke in, they said, in offended tones, when it was mentioned.

The vice chancellor appeared on the evening news, explaining that it had all been a misunderstanding. Exciting and highly successful medical research was being undertaken at the university using adult tissue. The public could look forward to significant announcements, advances that would bring hope to the sufferers of many intractable conditions. He hinted delicately about the possibility of the stem cells being derived from the patient's own body, a perfect match, in the future.

He came up to the lab and reported to the researchers that his interview had gone well, the camera team had needed only one take, and made it sound like an admonition to Lewis for getting things wrong in the first place.

From his position of mastery the vice chancellor considered inviting the protesters into the lab but that idea was swiftly vetoed by the Media Relations Unit, which said it would only cause more trouble. Eventually he settled for a core group of journalists and a meeting in his office. It turned out that the Media Relations Unit was doubtful on this one too, citing another university's disaster on student fees when the journalists had sought out the most militant and articulate protesters and smuggled them in among their photographers.

To reinstate himself, Lewis went and phoned the hack who

had covered the meeting with the local authority and told him they didn't use embryonic tissue. He came back assuring everyone he'd explained, there had been an apology and there'd be a retraction in tomorrow's paper. There was absolutely no requirement for further communication.

The hack was on the phone first thing the next morning. 'The thing is,' he said, 'there's been a further development. Patient groups are on your side. They say that if those demonstrators had seen how some people suffer they wouldn't begrudge them their only hope of a cure.' He had the courtesy to pause, leave a few seconds for decency's sake, then added, 'Any comment?' Under orders to keep his head down, Lewis switched off the phone.

That afternoon a police adviser came and took responsibility. He toured the building, identifying the least obvious entrances, and said they were to be used. Lewis had done the right thing in not making any comment to the newspapers and that was the way it should stay. He knew these people, he assured them. They didn't cause serious trouble. Deeply held beliefs were mentioned and acknowledged sombrely. Rhea watched him closely, but she couldn't tell where his own loyalties lay. He performed his duty with a scrupulously even hand.

Joe and Patrick wound their chains back around their bicycle wheels.

The foyer was quiet after Lewis left. He had neutralised their panic, like an alkali to an acid. Water and salt were what remained. They followed his instructions. The demos went on for a week and then they came to an end. No one knew whether the protesters felt they had achieved their objectives or just got bored. Joe thought they had probably moved on to another, less circumspect, location.

On Monday morning, the newspaper sent them some flowers. They were all white, roses, gypsophila and, mainly, lilies.

The florist had taken a lot of trouble with them. All the stamens had been snipped out so the pollen couldn't stain anyone who smelt them. When Rhea put her face into the waxy petals, they stuck to her cheeks. The smell was overpowering. Lilies always seemed just the far side of immaculate, predicting their own decay.

When Caroline came in to tidy the reception desk, she said they had been left over the weekend so the water had gone off. She threw them out.

Once things had settled down, there was a discreet phone call from Warren, wanting a meeting. He'd seen all the publicity, he explained, and would like a word with them. Rhea felt he could be invited to the lab but Lewis was nervous of intruders and, in the end, Warren's busy schedule dictated the terms: he offered to buy them lunch.

He waited for them in a booth in the restaurant. He was so well hidden that Lewis and Rhea were on the point of leaving, imagining they had made a mistake about the venue, when his head poked around the dark brown partition. They slid in beside him. After the demonstrations no one wanted to be seen with them in public. A vague distrust swirled around them wherever they went. No one had quite believed the VC's rebuttal on the news: it had smacked of cover-up.

Warren had seen it and felt confused. He took an investigative sip of his lime juice; its sharpness seemed to suit him because he managed a tight-lipped smile. 'We couldn't bear anything else to happen to Polly.'

It was a bald statement and brave. How often did men admit to love? Rhea waited, aware that more would follow. 'But your spokesman said stem cells could be made from the person's own body. We'd like Polly to be part of that trial.' He was a reasonable man; he had made every allowance for Amber's infertility treatment. There was an unspoken message that he was prepared to be involved, but in a limited fashion. Warren and Amber shared an enviable pragmatism.

Back in Rhea's world, the air crawled with noise. Outside the windows, seagulls screeched as they fought over food dumped in the campus bins. Inside the room, microfuges whirred on and off, faster and more purposeful than the birds but just as noisy, and all the students were chattering and joshing, while they slapped racks on and off holders. Even ramming her earphones further in and turning up her music couldn't shut it out.

Lewis was standing over her, pushing his face into hers. 'You weren't listening,' he complained.

'Yes, I was, Lew. To something else.'

Lewis was rehoming the cells. He needed an inventory of all the stocks they held for a patent application, and no one else would do it. In the final push to get everything in place, he'd become the most dispensable person in the team and had to shoulder the most menial jobs. He opened the lid of the liquid-nitrogen freezer and vanished in a mist of condensed water vapour. When he reappeared, he was clasping a straw of cells, tiny vials gripped in a metal holder.

'Look,' he said. 'I've found some of the cells from before we had all that dishwasher trouble. Do you think we should try them?' The misplaced cells smoked with cold, so that Rhea had to peer closely to see their date.

'SA 153, from last summer.' It seemed a world away, a world that had disappeared. Was it possible they'd ever been so naïve? So innocent? She felt much older now, yet here were the cells, preserved in their primeval state. 'Put them back,' she told him. 'They'll be ruined if you keep them out in the lab like that.'

But Lewis was handling the pristine straw thoughtfully, as though he was remembering, too, a time when they'd had a single clear objective: the quest for stem-cell yield. It was straightforward, next to the juggling of public concerns and patent issues, but monochrome, compared with the kaleidoscope of new experiences tumbling around them now.

'Do you miss the lab, Lewis?'

'No.' He dropped the straw back through the neck of the freezer into the top rack. 'I wouldn't want to be stuck in here now.' The insulated stopper slotted back into place.

But the lure of patient involvement pulled Rhea on. Back in the lab there was only the creeping staleness of routine. How could she tell Lewis that her own focus on his work was slipping?

She met Eleanor for lunch in the hospital refectory, chose a hidden corner behind a pillar but with a view of the door so she could check if anyone who knew her came in and told Lewis. No one was interested in them. The room was full of staff eating lunch, their minds still on the wards, close to their responsibilities. Who knew what might happen in the next half-hour? Urgent requests got in the way of mealtimes, so food was scarcely noticed.

When Eleanor talked about something, it was impossible to imagine it wouldn't happen. The way she concentrated made what she said seem real and solid. She sat with her back to the door, not watching over Rhea's shoulder for someone more important to speak to, or looking through her as though she was transparently insignificant. A grant application lay in its official envelope on the table between them. If it was successful, then also on the table, for Rhea, there was an independent lab in the Medical School.

'The synergy's there. We should go for it. I'll tell you what, Rhea.' Eleanor folded her hands decisively. 'It's a date. This summer you and I will have lunch together somewhere nicer than this and, with any luck, we'll be celebrating getting this grant.' She glanced at the clock. A consultant's time wasn't her own. It belonged to her patients and colleagues. 'I've got a clinic. Lunch again next week?'

'Eleanor?' A week seemed a long time to Rhea. Gossip passed from the hospital to the university at the speed of light. 'I don't want to be difficult but Lewis . . . I haven't told him yet.'

Eleanor rested her hands on the table while Rhea searched for signs of disgust or distrust, but there were none: only a bland, uncommitted appraisal of the situation.

'There's no need to go public about anything yet.' Eleanor braced her weight against her square hands and stood up. 'Let's see how it goes.'

Alone, Rhea stayed at the table for a few minutes, testing her feelings about a post in the hospital. All around her bleeps were going off and people were rushing, needed elsewhere. The immediacy woke you, made you know just how alive you really were. She couldn't imagine Eleanor feeling traumatised by the sight of the infertility website. She did something about it. Gave hope or, if there wasn't any, resolution.

CHAPTER 11

Eight a.m., and two weeks into the new IVF cycle. Even this high up and this far out, day was beginning to crack the chill of the early morning. It was starting to get light outside. The sun, still low on the horizon, had given the clouds great red under-bellies that scraped along the tops of the Flinbridge hills, but the land stubbornly clung to the browns and greys of twilight. Inside the outhouse at Snitter Heugh there was a tawny morning shadow. The open door gave a fuzzy rectangle of illumination and the windows cast faint light-shadows on the workbench, but still Amber had to wait for her eyes to adjust to the uncertainty of the light.

The night before she had pulped computer paper. Early drafts of Lewis's publications, shredded, were mashed into water until they were unrecognisable, a greyish mush with a thick crust rising to the surface.

'Best place for them,' Lewis said, giving them a final prod with a stick. 'It doesn't look much for all that work, does it?' He'd be expecting her to protest, to say that everything he did was important and would fit together in the long run, but she couldn't summon the energy. Somehow there didn't seem any-thing to do but agree with him.

Even now, after a night of fathomless, dreamless sleep, Amber felt tired and heavy. The crucible gave off an odour of sourness, like a fermentation that was just beginning. She had to take a deep breath before she plunged inside the room, and when she couldn't contain it any longer and finally breathed out, the exhaled air stirred the surface of the mash; it wasn't as solid as it looked. She wanted it as smooth as possible so she probed the crust with the stick and broke it up. A quick stir made a homogeneous paste and she bent over the crucible with her mould to scoop up the mixture. It ran comfortably into the frame. She lifted it, dripping, onto the bench and began to squeeze out the water, with practised strokes. This was the fifth time she'd made paper. The other times had been practice runs; the paper had been uneven, or the colour patchy, but now she knew she could rely on her judgement, certainly for small batches. This time she needed only a few sheets, but they had to be perfect. Flat, even sheets to match the wall hanging for the infertility unit, so that one could be framed and hang in the unit with her mother's name on it.

'And your name, Amber,' Stella had insisted. '*Paper by Amber*, here at the top.' With Warren on board, she had great plans for the stem-cell publicity. The embroidery would be the centre-piece, an unborn child held safe in a pair of hands.

The dirty, organic-looking mess would dry to a clean soft colour. She'd added some dye, blue like the sky, like the line on a pregnancy test. The passes her hands were making over the sur-face of the wet paper were steady; they would mould it smooth. By the door there was a sack of thistledown, collected from her own gateway. She dried her hands to touch it so that when she brought out a handful it didn't stick to her but floated away. Snatching it back from the air, Amber pressed it down into the surface of the paper, leaving a clear space in the centre for the writing. The wispy filaments were waxy; too light to stay down, they dampened and curled. Like babies' hair, she thought, as she covered it with the fine gauze that would support it until it dried.

She bent over the crucible to scoop up the final dregs of the mash, her breasts brushing lightly against the curved edge. She winced. It had hurt much more than it should. Her whole body felt jarred and touchy. The weight of her abdomen pressed down; it seemed too heavy to bear, and the smell of the damp paper left no air to breathe. Amber went outside into the light.

The river down in the valley was full, fed by the winter's rain, and she could hear the tumult of its rush to the sea. Already Amber had learnt to tell from the sound how high up the banks it would be. The deep boom that underpinned the shift and clicking of the stony riverbed meant that it had reached the arches of the bridge in the village. It would crush, choked, through the narrow gap and wouldn't widen or soften until it got to the estuary plain where it would spread out, and wander in dozens of rivulets, half sea, half river, for three or four miles. Vikings had come up that river once, looking for people like her. They'd sailed in long flat boats up the estuary. Whenever the water had got too shallow they had put down their oars, picked up the boats and carried them, swarming right up the valley. She could see a curve of water from where she was standing, silver, like a sword must have looked. Would she have stayed to fight, or would she have run? It might not have made much difference whether you fought or hid. If you saw that glint, that dark swarm, your life would never be the same.

The dozen or so steps across the yard felt much further, like a long journey. Rather than climb up to the bathroom she sat on a hard wooden chair and looked at the staircase. Rhea had dumped yet another pregnancy testing kit in the cabinet, pushing the aromatherapy-oil bottles to the back. 'At least you'll know, one way or the other,' she said, as though that was all there was to it, a simple knowing or not knowing.

The chair had uneven legs. Amber rocked on it, to and fro.

Knowing or not knowing, not knowing or knowing. How straightforward everything was for Rhea.

Not knowing, she decided. At least you could hope. She fended off despair. There wouldn't be many more chances, Eleanor Bonworth had explained. Medical science could only do so much.

Waking that morning, Amber had felt sick. Wasn't that how it happened? You woke up, you felt sick. But it had been only a hint of queasiness, like something flickering at the edge of your vision: a tic in your eye, tiredness from a longing that wouldn't settle down. It was mid-morning. Rhea was coming at about seven. That was a whole day's work away. By then Amber could know – she could know in the next five minutes. A few drops of urine: that was all it took. She could feel pressure in her bladder, mounting into an ache. She'd left the door open and the kitchen radio was talking quietly, working its way up to the news. Amber was all alone, inside her walls. If she screeched her lungs out, no one would hear her. No colleagues, no mother, no Rhea, no Lewis would look on with pity. The relief of it was like a deluge, clean and fast. She tried out her voice, where it couldn't be heard.

'No one will know,' she said loudly. 'Only me.' At that moment the radio pipped the hour, pinning her words to the kitchen wall.

She closed and locked the outer door before climbing the stairs, tentatively stepping on each tread as though it might give way and let her down.

The kit was still at the front of the cabinet, exactly where Rhea had left it last time. Amber didn't need to read the instructions: she'd had plenty of practice. I know more about this than Rhea does, she told herself, more than Lewis. A yank at her skirt. She was still wearing the waterproof apron for papermaking and it got in the way so she took it off and let it drop to the floor. Reluctant fingers grasping her knickers, Amber closed her eyes as she pulled. When she opened them again, it was there, the splash of fresh red blood that meant no baby.

The unused pregnancy test was still on the shelf, waiting to assault her with its certainties. What use were its antibodies against the prerogative of your own body? Biology had out-manoeuvred science once again. She remembered thinking she could scream and howl as much as she wanted and no one would hear her. Again it seemed a blessing. She had bared her pain to Rhea and Lewis but they hid their feelings from her behind the pretence that science had any answers.

She reached the best decision she could. What you couldn't beat, you had to join.

Her old office hadn't changed. Warren had bought a limited-edition series of urban prints to decorate the plaster walls. The New York skyline jutted, phallic, at various points around the room. Once Amber had thought it exciting, edgy and com-pelling. Now she realised it hemmed her colleagues in. Snitter Heugh, with its community of women and their attendant men always out, working on the farm or in the city, lay serenely in wait for her, but more than ever a child seemed the passport to its mercies. Without one she would have to return to work and join the metropolitan competition again.

She was lucky: no one was at her desk. Things were almost exactly as she had left them. Obviously Warren had meant it when he had said he wanted her back. You could never be sure in PR: you often said things that were decent approximations of reality.

Warren was out, expected back soon.

'But how are you?' the others asked, their voices tinted with the other question about pregnancy, like the mood-changing hint of colour in wall paint. If she had been pregnant it would have been so different. Her old chair, as she sat down in it, was still adjusted to suit her. She was glad it hadn't been changed by a replacement, but how much better if it hadn't still fitted her. If the back support was too high, or too low – she didn't know which to expect – to accommodate the bump of a baby. But it was perfectly comfortable. Unlike her friends, who were busy and didn't have time to waste with her.

Lewis was bringing Rhea home for dinner so she couldn't wait any longer for Warren, she explained. 'Tell him I popped in about the stem-cell project,' she called, as she left.

Warren's wife, Melanie, and Polly were on their way up. They waited at the bottom of the stairs, so she had a foreshortened view of the tops of their heads, Polly's soft brown curls and Melanie's bob. It must have given her a mistaken impression of how tall Polly was because she greeted her as a girl friend.

'Polly, darling,' she heard herself gush, and kissed her.

Polly flinched with embarrassment and turned to her mother in disgust. 'Who is that?'

Amber couldn't believe she had made such an exhibition of herself. To cover the awkwardness she said, 'I brought these for you.' She gave her a packet of Love Hearts, which she had meant to send to her with Warren. Once again Polly looked at her mother for guidance and Amber was made to accept how little she knew about children. Was thirteen too young or too old for Love Hearts? Melanie looked dismayed, as though she thought Polly both too young and too old to be exposed to such a degree of need. Her thin veneer of a smile had already dropped away and her eyes turned upwards towards the safety of the office.

'He's not in,' Amber said, and watched Melanie's discomfiture, and her own cruelty, with shameful malice. Polly led the way up. Step by slow step she brought her feet together and put distance between herself and the lunatic trying to entice her with sweets and kisses.

She's her mother's daughter, Amber thought, then wondered why she was surprised at that. Polly *was* Melanie's daughter, nothing to do with herself. A slow mud slide of despair threatened to engulf her, a feeling that without a child of her own she might go mad.

Katherine wanted Rhea to help her interpret the gel traces she had made from Rhea's cloned cells. She was bent over the light-box where the fluorescent tubes were throwing the light and dark lines into high contrast. Katherine had a good pair of hands and her work was always clean. The series of bands stood sharp and clear, although they had been through so many processes. Weeks it would have taken her to grow her cells, separate the membranes from the cytoplasm, and then separate the markers that made each of the cell types unique, but there was no blurring of the dozens of bands. They had remained distinct, their message intact.

'Have you shown them to Lewis?' Rhea asked, and got a decisive shake of the head.

'No, he hasn't time.'

They settled down together, the bar codes of lines for the test cells on one side, the control stem cells on the other. Rhea checked the intricate pattern to and fro, Katherine marking down the reference values. The two sides fitted neatly together: five, five; nine, nine; eleven, eleven. At least the traces weren't giving any problems; Rhea managed a smile in Katherine's direction and saw the twitch of excitement that pulled at her mouth. Katherine had worked hard to get these results out; she was hanging closely on Rhea's counting, but her face kept turning towards the door. She wanted Lewis to have a look at them. Second-best Rhea could see it in the scrawl of disappointment over Katherine's neat face when he didn't appear, but she went on reading steadily across the dense bands, moving her finger down the ladder, drawing Katherine with her.

By the time she was halfway down the patterns she had forgotten Katherine's disappointment and focused all her attention on the work. The hankering for symmetry, the matching of the pattern that showed both samples were stem cells was there, right down the run. She might have envied Eleanor her knowledge of fertility, but this was where Rhea's own expertise lay. She was going to have to upset Katherine. These results were far too good to be true.

Katherine radiated excitement. She held herself so still now that Rhea could feel the tension coming from her. She gave her most sympathetic smile into Katherine's coming disappointment. 'Kate, can you remember which cells you used ?'

Katherine shot her an angry look of disbelief. A sour reminder to Rhea of all the effort each experiment took.

'You must have used duplicate lots of the same cells. You'd better do them again,' she said, adding, 'Make sure you check the labels on the cultures.'

She didn't mean to tell Lewis about Kate's mistake when they were driving back to Snitter Heugh that evening. She'd meant to keep him out of it.

The weather was just on the turn. It was lighter in the evenings now; the convertible felt like a transparent bubble gliding across the countryside, instead of the darkly armoured capsule it had seemed on winter nights. Lewis was concentrating on manoeuvring round the tricky bends he negotiated every day of his life.

'The thing is, Rhea, we can't publish any of your stuff, not until the patent application's in. Next year, maybe.'

There was a pause, like the moment between a detonation and a building falling down.

'Christ's sake, Lewis. You never said it would take that long.'

Without a couple of decent publications from her current project, Rhea would never get her own funding. Never mind that she hadn't told Lewis she wanted some. His eyes flickered away from the road and towards her, his face exposed, the cover torn off.

The soft leather seats kept up their steady embrace. You could hardly feel that the car was moving at all.

He'd wrecked her chances of setting up her own team. The thought took up Rhea's entire mind. Lewis had kept everything to himself. She wouldn't be able to capitalise on any of the work she had done for him. 'You should have told me.'

'I'm telling you now. We're really on to something.'

His knuckles relaxed their white grip on the steering wheel. The car still went sanguinely on, as did Lewis. 'If we can get a decent patent, it'll be the making of all of us.'

The form for the Medical Research Council was tucked into her briefcase in the back of the car. Rhea thought of Eleanor and held her head steady now, fixed on the thought of independence. The run of Lewis's success couldn't pull her so easily off course. 'It'll be the making of you, Lewis, but I really need some publications.' She hesitated. 'My career can't afford two years in a row without anything.'

'Oh, don't worry.' The airy confidence of her success with the cloning made Lewis unsympathetic. 'If this pans out, there'll be plenty of money to keep paying everyone. Perhaps we won't even need paying.' Rhea raised her eyebrows. 'Under my university contract, I'll be entitled to a decent proportion of any patent income,' he explained. But he didn't explain how this would help Rhea.

She stayed quiet, pretending a calm thoughtfulness she wasn't feeling. She looked away from Lewis and out of the window. She ought to tell him straight, but there wasn't anything definite to say. They were driving up the coastal plain.

Great flat fields stretched away to either side, but the horizons were closing in on her.

Lewis put out feelers. 'We're almost there. Don't give up now.'

'No.' But her voice was already trailing off into complicity. With so many disappointments and dupings of her own behind her, it wouldn't take much to persuade her and she knew it.

'This morning . . .' she'd started. There was no stopping it now. '. . . Katherine thought we'd done it.' And she told Lewis what she had meant to keep to herself.

They were still talking about Katherine's mistake when they got home. The diversion made them falsely cheerful.

'We've all been there,' joked Lewis.

'We're probably still there,' said Rhea. 'We've just got better at covering it up.' She laughed as she said it.

'If only Kath had had it right,' Lewis said.

As they got out of the car, wind caught the door and slammed it, just as Lewis pressed the lock. The rear door stayed closed as Rhea tugged at it. They both looked through the window at their workbags in the well of the back seat.

'Leave them,' Rhea said. 'We won't get any more work done tonight. Amber won't let us.'

'Go on in.' Lewis's key released the door with a twitch of his thumb. 'I'll get them.'

For just a fraction of a moment Rhea caught his eyes over the roof of the car. She looked away, wary with complications. Papers from Eleanor pushed between her own. She could feel guilt mottling her skin. But Lewis wouldn't open her bag, would he? He leant into the recess, his back twisting awkwardly. 'I'll see to yours,' he called, into the enclosed space, so she went up to the house.

There was no need to ring the bell: the door wasn't locked. The kitchen was chilled, invigorating, as though the windows

213

were open and a sharp breeze had blown through, but it wasn't dishevelled. In fact, it was especially tidy, and Amber was wafting her hairdrier about, drying paper.

'You're late,' said Amber, probably auditioning for the role of put-on wife.

'It's me, not Lewis.'

'I know that. Lewis would have closed the door.'

She spoke as though Lewis was always closing doors, closing them on her. There was something about the set of her turned back that stopped Rhea trying to pass it off as a joke. Instead she all but closed the door in Lewis's face.

He dumped Rhea's bag at her feet and headed off to the study with his own, leaving the door swinging on its hinges. Rhea closed it with particular care and avoided Amber's eyes. She was tired and hungry. Lunch with Eleanor seemed to have happened to somebody else. She wondered what Amber had planned for dinner when she realised she couldn't smell cooking. She couldn't see any evidence of preparation either: no pans or peelings, only the sheets of paper, spread out, resolutely occupying the benches.

'I bet you're tired. I know I am. Maybe we could eat out.'

At last Amber turned around. 'I wouldn't mind. I'm not really hungry, but I don't fancy staying in.' Her hands and eyes were steady; Rhea wouldn't have known that anything was truly wrong if she hadn't looked at her mouth, the way it worked around words like 'mind' and 'not', as though they were stuck to her tongue. She's upset, Rhea thought. Things didn't show much on Amber, through the expert makeup, but the blusher on her cheeks stood out, lividly normal, at odds with her pallor.

Lewis was back, reading the paper, oblivious, but Rhea could feel the strain mounting in her sister. Outbursts were only a wrong word away.

Rhea tried to swing her mind round to the right words. What would Eleanor say?

'Are you going to tell Amber about the patent, Lewis, or shall I?'

Lewis shrugged uncomprehendingly, as though he had never heard of patents.

'Come on,' Rhea urged. 'She has the right to know.'

Still Lewis was silent. The two women looked down at him, while he glanced from one to the other. Rhea couldn't bear the tension. She turned to her sister. 'Lewis thinks if we can get a patent on some of the work, it could make a lot of money.' As she said it she became aware of that word, *we*. With Amber relying on her, she'd felt part of it again. She drew Amber close to her. 'Perhaps it'll pay for your renovations.'

At the mention of renovations Lewis joined in. 'If it goes well, you'll be able to have anything you want done.' 'Anything you want' sounded a bit much to expect. 'Why don't we treat ourselves to a takeaway?'

At the idea of a takeaway, Amber perked up. Yes, Lewis would run down to the village for it. He got up without a word and memorised the order: chicken tikka masala, Bombay potatoes, vegetable *saag*, *dahl* and, for Amber, poppadums; she couldn't eat a curry without a dry, crisp poppadum.

It was almost dark, but remnants of daylight reflected from the clouds so that Rhea could see Lewis walk to the car, turn and look back at the house. She waved, then Amber switched on the lights and Rhea caught sight of herself in the window, her brow furrowed with lines of anxiety. The night-time shuffles of the house settling itself against the cold paused for a moment, as if it held its breath, but Amber couldn't keep still.

She blundered around, as though she couldn't get out of her own way. And Rhea couldn't get out of Amber's way. She hadn't brought her car and would have to stay at Snitter Heugh. Amber pushed aside her paper to make room for the supper plates. The sheets were thick and smooth but they were still damp and clung to one against another. Rhea ran her fingers over them. They felt like fabric. Their mother shone through Amber's skin.

'So, there's no one special at the minute, Rhea? You've only got yourself to please.' Amber smiled, as if she'd known all along. She stopped sorting plates. Lewis had disappeared for her. Rhea sensed it, and felt the force of her interest. 'There'll be someone else,' Amber went on. 'You'll see, Rhea. You can't keep yourself safe for ever.' Then she sat down, suddenly tired, as if she didn't have the strength to stand for what she was going to say next. Rhea winced at some pain to come.

'The IVF hasn't worked again.' But this time Amber didn't cry. There was no flooding of tears and grief to wear her out. It was so quiet that the noise of a passing car made them both glance towards the door.

Rhea sat down and touched her sister's arm. 'I'm sorry.' The website kept popping up in her mind, confusing sympathy and guilt. She should have searched it more thoroughly. It might have given her some idea of what to say, some advice on how to help her. An irrefutable acceptance came over her. She realised she was a part of this, not an outsider.

'Rhea, I've been thinking.' Amber was watching the door again; she must be waiting for Lewis to get back.

'Have you told Lewis?' Rhea said as Amber said, 'I haven't told Lewis,' and there they were, both thinking like one person, the two little girls they used to be.

'You'll always have me,' Rhea said.

Amber shifted back to look her in the eye. 'You know that I can only have one more try, Eleanor says.' The idea of Eleanor was like a lifesaver. The way she bobbed up to rescue them. Her bouncing cheerfulness, the unremitting effort, was like a stiff drink.

'She's marvellous,' Rhea said. 'If anyone can do it, she can.'

'Would you do something for me, Rhea? Just now, while you don't have anyone else to worry about?'

Rhea put her arm around her sister's shoulders. They would get through this together. In a way, there was no need to involve Lewis: let him concentrate on work. She drew Amber close to her. 'We'll get through this, I promise.'

'There was something I wanted to talk to you about. I haven't told anyone.'

'What is it, Ambie?' How easily the baby name slipped out, like the days when Rhea had cared for Amber, hidden her away from the upset while their mother had nursed their father.

'You said you'd help me.'

'You know I will.' The thought of the grant application with Eleanor wrapped around Rhea. She might tell Amber; just the two of them would know; there was a space between the sisters where Lewis had no access.

'You could do it, Rhea. You could help me.'

As Rhea waited, Amber put her hands to her mouth, holding her words in, but they slid through her fingers to find their way out and hovered in the grey space between trepidation and confidence. When she let them fall her smile was terrifying.

'You know surrogacy? When someone else has your baby for you?'

Apprehension squeezed Rhea's chest, stopping her breath, but her words came hurtling along ahead of her thoughts. 'No. No, Amber.'

'What?'

'No.'

'Rhea . . .'

'Eleanor would never have anything to do with that.'

The smell of shock, acrid and sulphurous, as though an electric current had jumped the gap between them.

'You're not yourself, Amber.' Rhea could scarcely recognise her own voice, it was so weak with fear. Desperation bled out of every pore; she knew what was coming next. 'Don't ask me. I can't do that.'

But Amber was insensible to her revulsion; she wasn't even seeing her. Enthralled by her own compulsion, she saw only a mirror of herself everywhere. She radiated eagerness, conviction. 'Loads of people do it, Rhea, loads of them. They do, you know. They do.' Amber clutched Rhea's arm. She was saying, 'Sisters do. Of course they do. How could they not? Look at these.'

Amber rushed to the bookcase. From under the haphazard collection of files she drew out an envelope. Whatever it was, she had been saving it. She began by taking out just one sheet and laying it on the sofa in the space between them, a picture of two women, both young, both black-haired, with the startling blue eyes that occasionally come with such dark colouring, both looking at a baby that was suspended, as if by magic, between them. The baby had those same bright blue eyes, although it had no hair. Then Amber was slapping down another picture and another: all sorts of women, all sorts of babies, in a sort of desperate parade of maternity.

'They're all sisters who've helped each other,' she said. 'I got them from the net.'

At the bottom of each picture there was a web address, and a promise of sororal happiness. Amber's face shone with it.

Inside Rhea, a cold feeling was spreading, a freezing mist that hid her from herself and held her steady. She was afraid to let herself know what she felt – it reached too deep for her to fathom it. Amber's words held her in a pincer, *my* body, *her* baby.

But a jolt of realisation spun her round. This would be Lewis's baby too. Those eggs in their Petri dishes had been fertilised by Lewis's sperm. Not just a sharing of sisterly flesh, bodies that had come from the same womb, this would be Lewis's baby too. His flesh would invade her and drain the life-blood from her.

'I can't, Amber. I can't.'

But it was as if Amber couldn't believe her. 'You just need to get used to the idea. I thought it was weird at first, but once I'd thought it through . . .' Her confidence was impenetrable. 'It's only natural, Rhea.'

Rhea wrenched away. 'You shouldn't ask me, Amber. It isn't fair.' She tried to glare her sister away, but Amber came forward again.

'You're brave enough for anything. I know you, Rhea.'

But you don't know me, Rhea thought, struggling out of Amber's grip and staring out of the window. You think I can make everything all right? You don't have any idea what I had to do, because I couldn't go running to you to sort it.

The memory of another baby exploded through her.

When she turned back Amber was still watching her, oblivious to anything but getting her way.

Seeing her hold out her hands, Rhea was blinded by a searing flash of anger. Then in another moment she watched herself screaming at Amber to drop that shackle of a smile. She shook her sister and pummelled the soft wool of Amber's sweater scrunching under her hands as she dug for flesh, wanting to draw blood.

Engulfed with horror, suffocated by it, she threw Amber across the room so that her sister's head crashed against the cooker. She leapt back, away from the awful sight, and there was Amber, still sitting on the sofa, still holding out her hands.

It couldn't have happened.

Sweat prickled up through Rhea's hair; her legs shook. Her whole body quaked.

But her body had saved her. While her mind had torn her

sister apart, her body had stayed still, more to be trusted than she could have believed. The adrenalin surge hadn't left her yet: her muscles trembled with the trauma of what she hadn't done.

Still, Amber was defeated. She lowered her hands in a gesture of submission.

Rhea was in agony. She was terrified. She looked back at the darkness outside the window. How had it sprayed into the room like that? Was there a parallel universe out there, nearer than she could ever imagine, in which some other Rhea had really done that to Amber?

The lights of Lewis's car wobbled up the track. Now Amber was frightened too. She watched the door nervously. 'Rhea, don't say anything to him. Promise you won't tell him.' She came too close.

Rhea flinched away. She could only nod, too grateful to mind that Amber wanted her scheming kept secret, too shocked to trust herself to say anything. *I don't even know myself.* The hideous knowledge twisted round and round in her head.

CHAPTER 12

The warmth of the vial containing the cells, even though it was already at $-70°C$, made the liquid nitrogen crackle and fizz. The freezer was shaped like a futuristic amphora. A dense mist erupted from it and obscured the narrow opening, so that Rhea lowered the straw of cells by experience; she could scarcely see through her safety mask and the fog of frozen water vapour. She dropped the stopper into place, clumsily because of her thick gloves, and knew it had gone home when she heard the faint squeak of polystyrene on frozen metal.

Shaking her hands free of the gloves, she pulled up her visor and saw the last of the fog dissipate. Her breath was condensing in the air because the laboratory was so cold. She turned towards Lewis's office. There was no sign of him.

When she removed the safety helmet she could hear the throb of the condensers pounding to cool the air. They were running at the same speed as her heartbeat, a mirror image of the warmth underneath her white coat. If she stood still she could feel the matching throb of her pulse in her chest and neck, and even in her wrists, where it was lighter and threatening to flutter. She passed through into the culture suite. That was better. The culture suite was kept warm, womb-like, with no windows, and damp from the humidifiers in the cell incubators. Racks of bottles containing cell cultures exchanged gases with the atmosphere, turning from violent pink to yellow as the metabolic processes changed the medium from acidic to alkaline. Rhea took out the alkaline ones and began to check the condition of the cultures.

The phase contrast in the microscope adjusted reality. The cells she was checking were free-floating. They glowed orange and gold under the magnification: sunny spheres, looking healthy and benign, but that was only a property of the optical system. They drifted in and out of focus. A few groups of cells were still attached together after they had divided. Even as Rhea watched, the haloes around them coalesced, making them seem to float in an eerie bath of light. She bumped the microscope, and the cells spun away out of focus.

Her field of vision was left empty. It blurred before she could blink to disperse the tears that had started up from nowhere. Now her throat was constricting. She swallowed once, twice, in an effort to free the muscles. They must have constricted the internal carotid artery because she felt faint. She put her head down to relieve the dizziness, her hair falling around her face and shutting out the laboratory, the incubators and the waiting work. She hugged herself. She rocked and more tears welled up and spilt out of her, wetting her clothes, splashing onto the floor, but she was perfectly silent. Through all of this she could hear the quiet click and tick of the incubators switching on their warmth and the carbon dioxide that sustained all the cellular life around her.

Rhea knew that until now all those things had protected her from what was happening to her. Alone behind the curtain of her hair, she couldn't distract herself any longer: her mind turned to the termination she had arranged after Dave had left for Nottingham. When she had woken afterwards, she hadn't been sure she wasn't still waiting because she'd felt no different. There'd been a nurse hovering over her.

'Is it over?' Rhea had asked. 'Is it done?'

'Yes,' the nurse had answered. Hesitating and pretending to smooth the sheets, she'd added, 'It's all right if you cry. Most people do.' But Rhea had turned her head and set her lips so that no crying could possibly take place. The nurse had nodded kindly and left her alone to concentrate painstakingly on a mental diagram of the DNA helix. The multitude of genes that made it up registered separately in her mind as precious. Those same genes would appear not just in her and Dave but in other children all over the world. A sense of the connectedness of the universe engulfed and filled her mind with the thought that the soul that had accidentally lodged inside her had spun helter-skelter through the coils of its genes to freedom. 'Go to Amber,' she had whispered, and it had frolicked away to find its real home.

She was overwhelmed now in a way she hadn't been until then.

The parts of her didn't fit together any longer; some had changed shape; the others were thrown out of kilter. The room was cavernous around her. Usually Rhea liked to work, when it was quiet, but tonight she couldn't fill the empty space. Everyone else had left an hour ago; there was nothing left but to go home too. She returned the cell cultures to the incubator, turned off the microscope, checked the equipment and switched off the lights, the familiarity of the routine pacifying her body. She looked towards Lewis's office again. She hadn't seen him go and the light was still on, as though it was ready for him to come back. She left it to keep watch.

And all this took place alongside fear. Amber hadn't mentioned the surrogacy idea again. Don't let her ask me, Rhea prayed to some undefined Fate. I can't bear any more.

As she walked home the chestnut trees were in full leaf, their resolute green catching the last of the light. It was late spring and she could smell it, the undertone of stirring earth, disturbed by the movement of roots and thrusting foliage.

If Amber hadn't mentioned surrogacy again, it was because she was preoccupied by her final round of IVF, her expression determined, as if she could force a child into existence. *Even if she asks me again, I won't tell her about the termination,* Rhea vowed. She hadn't told anyone. Out of humiliation, she hadn't told Dave, but it was out of love that she hadn't told Amber.

Rhea had gone to the clinic alone, walked all the way, then watched other women being shepherded by mothers and sisters, only a few by boyfriends or husbands. She had felt relieved to take an anonymous taxi home.

I won't tell anyone now. But Amber's demand, her raised eyebrows and the set of her mouth, the expectation that she could use her sister's womb meant the edges of Rhea were fraying. She was tired, and her feet felt heavy as she walked. It seemed difficult to keep everything inside.

People said there wasn't any real friendship between men and women, that there was always a bedrock of sex in a platonic relationship, but she hadn't believed them. She and Lewis had been such loose, easy companions while she studied for her doctorate, linked by work and the lack of demands that their friendship involved. She'd been pleased when he'd met her sister, as though she had given them to one another. She had looked for it, idly, but hadn't found any reluctance to leave for the States. It was to be the start of her own life, Amber grown up, Lewis with his new wife. If there was a mystery it was in her return: the need to share with them all she had learnt while she was away, so that there would have been a point to it.

She counted her steps as she walked home, so she wouldn't think, and once inside the flat, she lay on the bed. Rather than know just how alone she was, she fell asleep.

The doorbell woke her. She knew where she was; she'd begun to pull herself together. The bedside clock said ten fifteen. By its light, she could see her reflection in the bedroom mirror; she monitored the dark circles under her eyes, the way the red had receded from the lids. I only look tired, she reassured herself. I'll be all right. The bell rang again so she pressed the intercom.

'It's Lewis. Let me in, Rhea.'

Lewis must have taken the steps three at a time, he was up the stairs so quickly. She only had time to wipe a moisturised tissue across her face. But it had a good clean smell and, automatically, she smiled as she opened the door. If Lewis noticed she was upset, he didn't show it. He barged forward, his glance flicking straight to the table where there was a pile of folders.

'They've finished our pictures. Just wait until you see these.' He groped in his inside pocket, where most men kept their wallet. He flung an envelope down, then grabbed it again as soon as it touched the table, his hands trembling. He began pulling out some photographs. The stiff paper caught on the flimsy envelope and tore it; Lewis swore softly. He didn't often swear. He slapped the photographs face down on the table; she recoiled as though the slap had been for her.

Amber had sent him to plead with her, armed with more photographs of surrogate mothers. And these weren't downloads from the net: they were real photographs of people Amber knew. Rhea's thoughts raced on. Amber had joined a support group: that would be just like her – she couldn't do anything by herself. She had to have a whole crowd of accomplices, whatever she was doing. The room seemed full of babies, they were packing the air all round her. She had to duck to escape them. The torn envelope fluttered to the floor; she and Lewis bent to retrieve it at the same moment.

'I came straight over to show you.' Lewis was back to the

photographs. He was pushing them forward right into her face, too near for her to focus.

'Lewis!' She was gasping, swatting them away.

'Rhea, it's fine. The SA 153s, they all stack up. They're ninety-five per cent pure. Katherine was right. We've done it.' He grasped the hair at the nape of her neck and held her head steady so that the photos hovered into view. Coloured electron micrographs. 'I've just got them back from the Electron Microscope unit.'

Rhea peered down as Lewis spread them out. She grasped at the table edge to steady her hands, flexing her fingers before she spoke. The photographs floated and swayed in front of her. She closed her eyes briefly, blocking out the image of those babies attacking, like a swarm of bees.

'Open your eyes, Rhea,' Lewis said. 'Look at them with me.'

He pulled out a chair and sat her down, pulled out another for himself. Together they picked up the proofs.

Gold-labelled antibodies clung to the surface of all the SA 153 cells, clustered around them, gleaming out of the photographs like uncovered crowns or precious torques. And all the other cells were bare, unburnished.

Only stem cells could sequester those antibodies and they were looking at the visual evidence, magnified a quarter of a million times.

Lewis put his hand over Rhea's, stilling its tremble. He bit his lip, like a child, and waited for her to say something to him. The photographs shone on in the quiet light, and Rhea let her gaze wander back to them. She let go of the panic she had felt. Fear changed places with relief. The air seemed irreproachable then, as though isinglass had passed through it and cleaned away all the impurities. Everything stood out clearly, bright-edged, sharp and true. A great and profound gratitude overcame her. It turned her weak.

'Oh, Lewis.' She could see the same salvation in him; the same dissolving of a rigid desperation. The same tears started in his eyes.

'Thank God.' They kissed.

When Dave had left, he had propped his shaving mirror by the basin, then forgotten to pack it. Rhea, shocked into tears, had stumbled into the bathroom, uncomprehending, and had seen herself, contorted and ugly, her humiliation magnified. She'd seen it again, creeping quietly home from the clinic. Hands and lips trembling, she had dropped it into the bin. She'd had no strength left to break it, to throw it at a wall and destroy it, so she'd picked it up, opened the cupboard door and, leaning on the unit for support, had let it fall into the rubbish. It had settled face up, still looking back at her, reflecting her hands and the length of her arms, so she'd closed her eyes and held her breath while she dropped in a pile of paper to cover it.

Ever since, Rhea had showered with her eyes closed. She would feel the soap around her body, inch by cleansing inch. She knew the knotty snags of her ribs under her breasts and the once strong – softening now – curve of her thigh where it met the pelvis. She could remember, in the slippery sweeps of her hands, the corrugated bones of her shins, the crannies of her toes and their blunt-cut nails.

Now she felt her own body through Lewis's fingertips. Her thoughts were Lewis's thoughts. That was how close they were. His moans were the ones she made herself, his eyes looked for her, sending her visions she didn't need to turn from.

This is me, this thinness, this transparency, the lightly worn sheen of warmth, as fine as gossamer, she thought. Lewis lay on her as lightly as she lay on him. The same person. Breath came easily now, deep and steady. It might always be so.

Lewis was lying by her side when Rhea woke: on his back,

his eyes open but his expression like that of a man deeply asleep. She was familiar with the vague ache deep in her pelvis, an odd comfort. She had often felt it after sex with Dave, the forewarning of the consequences: she was going to get cystitis. A white tidemark had appeared on the sheet: salt chromatographed from sweat. The steely taste of the cranberry juice, the changing of the linen, all the familiar post-coital paraphernalia: how extraordinary it ought to be; how bewilderingly ordinary it actually was.

The pulse in her neck throbbed blood to her brain, pumping up pictures of Amber. Rhea knew she should feel odious, sordid, but she didn't. She only felt dazzled: a blizzard had obscured the universe. And what did Amber need her for? To be protected against what? She had played the baby, had had to be pampered all her life. A sigh escaped Rhea and disorganised the light from the door. Dust motes spun on themselves, tiny recollections, glinting recklessly through the years: the times that Amber had cringed behind, refusing her share of the blame for some misdemeanour; her way of prancing forward when visitors arrived, rooting out kisses and endearments, planting her promises of future returns.

The sharp edges of reality softened into the ungraspable curves of dreams. And the reality that was Amber seemed a long way off. What Rhea felt now was peace, that some fearful trial had come to an end, that a difficult and onerous quest had been completed. The bedroom mirror reflected the sky through the window, and the window reflected the mirror and its sky. Backwards and forwards the light must be travelling, in precise lines, with a vagueness at the margin that took the hard edge off everything. If she sat up, she knew, because she'd done it many times before, that she would see the city lights, the spine roads radiating out towards the suburbs, but she lay very still, unable to disturb the calm that not seeing them brought. She held her breath, so that even that movement wouldn't disturb Lewis and jolt him out of his reverie. But perhaps that alerted him. He touched her, unfalteringly now, with the fingers that had felt like her own, but they were stronger, surer. They belonged truly to him. He interlocked them with hers.

'There'd be nothing without you. You know that, don't you?' His voice was thick and hot.

All the things Rhea knew became nebulous inside her. They lost their edges and blurred together. Without smiling, she gazed at Lewis. He kissed her.

'I'd better get home.' He was apologetic; there was sheepishness in his urgent buttoning and tying himself back together; he went into the living room. Rhea followed him, draping her dressing-gown around herself. Her skin was damp where she had lain next to him, the heat picking up between them. The central heating had been left on, as it wasn't supposed to be when you were in bed. A shiver took hold of her as she realised she was damp with Lewis's sweat and her own, mixed together. It made the fabric cling to her, so that she had to drag it around herself.

Lewis was gathering up the photographs, stuffing them into his pocket, preparing to leave.

'Will you tell Amber?' Rhea asked.

'There's no point,' he answered. 'She never understands anything about work.'

CHAPTER 13

Amber had borne the winter with its eternal winds and sharp frosts, but the confusion of early-summer rain and sun and unexpected chills made her falter. Driving to the clinic, she saw fronds of new bracken, uncurled across the moors like embryos, all head with their vestigial tails budding into bodies. Or they might have been question marks, thousands of them, all asking the same question. Amber was afraid of the answer. Because there was always room for deception, even if it meant deceiving yourself.

The staff wore green scrubs and, to give an impression of homeliness, white paper head coverings softened by printed sprigs of flowers. Nurses came straggling out of the treatment room, where they must have been making babies, with the same warm nonchalance that the village women had when they were baking. Last one out was Eleanor's registrar, a worried-looking woman, thin with nerves. Thank God Eleanor will see me herself, Amber thought. She could trust Eleanor to tell her the truth. Even so, she was panicky with doubt. The backs of her legs stuck to the plastic seat. Amber longed for clinic appointments and dreaded them.

She was sharing the waiting area with a shamefaced young couple, applying themselves assiduously to the faded hospital magazines. They hardly looked old enough to have put in the requisite two years of fruitless sex before you warranted infertility investigation. They ought to be enjoying themselves, not going through this meat machine. The girl put aside her reading and cautiously raised her eyes, as if sensing someone was thinking about her. Once she'd moved, the lad put his magazine down too, and then they waited, sitting side by side, forlornly gazing ahead into the indignities to come.

'Not long now,' the girl reassured her partner, just as the nervous registrar called their names, and they trotted off, guiding each other forward. The door closed behind them and Amber was left alone.

When she and Lewis had first come to the clinic, Lewis had mounted a campaign. He had burst through that same door, all businesslike effectiveness, primed to the gills with technical expertise. He had analysed the entire system of infertility investigation, first on the Internet and then in the university library. He knew more about it than the rookie doctor. Amber had seen her flounder in his tidal wave of technicalities. After that, the consultant had always dealt with their case, just as Lewis had intended. He hadn't known Eleanor then, of course. She'd been a stranger: stronger and more confident than her registrar. Eleanor openly enjoyed informing the assertive young chancer that, actually, she would be carrying out the primary investigations into him. Men were so much more straightforward, she'd said. So much easier, and cheaper – she had enjoyed emphasising the cost – than women. So it had been Lewis's turn first. But how intractable men's problems could prove. Eleanor had sighed deeply at the thought of what she might have to find out about Lewis. He would have to provide a sample, she'd explained. 'If you could give it to Nurse Evans.'

Lewis had looked so sick that Amber didn't press for the details, but that evening, on the phone, Rhea had been scientifically exact. The magazines in Reception weren't the only ones, she laughed, and made Amber laugh too, in spite of herself. Lewis wouldn't get any special consideration.

'And Nurse Evans, I wonder what she's like.'

They hadn't been able to decide whether they hoped Nurse Evans would be a dragon or a siren. Either would be awful for Lewis.

He had seemed quite subdued when he came home. The day that he and Amber had attended the clinic to get the result, Lewis had taken his briefcase with him, packed with the same sort of care that he displayed when he was off on a journey. He'd gone into the consulting room his face a blank, but he had come out beaming. He had been pronounced Grade A. The little devils were teeming everywhere, thrashing and swimming about like good 'uns. Not so little either, big ones, packing a massive punch of first-class genetic impetus.

Giddy with deliverance, he'd shown off shamelessly. They stood in silence on opposite sides of the lift, separated. For the first time Amber had felt that they weren't equal partners in this enterprise and now more of it seemed to be tipping in her direction. Through the prickly hospital garden and right out of the gate, the tests had released Lewis back into the land of the functional. Not only that, they had awarded him a certificate of merit, while she had still to bear the brunt of the unknown. He'd careered off down the path, back to work, pumped up with testosterone, leaving her to make her own way back to the office and to wonder what, exactly, Lewis's shock-troop sperm count meant to her.

But Rachel Fenbridgeter had the answer. Sitting close together in her tiny office, they had exchanged frank, unflinching words. Finally Amber had understood everything. Rachel wasn't like Rhea: she didn't blank you with her knowledge, talking for herself as though you weren't there. Where Rhea was black and white, Rachel was sable and ivory, linked by subtle shades of grey. 'It's never all or nothing,' Rachel had explained. 'If one gene isn't working, well, there are others that might take up the slack. And,' she'd gone on, inclining her head confidentially, 'sometimes we don't find anything unusual. Now and then – there's no knowing why – the chemistry between two people just doesn't work.' The idea of faulty chemistry lingered in Amber's mind like the laboratory smell Lewis didn't have any more.

She'd made the appointment and come by herself today. Rachel Fenbridgeter was on holiday and Amber had handed her urine sample to Nurse Evans with a miserable feeling of dislocation. Rachel was her person: with her there, she felt protected. She searched her body for some conniving sign of change, flexing her shoulders, manoeuvring her breasts so that they moved against the underwiring of her bra. Once, before all this disappointment, that would have made them tingle anyway, but not now. So much treatment had taken the edge off her feelings. At least the new regime had brought her back to some normality. It was almost a relief to feel ordinary; she had teetered on the edge, felt treacherously almost pregnant, for so long. The young couple was still cloistered; it must be their first appointment. They would be having the process explained to them in careful detail, having their hopes kept strictly within the prescribed limits.

'Mrs Norham, would you step in, please?'

Nurse Evans sat down behind Amber, leaving the floor to the consultant. Eleanor was out of scrubs now, wearing a blue shirt, looking like an ordinary, middle-aged housewife, and scanning Amber's notes. She looked up in surprise, past Amber to the nurse. Amber twisted in her chair to see what Nurse Evans was up to. The woman must have indicated something because Eleanor broke into a smile.

'Well,' she said, 'a positive test.'

A positive test? Amber's tongue was poised between her teeth, but she couldn't speak. Eleanor leant forward, raised her eyebrows in encouragement. Amber said nothing. She knew that Eleanor was skilled at handling her patients. She would wait for Amber to take it in, leaving a space into which the patient could throw out all the years of sadness, the memories of those leaking spots of blood that carried your hopes with them. Eleanor deserved this moment: she had earned it; she was expecting it. But Amber had lived too long with the unbridgeable gap between longing and reality. She stayed high and dry as the silence stretched around her.

'You're pregnant, Amber. You realise that, don't you?' But Amber couldn't believe it. Hope and fear cavorted together, taunting her.

'But it's only a test, isn't it?' There, she had said it: the awful unreality of everything that was happening, this trick of technology. Eleanor's face lost the glaze of understanding. It was washed away by concern. Amber could see her own doubt infecting that calm assurance: Eleanor was unnerved too, but she was quick to hide it.

'The tests are very reliable. We have every confidence in them.' She emphasised her confidence by closing her notes, drawing a line under the long effort.

Amber kept her gaze off the new nurse. Rachel, with her quick understanding, would have been sitting up with Eleanor, drawing her on.

'I was bleeding,' she said, 'a couple of weeks ago. Only a few spots. I did wonder.' It was out in the open. Eleanor reopened her file.

'Only a few spots? It's not so unusual, you know. I'll tell you what, if you pop next door on the couch, I'll have a quick look. Nothing to worry about, Amber.'

The nurse had the reluctant Amber popped onto the couch

in no time, unwrapped and laid out on the stiff paper roll for inspection. But Eleanor's hands weren't in any hurry. She must have done this so many times before, it seemed as though her fingers could brush as lightly as the thistledown yet still feel straight through skin and muscle and bone. Yes, she said, the womb would still be closed within the pelvic cavity at this stage, nothing to be palpated in the abdomen. Amber looked down at the convex curve of her own flesh and blenched.

'Can you tell?' She cringed from the all-seeing eyes, the all-feeling fingers.

'I'm as sure as anyone can be. You get dressed while I fill in the paperwork. We may as well get you booked in for a scan. If there's any more bleeding, straight on the phone, but I think things are going to be fine, you know.'

Amber didn't know. She had gained no weight, no sudden movement made her breasts twinge, she wasn't faint. In fact, she could sit bolt upright from a lying position with no effort at all, and she did it, there and then. 'You don't think it's just this new treatment that makes the blue line? You know, a false positive.'

The jar of alarm in Eleanor's face was like being picked up and thrown against a wall. The relief at the sudden lift, then the crump of shock. Amber gathered the hospital gown around her. The worst was happening. In front of her eyes, Eleanor receded. Professional caution hid her like a thick fog. Why had Amber thought that? Eleanor wanted to know. Had Lewis given her the idea? Her voice tailed off into wondering.

'No, not Lewis. I haven't even told him.'

The nurse had been listening, taking it all in. The drug company was paying her salary; she owed them their money's worth. Out came her pencil, but not as sharply as Eleanor's disapproval.

'If you would just go and recheck the test result for me, Nurse.'

The bossy nurse was straight to the point. 'I'm afraid I've disposed of the sample, Dr Bonworth.'

Amber was promptly dispatched to produce another; the nurse would give her the sample bottle. As she handed it over, she explained to Amber that these tests were almost foolproof.

'Your husband would tell you. He's in stem-cell research, isn't he?'

Since that newspaper article, Lewis's name must have been echoing around the hospital, the way he was always being mentioned. The vision of the woman taking Lewis's sperm sample from him, then meeting him later, as he was going about his work, made her cringe, and the way she would have folded back the record slip, stealing a look at the result. She probably knew Rhea too. Amber clutched the urine bottle. 'You'll be needing only a few drops,' she said, and withdrew.

The nurse did the test in front of Eleanor so there couldn't be any doubt. She held up the blue line, the same shade as her uniform. No mistaking that authoritative colour. She might have put it there with her own marker pen: that was how sure she was. Nurse Evans was ready with her notebook: the company record. But Eleanor's face was wary now: she was looking out for a pitfall, some problem she might have overlooked.

'There,' she said, bright as the kind of sunshine that shows up dirt on windows.

There were dark circles around Amber's nipples, and Eleanor had explained that that was right; everything was as it should be. Amber couldn't think why she didn't believe it. Halfway across the car park she almost turned back. If that nurse hadn't been there, she would have told Eleanor everything. She would have said the unspeakable words 'phantom pregnancy'. The dread that she wanted a baby so much she had imagined one into non-existence. But she couldn't say it in front of that nurse, with her dubious links to Lewis. The armies of his sperm swam

236

before her eyes when she thought of him disappearing back as soon as he'd had his result.

Once she was on home ground, inside the car, Amber pressed her hands to her cheeks and felt their heat. Eleanor had believed she was really pregnant. Next time she saw Lewis she would congratulate him. They might even congratulate each other on their success at getting Amber pregnant. They might smirk in professional complicity, taking the credit for her baby. If it was really true. The absence of Rachel Fenbridgeter had thrown her off balance. That other woman and everything about her drug company seemed to make a pregnancy less possible. But if you took her out of the equation, perhaps there was a baby.

Amber touched the softness of her abdomen. Could it hold that uncurling life? If it did, she wouldn't let any of them take it over. A catastrophe of a memory reminded her that she had wanted Rhea to feel this baby inside her. A baby that was hers and not hers. She'd wished this phantom pregnancy on herself; no wonder she couldn't believe in a real one. Rhea had been right to save her. A cautious spangling of excitement spread through her veins. Now the tendrils of the new life were already clinging to her own body, creating a delicate gauze of connection. Flyaway threads of spider silk were stronger than steel wire; she wanted to go home and be alone to feel the strengthening of that net. She couldn't bear anyone else to feel this flimsy tissue of attachment. Not even Rhea. Especially not Rhea. At the thought, the threat of a phantom pregnancy loomed up again. It would be driven away only when she had told Rhea herself and the awful surrogacy business could be put behind them.

The lab door was propped open and there was a press of people around Lewis's office. Rhea appeared; the crowd opened, took her in and assimilated her. She watched as the bodies shifted back around her sister, seeing the tight shoulders, the touching hips that closed the circle and kept interlopers out.

Amber was confounded by the unconcerned backs, the wall of jostling bodies cutting her off from Lewis and Rhea. Lewis's voice was low, quieter than anyone else's. A hush spread through the group as they tried to hear what he was saying. He was thanking everyone, lavishing gratitude on them; people were shaking hands. Some of the girls hugged one another. They moved apart.

'Amber. What are you doing here?' He didn't wait for an answer. He pushed towards her. 'We've done it.' Even as he pulled her forward, his gaze kept turning backward, reluctant to leave something, directing her to the desk. It was covered with the transparent negatives he and Rhea were forever examining. Everyone seemed intoxicated. They talked too quickly and she didn't understand what they were telling her, but then she saw Rhea, watching with the old look of worry and love she remembered from her childhood. Rhea struggling to smooth the edges of all the talk so that it couldn't grind in Amber's ears.

The crowd splintered and re-formed itself into discrete shapes, people she could recognise: Katherine, Andrew and Joe, Fazil, some medical students. Rhea and Lewis were looking at one another in surprise, as though they had existed only in a dream and hadn't managed to come to terms with the real world. Reborn and absolved, their faces seemed unmarred by all the disagreements and disappointments that usually dulled them. They had been polished so shiny that anything you threw at them would run off without a trace.

They made way for her so that she could reach the centre. Rhea gave her a seat, pressing her shoulders so that she sat down.

'It's all worked out the way we wanted it to,' she said.

Amber had thought that Rhea could read her mind: now she was sure. The day shimmered in its perfection.

Lewis placed a hand on her shoulder, the lightest of touches.

It might be like the touch of your guardian angel, and she, as he leant over her, breathed in the true smell of him: only the subtle resonance of his skin, hot, excited, mixed with the shower gel she had bought for him. She could feel the warmth of his body through her clothes.

The lab was empty, full of light. It brightened the spots of colour: the primary red of the culture medium, the nursery blue of the reagent bottle caps, chunky, like toys.

'It's so you can open them with one hand.' Rhea had demonstrated it often, unscrewing them easily with her left hand, pipette in the right.

She'd always been able to use her hands independently. Her mother used to turn away exasperated as little Rhea had patted her head and rubbed her tummy, forever showing off her party tricks. 'The trouble comes,' Stella would warn, with fatalistic presentiment, 'when your right hand doesn't know what your left hand is doing.' All the time her own hands would stitch more and more fabulous pieces, once her husband had gone.

Through the glass of his office, Rhea could see Lewis bending over the patent application. But would he see her? She resurrected the belief that Amber had clung to as a child, that if she couldn't see someone, they couldn't see her. She would sit in full view with her palms pressed to her eyes, convinced that she was invisible. Rhea had played that game herself. If I can't see him, he can't see me. But she'd been too knowing a child to believe that. She couldn't even pretend it now.

She closed her eyes against him, trying to blur his image through the interference patterns of her eyelashes, but he wouldn't disappear. Instead he was clearer, nearer. She opened them again fast, with no regard for the bright sunlight, and for a moment he became only a dark shape against the window. But her eyes couldn't help adjusting and soon he was back in focus again: this new Lewis, the unexpected translucence of his skin, so that he seemed truly naked in his office. You couldn't think of Lewis without his work; they were so intertwined.

She could still hear the whisper of Amber, before she left. 'Don't tell Lewis, I want to wait until he gets home, but I might be pregnant.' The sound stayed with her, its refrain the background of her afternoon.

It was as though what Rhea and Lewis had done had made Amber's baby possible. Tears of self-exoneration swam in her eyes and she raised her hands to the sides of her neck, pressing her fingers against her jaw as if to check that her head was still in place. She couldn't lose the sensation of lightness now. Wherever she went, gravity, that great warper of space-time, seemed to have no influence. She had to struggle to stay tethered to the earth. Rhea dropped her hands experimentally to her shoulders. Yes, her fingers still felt what Lewis had felt. Something transcendent had occurred; something had been distilled out of her. Lewis had been inside her, and when he had pulled away, he had taken something of her with him, taken it on himself.

But it hadn't burdened him. He looked unblemished.

The space between his desk and the poster wall used to constitute the whole of Lewis's territory. Now he took the coverings down – not because he suddenly felt entitled to blinds but because he felt entitled to stare outwards, to monitor the progress of the work in the lab. A feeling of inexhaustible potential took hold in him, the way it did when you were very young before reality cut you down to size and limited your options. The money and position that could accrue from this patent opened up his chances again. He felt he was standing in a high place where the air was thinned by altitude. In compensation, his heart beat faster, but no less powerfully. The same excitement infected everyone. When his researchers were working, he could sense the crackle of their synapses as the connections were made.

Right now, Lewis was hollow with hunger, but even this inconvenience was incorporated into the elation: the servicing of the flesh. If man couldn't live by bread alone, he couldn't live without it either. On the way to the refectory he had to walk past the photographs of the previous heads of department. One of them was rumoured to have only just missed a Nobel Prize. Just missed it in his sixties, for work he had completed in his thirties. Lewis was prepared to acknowledge that most great scientists had done their best work while they were young and had had to wait decades for the recognition it warranted. But he placed, with infinite tenderness, his faith in the patent system. Nowadays, the free market had dispensed with that lag. The world had to move faster and faster. With 95 per cent purity, Vic was back to finish the negotiations with the city fathers. According to him, a chair after forty was scarcely worth having.

When he got back, Rhea was in the lab, working, and at the same time keeping an eye on his office. Without the barricade of paper he watched her making a reconnaissance from her side of the glass, he from his.

He was lost in her. He rested himself in the subtlety of her colouring. White skin, dark hair made everything calm and beautiful. She stilled the jabbering world.

So many things had happened that they hadn't had a moment alone since last night when he'd been to her flat. The whirl of work and the celebrations had snatched them apart. A code of silence had surrounded what they had done: relief at first, then the sense of a reckoning that had been postponed. Now he felt the agitating threat of stasis. The speed of all these developments meant he had to keep moving. It was like riding a bicycle: if you didn't go fast enough, you fell off.

He went out into the lab and they were alone; the place was empty. Lewis had never had an affair before. It wasn't what he did. He was sure Rhea hadn't either. She was in front of him, the set of her shoulders charged with risk. He might be electrocuted by touching her. He couldn't ask her if she might get pregnant but there wouldn't be any need to: she took care of things, but she kept her thoughts private. He could see her but he had no idea what she was thinking, and was glad he didn't know. Amber told him everything, but not Rhea, and didn't he like that? Self-contained Rhea. It made things easier for him, he knew that, but pushed the reprehensible thought aside. There couldn't be any turning back now. He reached for her tentatively. It felt like strangers at first, but then, skin on skin, he plunged forward in a confusion of love and lust. He pulled her to him. She didn't falter. She just fitted into him and the bolt of nervousness was earthed. He felt for the cool respite that was Rhea.

There was a squeak of boots in the corridor. 'Not here, not now,' she said but he knew that neither of them was going to put an end to this. After all they had been through, there was no stopping.

Lewis thought that Vic had seen enough SA 153 cells – they all looked the same because they were, almost all anyway, so per-fectly the same – but the big man wanted another look and hunkered down to peer into the incubator. It was uncomfortable to watch a man of Vic's size squatting. There was the worry that he might not be able to get up again. But someone in Vic's posi-tion wouldn't want to lose a single gram of his weight. His bulk anchored him to the ground; it impressed on you just how much of him there was, how much weight he had to throw around.

'I'll get them out for you,' Lewis offered, but Vic shook his head. He raised himself smoothly upwards, never teetering from the strictly vertical.

'I want a word with the VC before we go up to City Hall. I'll see you there later, Lewis.'

Lewis's own name had an unfamiliar ring to him, in the displaced American accent. A knotted pain tightened his chest at the tension between his two worlds. Vic had brought the free-wheeling liberation of California into the lab with him. Could it thrive in the conventions of the old world? Leaning against the tall incubator, drawing an animal comfort from its warmth, Lewis watched the American leave.

Fazil nudged him aside, wanting to retrieve a bottle of medium he had set to equilibrate in the oven. He smiled at Lewis knowingly. 'Make the best of it. It won't last,' he said. Lewis looked back at him, alarmed, and Fazil laughed. 'Amber couldn't keep the news to herself. Once the baby's here, you'll always be leaning on something. You'll be too tired to stand up.'

Lewis managed a watery smile. 'It's ages yet.'

Fazil gave him the grimace of the experienced father. 'Your life will never be the same.'

In the library, Featley delivered his speech like a US politician, talking in a fast monotone as though he had a great deal of very important but obvious stuff to get through. The younger members of the department took their cue from him and adopted positions of engaged and proactive listening, leaning forward in their seats with their hands clasped before them on the table-top: the Washington intern pose. Only Vic, the solitary genuine American citizen, was sanguine enough to send out a message of disengagement from the entire process. He leant back in his chair, amused, his eyes fixed on the distance. Lewis angled his head to follow Vic's gaze and guessed that he was reading the notice the cleaner had stuck to the blind. *Please do not leave the window open*, it read. *The pigeons fly in and crap on everything.*

'A department like ours, always fully engaged in the quest for continuing development, both here and in complementary laboratories of international renown, is proud to have provided the essential and sophisticated infrastructure for some ground-breaking work.' Featley raced on, the backed-up pressure of the long list of non-existent urgent appointments hurrying the words out of his mouth.

When he'd first arrived and sought it out, Lewis had imagined the old library to be a hushed, oak-panelled sanctum. The university's state-of-the-art central library was stocked with electronic journals, computer stations and a coffee shop, with all its commotion and noise, so Featley had kept the old departmental library: a seedy room with one long, battered table. Lewis rarely went in there, but right at that moment, in the stale air, he felt he had lost his taste for the ancient and hallowed, and wanted to leave the burden of the past behind. Novelty beguiled him. Glee twitched in the corners of his mouth.

His colleagues were intent and earnest, except Glatton: they still harboured hopes that there might be something in this for them. Lewis tried to look hopeful too, as Featley's voice lifted to its climax: 'Team effort, inspiration, leadership and insight by workers who have relentlessly pursued their goals have led to further recognition for one member of our department. We must thank . . .'

There was a shifting around the table, then the tense stillness of anticipation as everyone understood that the announcement was here. Then, appallingly, it seemed that Featley had lost the script. He pecked forward short-sightedly, back to his default position. Of course, Lewis knew who had got Vic's money. He could feel Featley's pleading gaze in his own direction, wanting his help. In the embarrassed silence he could hear doors opening and closing in the corridor. His lips formed around his own name. 'Lewis,' he said.

When Lewis was a boy, barely thirteen, his father had placed a bet for him with a ticket at the racecourse. He had lost; the horse had come in third. Once he had the ticket in his possession, it had seemed impossible to Lewis that it wouldn't win. He could see it now, flimsy but certain. All around him people had thrown away their dud tickets and he had done the same. With a novice's vehemence, he had made sure he put his foot on it and ground it into the grass. His schoolmaster father had smiled complacently, as though he had taught an important lesson, but no one ever learnt that lesson, Lewis knew. Today everyone but him had one of those losing tickets. Their faces puckered at the chalky taste of it.

'Thank you, Lewis,' said Featley.

He went on to congratulate Lewis on having been awarded half a million pounds of Vic's start-up funding and refurbished lab space in the new Genetics Institute. Lewis composed his response. He gazed modestly around, angling for support, and had to make do with lukewarm congratulations. His colleagues made impatient little movements, wanting to leave, but they were trapped by Featley's need for departmental solidarity. When he eventually let them go, Lewis thought he heard the word *Napoleon* muttered, and when he turned to look, Stephen Glatton was walking away, but his other colleagues were standing still and looking back at him.

Rhea's 95 per cent had done the job. Half a million pounds, five hundred thousand. It had a modish sound to it. Not a huge amount, but his post-docs were safe, and that was hard for his colleagues to accommodate. Their own teams were going to look enviously at Lewis's now and wish they'd been on his. And the facility at the new Genetics Institute was a bonus. His people would be freer there, away from the constant surveillance of the departmental busybodies.

Featley's hand was straying to his stomach, rubbing it

tentatively. It's too much cheese, Lewis thought, vaguely queasy from the lunchtime moussaka. His colleagues were leaving without him. He started after them, but Featley stopped him. 'There's a drink in it for you, Lewis.'

As they crossed the uneven paving for the congratulatory drink in the staff club, he knew he would be visible from the lab. No longer just another aspirant, he grasped at his rightful place in the system and didn't look up for the approbation of his team.

Lewis had always hoped to be alone when the moment came, the moment of revelation that he was a true member of the establishment. He had imagined the feeling, the taking of a modest place in the history of scientific research: the grand isolation that this calling would involve. But here he was, pressing through a tide of undergraduates on their way to afternoon lectures. It was better than he had ever dreamt, the anonymous crowd parting around him.

But seeing his team again was like unwrapping a longed-for surprise: layers and complicated layers of crackling paper. Andrew, Joe, Fazil, Katherine. Then, at the heart of it, Rhea. The laboratory was a public arena; this was a private celebration, so they crushed together in Lewis's office. For once, he didn't even try to act cool.

'It's all ours,' he told them, 'five hundred fucking thousand,' while they huddled, shoulder to shoulder, arms pressed together in the confined space.

Katherine hugged Andrew, who hugged Rhea, and they shuffled awkwardly until they laughed and had just one wholehearted group hug. It wasn't even embarrassing: they just melded into a happy clutch. Katherine dabbed a kiss at his cheek; Rhea bent to his desk drawer. The long curve of her back unfolded in front of his eyes as she stood up with a bottle of champagne. When she raised it above her head, he felt the muscles of her arm tighten against the effort, as though they were his own.

'Vic brought it up while you were still with Featley,' she said, and for a sudden, disorienting moment, the clamour of success reverberated throughout Lewis's world. Even his celebration had been anticipated, organised, as though he had directed it without ever knowing. He couldn't remember feeling like this before; finally he had surpassed himself.

They drank the warm champagne in the office, slugged carelessly from disposable cups. It was fragrant and flowery in the heat, and if the beakers left a lingering aftertaste of plastic, it added only piquancy to the thrill. Curly sprays of bubbles hung suspended in the atmosphere and were breathed in, along with one another's exhaled air. This was their moment. The office windows steamed up, breath on glass, so that no one could see in and they couldn't see out.

In the huddle, Lewis put an arm across Rhea's shoulders and leant on her. He felt the rise of her body to support him and they rocked slightly, so that she bumped against Joe, who put his arm around her too. Andrew was crushed so he opened the door and they all tipped out into the laboratory.

'Work?' It was Andrew, closest to the edge.

'Good God, no.' Lewis wanted to hold on to this moment, not to have it swallowed by the effort of routine. 'Get real. Get to the bar.' Even Fazil, who didn't drink and always went home to his wife and children, nodded. Andrew shook Lewis's hand. Lewis knew it wasn't surrender, just a burying of the animosity, an understanding that Andrew's job was safe; he'd been brought back home, at least for the moment.

The move to the bar left Lewis behind. 'I'll see you all tomorrow.'

Rhea, too, lingered.

'It'll never be this good again,' Lewis said thoughtfully.

'Yes, it will. It will always be like this from now on.' She was watching him, complicated and too knowing. 'You should phone Amber.'

At the door everyone turned to wave. They would have heard Rhea's instruction because the bare surfaces in the laboratory made sure that voices carried as crisp, clear sound. They sent understanding smiles, because he couldn't come with them, shouldn't leave Amber alone. But the circle was such a perfect shape that Lewis couldn't bear to open it up and expose a gap. Without Amber, he'd have been straight into the bar with Rhea, getting beaten up by beer and noise all the way to oblivion. He felt sudden anger, and a longing for a simpler time before marriage had hemmed him in. He looked at Rhea, wanting her to insist they all celebrate together, but she was silent.

'I'd better get home,' he told her. 'What with everything.'

Painstaking attention to the smallest detail had finally paid off. Vic thought 96 per cent good enough to be going on with. Tonight, the continual reservations, the endless holdings back until she could be sure were falling away. Rhea shed them like an outgrown skin.

Lewis's arm across her shoulders. She could still feel its leverage, the steady emanation of success, as she walked back to the flat. She wrapped the warmth it generated close to herself as she fastened her coat against the evening cool. She hadn't joined the others in the bar. She wanted to walk by herself along the towpath. It wasn't lonely. There were plenty of places, crowded with people – she probably knew someone in every bar – but the solitary walk suited her.

Through the solace of achievement, the image of the amber-imprisoned insect kept resurrecting itself, prodding its way forward in her memory. Lewis likes being frightened of me. Amber had believed that, at least for a moment, when she'd said it. It's the only way he knows he is alive. It made Rhea uneasy. She'd just seen how absolutely Lewis had needed to stay with his group. He hadn't wanted to go home because his research team, the people who depended on him, were his home. She'd seen him consumed with longing to stay, and now she shivered, because she knew, with the certainty of total intimacy, that Amber would never recover from losing the tiniest part of Lewis, in the way she, Rhea, had got over losing Dave. Not without the baby to absorb her. She isn't me, Rhea thought, and it isn't Amber that Lewis is frightened of. He lives his real life in a world she knows nothing about, and he's terrified she'll find that out.

Behind her the lights shone out faithfully from the tall block of the Medical School, where other people were still busy, doing work that would help Amber keep her baby. Stay with Amber, she willed the child. You were made for each other. She had sent Lewis home to her sister so that she could accommodate her traitorous memories of him; adrenalin kept them safely at a distance.

Reflected light from the bars bounded across the water in the canal. Success had clutched at all of Lewis's team. The glitter dazzled and shimmered. Its naked intensity filled her with ela-tion and dismay.

When the scan had confirmed Amber's pregnancy, they all went out for a joint celebration of the baby and the project.

'It's your success too,' Amber urged. 'It wouldn't be the same without you.' The blunt edge of her voice pressed Rhea into compliance. In the event, Lewis decided to invite some col-leagues along, and Eleanor, naturally.

They sat around the table, among the wreck of the meal, sat-urated with superabundance: of food, of wine, of tremendous quantities of good fortune. Waiters whisked away the litter, the debris of the dinner, and too many empty bottles, but they couldn't remove the feeling of election that kept them at the table, not wanting the evening to end.

The stained cloth was swiftly covered with another that was clean and stiff, starched into a wide expanse of wholesomeness. Lewis smoothed it with his fingers, settling it in place. He looked past Eleanor to Rhea. 'If we had a company, would it foot the bill?' he asked, with his newly acquired cynical smile. He didn't wait for an answer. 'Next time.' He lifted his arms in an excited, extravagant arc right into the tray of a passing waiter.

Two macchiatos, destined for a couple seated just behind him, poured themselves straight down Lewis's back. Thick, gritty coffee and sweet, over-frothed milk spread in a mess across his jacket.

He leapt up, still smiling, and shrugged his way cheerfully out of the jacket, which would probably never be wearable again.

There wasn't any scrubbing with torn-off wads of kitchen towel in this restaurant. The waiters fielded soft, absorbent cloths to soak away the mess. Rhea looked on, conscious that somewhere in the city an anonymous, industrial laundry would wash those cloths. Every trace of the coffee would disappear into the underground drains, along with everyone else's stains, and the restaurant would take them back spotless. Apologies were murmured into the ears of the coffee-less diners; the girl sprawled forward, hands upturned in disappointment, to wait for the replacements. Then it was Lewis's turn. Concerned words poured into his unconcerned, civilised face: no lasting damage visible there.

How money mops up trouble, Rhea thought.

Other diners cast surreptitious glances in their direction, expecting to see signs of discomfort and a spoilt evening, but their table was a ring of faces all shining with the reflection of

Lewis's good nature: a charmed circle, impervious to ordinary unpleasantness. Lewis took his place again, in shirtsleeves, the coat spirited off stage. Coffee and yet more drinks appeared, slipped into their places by waiters who materialised out of the strategic twilight surrounding each table, beyond the glimmer of the candles. Amber had been here before, on her expense account. She had told Rhea it was quite the place to conduct affairs – the discretion of the waiters was legendary: you didn't notice them at all.

But they noticed Amber. How could they not, when she was so happy? They gravitated towards her, attracted by her frank delight in everything around her. Because there was no poison in Amber's chalice of fulfilment. She had her baby, her husband, and his stem-cell work to help Polly. Tonight was unadulterated by doubt, for her at least.

Hands toyed with glasses; there was a sense of expectation, a feeling that there should be a finale, the great something that would crown such an occasion. The colleagues kept their eyes decently on their brandy, warming the glasses, swirling thoughtfully. In the quiet, their expressions became reserved; they might have been contemplating their own opportunities, comparing them to Lewis's elevation.

It was Eleanor who raised her glass. 'Well done, Lewis. We always knew you had it in you.'

There was a general murmur of approval, mixed with relief at not having been the one to hand the crown to Lewis. Rhea caught the guilty eye of Stephen Glatton as he swivelled out of the loop, pulling at the collar of his shirt as though it was choking him.

But Lewis didn't flinch. He half stood up but then, with the tinge of worldliness that had crept into his repertoire, he eased back into his chair, ready to address them, yet leaning forward, looking down, then raising his head when he felt they were sufficiently attentive. He thanked them for their support. There were a few flickers of interest in his direction as people tried to remember what support, exactly, they had ever offered. He met their eyes with ersatz conviction. If there had ever been any, it would certainly be withdrawn now, was Rhea's guess.

'And it doesn't end there.' He got to his feet and swung the beaming spotlight of his achievement onto Amber.

'My wife' – he didn't mention her name; plainly this was a further triumph that belonged mainly on his CV – 'is pregnant. We'll be having a baby in the new year.'

There was a gracious relinquishing of the floor to Amber. Lewis bowed out as the double act came back into business: the golden couple, that fascinating circle of *yin* and *yang*. Congratulations were proffered, and accepted.

All evening Amber had been giving each of the guests her smiling attention, gift-wrapping her interest with diligent queries about their work, their home-renovation projects, their families. Now she had her reward. She was at the centre of unbounded enthusiasm. There had never been such a radiant example of a first-trimester pregnancy. As far as his colleagues were concerned, Lewis had been perfectly eclipsed. And they were pleased. Lewis and Amber were busy, offering themselves up for public consumption, accepting congratulations, leaving only Rhea to notice the falling away of camaraderie whenever their backs were turned. She smiled fondly, as she knew she ought.

Amber reached across and took her hand. 'Rhea will be god-mother,' she told everyone. 'She has to be, and so must Eleanor.'

Rhea could see Eleanor, her solid frame planted firmly on the baroque French chair, her comfortable shoulders spreading beyond the brocade back. She was laughing contentedly, seem-ing delighted with the whole situation. Lewis was leaning back.

His shoulders weren't as broad as Eleanor's; the greenish brocade made a sort of frame for his shape and he looked as though
he might be posing for posterity. Rhea tried to catch his eye, to
let him know that he should thank Eleanor. Perhaps it was for
the best that he didn't notice. Eleanor might not be ready to be
thanked: it was early days. But Lewis kept gazing straight
through the group, out into the fascinating mirage of his future
prospects.

It was the intensity of his self-belief that made him so exhilarating. Passion in him called out the matching feeling in her;
together in their private world, they were a powerful entity, so
powerful that she felt invincible.

The waiters had brought the jacket back, cleaned somehow.
Lewis put it on, reversing his arms into the sleeves while they
held it for him. Before Rhea realised it he had one of those arms
around her shoulders, the other around Amber's.

'My two girls,' he was saying. 'What would I do without you?'
Amber and her baby on one side, herself on the other. Rhea felt
the pull of his arm and turned inwards.

Amber hardly noticed: she was looking down at her stomach.
Her absorbed smile at the whole public pantomime excused
Rhea from any responsibility and she could scarcely believe that
the evening had passed so easily. It felt like vindication.

CHAPTER 14

Now that Lewis was safe, and his work approaching the patient trials, something everyone understood, Amber cut out of the paper the photo that had caused the demonstrations. She separated it from the beaming Brownies at their summer festival and the presentation of a book token to a volunteer librarian with thirty years' service at the hospital, and sent it to her mother. Stella wrote Lewis a nice little note, congratulating him, and phoned Rhea the same evening.

'Who was that girl with Lewis?' she wanted to know.

Rhea gave a huff of suppressed irritation. 'She's just some woman from the council. Lew was at a meeting about the Genetics Institute. You know. I told you.'

But Rhea knew what to expect. Stella was interested only in her son-in-law. She had no intention of being drawn into some discussion about a genetics institute. Instead, she gave a shrewd little cry. 'Frankly, Rhea, I didn't like the way he was looking at that girl. You don't think that there could be anything in it, do you?' Stella was at home, in Devon, but the acrid mist of her anxiety caught in Rhea's throat. 'He looked much too pleased with himself. He was smirking all over his face.'

Her mother could detect the slightest waver in a voice from continents away. Rhea always phoned her early, before she had sipped even one drink in the evening, to avoid censure. She

pushed her glass aside in a belated attempt to head off any discovery. But after what she had done, what did a glass of Vouvray
matter?

'What are you talking about, Mother? Of course there isn't.
He doesn't even know her.'

It was true, but that alone meant it would sound exactly like
a lie.

'You can't be too careful, you know, during pregnancy.' There
was a delicate silence as appropriate words were sifted in Stella's
mind. 'She's waited so long for this baby.'

Her tone made Rhea's blood turn viscid. The delusion of
Amber's self-involved happiness wavered before her. Lewis's
eyes looked away from her now, saddened. Stella went on,
'Amber's always on her own, these days. Whenever I ring,
Lewis is still at work. You know what she's like, she needs com-
pany. She doesn't need this.'

'What has she said?'

'She doesn't have to say anything to me, Rhea. I am her
mother.'

No one ever needed to say anything to her. Just by watching
you, Stella could unpick you like a piece of spoilt embroidery.
It took only the memory of those glances – looks tapering into
the seduction of her mother's silence – for Rhea to feel the
unravelling of her self-possession. Stella could do that, even
now. The Vouvray was back in Rhea's hands. She took a quick
gulp.

'No,' she said. Everything was fine. Lewis was busy at work.
'He'll have a family to provide for now. He has to make a go of
it.'

Her thoughts had to move fast to keep ahead of her mother's
intuition. Yes, fine. Stella could take the photograph to her bridge
club tomorrow, to trump some other mother-in-law's triumph.

*

Ninety-five per cent pure. Each of the cultures had been grown from a single cell, twice. The first cell had been 100 per cent pure. Ninety-five per cent meant that a few of the daughter cells had changed: those backsliders had lost the total flexibility that had distinguished them. What had made them so determined to turn into something else? Something lay dormant in those five per cent to single them out. One leaky pore in a membrane might take up the wrong message and contaminate a whole strain.

'We should stop this now,' she told Lewis.

In the suspended time between work and sleep he would follow her to bed. It had started like a project plan because no audit trail could be left to lead back to them: a fifteen-minute interval between their departures; cars parked at opposite ends of the building; duplicate keys so that he could never be caught punching the audio-phone outside her door. For Rhea it ended in elemental chaos. The pieces of her were flung so far apart she thought they might never be reunited. She wasn't sure that she wanted them to be. This abdication was the most empowering and harmonious thing she'd ever experienced. She moved from it to the lab, where doing half a dozen things at once felt natural and she was faintly and pleasurably tired. The row of clean glassware, the stacked order of her samples, the racks of tissue-culture flasks, labelled, at every stage of their development. All of them serving to legitimise this failure of jurisdiction over herself because the parts of her were never close enough together to let her wonder how Lewis got dressed and drove home to Amber afterwards.

Only a few months ago Lewis had been reluctant to come inside the culture suite, talking to her through the closed door. Now he squeezed into her workspace and made it his too. It was so small that he pressed up against her.

'Hmm,' he answered, and slipped his hand inside her white coat. Rhea rested her arm on his; the pipette held steady and

100 microlitres of solution fell accurately into each of the wells. You had to look at the plate from a particular direction to see the transparent wells clearly. It was a matter of perspective, but perspective was an illusion: you could make it play all sorts of tricks. 'We make a good team,' Lewis observed.

Too good, Rhea thought. An immense force was generated in this primal sex, powering their success. She was afraid to go on, for Amber's sake, and afraid to stop, because if she did the world might collapse in on itself.

'Have you noticed that Joe's abandoned his nose-ring?' Rhea asked. On the other side of the culture-suite door there was the pain of an emo band CD that meant Joe was working alone. He listened to obscure bands that no one else had ever heard of. He went to gigs that were more exclusive than private-invitation recitals. Joe was straightforward and easily shocked by emotional transgression in real life; the dissonant noise hid a lot. Lewis was put out, as though a nose-ringless Joe might threaten the balance of their lives. Rhea and he touched their fingertips together. But there were viewing windows in every door in the laboratory. Privacy wasn't supposed to be an issue here. Any moment you thought you had got for yourself might be interrupted by someone else. 'I ought to help him.'

Lewis was reluctant to let her go. The noise blanketed out the rest of the world. His hand moved, hungry, and Rhea wanted to disappear into him so she was invisible to everyone else. The spring-weighted door outside banged and the music was turned down.

'Be careful,' she warned.

Out in the lab Andrew was hovering over Joe, watching him. He glanced at Rhea and gave a knowing smirk. It might mean nothing, but Rhea thought otherwise. Andrew had guessed something about her and Lewis, or believed he had. It might not be long before that guess turned into certainty. Andrew could never leave a loose end dangling; his fearless determination was what made him such a good researcher. His committed search for the truth might have a downside now.

But existing in the moment was as much as Rhea could manage: at every moment of her days and nights she had something to do. She lifted one of the huge 10-litre volumetric flasks that she used for making up solutions and clutched it near to her body. They sucked all the warmth out of you but never heated up. She struggled to lift them; the taps weren't quite high enough for her to manoeuvre such tall flasks easily, but she'd mastered the knack. She set them to dry, pristine, without the slightest residue of detergent to contaminate her cultures.

If you couldn't escape other people, there were plenty of places to hide from yourself in a laboratory: behind the electrophoresis apparatus, between the big centrifuges, in the weighing room, with its balances and chemical smells, you could be part of the furniture. She could hide there from Amber, but she couldn't hide from Lewis. He was part of all those things too. Everything she touched, everything she did, bore an imprint of her brother-in-law.

They didn't work at weekends now. Saturday and Sunday opened out into a bubble of Amber's happiness. Rhea didn't need to confront the other part of herself, left behind in the lab. She had to believe in Amber and Lewis's happiness when they were together. It was unexpected, the gratification of the instant and the boon that Amber was so comprehensively protected by pregnancy: a pregnancy Rhea had wished on her.

Stella's voice had shattered the conviction.

They were the last remnant of Dave. Two tickets for *Rigoletto*, bought a year ago, lurked uneasily on the table. Amber was going to visit Mum, or she and Rhea would have had them.

'Well, that isn't going to stop you going.'

258

'Dave never really liked opera. He only went under sufferance.'

As far as Amber was concerned, Dave had forfeited any right to preferences when he had abandoned Rhea. She fingered the emblematic tickets. 'Look at the price. They've got your money but you'd have needed a crystal ball to know what you'd be doing in a year's time.' Her very kindness found the hurt and squeezed it. 'You'll have to go with her, Lewis. Look,' said Amber, 'she really loves opera. It takes her out of herself.'

The sudden unlooked-for pressure of the trap, enough to make you feel safe, enough to suffocate you; there wasn't a way out. Rhea knew she had created this snare for herself. She couldn't say no and make Amber suspicious; she couldn't say yes and betray her sister any further. This is the breakpoint, she thought. After this, it's over between Lewis and me.

She couldn't understand how music did so little for Lewis. He slunk into the theatre a condemned man. 'Hours of screeching,' he complained.

'At least you'll get a rest,' Rhea retorted. 'You don't have to do anything but sit still and let the music do the work.'

The foyer was noisy, too noisy to talk, and they moved straight into the auditorium where the acoustics dimmed extraneous chatter and only acknowledged sound from the stage. A man in the next seat took out the score and a tiny reading light so he could follow the notes. How could he immerse himself in the detail like that and not simply give himself up to the music? But then, she thought, probably he sat there matching the notes to the music so that he wasn't carried away, afraid of what it might mean to him if the distilled essence of wrongdoing and revenge poured straight into the receptors of his brain. Rhea shook her head as the house lights tactfully withdrew and each of them was left in their own private well of experience. The audience settled as the orchestra struck out into the restless overture with its premonition of the father's curse and she looked at Lewis. He was swivelling his head towards the stage, giving up his scrutiny of the audience for anyone he knew.

'Relax. Forget everything else.'

He moved his leg to press against hers and it stayed there through the rumbustious court scenes, firm and tense. It was only when the young heroine began her aria that she felt him soften. The soprano was wearing a primrose dress; there was none of the obvious vulgarity of white in this production, but a nudge towards the hidden joys of spring. Her fresh, pure voice filled the space with innocence and promise. There was no hint yet in the music of her fate. She must have sung that unknowing joy night after night without any taint of the ending. Rhea wondered how she did it. Did she forget every night that tragedy had overtaken her during the previous performance? Her face was radiant in her joyful present.

There was a pause when the interval lights came up while the audience, ambushed by emotion, extricated itself and remembered the need to get to the bar before the crush built up. Lewis was testy and didn't want the bother of a drink. They wandered across the downstairs foyer behind the smokers making for the exit and went outside. It was quiet and dark like the auditorium and held the same sense of suspended reality.

'The balance is off. The orchestra's just a little in front of the singers,' the vice chancellor commented.

His wife quickly contradicted him: 'No. I'm hearing the singers in front of the orchestra.'

At the sound of their voices Rhea couldn't move but Lewis couldn't stand still. He was anxious to join them, but she didn't want anyone to intrude on their evening. The VC's wife was a tall woman, handsome rather than pretty, and had a distinguished career in computing. The VC introduced Lewis to her.

'I've heard all about your work from Prof Featley.' She turned to Rhea. 'And you must be Amber.'

Illusion and counter-illusion felt so close in Rhea that she was temporarily unable to distinguish them. She couldn't think how to describe herself: Lewis's assistant, sister-in law, lover? The VC rescued her. It seemed she was one of his – one of our brightest biological scientists, Amber's sister, too, a family affair. His wife nodded sagely. She had been one of the first women to move into computing, in the sixties. If you can follow a knitting pattern, she had believed, you could write a program.

'You'll know what I'm talking about.' She included Rhea in her circle of women who had transcended their domestic origins. Kind, Rhea realised. With her bubbly hair and her smooth satin dress, she was like an amphipathic molecule, the mustard in salad dressing that emulsified the oil and vinegar, one part of her in each phase.

'We'll be keeping a close eye on your progress, Lewis. We're relying on you young people for the breakthroughs. We oldies are just turning the handle now.'

She cranked the air with her hands and at that moment an electronic melody called them back to the theatre.

'Ah, the division bell.' The VC hurried off to his own world and his distinguished wife followed.

From her seat in the stalls, Rhea could see the woman's enigmatic head strain from their box to see the nearside stage. 'We've got a better view from here,' she told Lewis.

He moulded himself to his seat, happy with his evening after all. The almost human voice of the cello began to expose the villain's duplicitous nature and this time Rhea felt Lewis let it take him over.

When the performers dropped back into their professional lives and presented themselves for applause, the spell broke. Blood soaked the young soprano's clothes and she stepped back into her own life, tired by Guilda's death, but Rhea could see she hadn't truly made her sacrifice. Once her audience applauded and stamped its feet she was consummately alive to her triumph. But Rhea had allowed herself to be seduced. She couldn't throw off the alternative reality. Only the thought of Amber kept pulling her back to the real world and Amber was gone, back home to Mother, to the shared motherhood that excluded her. When Lewis parked outside her flat Rhea drew him from the car.

'You don't need to go home tonight.'

With so much excitement swirling around him, Lewis felt feverish. At work, and at home, everyone was pleased with him: everyone, even the builders, whom Amber had back, working on the money sink. Snitter Heugh was benefiting from ever more expensive renovations. Now it seemed that the spring-water supply needed protection from the local animal life. Gleeful intakes of breath from Simon Pindon invariably warned of hefty bills. However much Lewis earned, it was whisked away on some necessity of country life. A part of him wondered if this was a payment, a sort of penance for what he was doing. It might be that this was a man's life. He'd given in to an impulse and now he didn't know what to do about it. He didn't suppose it would go on for ever. In fact, Rhea was already showing signs of disquiet; it might be for the best.

Amber was going to want to know what the Pindons had got done while she had been away visiting Stella. He had no idea, because he had stayed at Rhea's flat all week. He thought of her now, at home, still engulfed in a haze of sexuality. Perhaps she was lying in a bath, feeling the water touch her skin. His own skin softened as he thought of it, which reminded him of Amber too. He hoped, in a vague and unconvinced way, that Amber or Rhea would sort out this mess. They usually told him what to do, one or other of them. He fumbled with his briefcase; it held his patent application, almost completed. It was so vital to Amber's plans for the baby and all it would need. He could tell her that finishing it had meant it was very late when he'd got home: too late for him to go and check on Simon and Martin's progress. She would believe him and all would be well. The trouble was, Simon and Martin might have been checking on him.

The station foyer was packed with jittery people waiting to pick up relatives. Amber's train wasn't due for another quarter of an hour so he bought a newspaper and leant against a wall where he could keep an eye on the arrivals board. He scanned the headlines but a nudge at his elbow made him put the paper aside. There were too many people about, too close, brushing up against each other. There was always someone on the make, after something. A gang of hoodies was sniggering around the ticket machine. Lewis instinctively pressed his arm across the left-hand side of his jeans where he kept his wallet, then he let it go, mortified. Probably that was just what they wanted: they'd know which pocket to pick now. The grey shapes, with their fox faces half hidden, crossed the concourse. They were stalking a young lad, smartly dressed, who looked as if he had been to a job interview, with his air of having needed to please somebody. He turned and smiled ingratiatingly at a woman who knocked into him, and it was making him a target.

As the gang surrounded him he tried to squeeze between them, turning his body sideways, but the spaces kept closing. The victim was lost to Lewis's sight for a moment, hidden by a group of taxi drivers, gossiping with determined turned backs; they weren't going to witness anything. There was a flurry, the lad retreated, and the hoodies pressed on, pinning him into the corner by the taxi rank. Lewis leant forward. For a moment he wasn't sure whether he was trying to see or trying to help, but he looked for a policeman, someone to alert. He started pushing between the streams of unseeing people, but before he reached halfway across the concourse, the lad took out his wallet, a twenty-pound note was passed over and Lewis felt himself hesitate. This could be a drugs deal, or a debt, or just bog-standard begging with menaces.

Whatever, it looked like twenty pounds was enough: the hoodies had decided to let the lad off. They slipped away, sliding back into the washing stream of travellers without leaving a ripple. Their disappearing act left the victim with his back pressed up against the wall. He wasn't searching for help; you could almost feel the familiarity of the routine. This has happened to him before, Lewis realised, with an uncomfortable jolt of collusion. The lad studied the ground, all the way to the ticket barrier where he, too, disappeared from sight.

He needed to learn to stand up for himself. Lewis was sure he would have done something – he definitely would have – if it had gone any further. As it was, he had probably done the right thing by not creating any more drama. It would have been worse for the lad. He was out of it now, on his way home. Funny, there seemed to be policemen all over the place suddenly, standing smartly with their radios, blocking all the exits.

Lewis folded his arms around his paper and turned back to the arrivals board. The tinny voice from the speakers told him the train from Taunton terminated here: would passengers please be sure to take all their possessions with them. The hectoring tones singled him out from the crowd of waiting men, homing in on him, so that when he caught hold of Amber, smelling cleanly of soap and shampoo, he felt a distinct and manly sense of tarnish.

The kitchen stools had been bought in the days when Amber and Lewis had been a fashionable, newly married couple, without any thought for bodily comfort. They were elegant, minimal; they had no backs, so Amber had to concentrate on sitting upright. It was all she could do to fit her pelvis to the narrow perch. There were dirty dishes. The fine clear evening light showed the stains of neglected spills on the worktops, but she sat in transgressive idleness. The baby shifted uneasily, accommodating itself to her tiredness, and bringing out a reciprocal burst of tenderness in its mother. Phantom pregnancies didn't make smooth sweeps across your abdomen, reaching out from their world to yours.

They had been alone all day, she and the child, except for Simon and Martin. The builders had installed a solid metal cover over the manhole to the water supply.

'The cows won't be able to piss in it now,' Simon had assured her, stamping it into place. Beyond the field of cattle, below the line of trees, she could see a string of dainty pylons, holding their cables at arm's length, as though they felt there was something inherently distasteful about the discharge of electricity into the valley. Simon had commented on their fragility. What you need, he had advised, is a generator for when they go down in the winter storms. You don't want to be without power with a baby. He poked about in the outhouse where she made her paper. 'It'll fit in here, no problem.'

Self-sufficiency seemed to be turning Snitter Heugh into a private industrial complex. Last winter she had sat at this window and seen the orange glow of the motorway lights, an umbilical cord that connected her to the city and to Lewis. In the summer, the sun set so late that the lights never came on and she felt newly isolated.

The city was full of life. Rather than stay at Snitter Heugh alone, Amber sometimes drove down and roamed the streets. One day the traffic had been heavy, and then children were blocking her way. They walked in a broad swathe, hanging onto the hands of sixth-formers wearing red sweatshirts printed with a childish drawing of a house. It must have been a nursery school or something. Kids were being collected and taken somewhere to play until their parents had finished work. The teenagers could have been talking to one another, worrying about A levels, flirting, or arranging drug deals at the local under-age drinking den, but they weren't. They took notice of the children, two or three clustered around each of them, admiring their paintings, their new trainers or the gaudy backpacks they carried their school stuff in. They were doing what they were paid for, those youngsters. If I went back to work, Amber thought, I wouldn't mind my child being looked after by them.

One of Lewis's colleagues at the university had watched them from across the road. He rushed over, dodging cars. It was 4 p.m., shift change, and vehicles turning right were pulling out of the hospital across two lanes of traffic and causing difficulties. The man was able to take advantage of the jam and got himself across to reach the column of children as they gathered around a pedestrian crossing. He had bent down to one of the little boys, squatting in front of him so the child had to stop. The teenagers had surrounded him, but the man had still hunkered down. He began to protest: 'But I'm his dad.'

'Yes,' the little boy had agreed. 'He's my dad.' But he had a glum, wary look, and one hand clutched the trousers of his designated carer.

The big lad had shaken his head and ushered the child on. 'Sorry, mate, we're not allowed to let anybody talk to them.'

The pedestrian lights had changed to green, the bleep yammering over the car engines, and they all moved off in a disturbed cluster.

It'll be a divorce, Amber had thought. An absentee father. She had watched the children go, their guardians glancing behind them nervously.

Now a fly was trying to break in through the window glass; the dinner that Lewis hadn't eaten was congealed on the sill. Perhaps it was tormenting the fly. A fly couldn't understand the nature of glass, what it was that denied it the thing it wanted. Her mother's words wouldn't let her rest. *Take care. It's a dangerous time, with a husband*, as though men were inherently unreliable.

Amber decided she would phone the lab. She didn't know the number. Lewis's mobile was the only one on speed-dial at home. She had to find it in the book and that meant getting off the stool. Still, what did it tell you when someone answered their mobile? They could be anywhere, couldn't they? So getting the lab number was worth the trouble.

Poking at the digits on the keypad felt like her mother's probing questions, asking where Lewis was at this time of night. The lab phone had one of those old-fashioned rings that meant you could imagine someone wandering over to pick it up and holding it at arm's length while they finished what they were doing, not like the fast waver of a mobile, close to your body. She had almost decided to put it down again when Lewis answered.

'Hello,' he intoned cheerfully, with the high-low chord that was quite the fashion on campus, these days. Rhea did it too. It validated you as one of them and set up a barrier against outsiders. But to hear him really at work was a relief, in spite of the intimation of exclusion. It made her feel a trifle foolish now.

'Hello,' she mimicked, up and down, matching him. There was a pause, the length of time that it took someone to disentangle themselves from one situation and engage with another. She felt the effort it took in her own body.

'I won't be long, nearly done.' The words came freewheeling down the line, but Amber hadn't mentioned the time: there was an assumption of guilt in this automatic contrition. The same assumption of guilt as when she had mentioned how late he had worked while she was away. Simon and Martin had put in long hours during the light summer evenings, but they hadn't seen hide nor hair of him.

'Are you on your own?' she asked.

Lewis's voice took on a note of surprise. 'Yes. Why?' There was a pause when he might have been worrying about something. 'Are you all right?'

Then Rhea's voice came from further away. 'Has something happened?' she was asking. 'Lewis, is it Amber?'

There was a scuffle at the other end of the telephone; Rhea must have wrestled it away from him.

'Amber, what's the matter?'

So Lewis was on his own. Only Rhea was there. Amber shifted position. The baby stirred.

'There's nothing the matter, nothing at all. I just wondered when Lewis was coming home.'

That made Rhea laugh, just a small laugh, a bit too obliging. It didn't feel right, that laugh. Poor Rhea.

'I'll finish off here by myself and send him straight home.'

Rhea put the phone down. Lewis was obediently shovelling stuff into his briefcase, silent and avoiding her eyes.

'She shouldn't be on her own so much,' Rhea said: an echo of her mother. Lewis agreed by a slight movement of his shoulders, but he trailed his fingers down her arm while he looked at the vials incubating, warm in the water bath, as though he might be about to let them down.

'Don't leave them there. We can't afford to lose them.'

Once he had gone, Rhea let her head fall back and stared at the ceiling. Amber had been on the landline. No tenuous link for her. Lewis was attached to her by solid cables that had been laid years ago. None of the foggy insufficiency of the ether. The emptying of the lab left a gap which filled gradually, like a delayed reaction, with disquiet. Health and Safety directive required at least two people to watch over one another. She wasn't supposed to be working alone. She hadn't minded before, but she did now. Rhea let her thoughts drift around the past, trying to discover the line dividing the sanctioned from the prohibited. She had crossed it at some point to put herself at such risk but she couldn't tell where. All she saw were the infinite gradations of a grey area.

The array technology was still on Glatton's side of the lab. It had never found its way towards them, even if it was a communal resource. The time when she would have itched to try out the latest technology belonged to the past now, to a different Rhea. Vic wanted a read-out of the gene expression of the cells for the clinical trial. Part of the pre-patient checks. Can't be too careful, he explained, with people. Katherine had been keen to learn to use the arrays, challenge raising her voice. Or to co-operate with Stephen Glatton. Rhea agreed it was a probably a good idea.

On the way home she saw Katherine and Andrew pushing through the black hole that passed as the door of a club. It was dark inside and the pulse of the music was paced at something like a heartbeat, so insistent that all other sounds were muffled. Rhea hadn't been to a club for ages. It might be just what she needed: thoughtless comfort.

When she found them, Andrew was explaining to Katherine the difference between a scientist and a medic. It was like a re-run of her student days. She'd said the same thing herself, probably to Andrew in this very bar. 'Medics aren't rational,' Andrew shouted above the noise. 'If you give them a result that doesn't fit with their diagnosis, they say you've made a mistake in your analysis and just go ahead on their instincts.' Rhea's instincts were to go home, to bed and peace, alone. Her safest place, the one with her friends and colleagues, had grown dangerous. They could guess so much about her that she ought to avoid them now. But she'd been spotted. Katherine and Andrew bulked out their evenings with as much company as they could, probably not wanting to go home to chaos and unmade beds.

When they'd had enough of drinking and shouting, they filtered outside through the crowd and supported themselves against the wall. From this distance the music was kinder and smoothed the way for talk. Andrew leant across to her and said distinctly, 'Lewis told me you went to the opera together.'

Rhea watched a polystyrene cup blowing along the street. 'Yes. We had two tickets and Amber was away.' As soon as she'd said it she knew it was an admission of guilt. Explanations always were excuses, weren't they?

'*Rigoletto*.' Andrew pushed his advantage. 'Not a fan of opera, myself. Lewis said he didn't know when to clap. He'd thought it was over and the soprano was dead but she kept on singing.'

'Would you have known when it was over, Andrew?'

'No, Lewis and I have that in common, Rhea.'

It came to Rhea that the parts of her and Lewis that overlapped were all at work. In the rest of their lives they were apart. Their week after the opera had split into two entirely different experiences and she was tired of trying to reconcile them. Andrew looked at Katherine and laughed. 'We're hopeless, aren't we?'

A part of Rhea felt relief as she closed the door of her flat. Inside, everything was tidy, bare and manageable. There was a message from Amber on her phone. She wished her heart didn't thump every time she saw one.

Lewis didn't manage to come to the flat until Friday. It was an easy time to get away: Amber didn't come down for the demob drink at the end of the week any more, but she thought Lewis should still have one. 'Seeing him outside the lab keeps everyone on side', she said, perfectly misunderstanding his motivation. How easy she made their deceit, Rhea thought, and then, how difficult.

That Friday he brought a present with him, the right sort of present, she knew with redundant guilt. He would have paid for it in cash, no transaction to sully his bank statement. Amber probably checked it for him. Another CD of *Rigoletto*. There was one already on her bookshelf and she knew then that, while she was in the shower, he had never looked at what she listened to. Lewis didn't possess that sort of personal curiosity: he would have thought that your music collection was your own business. She wondered if he would take it home and pretend he had bought it for Amber. She promised herself that she would never look.

When she handed it back to him she told him, 'You have to go, Lewis.'

For a moment his eyes blazed with temper. It was his first instinct, and she knew he felt cheated of the few hours of oblivion Friday night owed him. But something else followed, a realisation of possibility, like a reprieve. His voice was flat, his feet dragged to the door, but he was pleased too. His shoulders were hunched as he left the flat but he got into the car straightforwardly and drove away.

She collected things from the bedroom, the laundry on the chair could go back in the drawer. The room took on its old, anonymous look. Perhaps you could believe that nothing had ever happened in it.

Rhea lay in the middle of the bed. She remembered Lewis in it. Or, rather, she didn't. People said no one could remember sex, that it was like weather. You couldn't bring the stinging blizzards of winter into a summer day. She couldn't call up the unbridled kissing and the absolution of Lewis's touch. It was a thing of the moment, lived through and gone when it was over. She thought of choosing another CD and letting the music mainline into her head so that she experienced the composer's feelings instead of the blank of her own, but she didn't. She fell asleep with her vacancy. At least she had ended it.

CHAPTER 15

Now that Amber's pregnancy had become a communal activity, Lewis was excused paternal angst. Almost everyone else was prepared to take on his share. Even the radiologist recognised him in the hospital corridors and gave him a special smile because she knew that everyone in the lab had installed the baby's scan as a screen saver. Each time Lewis glanced at a computer screen – a dozen times a day – he saw it, that entirely hidden thing, hauled into view. The baby was lying sideways, tiny fists clenched, its vestigial body merging into the electronic background. Only the head seemed substantial, disproportionably large, as though the child might be some cerebral giant brought back from the future to torment him. It unnerved him, seeming so unearthly and all-knowing: the splash of white where the sound had bounced from the forming curves, the dark lap of the amniotic fluid, and the shadows of the flesh solidifying, taking shape day by day. The single visible eye stared out from the screen, certainly guessing its father's wrongs. In response to his remorse, the screen pulsed with determination. He could never stare it out. But as soon as he touched his mouse the whole thing disappeared, the augury reverted to machine code, and Lewis could get on with his work.

Sometimes. At others he was having flashbacks. When the baby disappeared like that he sometimes remembered when he thought that Amber had almost died, trying to get pregnant. And how he had wanted to be dead too, if she was. He was afraid then that that click of the mouse would have some terrible consequence and the baby would disappear for ever.

The days stacked up, one on another, but they felt precarious. One tremor and the lot would be down. Outside the laboratory, so many things couldn't be kept under his control. He was like a bone being worried by a dog that wanted to kill it. But you couldn't kill a bone, could you? It was already dead, so the dog went on and on shaking and threatening and nothing changed.

He made a point of delivering the paperwork to the patent agent himself, driving to London with it on the back seat of the car. He should have stowed it in the boot but he couldn't bear to let it out of his sight. All the way it shifted and slewed across the leather. Like the baby, it had taken on a life of its own.

In another glass and steel office, just like the one where he and Amber had signed away their lives to Snitter Heugh, the accredited agent had taken the SA 153 patent into his charge. Asserting their ownership, the whetted eyes of the expert began the evisceration of his document. Lewis's chest clenched, and he felt such an ache of loss that he longed to have his destiny returned to his own hands. He clasped his fingers tightly together in case they snatched it back, squeezed them until they turned white, then realised he would have to get used to the grip of guilt around him.

'You might make some money out of this one,' the lawyer commented drily. Lewis smiled noncommittally, uncertain whether it was bad form to talk about profit in a lawyer's office. He'd come up against a distinct ambivalence throughout the university, but the agent openly fondled the possibilities of making money, feeling where the best advantage might lie. 'Just a pity it only lasts the twenty years,' he mused, 'but we'll apply for world-wide next.' His legal expertise circled the globe and homed in on the US. Lewis had it covered. He bent down to his briefcase, pulling out the ready-prepared list of American contacts, so the logic of the next question caught him unawares.

'Amber Norham. The cell donor wouldn't be a relative of yours, by any chance?'

The words were so unexpected that Lewis wasn't sure he'd heard properly. 'Sorry?'

The agent repeated himself gravely: 'Clarity is paramount. Allegedly,' he added.

Clarity and allegations were the very things Lewis wanted to avoid: not because it wasn't true that Amber had been the cell donor, not because it wasn't legal, but because it wasn't common knowledge. He hadn't told anyone from the lab that the SA 153 cells rescued from the bottom of the freezer were his wife's. Now he felt the need to explain, to unburden himself. 'She's my wife. She broke a tooth – it was ages ago – and I took the SA 153 line from there.'

'Clever girl! I see that she's negotiated a per cent of any profits from the patent in return for the broken tooth.' The lawyer paused to let his words sink in. Lewis swallowed, but couldn't speak. Of course Amber was clever as well as kind.

'Why shouldn't we benefit,' she had asked. 'They're my cells, anyway, every penny we spend on the house keeps some-one in work.'

In his study at Snitter Heugh, he had inserted Amber's name in the blank space left for it and rehearsed his explanation. Now that he had delivered it, he examined himself scrupulously. Had he been too anxious, too fast to come up with unnecessary details? All the complications and convolutions of his own life began to invade the lawyer's impersonal office, destroying its accommodating air of *sangfroid*. The agent kept his eyes on the papers, moving ahead. He cleared his throat and the discussion flowed forward, concerned only with legalities and the repeating of a professional mantra of caution.

'Well, I would advise you not to divorce her. You know that the US patent office doesn't recognise power of attorney. It demands that all the parties sign in person. I've known ex-spouses refuse. Revenge can be very costly in these cases.'

It was all so matter-of-fact, as though he dealt with such complexities every day of his life. But then again, Lewis thought, he probably did. There might be nothing very unusual about what he had done.

As Lewis left, he turned to close the door and saw his file being slotted tidily away, as though there was nothing exceptional. The lawyer wasn't interested in his marriage; there was something so aseptic about his separation of the legalities and the personal that Lewis felt refreshed, vindicated, even.

He drove home through a translucent sunset. It was as though the air had been washed clean of dust and pollen. Pregnancy had cured Amber's hay fever; there would be no wakeful night ahead, no fretting and waiting for winter this year. She had never been so well. The lawyer's office, with its clear divisions and sharp edges, connived with his longing for simplicity to beguile him. Lewis could feel the fearful curiosity that had made him take the cells from Amber, deserting him. It left a gap that was being filled by something too numb to feel fear. All the worry around Amber, her illness, her pregnancy had used him up. Rhea had practically taken over the running of his lab; he had only wanted to keep something to himself. He would have to tell Rhea, at least, the truth about where the cells had come from, but he could choose his time.

When he reached the village, the bus shelter was spewing out kids; the lucid air crackled with their racket. In the shadier corners of the village square, flares from lighters, urgently dug out after the journey, momentarily illuminated faces and caught the hidden stare of eyes as their owners lit cigarettes. Smoke and disorder surrounded them as Lewis crawled past. They watched him with rancorous insolence. He was sure that one would bolt from the pavement and jump under his wheels, just to put him in the wrong.

There was a lay-by a few hundred yards from the turn-off to Snitter Heugh. Rhea would be up at the house, keeping Amber company while he'd been away. The thought of them together, turning expectantly towards him when he went in, was suffocating him, closing his throat. He pulled off into the lay-by and sat still in the car, listening to the clicking of the cooling engine: quiet but irregular snaps and cracks. He remembered the spare, uncluttered legal office. Even the lab felt untidy and chaotic next to it, and Snitter Heugh a baffling paradox. He leant forward and let the wheel take the weight of his head.

Even through closed eyes he saw the glare of the huge full-beam headlights before he registered the unmistakable noise of Simon Pindon's flatbed. It stopped right alongside him, blocking the road, and he powered down the window. The Pindon head was looming over him. 'Problem, Lewis?' The Pindon voice held a huge swathe of contempt. How the brothers would love to have him at their mercy. How they would love to attach his convertible to their monster truck and haul him out of trouble, delivering him back to his house like a lost package.

'No problem. Took a phone call, that's all.'

The face beamed disbelief, even in the dusk. 'Busy man, then.'

As he drove off, the mockery of those few words made Lewis fume. The whole car heated up. He was a teenager again. His parents had sent him to empty the rubbish from a picnic basket into a lay-by bin. On top of the sandwich wrappers and banana skins there had been a pile of wank mags and an empty gin bottle. The bin had been placed in the shade but a gang of wasps had left the sunlight and clustered around the open neck of the bottle, crawling over one another to get at the oily alcoholic remains. When he'd poked at them with the edge of a crisp packet, they'd blazed up, angry and bewildered, but too drunk to find him and attack. A flush of excitement had coursed through him at the startling glimpse through this peephole into a hidden corner of adult life. Back at the car, Mum wondered if he was all right. A bit travel sick, he'd said. He felt sick now at the thought that Simon would surely be back tomorrow, peering from his high lookout, wanting to know what Lewis had been up to, hiding in a lay-by a couple of hundred yards from his house.

The more he thought of it, the worse it became, and he imagined the builders quizzing Amber tomorrow. She would smooth it over. Amber was fast on her feet, especially if any of the family needed defending, but there would be a momentary hesitation – she had been quick to ask him why the workmen hadn't seen him while she was visiting her mother. The Pindons would see that brief doubt with their prurient eyes, and remember. Next time he met them, he expected to see this ignominy wielded as though they had won a victory over him. Lewis allowed himself a thorough dislike of Snitter Heugh and all its grubby ramifications. With the image of the clean city office still plain in his mind, he wished he didn't have to wrestle with all the surveillance and censure of this countryside hole-in-the-corner.

The porch light switched on. Amber and Rhea would be there, expecting him, knowing just how long the drive should have taken him. They were probably sitting together, listening for his car. It had been a mistake to phone them from the service station, he saw that now. It had just kept him in their minds when he needed to have been forgotten for a few hours. Even when he was alone, he was never by himself any more.

A flat in town would solve a lot of this. Minimalist and impassive. Free of complications, because it would be big enough only for one. As soon as he thought of it, he started heading off the objections. No, he didn't want to put Rhea out by staying with her: she had her own life to lead. No, he didn't want Amber running her day around his work when she had a baby to think of. He could stay down there for a few nights during the week and come home at weekends, a sort of holiday for them all. The separation of work and home life might do them good.

The track up to the house was rutted and dusty after the summer, and when he swung the car through the entrance it bumped and scraped the ground. He opened the window and peered down to see the problem. Mare's tails, primordial as though the past was coming back – or had never quite gone away – had grown through the gateway during the hot weather and hid a deep gully; the front wheels had rutted down into it. Dried fronds moved in the night breeze, rustling against one another in malicious whisperings. He wanted the Pindons out of his house. He wanted his low-slung convertible out of this rut. He forced the accelerator down and, with a sudden outraged yowl, the car leapt forward. The noise disturbed the roosting birds and they splashed into the darkening sky, like stones thrown up by the churning wheels.

The door was open but the lights were off. When he went in, Amber and Rhea turned towards him with such wide-open faces that, for a moment, he could have believed they both knew and understood. But Amber looked towards the microwave. A moth couldn't resist the glowing LCDs: it fluttered around them, desperate to get closer to the light, bumping and banging on the metal casing.

'We were trying to get it out,' she explained. 'We put the lights off and opened the door but it only found something else to attract it.'

Lewis made a ball of his hands and enclosed the moth. He stretched his fingers as far as they would go, so that its wings wouldn't be damaged, and felt it flutter for a little while, then settle in his palms. When he walked out into the garden and let it go, he saw it shake itself out, make a perfect take-off and fly into the dark.

He watched it for a moment before he turned back to the house. Amber had come to stand in the doorway. She put out a hand and touched him. Then he brushed against Rhea as he passed. Mother, wife, lover, sister: his body went on in a confusion of feeling but his mind still turned the patent application over and over, testing it for snares.

'It's done,' he said. 'I've handed it all over to the authorities.'

In the new era of his work-life separation, Lewis judiciously imported aspects of one into the other. Managing expectations. Words that were bandied around the senior management team, like a new leisure activity, had a pertinent application in his home affairs. Amber was still under constant instruction from the Pindon duo; all the work they'd done at Snitter Heugh had made her an expert on building methods. She was keen to pass on their advice to Lewis for his own project, so he decided to let her see the Genetics Institute.

He helped her across the hot building site, holding her arm as she hobbled, big and unbalanced, in flimsy new sandals.

'I'm still me,' she protested, when he suggested sensible footwear. 'I'm still the same Amber. I'm not going to change just because of the baby.'

There was a deep puddle, left by the day before's rain, and Lewis stirred the mud with the toe of his shoe while he tried to think of a single significant way in which Amber hadn't changed since this baby business. Dead leaves piled up at the edge of the water; incredulity, scepticism and disorientation combined in his mind like all the colours of the spectrum mixed together. She was looking at him anxiously, wanting him to believe her. Amber hadn't been so vulnerable before. Always it had been him needing her, and she would turn away to sleep without noticing. He probed the myriad tiny wounds to his self-esteem. Whenever anyone phoned in the evening, late when he was home, Amber would leap from her chair to answer it. Esmé had called last night to offer Amber a dog: a wet-nosed, slobbering Labrador. With her eczema and asthma, it was the last thing they needed, but Amber had strung Esmé along, ignoring his shaking head and deprecatory gestures. It took a note, a written warning, about the health risks before she backed off. And then she had told Esmé that she was worried about the baby, coping and everything. Just being at Snitter Heugh was a full-time occupation to Amber: it used up all her energy and left nothing for him.

'Vic told me that in the States they keep finding shoes in the foundations of old buildings,' she said. 'They used to think that people's souls were in their shoes and buried the old ones to lay claim to the new land. We should put some in for luck.' She looked down at her jewelled and ribboned sandals. 'But I don't fancy walking back barefoot.'

Between the shale and the jags of swarf from the construction work on the new premises, Lewis thought blackly, there were plenty of opportunities for damaged soles. 'I don't suppose there's any need for blood sacrifices nowadays,' he offered, into the undefined, totally unknowable gist of Amber's meaning.

'Money!' She opened her purse and tossed fifty pence into the water. Lewis laughed with her at the aptness of her solution.

'Do you think it's enough?' he asked. 'Fifty pence?'

Amber held her purse aloft and emptied it. A few pennies fell at her feet and she eased the last dirty coins over the edge with her toes. 'We may as well be sure.' She paused, linked her hand with his, then said meditatively, 'But a little bit of our own blood is definitely worth it if it works, isn't it?'

It was quiet. The workmen were at the other side of the site, so far off they seemed to be playing with little boys' toys. No one but Amber could hear him.

'I ought to tell Rhea about the patent conditions,' Lewis said, 'before someone else does.'

The heat was drying the puddles at their feet, and there was a growing ring of caked mud around the edge where Amber had tipped her loose change. She scuffed at it, then angled her face to the sun. 'I can't see why not,' she said. 'I don't know why it had to be a secret in the first place.'

Lewis watched the purse disappear back into Amber's handbag. 'She might mind about the money. She won't be entitled to any of the royalty income, but you will.'

'Rhea won't mind. We can give some to her anyway. Who's going to stop us?'

Legal barriers, binding agreements, contracts rose in Lewis's head; the threat of exposure, litigation, stripped him down. 'Everybody,' he said.

'No, nobody. Get over it, Lewis. She's my sister. I'll give her whatever I want.' Amber started back across the rutted ground. The tempered leather of those sandals wasn't as flimsy as it looked.

The new car park had grown. The steel skeleton was covered with concrete tiles, but only in patches; in other places the bare bones were still protruding. The tips of the lift shafts pressed up into the sky. The building work was almost finished and they would soon move into their new laboratories.

'Do you think it would be a good idea if we bought a flat in town?' he asked. 'I could stay there in the week sometimes, when I'm busy. And you'll be busy with the baby.'

Amber was silent for a long time. She sat down on a half-built wall.

'No,' she said, at last. 'I've been thinking. We should sell Snitter Heugh.' Her voice picked up speed. 'We'll have made some money on the renovations and we'll buy another house down here. I've worked it all out. We'll be able to afford one big enough for a family.'

The new pragmatist in Lewis already saw the way that things would turn out. He would be rid of the interminable aggravations of Snitter Heugh; he and Amber would be happy again. He ran his fingers through his hair and was surprised – again – to find he hadn't got any. But Rhea had been right: you'd never expect the bristles to be so soft. He opened the car door for Amber and she felt for his hand, stroking him with a touch so sumptuous that it made saliva spring into his mouth. 'I'm sure it'll be all right, Lewis. Without all the commuting you'll have more time to get on with your work.'

'You wouldn't mind?' ventured Lewis, cautiously, feeling his way into good luck, testing that treacherous ground.

But Amber no longer harboured reservations. She grasped forward. 'Of course I won't. Come here, you. Feel the baby.' She placed his hand on her bulging abdomen. A series of kicks pranced up his arm. In the flesh, in Amber's flesh, the child was lively and strong: nothing like the usurping changeling in the scan picture.

'Do you think it's a boy or a girl?' he wondered.

'Why do you want to know?' Amber said. 'It'll be whatever it wants.'

Inside the car she pulled his hand towards her breast. 'Even if there had never been a baby, Lewis, especially if it was you who couldn't have one, I wouldn't have minded that much. It's you I want most.'

Lewis could see the new laboratories behind her. Workmen

282

were hauling equipment into the goods lift. 'It's all right. You're allowed to want something for yourself,' he said.

'I thought I had you,' Amber said sadly. 'You can't want what you've already got, can you?' She examined his face. Lewis felt clammy with the fear of exposure. But Amber only smiled. 'Once the baby's here, we'll be the same people again, Lewis. I promise.'

He said he knew, trying to fix the thought in his mind. Amber was firmly round; the baby was packed tight inside her. Her skin was calm and smooth, not flushed the way it had been when her eczema was bad. Even with the baby moving around, trying to stretch its cramped limbs, she was more in control than he could hope to be. He wondered if the baby felt it, and knew it, the way he did. Amber placed kisses on his palms and lifted them to his lips; Lewis thought that his fingers smelt of coins, used too often, grubby. But in his new workplace, with Amber next to him, pouring the money away, it might only have been the metal of the car keys.

Lewis could choose something from the bar's can-of-lager range.

'But I can't stand the smell of it since I've been pregnant.'

Amber's face hung over Rhea: the assured, spirited face that Amber used to have. And she was constantly attentive to Rhea's every need. 'Which water, Rhea? Shall I order still or sparkling?'

She must want something, Rhea thought. She looked steadily at Lewis to let him know she wasn't pleased, while Amber fussed over the water, exchanging sparkling for still. He looked steadily back at her, then raised his eyebrows in a gesture of surrender and let his eyes slide away, helpless in front of his wife's exuberance.

The bar was crowded and everyone wanted to eat outside so they had only been able to find a table next to the footpath, where passers-by surreptitiously eyed whatever they ate or drank.

'You should have come up to Snitter Heugh for lunch,' Amber said. 'You haven't been for ages.'

Everything was at its best. The university exams were over, the students gone to their homes or on holiday, and there was a general feeling of release. This year even the lab was quiet, and half empty as the equipment was moved to the new premises. 'You'll be able to get a sun tan this year,' Amber went on. 'And have a good rest before everything kicks off in the autumn.'

Lying in the garden at Snitter Heugh, half naked, with the rays of the sun pushing into every part of her, opening her out, was something that Rhea would never be able to do. She could feel the cradle of the lounger at her back and the wind from the hills, subdued in summer but with its unmistakable threat of hard weather to come, working on her memory, playing back scenes that shouldn't have happened. She might say anything, if she succumbed, but the seduction of giving in to relaxation was legitimate for pregnant Amber.

'It might be our last chance, you know.'

'I was going to decorate the flat.'

Amber and Lewis exchanged meaningful looks.

Intrigued, Rhea turned from one to the other. 'What?' she said.

Amber put out her big, warm hand and covered Rhea's. 'Don't do it just yet. We might have to stay with you for a while. I'm putting Snitter Heugh on the market.'

The waiter brought both sorts of water and the lager. All the questions that Rhea ought to ask welled inside her, kept tightly down because she didn't dare to voice them. There wasn't any way to ask, 'Is Lewis moving too?' Almost at once she thought better of it. How could he not be? Amber would get whatever she wanted.

'We're looking at a house in Benedict's Place. It's near to some of the best schools, it's close to Lewis's work and you'll be able to stay whenever you want, Rhea. There's plenty of room.'

Benedict's Place was well away from Rhea's flat. She understood how much she didn't want Amber near to her. It was no surprise, yet it was unexpected. During the time Amber had been out of the way at Snitter Heugh, Rhea had only her own feelings to contend with: she hadn't needed to consider Amber's too.

Amber's mouth opened again, then closed firmly, as though to say, 'And that's all there is to it.' But Rhea knew better. Those briefly parted lips told her there was something else, but it couldn't be that Amber had found out about her and Lewis. She wouldn't be sitting by the canal with them both, talking about Snitter Heugh as though it didn't matter to her, if she had any idea.

'Won't you miss the countryside?' she asked Lewis.

He didn't answer until he had looked at Amber, checking for her opinion. 'I never saw much of it anyway. You know that.'

You know that. It drove a chink between him and Amber – what Rhea knew – a small but hugely dangerous chink. If she put her hand into it, it wouldn't widen. Instead there would be a rumble and it would snap shut, trapping her.

Lewis opened his lager and Amber wrinkled her nose. 'Drink it over there,' she ordered, with the imperious power of the mother-to-be. Without a word, Lewis rose and went across to the water's edge where he stood rolling the can across his forehead, trying to cool himself. He looked back at Rhea and she knew what he was feeling: the heat of guilt. It weakened his face; she could hardly recognise him.

'I've got something to tell you,' Amber announced.

Lewis started and exchanged a look with Rhea. But he was prepared for whatever was going to happen and had already decided what to say. Out it came: over-rehearsed and pitch perfect. 'I'm sure you two have a lot to catch up on.'

Rhea jumped out of her seat. She grabbed his arm and held him fast, digging her nails in. 'I'm sure you'd like to hear too, Lewis.'

Amber smiled. 'The thing is, we can afford Benedict's Place now, Rhea. Lewis didn't say anything before because he didn't want to worry you, but those SA 153 cells, they're mine. He took them from my tooth.'

Once the words were said, Rhea saw that she had always known. How could it have been otherwise?

The buildings along the canal rose from low to high-rise in ascending steps. By the time she arrived at the university it seemed as if some pinnacle had been reached. The science blocks were the highest of all. Their walls soared from the ground like cliff faces, so convincingly that seagulls mistook them for the real thing and, creeping along the ledges, nested around the roof. Now those walls reared up, high, wide and white, around Rhea, crawling with a life that she had never taken into account. Nooks and crannies that she hadn't realised existed closed in on her. The consequences disoriented her. She hadn't lived the life she'd thought she had, she'd lived a different one; she would have to reconfigure history. It felt almost as though there had been two Rheas. The one she knew, capable, independent, working in an equal partnership, and another, the one Dave and Lewis had known, the same one her own sister knew, gullible, available to be used. She wondered which one everyone else saw, which one was the real Rhea. She didn't know if she could ever trust her version of reality again. Standing in front of the department, she was confronted by her reflection in the revolving doors. Half a dozen Rheas highlighted against the dark inside spun away from her, then melted back into one as she pushed the glass and walked in.

CHAPTER 16

Rhea didn't take the lead in the array technology experiments. Katherine, close to Glatton, was the obvious candidate.

'It's all yours.'

She wafted the laboratory air away from her face before she passed over the instruction manual. Andrew and Joe glared in disappointed fury at not being at the forefront of the team's progress.

Once, that childish game was what Rhea had wanted but the theoretical had lost its fascination. Each time she left the laboratory, her fingers on the door handle felt loose with the art of the possible. The grant at the hospital, working with the patients, gave her the chance of an independent existence. She couldn't raise any enthusiasm for the final stages of Lewis's project and hardly hid the fact.

Katherine rushed up to give her an envelope.

'It's the array-technology results. The SA 153s are nearly as good as the cord-blood cells.'

'The SA 153s are Amber's cells, Katherine.'

'How can they be?'

'Lewis took them from her tooth.'

Stephen Glatton stood behind Katherine, his stony face taking shape out of the background. He took her arm and removed her into the revolving doors, both of them together in the one compartment.

The envelope Katherine had given her was one of the reusable ones, passed throughout the university until they fell to pieces. This one had been around for some time and it was shabby. The address grid on the front carried the record of its life history. Admin, Economics, European Studies, Physics, Medicine felt like a varied and enjoyable life for an envelope. There was no address on her designation, just 'Rhea', which was fitting for someone in transit.

Rhea washed and fed the cultures. There was a necessity about the routine task; something deep in her knew she couldn't skimp on it. That would be like saying she hadn't existed, that all this work had done itself or, worse still, that Lewis had done it, when he certainly hadn't. But she dawdled over clearing up, not wanting to face the barrage of questions that must be waiting for her. Coffee time came and the noise in the general lab filtered away down the corridor, but no one came to call her. As she took off her gloves, the thin layer of latex peeled away from her skin, sticky and reluctant to release its hold. Face mask, hair covering, white coat, she dispensed with her protective clothing and went along to the tea-room. As she approached the door, she acknowledged to herself that this was better faced without Lewis.

Katherine was waiting, watching the door as though she knew that Rhea wouldn't be able to stop herself putting in an appearance. Andrew, that was no surprise, was prancing behind her, fascinated by the strength of her indignation. She's got a champion now, Rhea thought. She won't want to back down in front of Glatton.

There was a rustle as something was thrust aside. Rhea knew it would be Katherine's array results. She stretched out her hand and Andrew surrendered it, but with bad grace that he didn't try to hide. His face had a triumphant stare, as though just seeing her there meant he had gained a victory.

288

'I was going to mention . . .' It felt important to keep her voice neutral, as though it didn't really matter at all, but when Rhea put a hand to her mouth, her lips were dry and roughened. Shards of distrust, bright in Katherine's eyes, pierced her. 'I was going to talk to you about this, Katherine. I've only just realised, you know.'

There was a snort of derision from around the room. Not only Katherine: the whole team joined in the chorus of accusation. With the supporting crowd at her back Katherine was unflinching. 'Didn't you trust us to know?'

Rhea studied the printout so she didn't have to see her friends' disaffection. The cell-source identity had been changed: 'SA 153' had been replaced by 'A. Norham', ringed with black circles, thick, and forced down into the paper, so that she couldn't help but see Katherine making them, slowly at first, then faster and faster as outrage consumed her. You could see that it wasn't easy for Katherine to be difficult, even when she was right. Her face flushed with the effort. The memory of all the times they had worked together would be playing through her mind, just as it was through Rhea's. There was a cake on the coffee-table, iced with shells and scallops, like a wedding cake. It must be Fazil's birthday: his wife always sent them one. Rhea looked at it, amazed that a year had passed since the last time.

'Of course,' she said. 'Lewis just forgot.'

Fazil cut the cake and handed it round on pieces of kitchen paper torn from the roll. He had a special smile for Rhea, wanting to smooth things over. The cake, the wife, the children stabilised Fazil and made him less reactive than the others. Perhaps braver and more truthful too. Because the source of the cells wasn't the real issue on anyone's mind but Katherine's. While Andrew set about demolishing the pretty icing on the birthday cake, Fazil gave her the chance to rearrange things and put them straight.

'Did you know, Rhea, about the cells? We all thought they were bone samples.'

Bones, teeth? What difference did it make? They were hard, strong bits of you, with something soft and living at their centre. It wasn't the difference between bones and teeth that everyone was bothered about. It was the deception that mattered. Without meaning to, without actually caring, she defended Lewis. The ingrained reflex must still have been there. You could suppress it but perhaps it didn't disappear altogether.

'It doesn't make any difference, actually, where they came from,' she told them. 'You'll all get the same credit.'

No one spoke. There was a shuffle of disbelief, an effort to square up facts. God knew what they must have said when she wasn't there. Probably she'd have said the same in their place.

'Lewis didn't want to raise any false expectations, just keep everyone in work. He didn't even tell me.'

Rhea drank coffee and braced herself against the inevitable post-caffeine hypoglycaemia. In the still, private hollow of falling blood sugar, she followed the others back to the lab. The equipment that had been bought with Lewis's own funding had been packed and moved to the Genetics Institute. All the stuff that belonged to the department had been labelled with a red sticker and left in place.

Rhea heaved her gel tank out of its cupboard and onto the bench.

'That's departmental,' Katherine snapped, with avaricious need. Fighting over the odds and ends of equipment had turned into a family squabble over the thin pickings of an acrimonious divorce, the paltry gains representing much more than they were worth. Katherine marked the tank with one of the red labels. She looked at Rhea with the defiant but let-down expression of the terminally offended. 'I've applied for a job with Dr Glatton. I'll need a reference.'

Stephen Glatton was having their lab space when they moved up to the Genetics Institute. He'd walked around it, touching things with a pleasure and a tact that Rhea had never expected.

Katherine had shown him their equipment with flustered pride. 'There's a knack to the autoclave,' she'd explained, as he'd pushed at the controls, shrugging when nothing happened. 'You have to switch it on first.'

When they turned around and saw Rhea was still there, they looked at her as though she wasn't herself but some barely remembered ex-colleague who'd turned up wanting her job back.

Watching them, Rhea felt her chest constrict. It wasn't just that Katherine and Stephen were happy; they were happy against all the odds.

The team were down in the weighing room now, packing reagents, and the lab sweated chemicals, fusty and pungent. The freighted air pushed its way into her lungs, every breath heavy with the benefits of change. They would all get over this upset. Student murmuring, at a distance, had the comforting effect of road traffic during a sleepless night: a familiar background to the task of straightening things out.

'Before we move, you need to do a DNA run on the SA 153s, check them against some more cord cells so we have a complete set of information.'

Their grudging expressions loosened as the habits of work and the establishment of comprehensive data sets gathered strength in their minds and carried them past their impractical grievances.

In the half-empty lab the cleaners had done their stint and the late-afternoon sun reflected off the newly polished windows of Lewis's office so that she had no idea whether he was there or not.

She slid out the package from her briefcase. The letter from the Research Council was fat, weighty with its own message. Without opening it, Rhea knew that she and Eleanor had got their grant. Refusals came in slimline envelopes, unburdened with future responsibilities. Working at the hospital would be good. She would be out of the way of all this.

Lewis was in his office, deleting files from his computer. 'New lab, clean start,' he said. His fingers prodded the keys: delete; select; delete. His eyes stayed fixed to the screen – he was afraid to lose his place in the long list of redundant proposals. 'It's all thanks to Vic.' His fingers stopped, hesitating over the next item. 'Do you think we should apply to the university for another studentship?'

'I imagine they'll think we've had more than our share already.'

His fingers moved on, leaving the file for another day.

'Look at me, Lewis.'

He was afraid to. Rhea could see it in the slide of those fingers to the next key: afraid of what she was going to say to him.

'I've got some news for you. I'm not sure whether you'll like it.'

Lewis gasped, a scared, sharp sound, and dropped his head to his hands. Rhea's mind tingled with the truth. *He thinks I'm pregnant.* Her hands were so hot that the letter of acceptance wilted as she held it in front of him.

'I've got another job,' she said, 'with Eleanor at the hospital.' He looked at her, then. His smile was dazzling; it was meant to be. He didn't need to say anything. The arms around her were clumsy and pulled her too close. Shuffles and mutterings in the lab might mean someone was coming. She pushed him away, warning, 'It's more important than ever now.'

'Yes,' Lewis agreed. 'Contacts up at the hospital will be just what we need when it comes to clinical trials. And Andrew could have your post at the Genetics Institute. I'll get someone new on his grant.'

'You bastard! You used me!' she bawled.

Dumb, he shook his head, pulled her inside and closed the door. She watched him riffle through the file lists of his memory, then pull one out with an apologetic smile. 'No, I never once used you,' he protested. 'I didn't want you to get involved. I wanted to protect you, Rhea, and I have.'

He touched her, an empty touch: a habit that meant nothing. The empty bottles being stacked in the lab crashed together with a loud, reckless sound. Rhea's head rang with the clamour of Lewis enacting this patronising patience, the reasonable man, refusing to be implicated. She recognised it all too well. She couldn't defend him now.

'It's a pity to let the truth get in the way of a good story,' she said, because she wasn't going to allow him another word. Because it could only be one more lie.

Another Friday night and the bar was filling with students for the departmental freshers' bash. Over the years that Rhea had been coming to welcome parties they had hardly changed. The detail shifted: clothes, music, drinks had their own flowerings of celebrity, then shrivelled out of favour and disappeared, but the people remained much the same. Clumps of girls, basque-clad, tuffeted together for protection, came crowding down the stairs and wriggled themselves into places at the end of Rhea's table. They kept their faces turned down, like shrinking violets, but there was a thoroughly practised nonchalance in the way they ignored the calls 'Plenty of seats here,' from the men at the bar. The girls shied off, turned their exposed backs and kept smiling at Rhea, feathery hair ornaments nodding amiably at her presence, thanking her for providing them with a haven. They were indistinguishable to her. They all had straightened hair

293

and heavy artificial eyes, and made her feel old. The barman turned up the music a good ten decibels and seemed to look at her with distinct purpose. It was eight o'clock, time for the usual warning to the over-thirties that they were no longer welcome because the evening now belonged to the still young.

Joe came over, bringing her a glass of red wine. The girls looked up at last: a distinctive young man who could nonchalantly plant alcohol in front of a member of staff could pique the interest of any savvy fresher. Rhea couldn't afford to have her interest piqued by anything to do with next year's department and certainly didn't want her tongue loosened in front of the new students. Just to turn up to the party this year she'd had to make a much bigger effort than usual to remember what it was like to be a fresher, when the pinhole of light at the end of the long tunnel of A levels and university applications opened up into a kaleidoscope of colour. Those girls had stumbled down the stairs into the bar and burst into a new life. She didn't want to find herself patronising them with hackneyed old phrases like 'You'll soon make friends'; 'You'll soon find your way around'; 'You'll soon get used to it'. She might feel geriatric, but she wasn't ready to give anyone the satisfaction of hearing her sound it. It would be best not to drink the wine. She dealt with this tricky situation, as she had many times in the past, by recycling her drink. She moved it on with a discreet push and a rueful smile to the students. 'Driving,' she said.

'Drinking,' they answered, with the loose laughter of the young, and the wine disappeared into the boozy quagmire of undergraduate life. She gave up her seat to Joe: he would be hoping for just the same fate.

Over at the bar Katherine was squeezed between Patrick and Glatton, who was standing relaxed like a man at his own fireside, entertaining the new postgraduates who clustered around him. Rhea pressed a path through them and found a gap between Katherine and Glatton. She squeezed in and he shuffled a little further. The slight shift of his shoulders, the shrug of his leather jacket, not so very different from the ones she had just seen the students wearing, but softer and so very much more expensive, carried a presumption that he was entitled to the place she had just taken.

'Oh, well done,' he said. 'No Lewis?'

Rhea looked him straight in the eye. Her *coup de grâce* slid neatly between his primed neurons. 'No, he's at the vice chancellor's tonight.'

'Bugger,' said Glatton – probably his first honest reaction of the evening – and startled himself. Rhea laughed and he laughed back at the even score. 'I bet,' he said, 'that Amber got him the invite.'

Katherine reached across Rhea and placed a possessive hand on Glatton's arm. She shouted above the noise of the sound system, 'You know that Stephen's been made head of department.'

Glatton had the decency to give a self-deprecatory shrug. 'Safe pair of hands,' he explained. 'Featley's been made a dean. Restructuring.'

Rhea hung about, in spite of herself. Katherine was rosy. A happy summer glowed out from her. She reminded Rhea of the girl she herself had once been. And it nagged at her that there was something unfinished here: that Katherine shouldn't be leaving. She was the one who had first cultured the SA 153s. Could there have been some subtle technicality that had made them so successful? Something it was hard to say, like Rhea's own method of letting her cells have their way? She felt the link of the many overlaps in their careers, hers and Katherine's. It weighed down on her that they had quarrelled. It probably bothered Katherine too. Her face was creased by puzzlement. But her eyes were too bright. In the dull light of the bar, her pupils had expanded so they could take everything in, and that meant she was dazzled too: she saw only what she wanted. She wouldn't feel close to Rhea now, not after the trouble. But Katherine's wide eyes rested on her for a moment, and she sent Rhea a wry smile that meant she had discovered that an old pain and an old friend could feel much the same. After all, she'd taken up with Stephen Glatton.

Rhea's handbag was on the bar. She picked it up and redid her lipstick, a quick slash of crimson in the tiny mirror. She always wore makeup now. No one could peer into her face and find the sort of candour that Katherine's openly paraded. She went out into the warm evening. The sun hadn't quite set; its low rays were bleaching the colour out of the landscape. Rhea realised her own eyes must be dark-adapted too, pupils dilated by the semi-darkness in the bar, just like Katherine's. But outside in the clear evening, they were closing, narrowing, so that in one direction she could see her flat, at the top of the small block across the canal, and in the other, the university and the hospital. The Genetics Institute was just visible in the distance, on the other side of the orbital distributor road.

So, Lewis had been spun off from the centre with his five hundred fucking thousand pounds of start-up money. It wouldn't last long. Soon he'd be running back to Vic, begging for the next tranche.

Now that he was important, Stephen Glatton was automatically credited with impartiality and probity. Rhea wondered if he'd had a back-up supply of suitable attributes and his new title had just called them out, or if they had arrived in a package from Admin and hung loosely around his neck, along with his 'Head of Department' identity tag. It flapped about and he kept tucking it under the tie he had started wearing, now that he had been exalted.

Lewis's impartiality and probity, on the other hand, had to be demonstrated. For all sorts of reasons – medical, for the clinical trials; legal, for the patent; fiscal, for the money; and personal, because there were mutterings in the department along the lines of *Even his own team didn't know anything about it* – it was best proved that the cells were from his own wife's body.

Amber wasn't wearing any lipstick, in case of contamination. It made her mouth vulnerable.

'You don't have to do this,' Lewis said.

She sighed at him in an appeal, but the final huff sounded more like exasperation. 'Yes, I do. Nobody is going to accuse you of fixing this. SA 153s are my cells and I'm going to prove it.'

Stephen Glatton waited by the table. He rearranged his warranted store of implements in front of him, duplicate sets. Amber was determined that justice would be seen to be done, whatever it cost her.

In the end, Glatton couldn't take the buccal smear that would sample her DNA. As she opened her mouth, showing her teeth and tongue, he stepped back. 'You do it, Rhea. I'll sign to say it's all in order.'

While Rhea scraped the inside of Amber's cheek with a cotton probe, Lewis couldn't look. He stared out of the window.

'If there's no trust . . .'

'It's not personal.'

Glatton spoke in the neutral terms of the representative. It wasn't personal, obviously. The work had outgrown its makers and had to stand on its own feet, out there in the harsh world. He secured the duplicate samples and signed the seals. He gave one to Rhea and took the other away, a whole prototype of Amber, in its separate transparent plastic bag for his personal attention. It felt personal.

'Like she's a prisoner.'

Lewis couldn't do the check himself. Glatton would do one comparison of Amber's DNA with the SA 153 cells and Rhea, as an interested party but without her name on the patent, would do the duplicate.

It was the last thing she would do in the department because the move up to the Genetics Institute was almost complete. Complete at this end, but the labs were still half finished so there wouldn't be much actual work done there for a while. Before she set up the DNA runs Rhea wanted to protect the remnants of her efforts here. Her vials would be ready for transfer to liquid nitrogen. She sighed over them. A safety visor was hanging by its strap next to the row of spare white coats. Although it was difficult to see clearly through it, she put it on to check the level of liquid in the freezer. If the freezing nitrogen fell too low, and over the move she didn't know who was responsible for topping it up, the cells would be released from their suspended animation, and they would die. But it hadn't happened today. There was enough. She didn't need to fetch the container and fill it. But you can't close a liquid nitrogen freezer completely. You have to leave an escape route for the evaporating gas and be vigilant. It would hold out for another night, but she made a note to see to it tomorrow.

She tipped her head back to stare at the ceiling once more. The fluorescent lights were still flickering intermittently, as though they couldn't be bothered to gleam properly. Glatton's problem now. She lowered her vials through the narrow opening. As always, frozen water vapour swirled upwards, but there was a loud crack as one of the vials shattered and the cells scattered singly throughout the freezer.

She stirred the liquid nitrogen with the holder but there was too much condensation for her to see how deep the broken vial had sunk. Soft and flexible in the warmth of the room, it would have become brittle as it froze. The cells, their mitochondria, their organelles, their nuclei containing all their genes, would be spreading out, instantly frozen and dispersed.

Icy mist rose through the air. Condensed water vapour shone in the fluorescent lights. It spangled, sparkled, crackled. Then it was gone. Electricity arced through the laboratory. There was another burst and it sparked up again. The vapour thickened and thinned. The evanescent shimmer faded, but the thought remained sharp. Amber, transformed from warm and soft to hard and cold.

Amber would be dispersed throughout the room, a reversal of the time her sister had run towards Rhea across the grassy dunes after the hospital visit and she had been there to gather her up. Rhea couldn't remember the last time she had seen her father, the details had slipped out of reach, but the memory of that afternoon came back to her in a torrent.

Later, they had played on the seesaw. Amber had been a good deal lighter than Rhea in those days and, with her sitting at one end, Rhea had stood in the centre, astride the pivot, and shifted her weight backwards and forwards so that Amber clung to the hand rail as she was jolted up into the air, then thumped down to the ground. Her little girl's face had creased with a mixture of terror and excitement and she had screamed in ecstasy. Hesitation held Rhea still. Perhaps it had been only terror that had made her little sister shriek: the terror of being left out. Rhea had never felt the nervous foreboding that always plagued Amber, but she felt it now, uncomfortably late. After Dave's underhandedness, she wasn't sure that anything was what it seemed. The memory of Amber's shrieks had floated unexpectedly to the surface of her mind; she tried to move through it – had she chased off Amber's fright?

The affair with Lewis felt like a hallucination too. Rhea couldn't believe they had done any of it, not in this life anyway.

It didn't matter so very much that one of the vials hadn't

survived. One here or there, there were plenty more. The project must be almost fireproof now. She kept the last vial back to run the final DNA check against Amber's buccal smear before she lifted the visor of her safety helmet, slotted the cover back into place and gazed around the laboratory that had once felt like home.

Stephen's certified results exonerated them. Amber's fructuous teeth had given rise to a whole new tribe of stem cells. Even the four per cent gap that Rhea hadn't been able to keep on track had given in and the evidence was indisputable. The DNA run-outs of the SA 153s were a perfect match for the buccal smear taken from the inside of Amber's cheek.

Lewis had held up the vial of SA 153s he had given Glatton from the freezer, scruffy with age, and waggled it in his fingers. But it hadn't been an old vial: it had been a new one, put there the day Amber had been to the dentist. If it looked old, Lewis must have deliberately aged it. He must have scratched at the marker pen label with his fingernails, to disguise it. He must have written the wrong date on it deliberately.

The new vial that Rhea had just used for her analysis had some extra, unexplained DNA in it. Amber's certainly, but someone else's too. It took her a day and a night to be convinced that the extra DNA must have come from Lewis. He must have seeded embryonic cells from the fertility treatment into the tooth cells. They would have soon taken over the adult cells and produced the 96 per cent purity that had got them Vic's money.

As the new head of department, Stephen Glatton was entitled to an invitation to the presentation of the embroidery that Stella had made for the Fertility Unit, but Lewis was gritting his teeth at the thought of it.

'It's a family occasion, really,' he complained. 'Private.'

'We're having the family thing now. Just the . . . five of us.' Amber passed a hand over her bulge and smiled across to her mother as it swelled in acknowledgement of being included in the family.

'You know that we're talking about you, don't you?' Stella spoke to the baby, but smiled at Lewis. Even Amber had been diminished by the sheer grandeur of Lewis's achievements. She was prepared to forgive the father of her grandchild anything, Rhea thought. 'I don't very often get to see you all together,' their mother said and, suddenly remembering Rhea, 'Come and sit over here.' She made a space on the sofa, moving her sewing onto the arm. Amber smirked behind her back.

'Naughty seat,' she mouthed at Rhea, with just the right amount of vehemence to make it not seem like a joke.

'Mum, I ought to go now.' Even while she said it, Rhea knew this was a battle she had lost. Stella wouldn't have any of it. Her face unlocked itself into a reassuring smile. Her mother would never risk direct confrontation. She would ease your way, with her quiet adjustments and her soft movements, until you'd turned around and didn't know it. 'You'll have to stay here tonight, dear.'

Rhea was holding her glass in both hands. It was finally warm in Snitter Heugh and Lewis had opened the bottle early so that it could breathe. It must have been expensive wine, high alcohol content, because it was refluxing up the sides of the glass. Intoxicating fumes rose from its surface, filled the globe and then condensed, dripping back into the dark pool. She took a large mouthful, which left more room for the refluxing, and rubbed the sides of the glass with her palms to speed up the process. She might as well drink it. No one was going to let her drive home that night. She would have to lie awake in the usual spare room, with Lewis and Amber breathing all around her, and wonder what she was going to do.

'Amber has plenty of room and I never see you. You're not sleeping in that flat by yourself.'

The barbed reminder of her solitude stung, and the strain of Lewis's presence stiffened Rhea into an automatic, defensive response. But her mother looked anxious and small on Amber's huge sofa. There was a silence that felt like giving in. 'I'm fine on my own.'

'Don't imagine I don't know what it feels like. Since your father died.'

Another barb or another defence. It seemed it would go on for ever. Estrangement came back to Rhea from a distant past, before her father's death. She moved onto the seat next to her mother. 'You know, Mum,' she said, 'I missed you, when Dad had cancer.'

'You were a big girl even when you were little. I thought that you understood.'

Of course Rhea hadn't understood. She hadn't been a big girl: she'd been a child. But she had known about whispering; she remembered the too-quiet rooms and the smiles that shied away from becoming laughs, touches that never made it to hugs, as though she had lost her mother as well as her father.

'It wasn't cancer. It was liver failure. Grandfather couldn't bear to have it mentioned. His only son drank himself to death.'

Rhea and Lewis both placed their glasses on the table.

Only Amber kept on drinking her mango juice, safe for her baby. 'It doesn't matter,' she said, 'how he got it.'

Stella laughed bitterly at her. 'It doesn't matter now, Amber, I know that. But it mattered then. You have no idea how much something like that mattered then.'

The sadness of her mother's life opened itself out to Rhea. Her unwillingness to rejoin the world after her bereavement, her dependence on Grandfather, her constant anxiety for her girls. Her life had been reduced to that thin thread of existence because her husband had liked a drink.

'You shouldn't care what other people think, Mum,' she said.

Stella couldn't look at her. With her eyes to the floor she said, 'No, you shouldn't, but you do. You don't do anything wrong and then you have to feel guilty for the rest of your life.'

'Mum.' Rhea slipped an arm around her and Stella brushed herself down, as though something of the guilt might come off and cling to her daughter.

'It's done now, darling. I'm fine, honestly.' She looked at Lewis. 'But I think you should ask this Stephen to the presentation. Do the right thing and you won't have anything to regret.'

They walked down to the village for a last look at Snitter Heugh up on its rise. As they passed the churchyard Amber commented tenderly on the headstones. 'Imagine whole families laid to rest here, generations all together. And their friends around them. There's something wonderful about living all your life in one place.' Already she was creating a history for her child, weaving the story of the charming place where it had first been carried in her womb, loving Snitter Heugh even as she prepared to leave it.

Near to Rhea, Stella sighed.

Ready to be formally handed over to the Fertility Unit, Stella's embroidery was hanging on the waiting-room wall. Rhea gazed at it through a blur. She moved closer to hide the heave of her shoulders.

The foetus was floating in a soft blue lake; it almost moved as the breath fled out of her and brushed the delicate silk, silk so fragile that Stella had unwound the intertwined strands of the embroidery thread to make filaments fine enough to sew it. Rhea could see her undoing the spinning that had given them their strength. The threads would have sprung back together, twisting into themselves to resist her efforts, but she would have patiently teased them apart, again and again, until they lay separate on her lap, fine enough for Amber's embroidery. Her sewing room was white, and the pale walls and ivory furnishings would hold onto the last of the daylight, so that as evening fell she could sit there and sew, while her children grew up without her.

As Rhea was thinking of her mother, her resigned focus on the things nearest to her, someone placed a hand on her shoulder. She started. Eleanor had crept up, her approach masked by the noise of the party going on around them. The uncompromising solidity of her presence contrasted bluntly with the ethereal wall hanging; her voice was unruffled, matter-of-fact.

'I've never had any children myself, only all of these.' She indicated the wall of photographs, the babies who had been born because of the clinic. Rhea couldn't imagine Eleanor, the fertility specialist, going home to her own children. In the mornings Rhea saw mothers carrying their children to the crèche. They trod warily, seeing every crack in the pavement as a chasm of all the things they didn't have time to do. They were constantly anxious. Who would promote them if their children got in the way of project goals? For one thing Eleanor just didn't look scared enough. Rhea had never really thought of her outside the clinic, of the finite nature of her private dreams: the gradual attrition of her own desires by the demands of work.

'The new grant, I'm so pleased.' Eleanor's eyes crinkled in appreciation. 'We'll do very well between us, dear.'

'Did you . . . ?' Rhea hesitated. It wasn't something you should ask but Eleanor answered anyway.

'I can hardly remember now. It's just how things turned out.' She was smiling an uncomplicated smile. 'Your mother must be proud of you.'

Stella was still at the centre of a semi-circle of admirers, of herself or her wall hanging, she had never seemed to mind, and more were always welcome. While Eleanor praised it Rhea drifted towards the edge. There was a service area, full of pipes and conduits, in an alcove. She slipped inside. All around her the congratulations went on. Waves of billowing talk flowed towards her, as though she was a convenient safety valve through which all the overheated displaced air could escape.

Lewis brought her a glass of wine. Stephen Glatton was watching them but she didn't care who saw. She took Lewis out onto the landing.

'I know what you did with those cells.'

'Christ, don't say anything here. Someone might hear. We should go back in. We'll go over this in my office, in private.'

'Oh, don't worry,' said Rhea. 'They'll only think we're off having a fuck.'

'We're just getting some fresh air,' he told her. 'No one can prove it. Just deny everything. It's nothing to do with anyone else.' It was everything to do with everyone else. Once Vic knew, there'd be no clinical trial in the US if embryonic cells were involved. The patent would be null. Lewis would have to withdraw it and be ruined. He had everything to lose so he couldn't admit to anything. 'Anyway it's only for the moment. We'll soon have the tooth cells up to the same purity with your new methods. We just need to keep our heads down until then.'

Lewis centred his gaze through the window, towards the city. Rhea looked over the hand rail, down the deep stairwell to the ground floor.

'Don't exaggerate, Rhea, for God's sake. The methods are all in place. Other labs will be able to repeat our results with their own cells.'

Lewis might be right: perhaps the results could be repeated with any sample. Sometimes it happened like that. Things just came into their own. You'd had enough practice, everything was in place. But she didn't think so.

'And don't say anything to Amber. Just don't. There's no need for her to have anything more to worry about.' Lewis caught her arm and pulled her away from the rail. 'I kept you out of it, Rhea. I protected you. I made sure you had nothing to do with it. You've nothing to worry about.'

Lewis was himself again, taking care of her sister, taking care of her. There were a few moments when Rhea believed they might all be their old selves again. His certainty almost convinced her that there was nothing to worry about. He looked at her with the intense concentration that she had seen in the fertility suite but when she stared back, surprised, his glance darted fitfully away. She tried, Rhea tried not to know, but knowing forced itself on her. It wouldn't be turned away.

'It's not an adult stem cell line, is it, Lewis? You used Amber's fertilised eggs, didn't you?'

He didn't answer.

Lewis had made those eggs his own when he had hung over them in the fertility suite. He had stolen one. Only the real thing could act so much like a stem cell. No imitation could be so perfect.

'How could you do that?'

'If I did, Rhea, and I'm not saying I did, they're not just Amber's cells. They're mine too.'

Only half of the DNA in the latest vials of the SA 153 strain was Amber's. That was how Rhea knew the cells weren't from her sister's tooth. The other half was Lewis's.

'How are you going to tell her, Lewis?'

'Just believe me, you've nothing to worry about.'

'I've nothing to worry about? How do you suppose I'm going to work with Eleanor and pretend that those cells are an adult strain?'

'It won't be hard,' Lewis said, with a cold finality. 'You've kept things quiet before.'

The hospital establishment had strung safety nets from the landing on every floor, so no one could fall to the concrete below. One of the fastenings had come adrift. You could plunge through it, but the net below might hold you. Lewis would have this to worry about for the rest of his life because his name was on the patent.

He gave her a kiss, brisk and businesslike, one that anyone could see: a peck of affection they would believe was for his sister-in-law. But Rhea could feel the goodbye he had placed on her cheek, because the exciting, young Lewis had already gone. There would never be a time in the future when he would come back, trembling and raw, and say to her, 'Shall we? For old times' sake?' Wanting to recapture his youth. His eyes were already tangled with wrinkles, like those of someone staring into the horizon waiting for trouble to arrive. He needed a shave. A dark shadow of growth covered his cheeks and jaw, joining the stubble on his head. He bore the trademark designer stubble of the middle-aged academic. Rhea could see it plainly: the tetchy grey man Lewis would be twenty years down the line was already under his skin, filling him out and weighing him down.

'Go back in,' she told him. 'Mum and Amber will be looking for you.'

And she was right. Stella and Amber lit up to see him. They were both happy. When Lewis stood in front of Amber, Rhea couldn't see her. His body entirely encompassed his wife's. Rhea understood now the transcendental thing that Lewis had brought about in her. She recognised what he had lifted away. Amber. From now on, he would look after her. Rhea knew that her sister no longer needed her.

Warren and Melissa had brought Polly. There was a son too, but he had had the chance to go off with his mates to a rugby match and was, like, so not interested in babies. Melissa had been through childlessness, she said. She had been married for years before she had fallen pregnant and she wanted her Polly to see the embroidery. It represented what she once had been, after all.

'I'm going to try to use some of the cells from your body to help your leg,' Rhea told her. She shouldn't have raised Polly's expectations yet, the whole business was still too uncertain, but Polly gave a delighted squirm, which made up for any doubts. Warren passed round the draft flyer for the stem-cell publicity. Stella's needlework baby cupped in a child's hands. Polly's hands, Melissa explained. 'When you hold a baby you have to feel a sense of eternity.'

Polly was enthralled by this vision of herself.

Rhea could remember holding baby Amber, damp and sweet in her lap, but the emotions she had felt resisted her. They quailed, afraid to be remembered. They belonged elsewhere now. They didn't want to be the messenger from another time. You could have been killed once for bringing bad news.

Katherine came to tell her that she'd been missed at the university. 'Come back to visit,' she urged. 'You'll hardly recognise the place.' Rhea wondered what she could mean: there were so few variations on the arrangement of equipment in a laboratory. Katherine would see the difference because it fitted her own life. The invitation was a signal of her proud ownership, and reconciliation. Her kind face burbled on. 'I know you're busy, Rhea. Stephen wanted the DNA results you did on Amber's cells so I used your password and downloaded them from the analyser to save you from having to come up.'

Katherine had passed on the results that would incriminate Lewis to Stephen Glatton. She couldn't have any idea of what she had saved Rhea from.

Stella was animatedly pointing out the details of her stitching to Stephen, who moved to and fro to admire it. Lewis and Amber were standing by, waiting for her, holding back while she talked. They seemed passive and quietened next to her. Lewis had only one more night like this because Katherine's safe pair of hands had flicked lightly across the keyboard to bring him down. Stephen Glatton wouldn't have any choice but to make the results public now, and Rhea couldn't leave Katherine to bear the blame for something she hadn't done.

'I'll come up tomorrow,' she said, 'and see Stephen too.'

Instead of rejoining the party she went into the new lab in the fertility unit. It was spotless, gleaming and fresh for the new occupant. Empty like this, one lab was much like another. There was no trace of its past. The discoveries or disappointments that had unfolded here were gone, written into papers and published, or hidden under the stock phases of official failure in final, exonerating reports.

When you leave a lab, she thought, it's like leaving fairyland: you can't take anything away with you except the knowledge you've gained. Rhea would leave behind her notes, her methods and all her results, but she could take herself and everything that was in her head to the hospital. Polly couldn't have her clinical trial in the US now but Rhea could make her own cells here.

It was hard to imagine what would happen to Lewis. It could only be a matter of how quickly Stephen Glatton made the connection that would unravel him. The news would come in an email, or a phone call, when he least expected it. Perhaps some senior official would arrive at the Genetics Institute, hurrying in by a side door to be ushered discreetly to his room. She saw Lewis defiant, or in denial, not believing his accuser.

She also knew her own mistakes, her omissions and miscalculations. She owned them.

Eleanor came in with a click of the door. 'All ready for you,' she said.

The small, uncertain tenure that Rhea had on this room increased. There was nothing to show it had been meant for her.

The blank smell of cleaning fluids and the closed blinds would accommodate anyone who came along, but she could make it her own.

The smell of preservative curled through the air as Eleanor opened the cupboard. 'I cleared that one myself,' she said quietly. 'I didn't want anyone else to do it.'

It had held the department's ancient collection of miscarried foetuses, stored in formalin-filled jars. The room folded around them as if they were still there. Eleanor swept away the dust with a wad of paper. 'When those doctors were training, that was all they had to go on. No CGI and ultrasound scans then.'

There was something saddening about this study of developmental anatomy. Yet outside was Stella's entrancing, celebratory wall hanging and Eleanor's wall of baby photos, wearing their unconditional grins.

'What did you do with them?' Rhea asked.

Every year the hospital held a memorial service to honour the volunteers who'd left their bodies to medical science. 'We included them in that.'

As they left Eleanor switched off the light so that they stood for a moment in the dark, in homage. Then they gathered themselves for the party, and as she walked back along the corridor, to Stella, Amber and Lewis, Rhea was glad to think of the tiny remains nestled peacefully within the generosity of donated adult bodies. Science and love united in their long, close embrace.

ACKNOWLEDGEMENTS

I would like to thank a number of people for the help and guidance that I have received during the writing of this novel: Jan Carew, for her continuing enthusiasm, Stevie Davies, for her unstinting advice and wisdom, Tessa Hadley for her great generosity, Caroline Dawnay for her unfailing perceptiveness and the staff at Little, Brown for their sustained, expert work, especially Richard Beswick and Victoria Pepe, patient and constant editors. Thanks too, of course, my family and friends for all their encouragement, and my husband, Tony, for his unwavering support throughout the entire process.

Jennifer Cryer was born and grew up in a mining village. Married, she nows lives in South Wales.

After studying Biochemistry and working in hospital, university and industrial laboratories, she decided her interest in science in her first novel.

WD 3 10/15